Roy Crane

WASH TUBBS®
AND CAPTAIN EASY

WASH TUBBS
AND CAPTAIN EASY

VOLUME 6 1931-1932

BILL BLACKBEARD
Series Editor

© 1989 Newspaper Enterprise Association (NEA)
Wash Tubbs is a trademark of Newspaper Enterprise Association.

A Flying Buttress Classics Library
edition, © 1989 **NBM**.
Introduction © 1989 **Bill Blackbeard**.

ISBN 0-918348-62-5 hardcover
ISBN 0-918348-61-7 paperback
LC 87-062174

Design and Production: Amos Paine and Bhob

FLYING BUTTRESS CLASSICS LIBRARY
is an imprint of

NANTIER · BEALL · MINOUSTCHINE
Publishing co.
new york

COMING TO ROY CRANE AND Bill Blackbeard

To get a full perspective on the extraordinary thing Roy Crane was accomplishing in *Wash Tubbs* at the end of the 1920s, at the juncture of America's classic decade of plenty and classic decade of poverty, it is necessary to step back from the exciting immediacy of the daily episodes themselves and take a fresh look at the old, well-chewed subject of the history of the comic strip.

And I *do* mean a fresh look.

We're not going to start with the first definitive comic strip, Richard Felton Outcault's *Yellow Kid* episode of October 25, 1896, nor with the first pre-comic strip Yellow Kid vignette, nor with the first Outcault peek at New York slum kid life. This is vital material, but it doesn't concern the far further step back into graphic art history we are going to take here, and has only peripheral relevance to the new dimensions in adult drama Roy Crane was discovering for a long-stagnated art form in the late 1920s and early 1930s.

Nor are we going to try to trace comic strip foreshadowings in the general gag cartoon art of the nineteenth century, let alone the caricature broadsides of the eighteenth. Essentially established in the classic British *Punch* from 1841 on, the gag cartoon has always been a field unto itself,

TERMS WITH CARTOON ART:

with very little to do with what the comic strip represents as an art form. The attempt of some British historians to find early comic strip work in certain captioned magazine gag series centered on recurrent characters such as Ally Sloper in W.G. Baxter's cartoons of the 1880s, or John Thomas in the John Leech vignettes for *Punch* a few years earlier, is closer to the mark, although not—as we shall see—all *that* close. It was not, curiously enough, until the late 1920s that the British published any definitive comic strips at all, but that is another story for another time.

So we are not going to pay much attention to the magazine gag series of Leech, Maxwell, and their engaging ilk, either. We are after much bigger and much more relevant game. We are, in fact, going to pursue the crucial conceptual origin of the comic strip narrative form itself from its outset in book illustration in England at the close of the eighteenth century. Amazingly, that unstudied, unheralded origin, once perceived, seems the most obvious thing in the world: obvious in its direct relevance to Crane's alchemy of 1928 and later, obvious in its parallel development and decline to that of the American comic strip narrative form that succeeded it. So obvious that, like Poe's purloined letter, it has been altogether too visible to be noted.

The Comic Strip's Dickens of a Past

Before we hie back to the comic strip's conceptual twin, however, let's be sure we're of one mind on the meaning of the term *comic strip* itself. *Webster's* only definition, an absurd one, is "a group of cartoons in narrative sequence," which happens to describe the Bayeux Tapestry and the Trajan Column among other things. Such a definition (framed, of course, with a distracted eye on simplicity) has no functional use at all. The problem is that the comic strip, although a remarkable and self-possessed narrative device in and of itself, has links to so many other superficially similar and intrinsically simpler narrative and graphic forms that an effective and precise definition must of necessity be a bit verbose and at odds with the pithy substantive ideals of dictionary makers, in order to cite the crucial elements that are its strengths and differences.

To put it as simply as possible, then, the comic strip is any pictorial narrative intended to appear in printed sequential format for an indefinite period of time, linked by a single title or theme and featuring one or more recurrent characters, structurally removed from all external narrative text and dependent for comprehension on panel-enclosed balloon dialogue. The concluding point, of course, is the real zinger: It is the fast and sustained flow of crucial dialogue easily associated with the speakers in the panels that gives the comic strip its basic narrative competence, removing picture stories forever from the leaden restraints of printed or written blocks of text outside or inside the successive panels, to which the slowed reader must refer for dialogue, identity of speaker, volume and intonation of speech, etc., before looking back at the panels again.

These complications are basically silly, and the astounding thing is that it took so long for the strip form to be created (it would seem to have been a natural, as we shall see, for the English cartoonists of the Georgian period and later), and shake itself free of the dead hand of simplified prose that had always, prior to 1896, accompanied any pictorial narrative or cartoon sequence featuring a recurrent character (except, of course, for those instances in which artists eschewed *all* text and opted for pantomime, the other side of the pre-comic strip coin). Curious survivals of earlier non-strip forms ran in newspaper strip sections for decades, as in the pantomimic *Henry* and *Benny,* or in the still-appearing Sunday ruin called *Prince Valiant,* which only the doggedly masochistic bother to puzzle out. All of us call such oddities strips for convenience of general reference in the field, but it is always worthwhile to remember that they are about as relevant to the basic point of the comic strip as spittoons in a post-prohibition bar.

Clearly, the cutting free of a whole new narrative art form from the granite chunks of older ones should have called for the introduction of a fitting name. Unfortunately, the muddled way in which the comic strip slogged into eventual reality and its "lowbrow" arena of publication, away from most thoughtful intellects, left the form isolated to snag any apparently appropriate name thrown up in the casual comments of the public and the press. What emerged from knockabout references, of course, were such superficial tags as "funnies," "funny pages," "comics," and finally "comic strip." "Comic strip," as we all know, has turned out to be the most widely used term, and it has been a Sisyphean burden for the field ever since.

The reason is obvious. The term is a bathetic misnomer, imperceptive enough when coined during the early days of Sunday comics, but flatly wrong after Roy Crane's introduction of the adult adventure strip transformed the field in the early 1930s. Although the newspaper strip has retrogressed blatantly to near-universal gag comedy in recent years, the comic strip field in general has been anything but broadly comic since Crane's breakthrough, even though the form's demented name loudly proclaims the opposite. The effect is demeaning. As used in the present culture, the word "comic" is a stereotyping pejorative, meaning (at best) "light," and by inference, "trivial."

We can assess the real absurdity of the term if, for a moment, we imagine the general term for imaginative prose narratives to be "comic fiction" rather than simply "fiction." The uses would be risible: "Faulkner, one of America's leading writers of comic fiction, has just concluded a new novel of incest and murder..." Or, "Your assignment in English Comic Fiction this week will be to read the first chapter of Thomas Hardy's *Jude the Obscure*..." Or how about the obvious nonsense of this: "Dickens' *Martin Chuzzlewit* is the finest example of humorous comic fiction in English literature..." (We smile, but remember that the equally absurd term, "humorous comic strip," is almost routine usage in critical writing in the field.) Returning to the comic strip form, let's wrap up this point with an imagined graphic story panel featuring a gory-fanged vampire just lifting his encarnidined lips from the still-spouting jugular of his half-naked female victim and saying through a spray of blood, in stentorian, Melvillian words caught in a black-bordered balloon overhead, "Call Me Comic."

Enough. The futile point is made. At least we've taken a hard look at what a comic strip is and isn't, and we know that the field carries a name that for a great many intelligent people is the equivalent of a sign saying, "Kick me!" Bear with me, then, if I introduce a fresh new term for the—*uk*—comic strip form a little further along in our look at serious cartoon narrative art two centuries ago. It'll never get beyond these pages, of course, but God knows it'll be pleasant using a term that *fits* the subject, is as neutral in kindling preconceptions as the wonderful French *bande dessinée,* and cannot possibly hit its referent over the head every time it's used. See what you think of it.

Imagine the impossible. Conjure up a time and place in which cartoon art is the accepted *norm* in illustration, posters, and advertisements. All magazine covers and serial novel covers are the work of cartoonists. Cartoon art is accepted in oil and watercolor, and sells for top money in the best salons. Cartoon originals are prized on every level of society. Yet the word cartoon itself, as applied to this kind of art, is unknown to the broad public which revels in the cartooncopia that shapes the nature of popular and high art everywhere. Instead, the prevailing cartoon art is routinely called "illustrations," "book and magazine cover art," "poster art," etc., just as if such art were the natural way to develop such material and called for no special descriptive term of its own. Cartoons rule. It's a cartoon world.

A nice fantasy, you say? An engaging cloudland revery? And so it would seem to be—until we realize that this impossibility actually existed at the turn of the nineteenth century in England and continued to hold sway for the next fifty years. Some of the most eminent figures of English literature were intimately involved with this apotheosis of cartoon art: Dickens, Thackeray (himself a gifted cartoonist), Trollope, Reade, Ainsworth, Marryat, and a myriad of lesser lights, all of whom regarded the best of their cartoonist illustrators and collaborators as men of equal eminence and talent to themselves.

Several of the best-selling novels of the period developed from characters made famous by the books' illustrators—such once-renowned cartoonists as Thomas Rowlandson, George Cruikshank and his father Isaac, John Leech, and others—while publishers tried to recoup investments in poorly written fiction projects by spiffing them up with illustrations by one or another of the nation's top cartoonists, such as "Phiz" (Hablot Knight Browne, Dickens' illustrative collaborator) or Robert Seymour (whose art helped launch Dickens' career).

Rowlandson, Cruikshank, Phiz, Leech, Tenniel (the cartoonist who illustrated the *Alice* books), Seymour, and others were household names among the educated and the masses alike in the England of this enchanted half-century or so, and shelf after shelf of novels, poetry, children's books, books on war, books on naval exploits—you name it— in private homes were filled as much with prose as with cartoon art. *Punch,* the biggest magazine success of mid-century England, was jammed with little more than cartoon art, interspersed with pithy verse and commentary, and its imitators were legion.

Newsstands, crowded with the latest installments of thirty or more continuing novels-in-parts (the popular path of new fiction at the time), cheek by jowl with a bright-faced array of such author-edited journals as *Bentley's Miscellany, The Cornhill,* and *Ainsworth's Magazine,* and

Robert Seymour

"I am extremely anxious about 'The Stroller's Tale' . . . I have seen your design for an etching to accompany it. I think it extremely good, but still, it is not my idea; and as I feel so very solicitous to have it as complete as possible, I shall feel personally obliged to you if you will make another drawing . . . The alterations I want, I will endeavor to explain. I think the woman should be younger, the 'Dismal man' decidedly should, and he should be less miserable in appearance. To communicate an interest to the plate, his whole appearance should express more sympathy and solicitude; and while I represent the sick man as emaciated and dying, I would not make him too repulsive. The furniture of the room, you have depicted *admirably.*"

Charles Dickens

Figure 1

Fagin in the condemned cell.

edged with the continually-selling annuals and monthlies of such cartoonists as Cruikshank, Rowlandson, and Leech, turned bower-faces of cartoon fancy to a delighted public. Shops in every neighborhood hawked fresh lots of political caricatures and social comments by the nation's cartoonists in water-colored prints every week, while poster-bills for current dramas, comedies, vaudeville shows and revels run up on the blind sides of city buildings were wrought wholly in cartoon art. Water colors and occasional oils by Rowlandson, Cruikshank, Leech, Phiz, and others sold well in the London galleries and were hung in country houses across England. The sceptered isle was a sea of cartoon art in those years, and the public swam happily in it as if it would never end.

The word "cartoon" itself was used during most of this period only to refer to the preliminary sketches painters made before undertaking murals or easel oils. Light slang use of the term among artists for line drawings in general was taken up by writers at *Punch* in the early 1840s, and first appeared in print there as descriptive of a humorous drawing in an issue dated July 15, 1843. Popular use of the new term followed, but was limited for decades to come to gags or funny drawings only: Illustrations to popular novels, for example, even though done by artists drawing "funny pictures" in *Punch* in the same style, were not termed cartoon art until much later in the century. What we now call cartoon art in general, no matter how it was employed (even in so scarifying a work as *Maus),* was seen in the 1800-1850 period and later as simply a richly enjoyable *style* of art, applicable, as such, to any and all artistic themes or subjects without any sense of its use in some areas as inappropriate. Seen in such a light, cartoon art takes on a much larger significance that the twentieth century in general has seen fit to give it.

As a style, applied in nineteenth century novel illustration to tragic, suspenseful, tender, and horrific subjects as well as comic, cartoon art emerges as an attractively easy, open technique, utilizing various degrees of exaggeration for the depiction of all subjects, usually to enlarge and focus the effect and to provide the artist range for the application of individual graphic techniques in both figures and backgrounds. This last was useful in giving an artist's work instant recognition. In modern magazine fiction illustration as seen at its best in the *Saturday Evening Post* and *Collier's* in the 1930s and 1940s, most of the illustrators were visually indistinguishable from each other to the layman without checking signatures or making a close study of technique; in contrast, the English artists of 1800-1850 could be identified at a glance by anyone in any work they did. Strict reality was eschewed by the English artists, logically enough, as imposing restraints on stylistic freedom and forcing painstaking attention to detail which in the last analysis is usually irrelevant to mood or point.

Here we can illustratively contrast the work of the later Caniff with that of Crane in 1928 and later: As impressive and cinematically accurate as much Caniff detail was, Crane found most of it unnecessary detritus, distracting in its accuracy where a few lines of simple suggestion would suffice in developing the all-over composition. Crane also enjoyed an expansive use of exaggeration in characters, animals, and backgrounds when he felt his story called for it, while Caniff indulged such inclinations much more cautiously (as in the instance of Singh-Singh and elsewhere). Crane thus would have flourished in the English art world of 1800-1850, while Caniff would have seemed distinctly out of place, tending to drench his work in confusing detail and pursuing unnecessary imaginative restraint. The Caniff of 1934-35 would have been much preferred.

Never before, and never again, were artists and authors so closely and vitally linked at the highest levels of art and literature as during that halcyon English age. Famed artists depended on writers to illustrate *their* story and character concepts in appropriate text, as much as writers leaned on artists to bring their prose creations to vivid graphic life. Dickens, a touchstone through all of this period, began his career as a young author illustrated by the top cartoonist of the time (to insure the book's sale), turned to writing fiction continuity to carry the cartoon creations of another noted artist through their paces, and entered the major phase of his career working in close harness with a third great cartoonist on nearly a dozen shared novels for over twenty years.

Dickens' involved relations with these three cartoonists are typical of those which prevailed between many artists and authors of the time, and will serve to epitomize the primary aspect of this colorful era which concerns us here: the production of long narrative fiction in tight tandem cooperation between writer and artist with heavy emphasis on recurrent characters developing as written and drawn against deadline for weekly or monthly newsstand publication, a common undertaking at the time which almost exactly anticipates and parallels the newspaper and comic book strip work of our time.

From the first decade of the nineteenth century it became increasingly popular for new novels (whether inspired by artist or author or both) to be published in weekly or monthly parts bound with advertisements into stiff illustrated covers and sold in bookstores, news stalls, and similar places. When the authors and artists saw fit to wind up their often picaresque, loosely plotted narratives, the collected parts were often bound by the purchasers into permanent book form, while the original publishers issued other bound sets for bookstore sale.

As reprinted later through the century, the original illustrations were almost always included with the text; it was only after it became the "vogue" to publish fiction without illustrations in the 1880s or so (abetted

Figure 3

Mr. Nadgett breathes, as usual, an atmosphere of mystery.

Robert Seymour

"I'm dem'd if I can ever hit 'em."

by publishers who wanted to avoid the expense and an absence of illustrators with broad public appeal) that the manifold editions of Victorian and Edwardian fiction lacking the original illustrations we see everywhere today became the rule. The damage done to the structure of many of these works by dropping the original illustrations which author and artist had so carefully worked together to incorporate with the text as an integral part of the narrative has only recently been grasped by the critical world, notably in the cases of Dickens and Thackeray, and the art is returning to many new editions of these books. This century-long blindness to a matter of obvious importance at the time such novels were first printed only underscores the general disinterest in cartoon-styled graphics typical of our time, of course.

When a famous artist of the period, Robert Seymour, noted for his skilled comic handling of Cockney sportsmen, proposed an idea for a serial novel dealing with a middle-class hunting club in London taking off on a picaresque tour of the provinces and centering on the club's buffoonish founder, one Seth Pickwick, the artist's publisher thought of a bright young writer named Charles Dickens (who had just published a collection of humorous short stories called *Sketches by Boz*—Dickens' comic pen name—with illustrations by George Cruikshank) as a likely man to do the accompanying narrative text, with Dickens, of course, to take his story instructions from Seymour. The idea, normal for the time, worked out exactly in reverse. Dickens, ebullient and overflowing with comic ideas, overwhelmed the then-ailing Seymour with a three-chapter text for the first monthly number of *The Posthumous Papers of the Pickwick Club* (later simply *The Pickwick Papers*) that trampled his simple ideas underfoot in the soaring heights of fancy to which Dickens took them.

The publisher, like the public, was amazed at the new comic talent that had burst on the serial scene, and it was obvious to everyone but Seymour that Dickens had taken charge of the whole project. Now the artist had to draw to Dickens' demands, a situation so shocking to a man who had always been in charge of such undertakings before that he promptly died—partly of his illness, partly of simple dismay. Dickens was distressed at what had happened, seeing that he had been thoughtlessly careless in the cavalier way he had dealt with the famed cartoonist, and realized he would have to deal with his subsequent illustrator on *Pickwick* on a more evenhanded basis.

Happily, this proved to be no problem with the artist who signed aboard the novel by the time the fourth issue was due to be written: Hablot Knight Browne (who promptly dubbed himself "Phiz" to match Dickens' "Boz" byline on *Pickwick*) was a genial genius whose perceptions of character and drama meshed with those of Dickens from the first. So happily launched, their *Pickwick* rollicked on through another seventeen parts to become the widest-selling serial (and, later, book) of its time. The reputations of both artist and author were made; they were hot as a cracker, and only Dickens' obligation to a magazine publisher who serialized his next novel, *Oliver Twist,* and wanted Cruikshank as illustrator, caused him to part with Browne even briefly. With his following newsstand novel-in-parts, *Nicholas Nickleby,* Dickens rejoined Browne with gusto, and the two were not to part again until twenty years and another nine novels had rolled by.

On every level but the elimination of narrative text and the multiplication of Browne's cartoon panels to accommodate the flow of Dickens' dialogue, the activities and end results of the collaboration of these two matchless talents might as well have been stimulated by the production of a weekly newspaper comic strip or a monthly comic book strip. Detailed plotting and story outline by Dickens seldom extended more than two novel parts ahead, while Browne had to turn out his art in a fixed period of time each month as he received Dickens' precise suggestions for the illustrations. At the outset of a new novel, just as with a new comic strip, Dickens and Browne would huddle and work over graphic sketches of the principal characters slated to open the work, as well as over the elaborate cover design that identified the issues of each new novel on the newsstands.

Much of the fiction of this period—why not call it piction?—resembled newspaper strip story lines of the 1920s and 1930s with its rapid narrative swing between the comic and the melodramatic. Dickens' bizarre character comedy and fanciful plots in his novels before 1850 are much like E.C. Segar's; Captain Marryat's brutal and exciting sea stories, populated with both comic and horrific adventures, closely resemble Crane's work at its best; Thackeray's acid domestic exchanges and handling of social-climbing con-men parallel those in Harry J. Tuthill's *Bungle Family,* and the cartoon illustrations heighten the similarity. As one pages through the hundred and fifty year old bound volumes of these many novels-in-parts, it is as if time has stood still, so crisp and alive is much of the prose, so gripping the action, so undated the comedy, and it is easy to see the cartoon illustrations transferred to the Sunday comic pages of the 1920-1930 period, when strong story lines and comic characters developed in depth ruled the newspaper roost and the strip was at its brief apogee in the United States.

Martin Chuzzlewit and *The Old Curiosity Shop,* with their great cargos of classic human caricatures, from Mrs. Gamp, Mr. Pecksniff, and Sally and Sampson Brass, to Chevy Slyme, Montague Tigg, and the vicious Quilp, can easily be imagined as running for years in the color strip pages (Dickens' novels are wondrously long, like strips) beside

Figure 4

Secret intelligence

"Here's this morning's New York Sewer!" cried one. "Here's this morning's New York Stabber! Here's the New York Family Spy! Here's the New York Private Listener! Here's the New York Peeper! Here's the New York Plunderer! Here's the New York Keyhole Reporter! Here's the New York Rowdy Journal! Here's all the New York papers! Here's full particulars of the patriotic loco-foco movement yesterday, in which the whigs was so chawed up; and the last Alabama gouging case; and the interesting Arkansas dooel with Bowie knives; and all the Political, Commercial, and Fashionable News. Here they are! Here they are! Here's the papers, here's the papers!"

"Here's the Sewer!" cried another. "Here's the New York Sewer! Here's some of the twelfth thousand of to-day's Sewer, with the best accounts of the markets, and all the shipping news, and four whole columns of country correspondence, and a full account of the Ball at Mrs. White's last night, where all the beauty and fashion of New York was assembled; with the Sewer's own particulars of the private lives of all the ladies that was there! Here's the Sewer! Here's some of the twelfth thousand of the New York Swer! Here's the Sewer's exposure of the Wall Street Gang, and the Sewer's exposure of the Washington Gang, and the Sewer's exclusive account of a flagrant act of dishonesty committed by the Secretary of State when he was eight years old; now communicated, at a great expense, by his own nurse. Here's the Sewer! Here's the New York Sewer, in its twelfth thousand, with a whole column of New Yorkers to be shown up, and all their names printed! Here's the Sewer's article upon the Judge that tried him, day afore yesterday, for libel, and the Sewer's tribute to the independent Jury that didn't convict him, and the Sewer's account of what they might have expected if they had! Here's the Sewer, here's the Sewer! Here's the wide-awake Sewer; always on the look-out; the leading Journal of the United States, now in its twelfth thousand, and still a printing off. Here's the New York Sewer!"

"It is in such enlightened means," said a voice almost in Martin's ear, "that the bubbling passions of my country find a vent."

They made their way as they best could through the melancholy crowd of emigrants upon the wharf, who, grouped about their beds and boxes, with the bare ground below them and the bare sky above, might have fallen from another planet, for anything they knew of the country; and walked for some short distance along a busy street, bounded on one side by the quays and shipping; and on the other by a long row of staring red-brick storehouses and offices, ornamented with more black boards and white letters, and more white boards and black letters, than Martin had ever seen before, in fifty times the space. Presently they turned up a narrow street, and presently into other narrow streets, until at last they stopped before a house whereon was painted in great characters, "ROWDY JOURNAL."

The colonel, who had walked the whole way with one hand in his breast, his head occasionally wagging from side to side, and his hat thrown back upon his ears, like a man who was oppressed to inconvenience by a sense of his own greatness, led the way up a dark and dirty flight of stairs into a room of similar character, all littered and bestrewn with odds and ends of newspapers and other crumpled fragments, both in proof and manuscript. Behind a mangy old writing-table in this apartment, sat a figure with a stump of a pen in its mouth and a great pair of scissors in its right hand, clipping and slicing at a file of Rowdy Journals; and it was such a laughable figure that Martin had some difficulty in preserving his gravity, though conscious of the close observation of Colonel Diver.

The individual who sat clipping and slicing as aforesaid at the Rowdy Journals, was a small young gentleman of very juvenile appearance, and unwholesomely pale in the face; partly, perhaps, from intense thought, but partly, there is no doubt, from the excessive use of tobacco, which he was at that moment chewing vigorously.

He was intent upon his work. Every time he snapped the great pair of scissors, he made a corresponding motion with his jaws, which gave him a very terrible appearance.

Martin was not long in determining within himself that this must be Colonel Diver's son; the hope of the family, and future mainspring of the Rowdy Journal. Indeed he had begun to say that he presumed this was the colonel's little boy, and that it was very pleasant to see him playing at Editor in all the guilelessness of childhood, when the colonel proudly interposed and said:

"My War Correspondent, sir. Mr. Jefferson Brick!"

Martin could not help starting at this unexpected announcement, and the consciousness of the irretrievable mistake he had nearly made.

Mr. Brick seemed pleased with the sensation he produced upon the stranger, and shook hands with him, with an air of patronage designed to reassure him, and to let him know that there was no occasion to be frightened, for he (Brick) wouldn't hurt him.

"You have heard of Jefferson Brick I see, sir," quoth the colonel, with a smile. "England has heard of Jefferson Brick. Europe has heard of Jefferson Brick. Let me see. When did you leave England, sir?"

"Five weeks ago," said Martin.

"Five weeks ago," repeated the colonel, thoughtfully; as he took his seat upon the table, and swung his legs. "Now let me ask you, sir, which of Mr. Brick's articles had become at that time the most obnoxious to the British Parliament and the Court of St. James's?"

"Upon my word," said Martin, "I—"

"I have reason to know, sir," interrupted the colonel, "that the aristocratic circles of your country quail before the name of Jefferson Brick. I should like to be informed, sir, from your lips, which of his sentiments has struck the deadliest blow—"

"At the hundred heads of the Hydra of Corruption now grovelling in the dust beneath the lance of Reason, and spouting up to the universal arch above us, its sanguinary gore," said Mr. Brick, putting on a little blue cloth cap with a glazed front, and quoting his last article.

"The libation of freedom, Brick," hinted the colonel.

"Must sometimes be quaffed in blood, colonel," cried Brick. And when he said "blood," he gave the great pair of scissors a sharp snap, as if *they* said blood too, and were quite of his opinion.

This done, they both looked at Martin, pausing for a reply.

Mr. Jefferson Brick proposes an appropriate sentiment

Figure 2

Moon Mullins, Thimble Theatre, and *Dick Tracy,* and cozily bylined "Boz and Phiz." And one can readily imagine these illustrations, already so much like strip panels, being preceded and followed by story-linking panels, with dialogue balloons heavy-laden (in the delightful 1920-1930 manner) with the magical comic and dramatic exchanges of Dickens' raucous characters.

It is not easy to provide an effectively representative cross-section of cartoon art from these novels-in-parts to illustrate this discussion, partly because of space considerations—this volume is, after all, supposed to hold the usual rich serving of G. Washington Tubbs. However, I have a number of duplicate plates from some Dickens novels (plus a novel by a William Maxwell), and I have been able to make a somewhat typical selection of Phiz, Cruikshank, and Leech work from these.

Except for Cruikshank's horrific and classic portrait of Fagin in the condemned cell, none of these cartoons are bravura set pieces, nineteenth century splash-panel equivalents showing the artists at their frame-filling best, because our purpose here is to communicate a sense of the basic story-forwarding function of this narrative art as it was normally seen and relished by the readers of the time. Accordingly, the examples have been selected to demonstrate the routine use of cartoon art in 1800-1850 to illustrate any and all narrative moods or subjects as they emerged in the piction—a function, of course, largely denied cartoon art through the whole of the benighted century and a half following the 1850s.

The Cruikshank, from *Oliver Twist,* of course, speaks for itself. This is a case where even Dickens' words can barely evoke the paranoid aloneness and nail-biting fear of a man awaiting execution caught so nightmarishly in the inspired mesh of Cruikshank's superb lines. But this drawing, which stands so well alone, is not typical of the cooperative author-artist cross-feeding of art and text we will see in the following examples; it is here primarily to show a moving and unforgettable graphic rendering of a powerful emotion—total trapped fear—that our contemporary society feels a cartoonist could not possible portray (fig. 1).

The next example, "Mr. Jefferson Brick . . . ," (fig. 2) is accompanied by some lively slices of Dickens prose written to run with the Phiz drawing. We are presented in its accompanying chapter with the arrival in the rangy, rough-and-ready New York of pre-Civil War America of the hero of *Martin Chuzzlewit,* opening with his impressions of the ebullient New York press *(vide* today's *National Enquirer)* as hawked by newsboys, his meeting with the publisher of one of the papers, Colonel Diver, and the illustrated scene in the newspaper's office. The wild and wooly east coast America portrayed by Dickens may startle many of us, who are more used to the same kind of atmosphere after it moved a few hundred miles west to Medicine Bow and Wounded Knee. Certainly it infuriated his unsophisticated American readers of the time, but it seems to have been accurate enough, given Dickens' comic exaggerations in a text which is as much a written cartoon as Phiz's illustration is a drawn one.

Following this satiric turn, we next find Phiz sensitively catching the edgy, mean mood of a cache of scoundrels sounding out each other's motives and plots as their surface conversation maintains a largely polite tone. This is the "Mr. Nadgett" cut (fig. 3), again from *Martin Chuzzlewit,* portraying a London scene occurring during Martin's American excursion. Jonas Chuzzlewit, who will later murder the suave Montague Tigg who is applying the double brushes so dexterously to his sveltely barbered locks, has been momentarily crushed by some savage implications in Tigg's genial remarks, while the darkly listening party who stands apart in the background warming his scarf by the fire processes the gist of what he hears in terms of what he knows. He is the singly-named Nadgett, the first private eye in English literature, and a scurvy, skulking figure he is—exactly as caught by Phiz. A passage in this chapter, describing Jonas' reaction a bit later to a really alarming charge by Tigg, again gives us a neat sense of Dickens' bright, cartoon prose . . . and way with horror.

"[Tigg] beckoned to Jonas to bring his chair nearer; and looking slightly round, as if to remind him of the presence of Nadgett, whispered in his ear.

"From red to white; from white to red again; from red to yellow; then to a cold, dull, awful, sweat-bedabbled blue. In the short whisper, all these changes fell upon the face of Jonas Chuzzlewit; and when at last he

GEORGE CRUIKSHANK

John Leech

Figure 5

Mark Antony saving the life of the Voltigeur.

laid his hand upon the whisperer's mouth, appalled, lest any syllable of what he said should reach the ears of the third person present, it was as bloodless and as heavy as the hand of death."

In a grim scene from the London underworld, "Secret Intelligence," from *Dombey and Son* (fig. 4), Phiz demonstrates the brutal realism with which the cartoonist illustrators of the time would depict poverty. In this drawing there is not the least flinching from the grubby ugliness of life obviously lived in one room. Again, the dramatic tension of a Dickens scene is perfectly caught, with the shrill importunities of the bonneted harridan, the echoing gabble of the caged parrot, and the despair of the couple seated at the table, unaware of the lowering presence of Mr. Dombey at the door. It is a scene Harold Gray could have caught perfectly as well in illustrating *Dombey,* just as Phiz could have depicted the story line of *Orphan Annie* without ever losing the mood or drama of Gray's actual art.

Finally we have a drawing by John Leech from a picaresque war novel by William Maxwell called *Hector O'Halloran* of 1843 (fig. 5), in which the arbitrary violence and bloodshed of troops shot down by guerillas in a village street is sharply caught; it is a scene Crane could have handled as well or better, if we imagine a pleading Wash telling the guerillas that a uniformed Easy is really on their side, despite appearances. (The comic village figures in the background would, of course, be routine for Crane.)

We have seen the art of piction at its height in this half century of cartoon art's exhilarating reign, but we will have to deal next with the black epoch which followed after the 1850s, a ying-yang movement from the open, broad art of cartooning to the closed, rigid art of realism which has been sadly echoed in the newspaper and magazine strip work of our own time. This will be discussed in the introduction to Tubbs #7, together with a close look at such cartoon art as survived through the 1860-1930 period in popular magazine illustration, including the dime novels and pulps of Crane's youth.

Bill Blackbeard

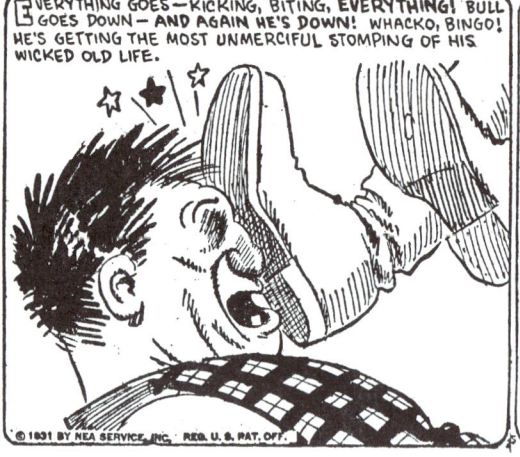

JULY 1931

EASY CAN HARDLY BELIEVE HIS EYES WHEN HE READS WASH'S FAREWELL NOTE.

UNSELFISHLY, HE HAS SACRIFICED THE FINEST FRIENDSHIP OF HIS LIFE SO THAT OTHERS MIGHT PROFIT AND BE HAPPIER BY HIS LOSS.

HE PAUSES TO ADD THE GENTLEMANLY TOUCH WHEN HE REACHES THE EDGE OF HIS HOME TOWN.

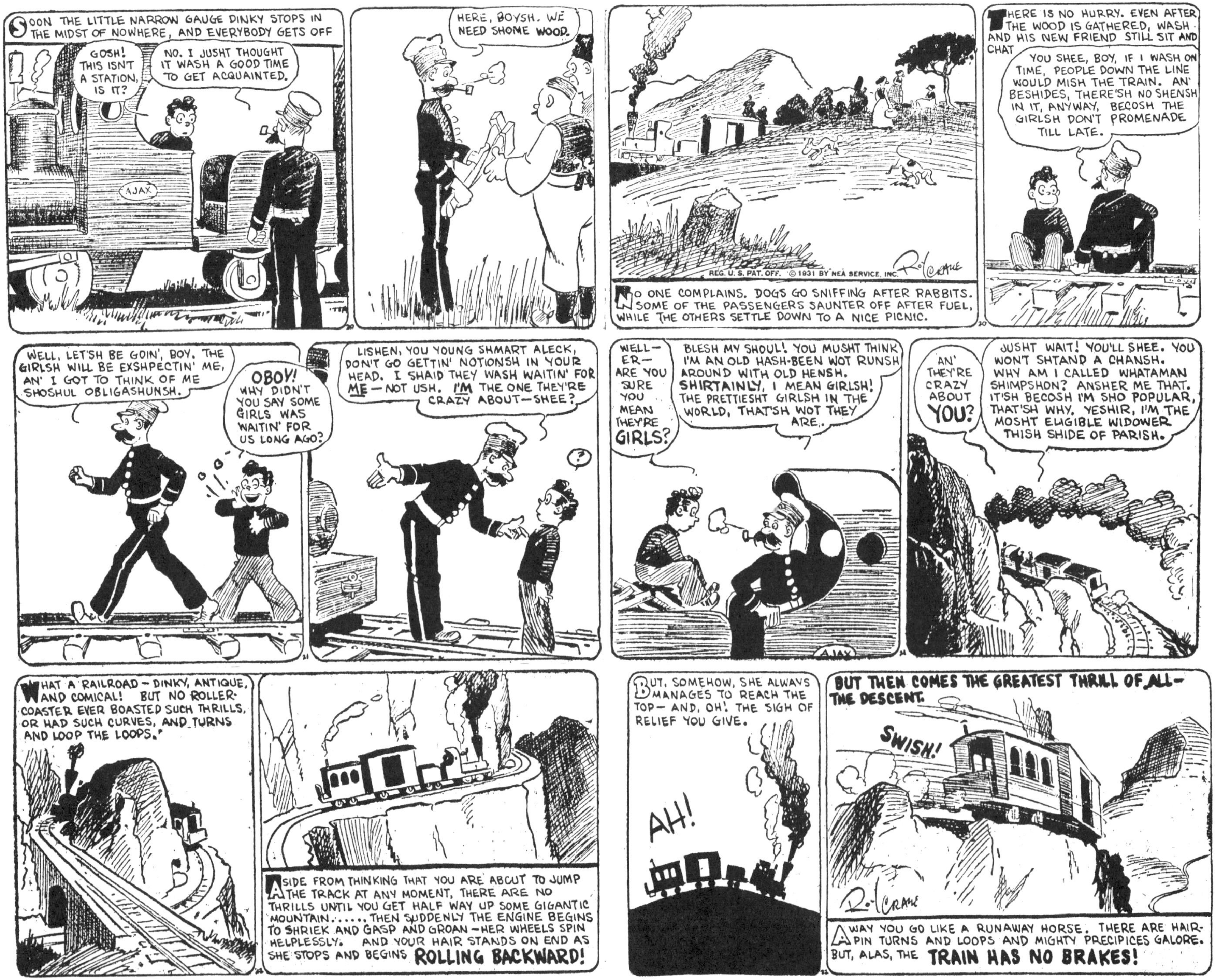

TOOT!
DEPOT
AJAX
TO YOU, PERHAPS, THE TRANS-ALPINA EXPRESS IS A GREAT JOKE. BUT NOT TO THE PEOPLE OF BELCHIA AND SNEEZIA. NO, INDEED. TO THEM IT IS THE EIGHTH WONDER C THE WORLD.
IT HAS BEEN THE TALK OF THESE DREAMY, OLD-WORLD COUNTRIES FOR 20 YEARS, AND, EVERY DAY, FOLKS GATHER FROM MILES AROUND JUST TO VIEW ITS THUNDEROUS ARRIVAL.
NOWHERE, SURELY, IS THERE A WHISTLE SO LOUD, OR CARS SO BRIGHTLY PAINTED, OR AN ENGINE SO FLEET AND POWERFUL AS THEIR AJAX. HOW THEY MARVEL AT ITS SPEED IN MAKING THE ROUND TRIP BETWEEN BELCHIA AND SNEEZIA IN ONLY ONE DAY.
THINK OF IT! SEVENTY TWO MILES — WHY, NOT EVEN A HORSE COULD GO SO FAST.
REG. U. S. PAT. OFF. © 1931 BY NEA SERVICE, INC.
INDEED, NO HOME IS COMPLETE WITHOUT A PICTURE OF THE TRANS-ALPINA EXPRESS. IT IS AN OBJECT OF PRIDE AND JOY— ALMOST A NECESSITY.
AND IF YOU WERE TO TELL SOME ONE THAT THERE ARE RAILROADS HAVING MORE THAN ONE LOCOMOTIVE, HE WOULD LAUGH IN YOUR FACE AND TELL HIS FRIENDS OF THE AWFUL LIAR HE HAD MET.
YOU SHEE, BOY, THERE ISHN'T ANY BRAKE, SHO YOU JUSHT PUT IT IN REVERSH WHEN YOU WANT TO SHLOW DOWN.
WASH ASKS A MILLION QUESTIONS ABOUT THE RAILROAD, THE COUNTRY, AND HOW TO RUN LITTLE AJAX.
HE'S HAVING THE TIME OF HIS LIFE, AND WHATAMAN EVEN LETS HIM BE ENGINEER FOR AWHILE.
BUT WASH IS ALL EYES AS THEY NEAR THE BELCHIAN CAPITOL— A TINY FAIRYLAND PLACE OF TINKLING MUSIC, TOWERS, SPOTTED GOATS, AND TUMBLE DOWN CASTLES ON A SKY-BLUE MOUNTAIN LAKE.
HERE, HERE! WHAT'SH THE IDEAR?
THE TRANS-ALPINA EXPRESS RATTLES OVER THE BRIDGE COMING INTO THE BELCHIAN CAPITOL, AND TWO GIRLS SURPRISE WASH BY JUMPING ON THE ENGINE.
AW, WHATAMAN— PLEASE!
NOSHIR! GIT OFF AN' SHTAY OFF! HOW MANY TIMESH MUSHT I TELL YOU OLD HENSH TO QUIT PESHTERIN' ME?
AJAX
MY GOSH! DO YOU CALL THEM BABIES OLD HENS?
ABSHOLUTELY! WALL-FLOWERSH, THAT'SH WHAT THEY ARE, WALL-FLOWERSH. THEY PESHTER ME TO DEATH. AH, WELL! I SHPOSE THAT'SH WHAT I GET FOR BEIN' SHO POPULAR.

WELL, I'MA THREE-LEGGED DUCK! TH' OLD WALRUS WASN'T LYIN' AFTER ALL.
NOW, NOW, GIRLSH! YOU MUSHN'T BE TOO IMPULSHIVE. AND HOW MANY TIMESH MUSHT I TELL YOU TO SHTOP GIVING ME CANDY? I'M SHICK OF IT.
TO WASH'S AMAZEMENT, HALF A DOZEN BEAUTIES NEARLY GO WILD AT THE SIGHT OF WHATAMAN WHEN THEY REACH THE LINE'S END.
WELL, I SURE GOTTA HAND IT TO YOU, BIG BOY. YOU'RE A WONDER. I NEVER SAW SO MANY SNAPPY BON BONS IN MY LIFE.
OH, THOSH WASH JUSHT A FEW OF MY ADMIRERSH. WE'LL MEET THE RESHT AFTER WE PUT UP THE TRAIN.
REG. U. S. PAT. OFF. © 1931 BY NEA SERVICE, INC.
WOTTA YOU DOIN' THAT FOR ?
THAT, BOY, ISH MY SHECRIT WAY OF LOCKIN' UP OLD AJAX. YOU SHEE, I PUT THISH ROD BETWEEN THE SHIDE BARSH, WHICH LOCKSH THE WHEELSH. IT KEEPSH THE KIDSH FROM PUSHIN' IT DOWN HILL EVERY NIGHT SHO ASH TO MAKE ME WALK AFTER IT.
AJAX
ROY CRANE
THE PLAZA OF THE BELCHIAN CAPITOL — UNKNOWN TO HURRYING TOURISTS. UNSPOILED. COLORFUL. ROMANTIC.
TWILIGHT, AND THE DREAMY ENCHANTING ODORS OF PEPPERMINT AND LEMON TREES. QUEER, SAGGING HOUSES, AND THE CRUMBLING RUIN OF A ROMAN TEMPLE. YOUTHFUL LAUGHTER. GAYETY. AND THE LIVELY, EXOTIC STRAINS OF A GYPSY ORCHESTRA.
GIRLS — BRIGHT-EYED AND GRACEFUL — SWISHING THEIR SKIRTS SAUCILY AS THEY PARADE BEFORE THE ADMIRING EYES OF MORE BASHFUL MALES.
HERE'S WHERE WHATAMAN BRINGS WASH, AND WASH IS CAPTIVATED BY THE CHARM OF THE PLACE.
OBOY! IF ONLY I HAD A GIRL.
WAL, THERE'SH SHOME VERY SHTRANGE CUSHTOMSH IN THIS COUNTRY. JUSHT SHTART WALKING ABOUT — IF THE GIRLSH LIKE YOU, BOY, THEY'LL GRAB YOU.
YOU SAY ALL I GOTTA DO IS TO START WALKIN' ABOUT TH' PLAZA AN' TH' GIRLS WILL START FLIRTIN' WITH ME.
OH, NO. IT ISHN'T FLIRTIN' EGSHACKLY. IT'SH A CUSHTOM. INTRODUCTIONSH ISHN'T NESHESHARY.
YOU SHEE, IN THISH COUNTRY IT'SH THE GIRLSH WOT DUSH THE COURTIN' — NOT THE BOYSH.
WELL — DO THEY SEND CANDY TO TH' FELLAS, AN' BUY 'EM SODAS AN' THINGS?
ABSHOLUTELY! ALL A BOY DUSH ISH TO COME TO THE PLAZA, LET SHOME GIRL SHELECT HIM FOR A DATE — AN' THEN HE SHESH HE'SH HUNGRY OR THIRSHTY. OH, IT'SH SURE A GREAT CUSHTOM.
OBOY! SAY, I LIKE THAT.
LISSEN, WOULDN'T IT HELP IF I SMILED AT 'EM FIRST — Y'KNOW, JUST TO ENCOURAGE 'EM, KINDA?
OH, IT MIGHT. BUT A FIRSHT CLASH MAN WILL SHOMETIMESH HAVE 4 OR 5 GIRLSH WITHOUT EVEN TRYING. MYSHELF, I GENRULLY MAKE FAYSHESH AT 'EM, SHO ASH NOT TO BE TOO ATTRACTIVE.
ROY CRANE
REG. U. S. PAT. OFF. © 1931 BY NEA SERVICE, INC.

WASH STARTS OUT, BRIGHT AND CONFIDENT, EAGER TO ENJOY THE STRANGE BELCHIAN CUSTOM OF BEING SELECTED BY SOME GIRL AS A DATE.
OBOY! WATCH ME STRUT.
TO HIS DELIGHT, MOST OF THE GIRLS ARE KNOCK-OUTS. BUT SOON HE BEGINS TO LOOK WORRIED.
'AT'S FUNNY. NOBODY'S EVEN GIVEN ME A LOOK YET. MAYBE IT'S MY CLOTHES, OR MAYBE THEY DUN'T LIKE CURLEY HAIR, OR SUMPIN.
AN HOUR LATER HIS LUCK IS EVEN WORSE.
WELL, YOU NEEDN'T LAUGH ABOUT IT, Y'BIG SIMP.
MY SHTARSH! BUT I THOUGHT YOU WASH A LADIES'H MAN. AR, WELL! DROP THE OLD CROW, AN' COME ALONG WITH ME. I GESH I GOT ENOUGH FOR THE TWO OF USH.
©1931 BY NEA SERVICE, INC. REG. U. S. PAT. OFF.
HEY, BABY! WAN'T ME TO DO SOME TRICKS FOR YA? HEY! LISSEN!
EVEN WITH HIS FRIEND, WHATAMAN, TO PUSH HIM SOCIALLY WASH CONTINUES TO BE IGNORED. IT'S VERY HUMILIATING, FOR THE GIRLS SIMPLY FLOCK AROUND OLD WHATAMAN.
WASH CAN'T UNDERSTAND IT. HE'S DUMBFOUNDED. ALWAYS, UNTIL NOW, HE HAS CONSIDERED HIMSELF QUITE A HAND WITH THE LADIES.
IT BURNS HIM UP THAT A HOMELY, SEMI-TOOTHLESS, OLD FOSSIL LIKE WHATAMAN CAN BE SO POPULAR. IT'S UTTERLY RIDICULOUS.
AND THE MORE HE THINKS ABOUT IT, THE MADDER HE GETS.
BAH! THESE DAMES IS CRAZY! PLUMB CRAZY!
WASH IS JEALOUS, MAD, AND HURT. OLD WHATAMAN CERTAINLY HAS THE PICK OF THE TOWN—NO OTHER GIRLS CAN COMPARE WITH HIS.
WELL, THEY'S ONE CONSOLATION—TH' RESTA THESE BIRD'S ARE BURNIN' UP, TOO.
HEY! PSST-
FINALLY, WASH CAN STAND BEING IGNORED NO LONGER. HE SWALLOWS HIS PRIDE, AND CALLS HIS FRIEND ASIDE.
LISSEN. FOR GOSH SAKES, MR. SIMPSON, HOW DO YOU DO IT? I NEVER SAW A GUY WITH SO MANY SNAPPY BON BONS IN ALL MY LIFE.
WELL, BOY, IT'SH LIKE THISH: TAKE YOU FOR INSHTUNSH, YOU GOT AN HONESHT FAYSH. YOU AIN'T A BAD LOOKIN' LAD, AN' YOU GOT YOUTH.
BUT YOU LACK SHEXSH APPEAL. THAT'SH WHAT IT ISH, SHEXSH APPEAL. ON THE OTHER HAND, MY BOY, LOOK AT ME. I GOT SHEXSH APPEAL GALORE, AN' WIMMIN ISH SHIMPLY WILD ABOUT ME. THAT'SH THE SHECRIT.
?

WELL, I'M NOT GUNNA HAVE THEM DIZZY DAMES TURNIN' UP THEIR SNOOTS AT ME ANY MORE. I'M GUNA FIND A GOOD BOX SOME PLACE, AN' GO TO SLEEP.
NOSHIR, RIGHT UP TO MY ROOM, BOY.
OMAR
PUNCH
GARDEN
MUSK
NO GUESHT OF MINE ISH GOIN' TO SHLEEP IN A BOXSH. YOU'LL SHTAY WITH ME AT THE INN. AND HERE'SH A FEW DOLLARS TO TIDE YOU OVER.
POOR WASH PUZZLES FOR HOURS ON HOW A MOTH-EATEN OLD ROOSTER LIKE WHATAMAN CAN SHOW HIM UP WITH THE GIRLS.
IT'S BECAUSE I'M SO LITTLE, 'AT'S WHY. EVERYBODY THINKS I'MA RUNT.
REG. U. S. PAT. OFF. © 1931 BY NEA SERVICE, INC.
MY HERO!
NEVER HAS HE FELT SO UNHAPPY. BUT AT LAST HE GOES TO SLEEP, AND DREAMS THAT BY WEARING STILTS, HE BECOMES THE HIT OF THE TOWN.
WHAT! YOU AIN'T GOIN TO RIDE ON THE TRAIN WITH ME TODAY? NOT EVEN IF I LET YOU RUN IT?
NAW. I FEEL KINDA SICK. I GOTTA HEADACHE.
BUT AS SOON AS WHATAMAN LEAVES, WASH COMES TO LIFE.
HA! I'LL SHOW HIM. I KNOW WHY TH' GIRLS ARE SO COO-COO ABOUT 'IM.
I WUNTA BUY A SUIT, MISTER. ANY KIND OF A SUIT SO LONG AS IT'S GOT LOTSA BRASS BUTTONS.
BOOTIES, PANTIES, VESTIES
AHEM!
BUT NOT EVEN THE GLITTERING BRASS BUTTONS SEEM TO MAKE MUCH DIFFERENCE. WASH IS BEWILDERED. COMPLETELY BAFFLED
WASH IS STUMPED. EVEN AFTER HE HAS BOUGHT A SUIT WITH NUMEROUS BRASS BUTTONS, THE GIRLS STILL IGNORE HIM.
DAWGUNNIT! I GOTTA FIND OUT WOT MAKES OLD WOTTAMAN SO POPULAR. SOMEBODY'S BOUND TO KNOW.
LISSEN, FRIEND, HOW TH' HECK CAN AN OLD CROW LIKE WOTTAMAN SIMPSON GET ALL TH' BEST LOOKIN' GIRLS IN THIS TOWN?
MISHTER, I MYSHELF WOULD GIVE HALF MY LIFE TO KNOW THAT.
WUNSH, I WUSH THE MOSHT POPULAR MAN FOR MILESH AROUND. BUT WHEN THAT BLASHTED SHIMPSHON CAME ALONG, THE GIRLSH PLUMB DESHIRTED ME. YESHIR, LEFT ME COLD.
?
REG. U. S. PAT. OFF. © 1931 BY NEA SERVICE, INC.
I THOUGHT IT WUSH BECOSH HE TALKED FUNNY. I WUSH DESHPRIT. I GREW A MUSHTACHE, AND HAD ALL MY TEETH PULLED OUT SHO I WOULD TALK JUSHT LIKE HE DUSH. BUT WUSH IT A SUCSHESH? NO, SHIR, IT WUSH NOT. I NOT ONLY LOSHT MY GIRLSH, BUT MY TEETH ASH WELL.

WHATAMAN ARRIVES EAGER FOR ANOTHER PARTY, BUT WASH HAS HAD ENOUGH.
NIX. THESE DAMES GIMME A PAIN. I'M GOIN' T'BED.
?
AJAX
NEXT MORNING:
WOW! IT MUST BE LATE. WOTTAMAN'S ALREADY GONE— AN' I WAS PLANNIN' ON RIDIN' WITH HIM TODAY.
HE'S NOT AT TH' DEPOT. MAYBE HE'S STILL AT TH' YARD, FIRIN' UP.
TO HIS SURPRISE, THE ENGINE IS STONE COLD, SO HE SITS DOWN TO WAIT. HOURS PASS, AND STILL HIS FRIEND DOES NOT SHOW UP.
GEE! I'M BEGINNIN' TO GET WORRIED.
Roy CRANE
ALL DAY LONG, THE TRANS-ALPINA EXPRESS STANDS IN THE YARD WITHOUT MAKING ITS SCHEDULED TRIP.
AT FIRST WASH IS UNEASY, BUT FOLKS LAUGH AND ASSURE HIM THAT IT IS NOTHING UNUSUAL FOR WHATAMAN TO TAKE A DAY OFF WHEN THE FISH ARE BITING.
BUT WHATAMAN IS MISSING THE NEXT DAY, ALSO, AND WASH IS GETTING REALLY WORRIED.
OBOY! MAYBE 'AT'S HIM AT TH' DOOR NOW.
NO, MR. SIMPSON ISN'T IN. I'M HIS GUEST.
WELL, TELL HIM THE PROPRIETOR SAYS IF HE DOESN'T COME ACROSS WITH THE RENT TODAY OUT HE GOES!
REG. U. S. PAT. OFF. © 1931 BY NEA SERVICE, INC.
. MY GOSH! WOT'LL I DO? EVERY TIME I TURN AROUND I PICK UP NEW TROUBLES.
WELL, Y'NEEDN'T GET SO ROUGH ABOUT IT. IT WASN'T MY OLD ROOM.
ON THE THIRD DAY OF WHATAMAN'S MYSTERIOUS ABSENCE, WASH GETS KICKED OUT OF THE INN FOR NON-PAYMENT OF RENT.
OH, WELL! I WAS GOIN' OUT ANYWAY. I GOTTA FIND OLD WOTTAMAN. FOR ALL I KNOW SUMMA THESE JEALOUS ROMEOS MIGHTA KIDNAPPED HIM OR SUMPIN.
HEY! WOT'S ALL TH' WEEPIN' AN' WAILIN' ABOUT, SISTER? HAS SOMEBODY DIED?
BOO HOO! OUR WHATAMAN'S GONE.
HE'S ELOPED!
HE MARRIED THAT SILLY LOOFER GIRL FOR HER MONEY.
Roy CRANE
ELOPED!!
MY GOSH! NOW I AM IN A FIX. NO ROOM— NO MONEY— AN' NOW MY ONLY FRIEND'S GONE. TO MAKE MATTERS WORSE, I CAN'T EVEN HOP A TRAIN OUTA THIS DUMP.

ON THE THIRD DAY OF WHATAMAN'S ABSENCE, THE BELCHIAN PRESIDENT CALLS A CABINET MEETING AT HIS STORE TO CONSIDER THE EMERGENCY.
GENTLEMEN, A GREAT CALAMITY HAS BEFALLEN US. OUR ONLY RAILROAD ENGINEER HAS ELOPED.
ALL ABOARD!
AND AFTER MANY HOURS OF DEBATE THEY DECIDE TO HITCH A MULE TO THE TRANS-ALPINA EXPRESS.
BUT THERE IS A FLAW IN THEIR PLAN. THE MULE KEEPS STEPPING THRU THE TIES ON ALL THE BRIDGES.
HEAVE HO, BOYS!
AND THE PASSENGERS GET SORE WHEN THEY HAVE TO PUT THE MULE IN THE COACH AND PUSH HIM OVER EACH BRIDGE.
JUST THINK — 334 BRIDGES. WE'LL NEVER GET TO SNEEZIA.
BAH! AND I PAID MY FARE FOR THE PRIVILEGE OF PUSHING A MULE.
ON THE FOURTH DAY OF WHATAMAN'S ABSENCE, ANOTHER CABINET MEETING IS CALLED. THIS TIME IT IS DECIDED THAT HAND CARS ARE TO PULL THE TRANS-ALPINA EXPRESS.
BUT SO STEEP ARE THE GRADES THAT ALL THE PASSENGERS MUST WORK ON THE HAND CARS IN ORDER TO PULL THE EMPTY COACH.
THEN, WHEN THEY START DOWN HILL THE HAND CARS ARE NOT FAST ENOUGH TO GET OUT OF THE WAY OF THE FLYING COACH.
HELP! SHE'S GOING TO RUN US DOWN.
JUMP FOR YOUR LIVES!
ANOTHER FAILURE! THE EXPRESS SOON JUMPS THE TRACK AND EVERYBODY HAS TO WALK HOME.
FIVE LONG DAYS HAVE PASSED SINCE THE TRANS-ALPINA EXPRESS MADE ITS LAST DAILY TRIP TO SNEEZIA.
THE DEPOT, ONCE THE GAYEST SPOT IN ALL BELCHIA, IS NOW DESERTED AND STILL.
THE PEOPLE LOVE THEIR WHEEZY OLD LOCOMOTIVE. THEY LOVE ITS FRIENDLY WARMTH, ITS OILY SMELL, ITS FUNNY GURGLES AND CLANKINGS, ITS SCREECHING WHISTLE. SOMEHOW, LIFE WITHOUT OLD AJAX CLATTERING ABOUT SEEMS SORT OF SAD AND LONELY AND EMPTY.
ALL BELCHIA IS HEART-BROKEN. THE PRESIDENT IS FRANTIC.
BEWARE OF DOG
BUT WASH IS HAVING TROUBLES OF HIS OWN. HE HAS LONG SINCE BEEN FORCED TO HOCK HIS NEW BRASS-BUTTONED SUIT, AND HAS MOVED INTO AN ABANDONED DOG HOUSE.

THE LITTLE REPUBLIC OF BELCHIA IS FACE TO FACE WITH THE GRAVEST CRISIS IN YEARS. DAYS HAVE PASSED SINCE THEIR ONLY ENGINEER ELOPED, AND THEREBY PUT THE RAILWAY ON THE BLINK.
THE HIGHEST OFFICIALS IN THE LAND, EVEN THE PRESIDENT, LEAVE THEIR FARMS AND STORES IN A PATRIOTIC EFFORT TO GET OLD AJAX STARTED ONCE MORE.
WHAT DO WE DO FIRST? BUILD A FIRE?
I THINK YOU PUT WATER IN THE BOILER FIRST.
HOW DO YOU GET IT IN THERE? I DON'T SEE ANY HOLES.
MAYBE YOU POUR IT DOWN THE SMOKE STACK OR THE WHISTLE.
AJAX
THEY GET IT STEAMED UP WITHOUT SERIOUS MISHAP, BUT IN SPITE OF PULLING LEVERS AND TURNING ALL THE GADGETS AND DOODADS IN SIGHT, OLD AJAX REFUSES TO BUDGE.
ALL TOGETHER, BOYS— PUSH.
TRY BLOWING THE WHISTLE AGAIN, ADOLF.
NO. SIT ON THE SAFETY VALVE. WE HAVEN'T TRIED THAT YET.
WELL! WELL! LOOKS LIKE I'M GUNNA COME IN HANDY.
WASH IS AMUSED AS THE GOVERNMENT OFFICIALS TRY IN VAIN TO START THE TRAIN. FINALLY, HE WANDERS OVER TO THE PRESIDENT.
SAY, I KIN START OLD AJAX. I KNOW ALL ABOUT ENGINES.
!
WHAT? YOU CAN RUN A TRAIN? HERE—HOLD THIS BOY! DON'T LET HIM GET AWAY—HE'S OUR NEW ENGINEER.
EVERYBODY CROWDS AROUND TO GET A BETTER VIEW OF THE SAVIOR OF THE RAIL ROAD. THEY SHAKE WASH'S HAND, CHEER HIM, TAKE HIS PICTURE, AND LITERALLY PUSH HIM INTO THE CAB.
GEE! I ALMOST WISH I HADN'T SAID ANYTHING— I SURE HOPE EVERYTHING GOES AWRIGHT.
AJAX
HIS KNEES SHAKE SO BADLY THAT HE CAN HARDLY GET INTO THE GAUDY UNIFORM SOMEONE HANDS HIM.
LE'S SEE, NOW—MUSTN'T FORGET ANYTHING. STEAM'S O.K. FIRE'S OK. BUT LOW ON WATER. THANK GOODNESS, OLD WOTTAMAN SHOWED ME HOW TO WORK THE WATER INJECTOR.
AJAX
GEE! I SURE HOPE I REMEMBER EVERYTHING HE TOLD ME ABOUT RUNNIN' THIS OLD THING.
JAX
THE OFFICIALS LOOK ON IN BEWILDERMENT AS WASH REMOVES WHATAMAN'S SECRET "LOCK", USED TO PREVENT THE BOYS FROM PUSHING OLD AJAX DOWN HILL.
CHUG!
OH, THE SIGH OF RELIEF THAT HE GIVES WHEN IT ACTUALLY STARTS, AND THE CROWD YELLS WITH DELIGHT.
HE'S TERRIBLY RATTLED, BUT MANAGES TO SWITCH A FEW CARS AND RUN THE TRAIN DOWN TO THE DEPOT LIKE A REAL VETERAN. IN FACT, HE PULLS BUT ONE BONER.
HEY! YOU FORGOT TO WAIT FOR THE PRESIDENT.
Roy Crane

AT THE DEPOT A HUGE, CHEERING CROWD GATHERS TO CELEBRATE THE RENEWAL OF TRAIN SERVICE. IT IS A DAY OF REJOICING. THERE ARE SPEECHES. BOTH BANDS ARE OUT, AND THE POPULACE IS CUTTING UP LIKE ALL GET OUT.
DEPOT
OUR OLD FRIEND, WASHINGTON TUBBS, IS THE NEW ENGINEER—THE MAIN ATTRACTION. HOW THEY CHEER HIM. ONE OF THE BANDS, OCCUPYING TWO ENTIRE FLAT CARS, IS GOING ALONG JUST TO MAKE SURE THAT HIS FIRST TRIP IS A ROLLICKING SUCCESS.
AND TIME AND AGAIN, OLD WASH IS CALLED UPON TO ACKNOWLEDGE THE CHEERS. BOY, HOW HE LOVES IT!
PWEEEK!
WASH GIVES TWO THUNDERING BLASTS ON THE WHISTLE, AS THE TIME ARRIVES FOR THE TRANS-ALPINA EXPRESS TO DEPART.
OLD AJAX GIVES A MIGHTY JERK, AND THE CHEERING CROWD GOES WILD. CAPS ARE THROWN IN THE AIR. DOGS BARK. BOTH BANDS STRIKE UP LIVELY TUNES, AND SOMEBODY FIRES AN OLD CANNON.
HI HO! I AIN'T MAD AT NOBODY!
OLD WASH GRINS WITH PRIDE AS HE NOTICES THAT ALL EYES ARE TURNED ON HIM.
BUT BEST OF ALL, A GROUP OF ADMIRING BEAUTIES HAS GATHERED TO WAVE HIM GOOD BYE.
WITH WASH AT THE THROTTLE, THE TRANS-ALPINA EXPRESS RATTLES OFF TOWARD SNEEZIA IN MAGNIFICENT STYLE.
OBOY! I'M BEGINNIN' TO FEEL AT HOME IN THIS THING- I GUESS I'LL SHOW 'EM SOME SPEED.
EVERYONE IS IN A GALA MOOD — THE BAND STRIKES UP A SNAPPY MILITARY MARCH.
THEN A SHARP CURVE!!!
AND THE MUSIC SUDDENLY STOPS!
SPLASH!

GEE, BOYS, I'M AWFUL SORRY. I'LL BE MORE CAREFUL NEXT TIME. HONEST, I WILL.
BAH! THERE WON'T BE ANY NEXT TIME.
WASH FEELS PRETTY BAD ABOUT TAKING A CURVE TOO FAST AND THROWING THE BAND IN THE LAKE.
AND FOR AWHILE IT LOOKS AS THO THE BAND WILL SPOIL THE CELEBRATION BY WALKING HOME.
NOSIR! WE'RE THRU. NO MORE FLAT CARS FOR US, AND THAT'S FINAL.
AW, NIX, FELLAS, PLEASE. LISSEN, I GOT A GREAT IDEA. WHY DON'T YOU RIDE ON TOP OF TH' TRAIN?
AH! THIS IS BETTER.
THAT NEW ENGINEER ISN'T SUCH A BAD SKATE AFTER ALL.
© 1931 BY NEA SERVICE, INC. REG. U. S. PAT. OFF.
SOK!
SWISH!
AJAX
ASIDE FROM LOSING THE BAND A COUPLE OF TIMES, WASH'S FIRST TRIP AS ENGINEER ON THE TRANS-ALPINA EXPRESS IS PRACTICALLY UNEVENTFUL. HE JUMPS THE TRACK BUT ONCE.
POW!
ONLY ONE MORE MISHAP MAY BE CONSIDERED WORTH MENTIONING. UPON REACHING THE END OF THE LINE, HE BECOMES CONFUSED AND NOSE DIVES THRU THE CITY HALL.
POOR WASH!
HE SURVEYS THE AWFUL WRECKAGE, AND WAITS DEJECTEDLY TO BE FIRED.
I GUESS I JUST WUZN'T CUT OUT TO BE AN ENGINEER, 'AT'S ALL.
WELL, WHEN DO I GET FIRED?
FIRED? MY DEAR BOY, NEVER! YOU'RE THE GREATEST ENGINEER IN THE HISTORY OF THE RAILROAD.
BUT I WRECKED THE TRAIN TWICE, AN' TH' CITY HALL, AN' LOST TH' BAND, AN' ALMOST KILLED EVERYBODY ABOARD.
TUT TUT! THAT'S WHAT THIS COMMUNITY LOVES, SIR—EXCITEMENT! GIVE THE PUBLIC WHAT IT WANTS, AND THE MORE WRECKS, THE MERRIER.
YOU'RE A SENSATION. FOR THRILLS, MY BOY, YOU'VE GOT A ROLLER COASTER BACKED OFF THE MAP. COME, LET'S GET STARTED—HALF THE TOWN IS YELLING TO RIDE BACK WITH YOU.
Roy CRANE

OOPS! ANOTHER ONE.
CLANK!
DOZENS OF THRILL-SEEKERS FIGHT THEIR WAY ABOARD WASH'S TRAIN, EAGER FOR WRECKS AND EXCITEMENT.
TO THEIR DISGUST, THO, WASH IS LEARNING TO MASTER OLD AJAX, AND ONLY MINOR MISHAPS OCCUR.
OBOY! AIN'T I HAPPY?
BUT, OH! HOW THE GIRLS GO FOR WASH THAT NIGHT! HE'S THE HIT OF THE TOWN— A SENSATION. NEVER WAS OLD WHATAMAN HALF SO POPULAR. NEVER DID ANYONE IN BELCHIA HAVE SO MANY GIRLS.
Dear Easy-
Well old Pal I guess by now you are an old hen pecked sissy and have to dry the dishes every night.
Ha Ha! Look at the inclosed picture of me you big cheese & see what you are missing as I am a Big Shot now & these are only a few of my hundreds and hundreds of beautiful admirers.
Well I guess you think I am a big windy as you use to think you were the whole works but I guess this picture proves I'm no dummy, old Pal. I am considered such a great guy I call the president by his first name which is Oscar.
I am now in the railroad business.
I am surprised I never got in the Railroad business ~~before~~ before as I am such a success. I am an Engineer, Easy. My train is an Enternational express train & it is the biggest and finest train in this part of Europe no kidding & I am such a success they say the whole line would be paralized if it wasn't for me to run that train.
Well old pal I will write again to tell you of any of my new successes.
your old Pal
W. Washington Tubbs
PRESIDENT
TIME PASSES, AND ONE AFTERNOON THE MOST POPULAR MAN IN BELCHIA IS TORN AWAY FROM HIS LADY LOVES TO TAKE THE PRESIDENT ON A MILITARY INSPECTION TRIP.
IT BURNS WASH UP, TOO, UNTIL HE TUMBLES TO THE FACT THAT A STRANGE GIRL IS ABOARD.
WOW! WOT EYES!
IMMEDIATELY, HIS OTHER GIRLS ARE FORGOTTEN. WHO CAN THIS LOVELY CREATURE BE? WHY HAS HE NEVER SEEN HER BEFORE? AH, HOW HE WOULD LIKE TO MAKE AN IMPRESSION!

Panel	Text
1	THE PRESIDENT AND HIS PARTY WANDER OFF TO INSPECT A FRONTIER FORT. ONLY THE GIRL — AND WASH — REMAIN.
2	POOR WASH! NOW IS HIS CHANCE TO GET ACQUAINTED. BUT SO STRUCK IS HE WITH HER BEAUTY, THAT HE GETS STAGE-FRIGHT, AND IS AFRAID TO SPEAK.
3	HOWEVER, THE GIRL SOON BREAKS THE ICE. "WHY DON'T YOU COME AND SIT BESIDE ME?"
4	FROM THEN ON, WASH IS HOPELESSLY LOST. EVERY TIME SHE FLASHES THOSE EYES AT HIM, HIS HEART DOES FLIP-FLOPS. AND WHEN SHE BRINGS OUT A BASKET OF FOOD — WELL, HIS HEART IS GONE. IT IS NO LONGER HIS.
5	WHEE! WASH IS IN LOVE!! THE IDOL OF HIS DREAMS IS NONE OTHER THAN THE ONLY DAUGHTER OF THE PRESIDENT OF BELCHIA.
6	SHE IS AN ANGEL, THINKS WASH. HER NECK IS LIKE THAT OF A BEAUTIFUL SWAN. HER EYES ARE LIKE STARS, AND HER LIPS LIKE A RED, RED ROSE.
7	AH! AH! NO WONDER HE FALLS FOR THIS WONDROUS CREATURE. NO WONDER HE IS SO SAD AT PARTING, AND GIVES THE OTHER GIRLIES THE GO-BY THAT NIGHT SO THAT HE MAY BE ALONE WITH HIS MEMORIES.
8	FOR A WEEK AFTER WASH MEETS THE FAIR DAUGHTER OF THE PRESIDENT, RAILROAD SERVICE IS ALMOST AT A STANDSTILL. THE BOY ROMEO IS HAVING FAR TOO GOOD A TIME TO BE BOTHERED WITH BUSINESS. NO TRAIN TODAY. GOTTA DATE
9	HE DOES THINGS IN STYLE, TOO. EVERY NIGHT HE HIRE'S A BAND AND TAKES HIS LADY LOVE ON WONDERFUL MOONLIGHT RIDES THRU THE MOUNTAINS..... HIS WHIRLWIND COURTSHIP IS THE TALK OF THE COUNTRY.

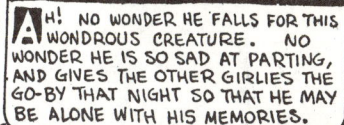

OCTOBER 1931

OF ALL OF WASH'S GIRLS, ONLY ONE NOW NOTICES HIM.
WHY AREN'T YOU IN THE ARMY LIKE ALL THE OTHER MEN?
SHOO! I DUN'T EVEN KNOW WOT THEY'RE FIGHTIN' ABOUT.
GEN. DE PRESHIN
WHY, IT'S ABOUT THE RAILROAD. YOU SEE, THIS IS THE FIRST TIME THAT THE RAILROAD'S EVER MADE MONEY. AND SINCE MORE OF THE LINE'S IN SNEEZIA THAN IN BELCHIA, SNEEZIA DEMANDS MORE THAN HALF THE PROFITS.
RATS! WOTTA I CARE WHO GETS TH' PROFITS?
B'SIDES, I DON'T FIGHT WITH ANY O' THESE AMATEUR CLUBS. I'M A PRO– A BIG LEAGUER. AN' I HEAR SOLDIERS OVER HERE DUN'T GET ANY PAY.
CERTAINLY NOT! THEY FIGHT FOR THE SPORT OF IT.
OH, HO! THEY THINK IT'S SPORT TO HAVE BULLETS BOUNCED OFFA THEIR DOMES, EH? WELL, NOT ME SISTER. I BIN IN WARS BEFORE.
YOU TRAITOR! YOU SLACKER! YOU'LL GET SHOT FOR THIS.
REG. U. S. PAT. OFF. © 1931 BY NEA SERVICE, INC.
THERE HE IS– HE WON'T JOIN THE ARMY.
YA-A! HE'S YELLOW. HE'S AFRAID TO FIGHT.
HELLO, SLACKER!
?
WHO SAYS I'M YELLA?
SHOO! I WOULDN'T SEE THIS MUCH FIGHTIN' IF I WAS AT TH' FRONT.
HORSES ONLY
WITHIN AN HOUR WASH LOSES THREE FIGHTS, AND CONCLUDES THAT SOMETHING OUGHT TO BE DONE ABOUT IT.
SLACKER! COWARD!!
I'LL SHOW 'EM.
WASH IS BURNING UP. ALL HIS SWEETIES HAVE JILTED HIM FOR THE BRAVE SOLDIER LADDIES.
GIMME A UNIFORM AN' A GUN. I WUNTA FIGHT.
TUT TUT, MY BOY! YOUR PLACE IS AT THE THROTTLE. HOW ON EARTH WOULD WE EVER GET THE TROOPS TO THE FRONT WITHOUT YOU TO RUN THE TRAIN?
RECRUITING OFFICE
YOUR COUNTRY NEEDS YOU
BELCHIA EXPECTS EVERY MAN TO DO HIS DUTY.
WHY, WE WOULDN'T THINK OF LETTING YOU JOIN THE ARMY.
ZAT SO? WELL, WOT IF I GO ON A STRIKE, AN' REFUSE TO RUN TH' TRAIN?
IN THAT CASE, SIR, YOU WOULD BE SHOT AS A TRAITOR!!
SO WASH RUNS THE TRAIN. BUT HOW HE BURNS!!
REG. U. S. PAT. OFF. © 1931 BY NEA SERVICE, INC.

THEY OUGHTA START A WAR ABOUT SOMETHING.
WARS BETWEEN BELCHIA AND SNEEZIA ARE QUITE COMMON. ALSO VERY STRANGE. NOBODY REALLY GETS MAD, BUT IT'S A NICE FORM OF AMUSEMENT WHEN THE FISHING GOES BAD.
THE OBJECT SEEMS TO BE TO MAKE MORE NOISE THAN THE OTHER SIDE, AND THE GUNS ARE LOADED WITH ROCKS, OR MUD, OR MOST ANY OLD THING. HARDLY EVER IS ANYONE KILLED, BUT THINK OF THE FUN THEY HAVE.
POW!
WARFARE IN BELCHIA IS NOT SOLELY A MAN'S SPORT EITHER. NO INDEED!
IT MAKES A BIG HIT WITH THE YOUNGSTERS AND WOMEN FOLKS, WHO COME OUT ON PICNICS TO ENJOY THE NOISE AND TO ADMIRE THE DASHING UNIFORMS OF THE GALLANT "HEROES."
I HEAR THE SNEEZIANS ARE SHOOTING BLANKS THIS YEAR ON ACCOUNT OF THE DEPRESSION.
DO HAVE ANOTHER PIECE OF CAKE.
WHERE'S THE LEMONADE?
BAM!
ROY CRANE
THE WAR MAY BE A BIG PICNIC TO THE BELCHIANS, BUT NOT TO WASH. HE'S MAD. NOT ONLY HAVE THE GIRLS JILTED HIM, BUT HE WORKS SIXTEEN HOURS A DAY HAULING TROOP TRAINS AND SUPPLIES.
BAH! I DO ALL TH' WORK, AN' TH' OTHER GUYS GET TH' CREDIT.
SO FAR, THE OUTSTANDING HERO OF THE WAR IS A CLUMSY BOZO WHO FALLS OUT OF A TREE AND BREAKS HIS LEG.
AND EVERYBODY MAKES QUITE A FUSS WHEN THE RED CROSS TRAIN ARRIVES FROM THE FRONT WITH THE "WOUNDED."
DON'T SHOOT
HOSPITAL CAR
ROY CRANE
© 1931 BY NEA SERVICE, INC. REG. U. S. PAT. OFF.
WASH IS DISGUSTED.
BOY, JUST WAIT. I'M GUNNA SHOW THESE DAMES WOT A REAL HERO'S LIKE.
THE PRIDE OF THE BELCHIAN ARMY IS AN OBSERVATION BALLOON, BUT NO ONE SEEMS TO KNOW HOW TO USE IT.
LISSEN, COLONEL. WHY DON'T YOU TIE IT TO MY TRAIN? THEN WE CAN MOVE IT TO ANY PART OF TH FRONT WE WANTA.
?
SO THE BALLOON IS ATTACHED TO THE TRAIN, AND EVERYTHING GOES WELL UNTIL A CANNONBALL WHIZZES BY.
ZIPEEEEE!
JUMP FOR YOUR LIVES!
REG. U. S. PAT. OFF. © 1931 BY NEA SERVICE, INC.
HEY!
SNAP!
AND, ALAS, TWO FLAT CARS AND THE BALLOON GO SAILING OFF TOWARD SWITZERLAND..... AND POOR WASH GETS THE BLAME.

ON ONE MOUNTAIN IS THE BELCHIAN ARMY. ON ANOTHER IS THE SNEEZIAN. AND FAR BENEATH EACH ARMY RUNS THE RAILROAD. WASH KNOWS THIS.
ONE NIGHT HE STEALS CAREFULLY ACROSS THE HIGH BRIDGE IN NO MAN'S LAND— THEN INTO THE INKY TUNNEL BENEATH THE ENEMY LINES.
AND A COUPLE OF SENTRIES GIVE HIM THE SCARE OF HIS LIFE.
HALT!!
BANG!
HOWEVER, HE SEEMS WELL SATISFIED WITH THE DISCOVERY THAT THE TUNNEL, APPARENTLY, IS NOT BLOCKED IN ANY WAY.
OBOY! I COULD RUN MY TRAIN THRU THERE EASY AS PIE.
BANG! BANG!
WASH IS DESPERATE TO BECOME A BIG HERO, AND WIN BACK THE HEARTS OF HIS LADY FRIENDS.
OBOY! I GOTTA IDEA 'AT'LL WIN TH' WAR. I'LL BE FAMOUS.
IT'S THIS WAY, COLONEL. FIRST, Y'FILL MY TRAIN WITH SOLDIERS, SEE. THEN DASH 'EM THRU TH' LINES AN' CAPTURE TH' ENEMY CAPITOL WHILE NOBODY'S THERE.
EXCELLENT. I MUST TELL THE GENERAL.
LISTEN, GENERAL, I JUST THOUGHT OF A PLAN TO WIN THE WAR. ETC. ETC.
I HAVE A GREAT IDEA, TUBBS. IT'LL WIN THE WAR. ALL YOU HAVE TO DO IS TO RUN A TRAIN LOAD OF TROOPS THRU THE ENEMY LINES SO THEY CAN CAPTURE THE CAPITOL.
!
FORTY DARING WARRIORS, THE PICK OF THE BELCHIAN ARMY, ARE ABOARD WASH'S TRAIN. HOW BRAVE THEY ARE! HOW THE CROWD CHEERS! OH, IT'LL BE A NIFTY JOKE ON SNEEZIA WHEN THEY SWOOP DOWN AND CAPTURE ITS CAPITOL.
BOOM!
WHOOPEE! THEY'RE OFF. SUCH A DIN OF SHOUTING AND SHOOTING YOU'VE NEVER HEARD. STRAIGHT ACROSS NO-MAN'S-LAND THEY RATTLE. STRAIGHT FOR THE INKY TUNNEL BENEATH THE ENEMY LINES.
REG. U. S. PAT. OFF.
© 1931 BY NEA SERVICE, INC.

SUCCESS! RIGHT BENEATH THE SNEEZIAN ARMY STEAMS OLD AJAX, CARRYING THE PICK OF BELCHIA'S WARRIORS.
CLICKETY CLICK—DOWN HILL AT 40 MILES AN HOUR—AROUND CURVES—THRU TUNNELS—NOTHING STOPS 'EM.
THEY'VE BROKEN THRU THE ENEMY LINES!! THE SNEEZIANS ARE DUMBFOUNDED! SPEECHLESS!
! !
THEN TELEGRAPH WIRES FLASH THE TERRIFYING NEWS TO THE UNPROTECTED CAPITOL
ROY CRANE
STRANGE TO SAY, THERE IS NO PANIC WHEN NEWS COMES TO THE SNEEZIAN CAPITOL THAT WASH AND A TRAIN-LOAD OF SOLDIERS HAVE BROKEN THRU THE LINES.
NAY, THE BUXOM WOMEN OF SNEEZIA ARE MADE OUT OF STERNER STUFF.
NO PESKY SOLDIERS ARE GOING TO MESS UP MY KITCHEN.
WE DON'T CARE HOW MANY GUNS THEY GOT.
THEY GRAB BROOMS, ROLLING PINS, AND PITCHFORKS, AND SET OUT TO REPEL THE INVASION.
ALL TOGETHER, GIRLS. GET READY FOR BATTLE.
AND SOON A GREAT SHOUT RINGS OUT AS THEY HEAR OLD AJAX RATTLING DOWN A HILL NOT HALF A MILE AWAY.
REG. U. S. PAT. OFF.
© 1931 BY NEA SERVICE, INC.
ROY CRANE
TOO LATE, WASH SEES THAT THE TRACK HAS BEEN TORN UP.
!
AJAX
HE BARELY HAS TIME TO THROW OLD AJAX IN REVERSE — THEN—
KER-PLUNK!
©1931
ROY CRANE

POOR OLD AJAX PLUNGES INTO A WATERY GRAVE, AND WASH AND THE BRAVE SOLDIER LADDIES FLOUNDER TOWARD THE SHORE.
THEN THEY BEHOLD THE BEVY OF BUXOM BELLES WAVING BROOMS, PITCHFORKS, AND ROLLING PINS AT THEM.
SURRENDER, YOU MUGS OR SINK!
AND, ALAS FOR THE FIRST TIME IN HISTORY THE PROUD AND DASHING WARRIORS OF BELCHIA BECOME THE PRISON ERS OF WOMEN.
OH, THE SHAME AND DISGRACE!
OH, THE HUMILIATION OF THEIR AWFUL DOWNFALL!
OF ALL THE ARMY, WASH ALONE DEFIES CAPTURE AT THE HANDS OF THE EN-RAGED SNEEZIAN HOUSEWIVES.
BY GOLLY! I'LL SINK FIRST.
WOW! I GOTTA TAKE OFF THESE BOOTS AN' THINGS OR I'LL NEVER MAKE IT.
HE STARTS OUT BRAVELY ENOUGH TO SWIM THE LAKE, BUT BEGINS TO WEAKEN HALF WAY ACROSS.
IMAGINE HIS DISMAY, AFTER REMOVING HIS CLOTHES, WHEN HE SEES A BOATLOAD OF WOMEN COMING AFTER HIM.
DON'T LET HIM GET AWAY, GIRLS. FASTER!!
OMY GOSH! THEY'RE GAININ'! WOT'LL I DO? HELP!
'TIS THE MOST EMBARRASSING MOMENT OF OUR YOUNG HERO'S LIFE.
SURRENDER!!
STICK HIM AGAIN, MABEL. DON'T LET HIM ESCAPE.
SURRENDER, YOU MUG, OR I'LL--
OUCH! HELP! PLEASE, LADIES, I-I CAN'T SURRENDER! I HAVEN'T ANY CLOTHES ON.
HASTILY, THE SNEEZIAN HOUSEWIVES CALL A CONFERENCE OF WAR.
NO CLOTHES ON! HEAVENS! WE CAN'T CAPTURE A MAN LIKE THAT.
OH, OH! WHAT'LL WE EVER DO?
MY DEAR, SOMEBODY WILL SIMPLY HAVE TO LOAN THE POOR MAN A PETTICOAT.
TEE HEE
TEE HEE
HOHO HA HA!
ROY CRANE
© 1931 BY NEA SERVICE, INC. REG. U. S. PAT. OFF.
AND, TO WASH'S DYING DAY, HE'LL NEVER FORGET HIS AWFUL AND HUMILIATING CAPTURE.

Panel	Text
1	**WOT? DON'T I GET NO PANTS?** — Wash's imprisonment is a nightmare even worse than his capture. He is given nothing to replace the petticoat.
2	And his cell is on the ground floor. Oh, it's awful. All day long the Sneezian women stand at his window and giggle at his embarrassment. "TEE HEE!" "GO 'WAY, PLEASE! HAVVA HEART." "HEE HEE!"
3	"TEE HEE!" "HE'S A SCREAM!" — What fun they have! How they delight at his blushes.. In vain he pleads for some pants, a shirt, or even a pin.
4	And laughingly they bring him dainty little pink things. Poor Wash! He had dreamed of attaining fame, glory, honor — and this is his reward.
5	Wash's capture gives the Sneezians ideas. Big ideas. Ha! They'll show those Belchians a trick or two. Yessir, they'll pull Ajax out of the lake and put old Wash to work, that's what.
6	But poor old Ajax is buried deep in the mud and all they recover is the smokestack.
7	**GLOOM** overcomes them! They know not what to do.
8	Then, in desperation, they empty the treasury, and rush a man to Austria to buy a new locomotive, at any cost.
9	"AH HA!" AMERICAN NARROW GAUGE A.D. 1860 VERY RARE. HANDS OFF — Well, sir, the Sneezian agent finds a locomotive. And it's a dandy, too. A genuine antique. The pride of a famous museum in Budapest.
10	Twenty thousand dollars in gold it costs — but what an engine! It's trimmed in real brass, and has a bell and a cow-catcher, and a whistle twice as big as Ajax's. SOLD
11	"I CHRISTEN THEE 'HERCULES.'" No wonder the populace wildly acclaims its arrival.

SH-H — NOT SO LOUD.
NOW, THERE SEEMS TO BE QUITE A BIT OF MYSTERY AND SECRECY AS TO WHAT THE SNEEZIANS ARE GOING TO DO WITH THEIR NEW ENGINE.
BUT ONE THING IS CERTAIN. OLD WASH IS GOING TO BE THE ENGINEER.
JAIL
NOSSIR! I DEMAND SOME PANTS.
SHUT UP!!
DANGER
DYNAMITE!
NO SMOKING.
GUN POWDER
DANGER!
HIGH EXPLOSIVE
!
NOBODY ENVIES HIM HIS JOB EITHER. DYNAMITE! GUN POWDER! WOW! A WRECK WITH A LOAD OF THAT STUFF — AND GOODBYE WORLD.
EVIDENTLY THOSE FOXY SNEEZIAN GENERALS HAVE SOMETHING UP THEIR SLEEVES BESIDES ELBOWS.
REG. U. S. PAT. OFF.
© 1931 BY NEA SERVICE, INC.
OMY OME!
WOW! HERE COMES THE BELCHIAN SPY WITH ALARMING NEWS FROM SNEEZIA.
IT'S AWFUL, GENERAL. THEY'RE GOING TO MAKE TUBBS RUN A TRAIN LOAD OF DYNAMITE THRU THE LINES. I'M POSITIVE! OW, THEY'LL BLOW BELCHIA OFF THE MAP.
OH HO! THEY WILL, EH?
WE'LL SHOW THOSE MUGS. GET MORE CANNON. GET 'EM ALL. HA! I'D LIKE TO SEE 'EM TRY TO RUN A TRAIN LOAD OF DYNAMITE THRU OUR LINES.
IF I COULD ONLY GET RIDDA THESE DUMB SOLDIERS — BOY, I'D SHOW 'EM!
HERCULES
DANGER!
DYNAMITE
NO SMOKING
THE TRAIN HAS BEEN READY TO GO ON ITS MYSTERIOUS TRIP FOR SOME TIME, BUT WASH PRETENDS THAT SOMETHING IS WRONG.
AT LAST, THE SOLDIERS TIRE OF WATCHING WASH, AND ALL BUT ONE WANDER OFF.
CANTINA
HA! NOW'S MY CHANCE!
PLOP!

BYE BYE, SNEEZIA.
WASH HOPS QUICKLY INTO THE CAB, AFTER SMACKING OVER HIS GUARD.
POW!
AND JERKS THE TRAIN INTO A FLYING START.
FOR A MOMENT THE NEARBY SOLDIERS STARE STUPIDLY. THEN GO TEARING AFTER HIM.
HELP! HE'S STEALING OUR TRAIN!
HALT!
STOP HIM!
ROY CRANE
BOY, HERE'S WHERE I BECOME A HERO, OR BUST.
DANGER NO SMOKING
HERCULES
SOK!
DYNAMIT
WASH STEALS TRAIN!
SOLDIERS ARE CHASING HIM. BUT AS FAST AS THEY HOP ABOARD HE BATS THEM OVER THE HEAD WITH FIRE WOOD.
YA YA YA!
REG. U. S. PAT. OFF. © 1931 BY NEA SERVICE, INC.
FASTER AND FASTER HE GOES. THE SOLDIERS ARE LEFT BEHIND, AND WASH IS WILD WITH JOY.
HOWEVER, A LONE SOLDIER HAS CAUGHT ONTO THE BACK END, AND COMES CRAWLING OVER THE BOUNCING BOX CARS.
DYNAMITE! DANGER!
DEAD OR ALIVE, BOYS.
WASH IS ELATED AT HIS EASY ESCAPE. BUT THERE ARE DANGERS STILL IN STORE. AHEAD, LIE THE FRONT LINES AND SOLDIERS GALORE. BEHIND, COMES A TROOP OF CAVALRY IN HOT PURSUIT.
HA! I GOT YOU, BUDDIE! STOP, OR YOU'RE A DEAD UN.
!
HERCULES
AND THE LONE MUSKETEER, WHO BOARDED THE STOLEN TRAIN, IS NOT TO BE FORGOTTEN, EITHER. NO, INDEED.
REG. U. S. PAT. OFF. © 1931 BY NEA SERVICE, INC.

THE LONE SOLDIER, WHO HAS HOPPED THE STOLEN TRAIN, TRIUMPHANTLY AIMS HIS GUN AT WASH AND ORDERS HIM TO STOP.
AND WASH STOPS!
DANGER
DYNAMITE
DYNA
HERCULES
BUT WITH SUCH A VIOLENT JERK THAT THE TROOPER TUMBLES CLEAR OVER THE ENGINE CAB.
HA! I GUESS I SHOWED THAT BABY. NOW TO CUT TH' TELEGRAPH WIRE.
HOPE I'M NOT TOO LATE— THIS IS CERTAINLY ONE TIME I DON'T WUNTA GET WRECKED.
POP!
FASTER, BOYS! WE GOT 'IM.
THEY ALMOST CATCH OLD WASH AS HE STOPS ON A STEEP GRADE TO CUT THE TELEGRAPH WIRE.
BUT OUR WEE HERO IS NOT TO BE CAUGHT SO EASILY. NO INDEED! HE UNCOUPLES A BOX CAR.
JUMP FOR YOUR LIVES!
DANGER!
DYNAMITE!!
R. CRANE
REG. U.S. PAT. OFF.
© 1931 BY NEA SERVICE, INC.
NOT ONLY DOES HE SCATTER HIS PURSUERS, BUT THE SNEEZIAN CAPITOL, TWO MILES BACK, IS NEARLY BLOWN OFF THE MAP.
WASH FEELS PRETTY COCKY OVER HIS SUCCESS THUS FAR. HE'S NOT GREATLY BOTHERED, EVEN WHEN A SQUAD OF SOLDIERS TRIES TO AMBUSH HIM.
BANG! BANG!
DANGER
DYNAMI
IN FACT, HE ENJOYS RUNNING OVER THE SWAYING TRAIN, AND UNHOOKING CAR LOADS OF DYNAMITE TO ROLL BACK AT HIS ENEMIES.
AND THE DYNAMITE IS CERTAINLY PLAYING HECK WITH TUNNELS AND BRIDGES.
WHAM!
R. CRANE
HOWEVER, THE EXPLOSIONS ARE HEARD AT THE FRONT. AND THE ENTIRE ARMY HASTILY PREPARES FOR TROUBLE.

HERE HE COMES!
THE SNEEZIAN TROOPS HAVE PREPARED A NICE LITTLE RECEPTION FOR WASH.
ALL TOGETHER, BOYS. LET 'EM GO!
HEY! WOT TH'-?
WHAM! BAM! TEN TONS OF BOULDERS COME THUNDERING DOWN AT WASH AND HIS TRAIN-LOAD OF DYNAMITE.
HI HO! WOT'S TH' LOSS OF A SMOKESTACK?
WASH HEAVES A SIGH OF RELIEF AS HE RACES THRU THE BARRAGE OF STONES, WITHOUT BEING BLOWN TO KINGDOM COME.
BUT A MOMENT LATER HE IS PETRIFIED TO BEHOLD THE ENTIRE SNEEZIAN ARMY WAITING FOR HIM.
POOM!
BANG!
PAM!
BAM!
BANG!
BLOOIE!
RATTY-TA-TAT!
BINGO
BAM!
BUM!
HE KNOWS WHEN HE'S LICKED. HE JUMPS. AND JUST IN TIME, TOO, FOR HERCULES IS RIDDLED WITH HUNDREDS OF BULLETS.
FOUR HUNDRED SNEEZIAN TROOPS OPEN FIRE AND WASH PROMPTLY QUIT HIS TRAIN.
I KNOW WHEN I'M LICKED.
?
IMAGINE HIS SURPRISE WHEN HE LANDS ON A RAILROAD TRACK. AND THEN SEES HIS TRAIN COMING AROUND ONE OF THOSE CRAZY LOOPS.
OBOY! THIS IS MY LUCKY DAY.
HERCULES
WHOOPEE! H'RAY! I'M FREE!
DANGER DYNAMITE
© 1931 BY NEA SERVICE, INC. REG. U. S. PAT. OFF.
SUCCESS SEEMS ASSURED. THE LAST OF HIS ENEMIES ARE LEFT BEHIND.

WHOOPEE! HERE I COME.
DANGER!
DYNAMITE
HOORAY! WASH BREAKS THRU THE SNEEZIAN LINES. HE'S FREE! TRIUMPHANTLY HE RACES ACROSS NO MAN'S LAND.
BUT THE BELCHIANS BELIEVE IT IS THE LONG AWAITED ENEMY ATTACK.
FIRE!
REG. U. S. PAT. OFF. © 1931 BY NEA SERVICE, INC.
WASH ESCAPES SNEEZIANS!
RACES TRIUMPHANTLY ACROSS NO MAN'S LAND.
THEN, HORRORS! 42 BELCHIAN CANNON BOOM TO REPEL WHAT THEY TAKE TO BE AN ENEMY CHARGE.
HEY! HELP!! CUT IT OUT!
POW!
HERCULES
BAM!
BINGO!
HEY! STOP SHOOTIN'. IT'S ONLY ME—OLD WASHIE.
BAM!
BLOOEY!
BOOM!
BAM!
POWEE!
HERCULES CRUMPLES UNDER A BARRAGE OF CANNON FIRE, BUT THE BELCHIANS ARE TOO EXCITED TO HEAR WASH'S FRANTIC YELPS TO CEASE FIRING.
GIVE IT TO 'EM AGAIN, BOYS.
BURROOM!
A DIRECT HIT! AND TWO CARLOADS OF DYNAMITE FINISH NO MAN'S LAND FOR KEEPS.

THEY PICK WASH UP, LIMP AND BLEEDING, AFTER THE DISASTROUS END TO HIS TRAIN RIDE.
NOBODY LAUGHS AT HIS PETTICOAT. THEY ARE SILENT, THOSE SNEEZIANS. THEY BOW THEIR HEADS IN SHAME, FOR THE LITTLE FELLOW THEY SO RECENTLY JEERED, AS BEING YELLOW, IS NOW THE HERO OF THE WAR.
CAREFULLY, THEY PLACE HIM IN AN IMPROVISED AMBULANCE, AND SPEED TOWARD THE CAPITOL.
12
© 1931 BY NEA SERVICE, INC. REG. U. S. PAT. OFF.
Roy Crane
THE WAR IS OVER! BELCHIA WINS! THE ARMY MARCHES HOME, TRIUMPHANT.
HOO RAY FOR TUBBS!
HE WON THE WAR.
13
YOO HOO! WASHIE! WE BROUGHT YOU SOME CANDY.
HOSPITAL
OUTSIDE THE HOSPITAL, WHERE WASH LIES WOUNDED, ALL THE BELLES OF BELCHIA ARE GATHERED, BEGGING ADMITTANCE.
INSIDE, WASH IS IN HIS GLORY.
HA! SO I'M TH' HERO OF TH' WAR, EH? THEN KICK 'EM OUT. I'LL SHOW 'EM — NO DAMES KIN TWO-TIME OLD WASH TUBBS.
BUT THE PRESIDENT'S DAUGHTER, SIR — SHE IS WEEPING AND PLEADING.
WEEPIN'? 'AT'S GREAT! I NEVER DREAMED I'D HAVE A CHANCE TO STICK UP MY NOSE AT TH' DAUGHTER OF A PRESIDENT. YEH, BOOT HER OUT, TOO.
Roy Crane
© 1931 BY NEA SERVICE, INC. REG. U. S. PAT. OFF.
OW! STOP PULLING MY HAIR!
WASH IS MINE!
HE'S NOT! YOU JILTED HIM FOR A GENERAL.
AH, JUST LISTEN TO THAT.
HOSPITAL
KEEP OUT
WOTTA MAN! THE LADIES' CHOICE. THE HERO OF THE WAR. LET 'EM FIGHT — BOY, I'M WORTH FIGHTIN' OVER. I'M CLASS. I'LL GO DOWN IN HISTORY.
To my hero
SHOO! WHO'S THIS GUY, NAPOLEON? I BET HE NEVER WON ANY WARS SINGLE HANDED.
AND AS FOR THOSE DAMES 'AT JILTED ME — HA! I'LL SHOW 'EM. I'LL BUST THEIR HEARTS. I'LL MAKE 'EM WEEP PLENTY BEFORE I'M THRU.
14
© 1931 BY NEA SERVICE, INC. REG. U. S. PAT. OFF.
Roy Crane

Dear Easy:
Well old pal I am a big success. I am the Greatest hero that ever lived here, as I have just gone out and won a war Single handed, and I am the idle of all the People.
WASH STARTS A LETTER.....
AND FALLS ASLEEP, DREAMING OF THE MEDALS FOR HEROISM HE IS SO CONFIDENT OF WINNING.
HOSPITAL
SH-H! ALL OUT.
ROY CRANE
IN THE MEANTIME, A CART STOPS IN FRONT OF THE HOSPITAL.
WOT TH'—?
SHUT UP! ONE WORD OUT OF YOU, MR. HERO, AND YOU'RE A DEAD ONE.
BUT LISSEN, FELLAS. THERE MUST BE SOME MISTAKE. WHY, I'M WASH TUBBS. I'M TH' GUY 'AT WON TH' WAR.
PILE OUT! WE KNOW WHAT WE'RE DOING
BUT I'M WOUNDED! GEE WIZ, WHY I---
GRAND STAND STUFF! YOU'RE NO MORE WOUNDED THAN MY AUNT SUSIE. GET INTO SOME CLOTHES, AND SHUT UP.
AW, HAVE A HEART. LE'S TALK THIS OVER PEACEFULLY, FELLAS. I HAVEN'T DONE NUTHIN, HONEST I HAVEN'T.
SILENCE!
AH, I KNOW. YOU'RE SNEEZIANS. YOU'RE SORE BECAUSE I LICKED YOUR WHOLE ARMY. WELL, YOU SURE BETTER LOOK OUT. I'M TH' GREATEST HERO BELCHIA EVER HAD. HA! JUST WAIT'LL THEY FIND OUT ABOUT THIS OUTRAGE. THEY'LL--MFF-
THAT'S THE STUFF, OSCAR. GAG HIM.
Wash is Kid-Naped AND TAKEN FAR OUT INTO THE COUNTRY.
ALL RIGHT, BOYS. KICK HIM OUT.
YOU BUMS! JUST WAIT'LL TH' PRESIDENT OF BELCHIA HEARS ABOUT THIS.
BOUNDARY
BELCHIA
AUSTRIA
PLOP!
SIR! IT MAY INTEREST YOU TO KNOW THAT I AM THE PRESIDENT OF BELCHIA, AND THAT THESE GENTLEMEN ARE MY CABINET.
OH! THEN IT'S ONLY A JOKE. HA HA! THAT'S A GOOD ONE ON ME.
IT IS NOT A JOKE, FOOL! YOU'RE GOING TO BE HORSE-WHIPPED AND RUN OUT OF THE COUNTRY.
ROY CRANE

WHAT! YOU'RE GUNNA HORSEWHIP ME OUTA TH' COUNTRY, AFTER I WENT AN' WON A WAR FOR YOU?
EXACTLY!
BUT I DON'T UNDER-STAND. I --
FOOL! DON'T YOU KNOW WHAT BELCHIA WAS FIGHTING FOR? THE RAILROAD, THAT'S WHAT. AND WHAT HAPPENED TO THE RAILROAD?
YOU BLUNDERING IDIOT, YOU WRECKED THE TRAINS, BLEW UP THE TUNNELS, DESTROYED THE BRIDGES—YOU UTTERLY RUINED THE VERY THING WE WERE FIGHTING FOR. WHAT GOOD IS THAT KIND OF A VICTORY, HEY?
REG. U. S. PAT. OFF. © 1931 BY NEA SERVICE, INC.
A HERO—BAH! YOU'RE LUCKY THAT WE DON'T STRING YOU UP TO A TELEGRAPH POLE.
ROY CRANE

HEY! OUCH!
ALL RIGHT, BOYS, LET'S GIVE HIM THE WORKS.
RUN, DERN YOU, RUN!
WE'LL TEACH YOU TO SPOIL OUR RAILROAD.
POP!
CRACK!
A FINE WAY TO TREAT A WOUNDED HERO.
AND LET THAT BE A LESSON — KEEP OUT OF BELCHIA, IF YOU VALUE YOUR LIFE.
YOU MAY BE A HERO TO THE LADIES, YOU MUG, BUT YOU'RE ONLY A PAIN IN THE NECK TO US.
© 1931 BY NEA SERVICE, INC. REG. U. S. PAT. OFF.
ROY CRANE

OH, WELL! BELCHIA WASN'T MUCH OF A COUNTRY. I SHOULD WORRY IF THEY RAN ME OUT.
I GOT NO KICK. IT WAS FUN WHILE IT LASTED. I GOT DOUGH, TOO. AT LEAST THEIR OLD PRESIDENT WAS SPORTY ENOUGH TO SLIP ME MY WAGES.
AN' THOSE GIRLS! HA! I SURE BUSTED THEIR HEARTS, I BETCHA. I SHOWED 'EM. THEY'LL WEEP PLENTY OVER ME.
OBOY! A ROAD! 'AT MEANS HOUSES AN' FOOD. 'N'ALL I NEED TO MAKE ME PERFECKY HAPPY IS A BIG MESS OF GOOD OLD HAM'N EGGS.
ROY CRANE

WASH IS HUNGRY. MISERABLY, HE PLODS ALONG THE MUDDY, DESERTED ROAD. IT IS ALMOST DECEMBER, AND A COLD DRIZZLE CHILLS HIM TO THE VERY BONE.
BR-R!
LOOKS LIKE A DESERTED CASTLE.
IT SEEMS AGES BEFORE HE COMES TO A BLEAK, LONELY PLACE BESIDE A RIVER.
NO. CAN'T BE DESERTED. THERE'S SMOKE.
HE HESITATES SEVERAL TIMES BEFORE APPROACHING. STRANGELY, SOMETHING HAS GIVEN HIM A WEIRD, CREEPY FEELING.
THEN HE HEARS LAUGHTER AND VOICES INSIDE. AND THE THOUGHT OF WARMTH AND FOOD OVERCOMES HIS TIMID FEARS.
SHOO! ANY OLD PORT IN A STORM.
ROY CRANE
REG. U. S. PAT. OFF. © 1931 BY NEA SERVICE, INC.
THE HOUSE BESIDE THE LONELY ROAD PROVES TO BE AN INN, AND WASH BOLDLY ENTERS.
GASTHAUS
CONVERSATION AND LAUGHTER INSIDE COME TO AN ABRUPT STOP. SIX MEN TURN SLOWLY AROUND AND STARE HIM UP AND DOWN, WITH ICY INSOLENCE.
AT LAST THE PROPRIETOR STEPS FORWARD, AND CONVERSATION IS RESUMED IN AN UNDERTONE.
VELL? VOT YOU VANT?
THREE ORDERS HAM'N' EGGS. I'M STARVED.
REG. U. S. PAT. OFF. © 1931 BY NEA SERVICE, INC.
THREE ORDERS! HMMM!
UND NO LUGGAGE. MAYBE YOU VOULD LIKE TO PAY IN ADVANCE. JA?
RATS! GET BUSY. I GOT TH' DOUGH- PLENTY OF IT.
MONEY!! AGAIN WASH FEELS THAT UNCOMFORTABLE STILLNESS, AND THE SIX PAIRS OF EYES BORING INTO HIM.
MAYBE, VEN YOU FINISH DER EGGS, YOU LIKE A NICE ROOM, HEY?
ME SLEEP IN THIS DUMP? NOSSIR, I VALUE MY LIFE.
ACH! BUT IT ISS RAINING HARDER DAN EFFER OUTDSIDE. IT ISS TURNING COLDER. YOU ARE VET UND TIRED.
O, WELL! WOTTA I CARE? SHOW ME TH' ROOM.
DER BEST IN DER HOUSE, DOT'S VOT IT ISS. AN OUTSIDER MIT STAIRCASE.
WASH BOLTS THE DOOR, HANGS HIS CLOTHES ON A QUAINT OLD PORCELAIN STOVE TO DRY, AND HIDES HIS MONEY. HE IS ASLEEP IN NO TIME.
Z-Z-Z
ROY CRANE
© 1931 BY NEA SERVICE, INC. REG. U. S. PAT. OFF.

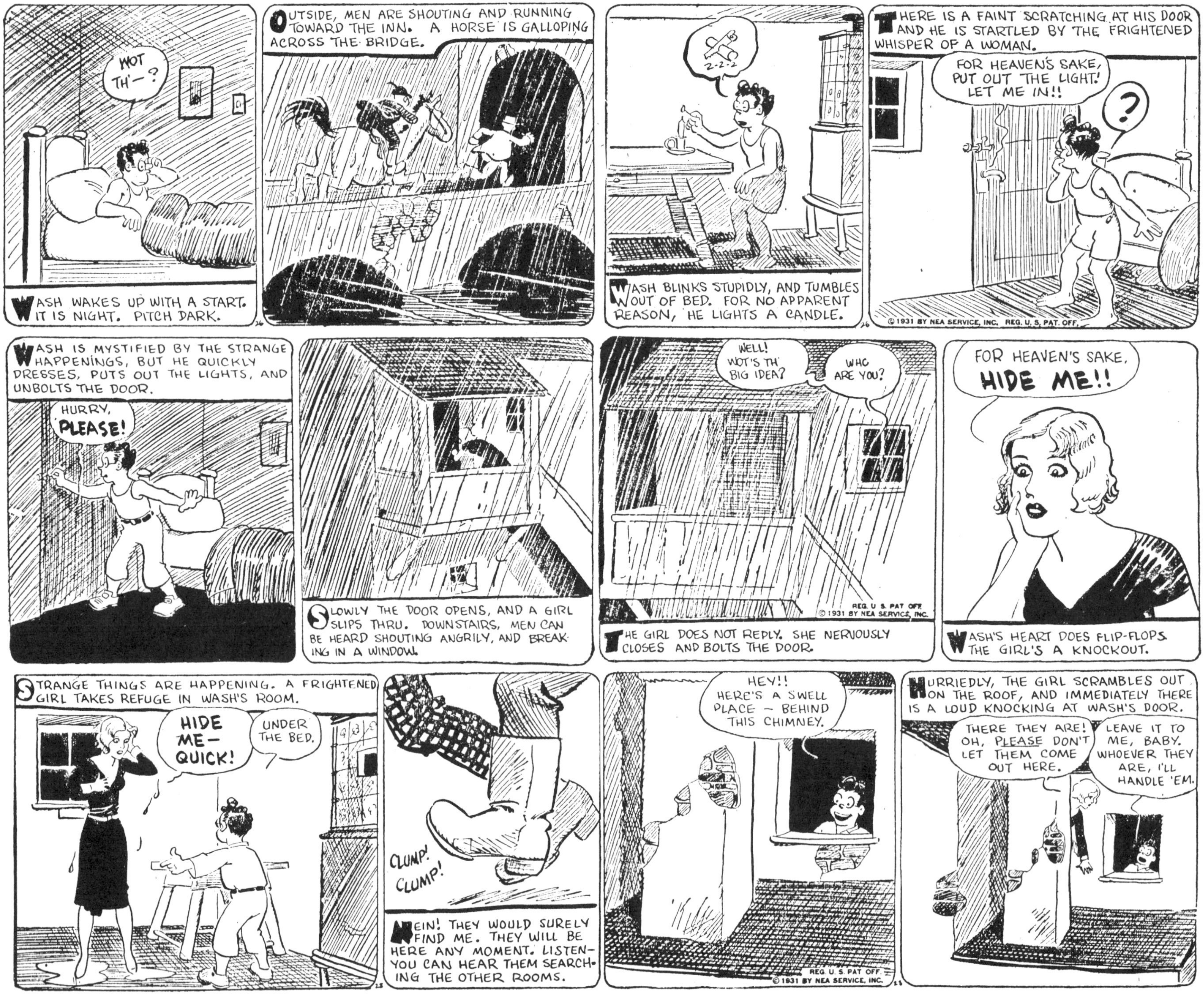
WOT TH'—?
WASH WAKES UP WITH A START. IT IS NIGHT. PITCH DARK.
OUTSIDE, MEN ARE SHOUTING AND RUNNING TOWARD THE INN. A HORSE IS GALLOPING ACROSS THE BRIDGE.
Z-Z-Z
WASH BLINKS STUPIDLY, AND TUMBLES OUT OF BED. FOR NO APPARENT REASON, HE LIGHTS A CANDLE.
THERE IS A FAINT SCRATCHING AT HIS DOOR AND HE IS STARTLED BY THE FRIGHTENED WHISPER OF A WOMAN.
FOR HEAVEN'S SAKE, PUT OUT THE LIGHT! LET ME IN!!
?
© 1931 BY NEA SERVICE, INC. REG. U. S. PAT. OFF.
WASH IS MYSTIFIED BY THE STRANGE HAPPENINGS, BUT HE QUICKLY DRESSES, PUTS OUT THE LIGHTS, AND UNBOLTS THE DOOR.
HURRY, PLEASE!
SLOWLY THE DOOR OPENS, AND A GIRL SLIPS THRU. DOWNSTAIRS, MEN CAN BE HEARD SHOUTING ANGRILY, AND BREAKING IN A WINDOW.
WELL! WOT'S TH' BIG IDEA?
WHO ARE YOU?
REG. U. S. PAT. OFF. © 1931 BY NEA SERVICE, INC.
THE GIRL DOES NOT REPLY. SHE NERVOUSLY CLOSES AND BOLTS THE DOOR.
FOR HEAVEN'S SAKE, HIDE ME!!
WASH'S HEART DOES FLIP-FLOPS. THE GIRL'S A KNOCKOUT.
STRANGE THINGS ARE HAPPENING. A FRIGHTENED GIRL TAKES REFUGE IN WASH'S ROOM.
HIDE ME—QUICK!
UNDER THE BED.
CLUMP! CLUMP!
NEIN! THEY WOULD SURELY FIND ME. THEY WILL BE HERE ANY MOMENT. LISTEN—YOU CAN HEAR THEM SEARCHING THE OTHER ROOMS.
HEY!! HERE'S A SWELL PLACE — BEHIND THIS CHIMNEY.
REG. U. S. PAT. OFF. © 1931 BY NEA SERVICE, INC.
HURRIEDLY, THE GIRL SCRAMBLES OUT ON THE ROOF, AND IMMEDIATELY THERE IS A LOUD KNOCKING AT WASH'S DOOR.
THERE THEY ARE! OH, PLEASE DON'T LET THEM COME OUT HERE.
LEAVE IT TO ME, BABY. WHOEVER THEY ARE, I'LL HANDLE 'EM.

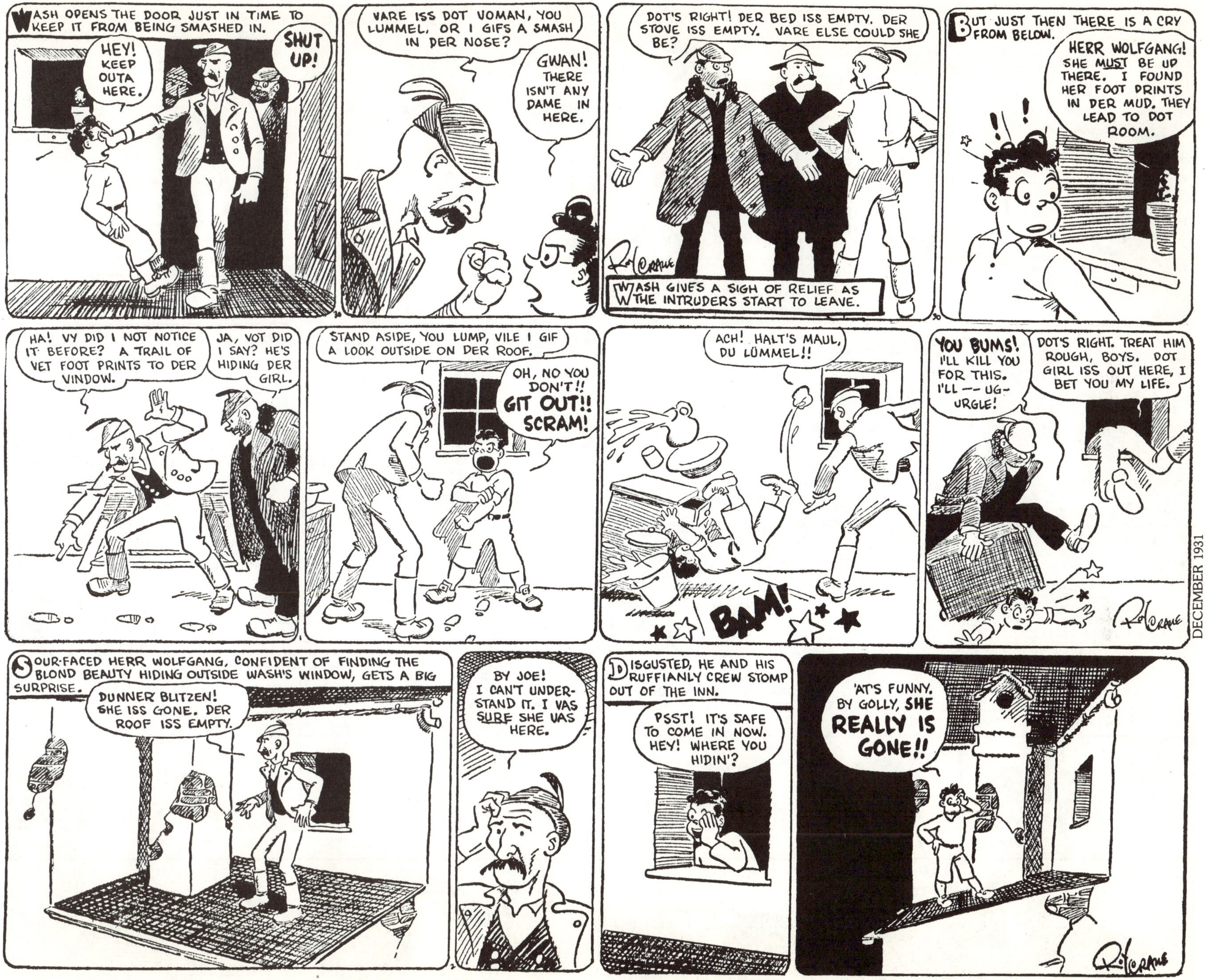

DECEMBER 1931

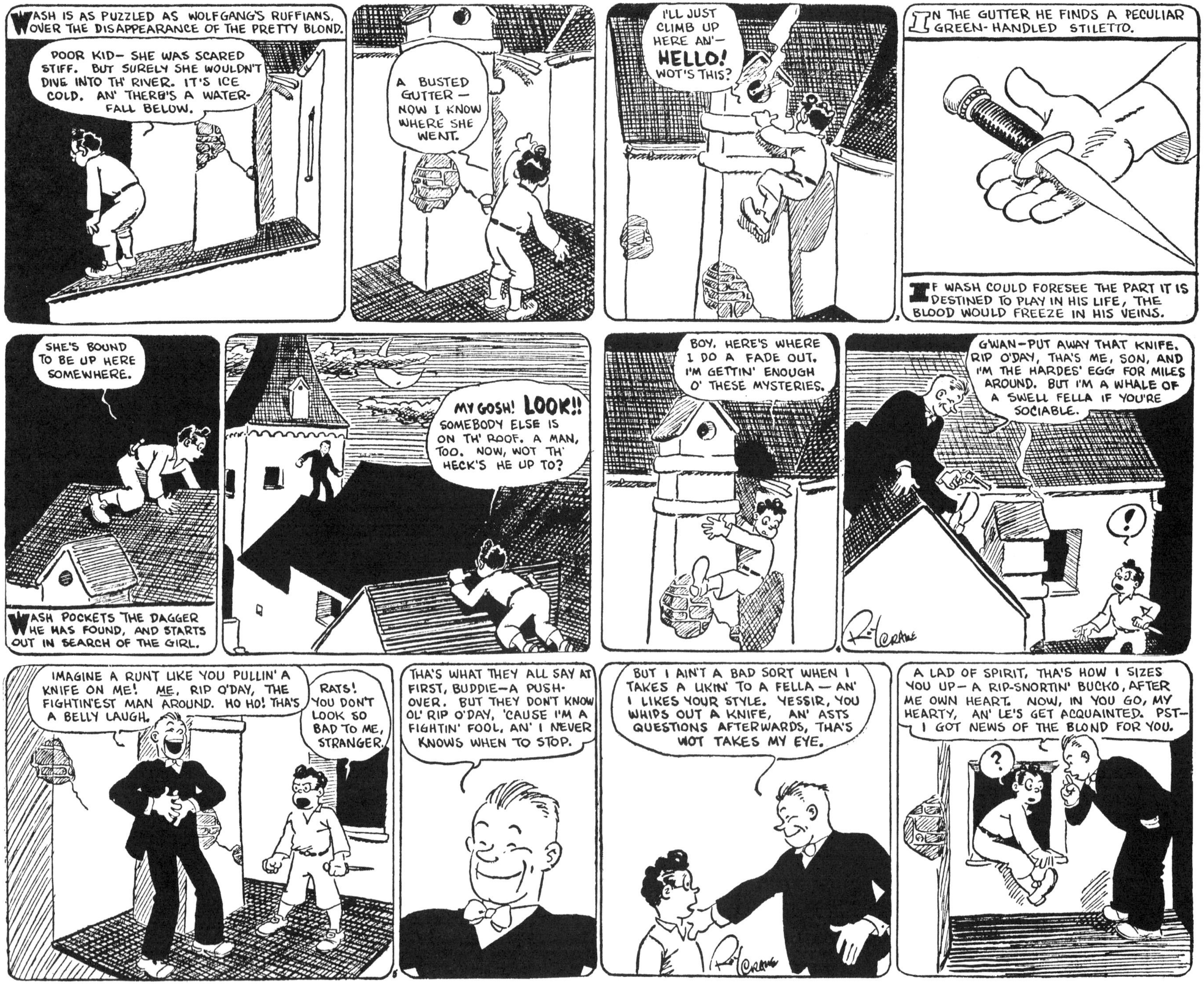
WASH IS AS PUZZLED AS WOLFGANG'S RUFFIANS, OVER THE DISAPPEARANCE OF THE PRETTY BLOND.
POOR KID— SHE WAS SCARED STIFF. BUT SURELY SHE WOULDN'T DIVE INTO TH' RIVER. IT'S ICE COLD. AN' THERE'S A WATER-FALL BELOW.
A BUSTED GUTTER — NOW I KNOW WHERE SHE WENT.
I'LL JUST CLIMB UP HERE AN'— HELLO! WOT'S THIS?
IN THE GUTTER HE FINDS A PECULIAR GREEN-HANDLED STILETTO.
IF WASH COULD FORESEE THE PART IT IS DESTINED TO PLAY IN HIS LIFE, THE BLOOD WOULD FREEZE IN HIS VEINS.
SHE'S BOUND TO BE UP HERE SOMEWHERE.
WASH POCKETS THE DAGGER HE HAS FOUND, AND STARTS OUT IN SEARCH OF THE GIRL.
MY GOSH! LOOK!! SOMEBODY ELSE IS ON TH' ROOF. A MAN, TOO. NOW, WOT TH' HECK'S HE UP TO?
BOY, HERE'S WHERE I DO A FADE OUT. I'M GETTIN' ENOUGH O' THESE MYSTERIES.
G'WAN—PUT AWAY THAT KNIFE. RIP O'DAY, THA'S ME, SON, AND I'M THE HARDES' EGG FOR MILES AROUND. BUT I'M A WHALE OF A SWELL FELLA IF YOU'RE SOCIABLE.
!
IMAGINE A RUNT LIKE YOU PULLIN' A KNIFE ON ME! ME, RIP O'DAY, THE FIGHTIN'EST MAN AROUND. HO HO! THA'S A BELLY LAUGH.
RATS! YOU DON'T LOOK SO BAD TO ME, STRANGER.
THA'S WHAT THEY ALL SAY AT FIRST, BUDDIE—A PUSH-OVER. BUT THEY DON'T KNOW OL' RIP O'DAY, 'CAUSE I'M A FIGHTIN' FOOL, AN' I NEVER KNOWS WHEN TO STOP.
BUT I AIN'T A BAD SORT WHEN I TAKES A LIKIN' TO A FELLA — AN' I LIKES YOUR STYLE. YESSIR, YOU WHIPS OUT A KNIFE, AN' ASTS QUESTIONS AFTERWARDS, THA'S WOT TAKES MY EYE.
A LAD OF SPIRIT, THA'S HOW I SIZES YOU UP— A RIP-SNORTIN' BUCKO, AFTER ME OWN HEART. NOW, IN YOU GO, MY HEARTY, AN' LE'S GET ACQUAINTED. PST— I GOT NEWS OF THE BLOND FOR YOU.
?

SA NICE DUMP Y'HAVE HERE, SHIPMATE.
LISSEN, WOTTA 'BOUT TH' GIRL?
OH, YEAH—BLONDIE. NICE KID, BLONDIE. YA SEE, SHE CLIMBS ACROST THE ROOF AN' I HELPS HER IN MY WINDER, AN' SHE TROTS ON HOME AS SAFE AS YER AUNT SUSIE. SHE AST ME TO TELL YOU.
POOR KID! SHE WAS SCARED SILLY AT THOSE MEN CHASIN' HER. WHO ARE THEY?
I DUNNO, BUT SHE'S AFRAID SHE GOT YA IN TROUBLE.
I GUESS SO, DAWGUNNIT! SEEMS LIKE I'M ALWAYS IN TROUBLE
YEAH? SAY, THA'S GREAT, FELLA. I SEES WHERE ME AN' YOU'S GUNNER GET ALONG GREAT GUNS, 'CAUSE IF THEY'S ANYTHING I LOVES, BOY, IT'S TROUBLE.
CHRISTMAS GREETINGS 1931
AFTER AN HOUR OR SO, WASH AND MR. O'DAY ARE GETTING ALONG FAMOUSLY.
YEAH, WE SURE GUNNA HAVE SOME GREAT TIMES TOGETHER, 'CAUSE THEY'S NOTHIN' I LOVES BETTER'N TROUBLE.
BUT LISSEN, RIP. WHO'S THIS GIRL WE BIN PROTECTIN'?
AW, I DUNNO, SPORT. JES ANOTHER DAME, I GUESS. THE WORLD'S FULLA DAMES.
YEH, BUT THIS GIRL'S CLASS. GEE, I WISH I KNEW WHY THOSE MEN WERE AFTER HER.
I DUNNO. I JES BLEW IN, MYSELF. MAYBE ONE OF THEM'S HER HUSBAND.
THERE SURE IS A MYST'RY AROUND HERE, RIP. THIS DAGGER, F'RINSTANCE. WHO'S IS IT? AN' HOW COME IT WAS UP ON TH' ROOF?
HMM! THAT DAGGER—NOW THA'S MORE IN MY LINE. GREEN-HANDLED, AN' GOT FOREIGN WRITIN' ON IT. SAY—THA'S WORTH REAL MONEY, SPORT. FI'TEEN, TWENNY DOLLARS, I BETCHA. MAYBE MORE.
WASH AND HIS NEW FRIEND ARE GABBING QUIETLY ABOUT THE GREEN-HANDLED STILETTO WASH FOUND, WHEN RIP APPARENTLY GOES COO-COO.
QUICK—LEMME YER STOOL, LAD.
WOT TH'—?
KRASH!
TINKLE! TINKLE!
WOT TH' HECK IS THIS? A JOKE?
OH, I JES LIKES TO BUST WINDERS. AN' BESIDES, THERE WAS A TOUGH-LOOKIN' GUY PEEPIN' IN AT US.
SHUX! I MUST OF MISSED HIM—HE'S GONE. OH, WELL! MAYBE HE'LL GIT MAD AN' BRING BACK HIS FRIENDS—THEN WE'LL HAVE SOME FUN.
© 1931 BY NEA SERVICE, INC. REG. U. S. PAT. OFF.

WASH IS AT BREAKFAST WHEN IN STRIDES HERR WOLFGANG, SCOWLING.
WELL! WOTTA YOU WANT? STILL LOOKIN' FOR TH' BLOND?
I VILL TROUBLE YOU, MY FRIEND, FOR MY DAGGER.
WASH DECIDES TO PLAY CAGEY.
WOT DAGGER?
YOU KNOW VOT DAGGER! DER GREEN-HANDLED VUN DOT YOU VAS SHOWING YOUR FRIEND LAST NIGHT. IT ISS MINE.
NO SPIKKA LA DUTCH. BEAT IT!
BAM! BAM!
REG. U. S. PAT. OFF. © 1931 BY NEA SERVICE, INC.
HAF A CARE, MY FRIEND. UNLESS YOU GIF IT QUICK, DOT DAGGER ISS GOING TO CAUSE YOU A LOT UF TROUBLE.
LISSEN, FELLA! I DON'T LIKE YOU—I DON'T BELIEVE YOU—AN' I DON'T GIVE A SNAP FOR TROUBLE. SO ON YOUR WAY! SCATTER!
Roy Crane
LISSEN! ARE YOU TRYIN' TO THREATEN ME?
ACH, NEIN! BUT DOT DAGGER ISS MINE. IT VAS STOLEN FROM ME. HAF CARE—IT COULD GIF TROUBLE.
STOLEN, EH? THEN I BETTER TURN IT OVER TO THE POLICE.
NEIN, NEIN! NOT THAT! COME, I AM A FAIR GENTLEMAN, I VILL GIF A NICE REVARD FOR IT.
CHRISTMAS GREETINGS 1931
HERE ISS FIFE DOLLARS.
NIX! THERE'S A GIRL MIXED UP IN THIS. I'M GUNNA SEE WOT SHE HAS TO SAY ABOUT TH' DAGGER BEIN' YOURS.
NEIN! SHE VOULD ONLY LIE! COME, MY FRIEND, HERE ISS TWENTY FIFE DOLLARS. NO, I VILL BE GENEROUS—I GIF FIFTY DOLLARS IN GOLD!
AH! IT MUST BE MORE VALUABLE THAN I THOUGHT.
Roy Crane
BUT HOW DO I KNOW TH' DAGGER I GOT B'LONGS TO YOU?
AH, PERHAPS A REWARD UF $50 ISS NOT ENOUGH, EH? VOT IF I GIF YOU VUN HUNDRED DOLLARS, MY FRIEND? HOW ISS DOT?
?
NAW, I THINK I BETTER CONSULT TH' GIRL FIRST. AFTER ALL, SHE'S TH' ONE 'AT LOST IT.
NEIN! NEIN! I GIF $200.
OR PERHAPS I OUGHTA TURN IT OVER TO THE POLICE, AN' LET THEM SETTLE IT.
NEIN! THREE HUNDRED!!
Roy Crane
ON SECOND THOUGHT, THO, I THINK I'LL KEEP IT MYSELF. I HAD NO IDEA IT WAS SO VALUABLE.
ROBBER! THIEF! $500 UND NOT VUN CENT MORE! ACH HIMMEL! I VAS A FOOL NOT TO STEAL IT FROM YOU IN DER FIRST PLACE.

WASH OFFERED BIG REWARD!
GREEN-HANDLED DAGGER PROVES SURPRISINGLY VALUABLE.
HERR WOLFGANG BOOSTS OFFERS TO NO AVAIL.
I WISH THAT GUY WOULD START SOMETHING.
LOOK! EXAMINE IT! ACH, A STEEL BLADE MIT A PAINTED HANDLE—VORTH $10, UND I OFFER $575. HIMMEL, VOT A DUMMER YOU ARE.
OH, I'M NOT SO DUMB. NOBODY PAYS 'AT MUCH FOR A $10 KNIFE UNLESS HE'S GOTTA DERN GOOD REASON. AN' I WUNTA KNOW TH' REASON.
SIMPLE, MY FRIEND. VERY SIMPLE. IT'S AN HEIRLOOM. ONLY BECAUSE IT ISS IN MY FAMILY SIX GENERATIONS DO I VANT IT.
B'LONEY! YOU GOTTA BETTER REASON THAN THAT, AN' I'M NOT SELLIN'.
VOT! YOU REFUSE? THEN, BY JOE, I'LL—
OH, NO YOU DON'T! REACH FOR THAT PISTOL, YOU BUM, AN' YOU'LL GET THIS KNIFE FOR NUTHIN'!
ATTABOY! ATTABOY!! LE'S START TROUBLE.
ROYCRANE
ROBBERS! I VARN YOU! I'LL GET DOT DAGGER IF IT COSTS ME MY LIFE.
WHY DON'T YOU COME BACK 'N' TAKE IT? I DARE YOU TO.
WOW! 'AT GUY GIVES ME TH' CREEPS, RIP. I ALMOST WISHT I'D SOLD IT TO HIM.
SHUX! DON'T LET A SOFTIE LIKE HIM SCARE YOU. HE COULDN'T WHIP NOBODY.
ROYCRANE
WELL, ANYWAY, HE OFFERED ME $575 FOR IT, AN' THAT'S A LOTTA MONEY.
$575 FOR THIS DAGGER? SAY, EITHER THAT MUG'S PLUMB CRAZY, OR HE'S A HEAP SMARTER THAN HE LOOKS. I'LL KISS A PIG IF IT'S WORTH MORE'N $20.
BOY, I BETCHA WE HEAR MORE OF HERR WOLFGANG. HE'S PLENTY MAD.
THA'S THE WAY I LIKES 'EM. 'CAUSE I'M RIP O'DAY, AN' THEY'S NUTHIN' I LOVES LIKE TROUBLE.
YOU'LL GET IT, BUDDIE. JUST STICK AROUND.
I FIGHTS TO LIVE, 'N' LIVES TO FIGHT, SO BRING ON YOUR TROUBLES. BRING ON YOUR FIGHTERS. I LIKES 'EM BIG 'N' I LIKES 'EM BAD—ALONE, OR BY THE DOZENS.
HAND 'EM EACH A RAZOR 'N' A GATLIN GUN 'N' PUT A WILDCAT UNDER THEIR ARMS, 'CAUSE IF THEY'S ANYTHING I HATES, IT'S A SET-UP.
THE TOUGHER THEY ARE, THE HARDER THEY FIGHTS, 'N' THE HARDER THEY FIGHTS, THE MORE FUN I HAS. SO BRING 'EM ON, 'CAUSE I'M A RIP-ROARIN' TOOTER 'N' I AIMS TO ENJOY MYSELF.

A PRETTY GIRL, HERR TUBBS, ASKED ME TO GIF YOU DIS.
?
AH HA! A MASH NOTE.
I BET IT'S FROM THE BLOND.
OBOY! SURE ENOUGH! SHE WANTS ME TO COME OUT TO SEE 'ER. SHE WANTSA THANK ME.
SAY, THA'S GREAT. WE'LL START AT ONCE.
OH, NO YOU DON'T. I'M TH' ONE SHE WANTSA SEE. YOU WEREN'T EVEN MENTIONED.
OH, AWRIGHT. BUT I WOULDN'T TRUST THAT DAME, SPORT. YOU BETTER TAKE MY ROD.
WHAT! TAKE A PISTOL WHEN I CALL ON A GIRL? POO! THIS IS ROMANCE, YOU FAT HEAD, NOT A BATTLE.
I'M GLAD I LEFT RIP BEHIND. HI HO! WOT DOES 'AT BIG HAM KNOW ABOUT LOVE? OR ROMANCE?
TAKING HIS GREEN-HANDLED DAGGER, WASH BORROWS A BIKE AND DASHES OFF TO SEE THE PRETTY BLOND.
AH, HERE'S TH' PLACE. HER NOTE SAYS SHE LIVES A MILE UP TH' RIVER ROAD.
MY GOSH! WOTTA DUMP! LOOKS DESERTED. WHY, THIS CAN'T BE IT.
© 1931 BY NEA SERVICE, INC. REG. U. S. PAT. OFF.
BUT IT MUST BE! I COULDN'T OF MISSED IT. BUT I—WELL, I KINDA THOUGHT A NICE GIRL LIKE HER WOULD AT LEAST PICK UP TH' TIN CANS.
THERE MUST BE SOME MISTAKE. I CAN'T B'LIEVE A NICE KID LIKE "BLONDIE" WOULD LIVE IN A DUMP LIKE THIS.
NOK! NOK!
TO WASH'S SURPRISE, THO, A FEMININE VOICE ANSWERS HIS KNOCK.
COME IN.
?
PLOP!
CAUTIOUSLY, HE ENTERS. WHAM! SOMETHING STRIKES HIM OVER THE HEAD, AND HE FALLS TO THE FLOOR.
THEN A GRUNT OF SATISFACTION, AND THE DOOR IS SLOWLY CLOSED.

I'LL JES CIRCLE AROUN' BEHINER.
SHORTLY AFTER WASH LEAVES TO CALL ON THE BLOND, RIP IS SURPRISED TO SEE HER HIDING NEAR THE INN.
HOW YOU FRIGHTENED ME!
AW, THA'S AWRIGHT. SAY, WHERE'S TUBBSY?
YOU MEAN THE LITTLE CHAP WITH GLASSES? WHY, I HAVEN'T SEEN HIM.
THA'S FUNNY. DIN'T HE COME OUT TO YOUR HOUSE LIKE YOUR NOTE AST HIM TO?
MY NOTE? HOW ABSURD. I'VE WRITTEN NO NOTES.
WHAT?
WHAT! YOU NEVER WROTE WASH A NOTE ASTIN HIM TO COME TO YOUR HOUSE ON THE RIVER ROAD?
CERTAINLY NOT. I DON'T EVEN LIVE ON THE RIVER ROAD.
THEN I GOTTA BEAT IT.
RIP SEES THE ENTIRE PLOT. WOLFGANG, UNABLE TO BUY THE GREEN-HANDLED DAGGER, HAS LURED WASH TO A LONELY SPOT WHERE HE CAN TAKE IT BY FORCE.
HERE'S TUBBSY'S BIKE. I CERTAINLY HOPES I AIN'T TOO LATE FOR A NICE FIGHT.
HERR WOLFGANG—LOOK! IT ISS DOT OTHER AMERICAN, SNOOPING MITOUT.
GOOT! UNLATCH DER DOOR. HA! VE LET DOT DUMMER VALK IN UND—BAM!
OLD WOLFGANG MUSTA SEEN ME. THEY LOCKED THE DOOR.
CLICK!
OH, NO! THEY UNLOCKED IT. THEY'RE BIG 'N' THEY'RE BAD 'N' THEY WANTS ME TO COME IN, SO'S THEY CAN CRACK MY NOODLE. HA HA! FAT CHANCE OF TRICKING OLD RIP O'DAY.
I'LL JES SLIP IN THE BACK DOOR AN'— —SAY!! THA'S FUNNY. THERE AIN'T ANY BACK DOOR. NOW, THA'S A PROBLEM.
OR MAYBE IT'S A BIG HELP. WITH THIS OL' ROPE I FOUND, IT LOOKS LIKE I HAS THE UPPER HAND.

SEVERAL MINUTES PASS BEFORE WOLFGANG AND HIS MEN REALIZE THAT RIP HAS IMPRISONED THEM.
HIMMEL! DER DOOR ISS TIED.
QUICK! OUT DER VINDOW, BEFORE HE RETURNS MIT HELP.
SILENCE, YOU LUMPS! UND PULL ON DER DOOR. DOT'S IT. NOW, I SLIP DER DAGGER THRU, UND CUT DER ROPE.
HA! VOT A DUMMER DOT RIP ISS. NOW, OUT VE GO, UND EFRYBODY SCATTER.
EEYI! YOU BETTER SCATTER! 'CAUSE I'MA RIP-SNORTING CYCLONE 'N' IT'S MY TIME TO BLOW.
POW!
© 1931 BY NEA SERVICE, INC. REG. U. S. PAT. OFF.
RIP O'DAY, THA'S ME, 'N' I SPECIALIZES IN LAYING OUT MUGS LIKE YOU.
!
NO TIME IS WASTED IN RELIEVING WOLFGANG OF HIS REVOLVER, AND IN RECOVERING THE GREEN-HANDLED DAGGER.
THEN WOLFGANG'S MEN GET INTO ACTION FROM ACROSS THE ROAD. RIP FORGETS THE FALLEN LEADER AND SCRAMBLES FOR COVER.
BANG!
BAM!
SCATTER, YOU BUMS, AFORE I COMES OVER AFTER YOU.
BANG!
IN A MOMENT THEY TURN AND RUN, BUT NOT BEFORE WOLFGANG IS ON HIS FEET. A STRANGE WOMAN DASHES OUT OF THE CABIN, AND THE TWO DISAPPEAR.
RIP DOES NOT GIVE CHASE. HE IS WELL CONTENT WITH A MORAL VICTORY AND THE RECOVERY OF THE DAGGER.
HI HO! NOW TO SEE WHAT'S HAPPENED TO OL' TUBBSY.
WOTTA SAP I WAS! TH' BUMS! THEY CRACKED ME OVER TH' NOODLE, AN' TOOK MY DAGGER, RIP.
S'ALL RIGHT, FELLA. LOOK— I GOT IT BACK.
GIMME CREDIT, SPORT. AIN'T I THE NIFTIEST FIGHTER YA EVER LAYS EYES ON?
WELL, YOU SURE DID PLENTY OF HOLLERIN' AN' SHOOTIN'. DID YOU BUST ANY BONES, OR HIT, OR CAPTURE ANYBODY?
WELL, NO — BUT I GOT BACK THE DAGGER, DIDN'T I?
SHOO! I DON'T CALL 'AT FIGHTIN'. NOT REAL FIGHTIN'. I HAD A BUDDIE WUNCT, NAMED EASY — AN' BOY! HE COULD LICK ANYTHING — MEN, ARMIES, CYCLONES, ANYTHING!
REG. U. S. PAT. OFF. © 1931 BY NEA SERVICE, INC.
OF COURSE IT WAS MIGHTY SWELL TO GET BACK MY DAGGER, RIP, BUT I BETCHA OL' EASY WOULDA LAID OUT TH' WHOLE GANG. I BETCHA HE — —
EASY? I NEVER HEARD OF THE MUG! ANYWAY, I BETS I KIN SMEAR HIM PLENTY, 'CAUSE I'M RIP O'DAY, 'N' I NEVER SEES NUTHIN ON LAND, OR SEA, OR SKY KIN HOLD A CANDLE TO ME. I'M GOOD 'N' I KNOWS IT.

AFTER RECOVERING THE GREEN-HANDLED DAGGER, WASH AND RIP RETURN TO THE INN.
HEY! LOOK— SOMEBODY'S BIN SEARCHIN' MY ROOM AGAIN.
WOLFGANG!
WELL, THEY AIN'T NUTHIN TO GET EXCITED ABOUT, SPORT. HE PROB'LY DONE IT HOURS AGO.
SURE! LONG BEFORE HE EVEN TRIED TO BUY MY DAGGER, I BETCHA.
KACHOO!
A SNEEZE! INSTANTLY, WASH AND RIP LEAP INTO ACTION.
IT ISN'T WOLFGANG— MY GOSH! IT'S A GIRL!
!!!
ROY CRANE
OH HO! THE BLOND!
HA! BIN SEARCHIN' MY ROOM, HAVE YOU?
HELP! LET ME GO!
NOT ON YER SWEET LIFE! YOU'RE GUNNA STICK AROUN' TILL YOU TELLS WHAT YOU WAS AFTER.
YOU WRETCH! HOW DARE YOU?
SHOO! I BET I KNOW WOT SHE WAS AFTER— IT'S THIS DAGGER.
WHERE DID YOU GET THAT? IT'S MINE!!
ROY CRANE
THA'S NOT WHAT WOLFGANG SAYS, 'N' I AIMS TO GET TO THE BOTTOM OF THIS. CRY ALL YOU WANTS, MA'AM, BUT YOU'RE GUNNA SET HERE TILL YOU SPILLS THE WORKS, SEE?
YOU BET! WE'RE GUNNA KNOW WHY AT DAGGER'S SO ALL-FIRED VALUABLE.
PLAY FAIR WITH US, AN' WE'LL SHOOT SQUARE WITH YOU.
THA'S RIGHT, MA'AM. WE AIN'T THE SORT AS GOES AROUN' TAKING VALUABLES AWAY FROM PRETTY DOLLS, SEE. BUT WE DEMANDS EXPLANATIONS 'N' PROOF AFORE WE TURNS OVER ANY DAGGERS.
ALL RIGHT. I'LL— I'LL TRUST YOU. BUT YOU'LL SIMPLY HAVE TO BELIEVE ME. I CAN'T PROVE MUCH.
IT'LL BE SAFE.
FIRST, THO, I MUST EXPLAIN HOW THE DAGGER CAME TO BE ON THE ROOF. YOU SEE, I WAS TERRIBLY FRIGHTENED WHEN WOLFGANG WAS AFTER ME, SO I HID IT.
WHEN YOU BOYS LEFT THE INN, I SAW MY CHANCE TO GET IT BACK. BUT THE DAGGER WAS GONE! I WAS PETRIFIED! I BEGAN SEARCHING FOR IT— —AND YOU CAUGHT ME.
?
HELP!
ROY CRANE

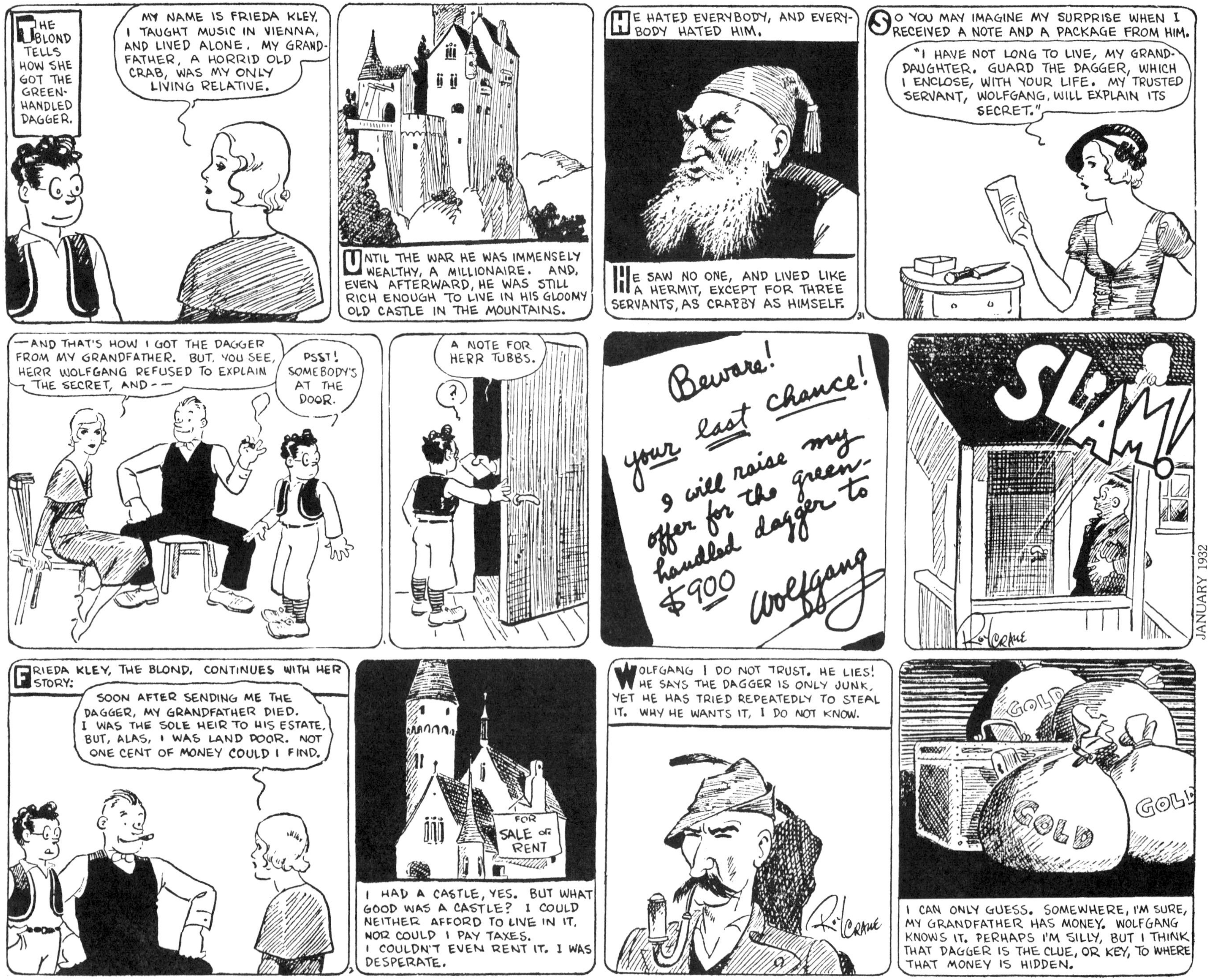

JANUARY 1932

THE BLOND CLAIMS:
1. THAT SHE RECEIVED DAGGER FROM GRANDFATHER.
2. THAT HE DIED, LEAVING HER HIS ESTATE.
3. THAT DAGGER IS KEY TO HIDDEN WEALTH.
4. THAT WOLFGANG IS FORMER SERVANT OF GRANDFATHER AND KNOWS IMPORTANCE OF DAGGER.
WELL, THAT'S MY STORY. BUT I'M AFRAID ALL I CAN REALLY PROVE IS THAT THE ESTATE IS MINE.
PICKLE MY BONES! I B'LIEVES YA, MA'AM. THA'S ALL THE PROOF I WANTS.
ME, TOO. I NEVER DID B'LIEVE WOLFGANG'S YARN, ANYWAY! TH' DAGGER'S YOURS.
REALLY? OH, HOW KIND!
AN' NOT ONLY THAT, MA'AM, BUT IF YA NEEDS US TO LAY OUT THIS MUG, WOLFGANG, JES SAY THE WORD.
OH, YOU DARLINGS! HOW CAN I EVER, EVER THANK YOU?
AW, THA'S AWRIGHT. SQUARE SHOOTERS, THA'S US, MA'AM, 'N' WE LOVES TO FIGHT.
YEH. AN' BESIDES, WE GOT SCORES TO SETTLE WITH 'AT BIG BUM.
OBOY! IF THIS OLD DAGGER IS REALLY TH' KEY TO A HIDDEN TREASURE, LE'S FIND OUT TH' SECRET.
ATTABOY, TUBBSY. TAKE OFF THE HANDLE. MAYBE THERE'S A MAP INSIDE.
IT'S NO USE, WASH. I'VE TRIED TO TAKE IT OFF A THOUSAND TIMES.
OH, BUT YOU'RE ONLY A GIRL AN' I'M A — — WOW! IT MUST BE RUSTY.
MAYBE A GIRL CAN'T DO IT 'N' MAYBE A MAN CAN'T, BUT OLD RIP O'DAY KIN DO ANYTHING, SO STAN' BACK, FOLKS, 'N' GIMME ROOM.
THA'S FUNNY! I'M BIG 'N' STRONG 'N' I TEARS OUT TREES BY THEIR ROOTS — I KIN TOTE A HOSS, BUT I CAN'T TAKE THIS LI'L' OL' HANDLE OFF.
SHOO! I BET EASY COULD.
OOF!
UGH!
WELL, PICKLE MY BONES 'N' BUST MY NECK! I MUS' BE GETTIN' WEAK 'N' PUNY. A LI'L' OL' HANDLE LIKE THAT, 'N' I CAN'T GET IT OFF.
BUT IT'S BOUND TO COME OFF, RIP. THAT IS, IF TH' DAGGER'S REALLY TH' KEY TO A HIDDEN TREASURE.
MAYBE THERE'S A TRICK TO IT.
YEAH. 'N' THERE'S SOME FURRIN WRITING ON THE BLADE. MAYBE THA'S A CLUE.
NO, I'VE HAD IT TRANSLATED, AND IT ONLY TELLS THE NAME OF THE MAKER. OH, I'VE TRIED EVERYTHING — SIMPLY EVERYTHING. I-I DON'T KNOW WHAT TO DO NEXT.
WELL, RIP O'DAY AIN'T QUIT. LEAVE ME TAKE THE DAGGER TO MY ROOM, MA'AM, 'N' I'LL KISS A PIG IF I DON'T FIND THAT SECRET.
OH, PLEASE DO! YOU SEE, I'M DESPERATE.
ROY CRANE

AS RIP TAKES THE DAGGER TO HIS ROOM, HIS ALERT EYES GLIMPSE A SLINKING FIGURE NEARBY. "PROB'LY WOLFGANG," HE GRUNTS AND PASSES ON.
'N' JES TO PLAY SAFE, I'LL PULL DOWN THE SHADES 'N' PUT MY ROD IN EASY REACH.
FOR HOURS HE WORKS METHODICALLY, TRYING TO PRY OFF THE HANDLE OF THE DAGGER. THEN FOR HOURS MORE HE SCRIBBLES ON SHEET AFTER SHEET OF PAPER.
AT LAST THE MORNING SUN PEEPS THRU THE FOREST. RIP YAWNS, POCKETS THE DAGGER AND GOES OUT, SMILING.
!
SHH! HERE HE ISS.
?
WASH COMES DOWN STAIRS TO BREAKFAST. TO HIS AMAZEMENT, HE FINDS RIP IN A HUSHED CONFERENCE WITH WOLFGANG AND HIS RUFFIANS.
BAH! I NEVER EXPECTED TO SEE YOU HANGIN' OUT WITH THESE BUMS.
WELL—I RECKON YOU MIGHT AS WELL LEARN THE NEWS NOW AS LATER, SPORT— I'M SELLING THE GREEN-HANDLED DAGGER.
ROY CRANE
WOT? YOU'RE DOIN' WOT?
I SAYS I'M SELLING THE DAGGER TO WOLFGANG! AW, DON'T GIT SORE, KID. $900 IS $900, 'N' I'M SHORT O' CASH. I'M NO SAP.
BUT, RIP, YOU'RE MY PAL. TH' DAGGER ISN'T EVEN YOURS. IT'S FRIEDA'S. WHY, YOU CAN'T SELL IT!
BLISTER ME! I AM SELLING IT, AIN'T I?
BUT TO WOLF-GANG! OF ALL PEOPLE!
WHY NOT? HE'S GOT $900—AND THE BLOND'S DEAD BROKE. BAH! I'M NO SAP. $900 IS $900.
NOW, LISSEN, KID! I LIKES YOU 'N' I LIKES YER STYLE, BUT YOU KEEP OUT O' THIS! SCRAM!
YOU CHEAT! YOU DOUBLE-CROSSIN' CROOK! YOU'LL NEVER SELL 'AT DAGGER!
POW!
!
ROY CRANE

WASH'S EFFORT TO KEEP RIP FROM SELLING THE GREEN-HANDLED DAGGER COMES TO NAUGHT.
YOU CROOK! I'LL GET YOU YET.
OH HO! YA THINKS YA KIN TRIM OL' RIP O'DAY, THE FIGHTING FOOL, EH?
DOT BUMMER! VE OUGHT TO CRACK HISS EMPTY NOODLE.
BLISTER ME! YA SEES HIM SOCK ME WITH A CHAIR, 'N' BOWL ME OVER, DIDN'T YA? WHY, THA'S THE KIND OF A PAL I LIKES.
BUT HE ALMOST GOT AVAY MIT DER DAGGER.
SURE, 'N' HE'S LIABLE TO DO IT YET. HE'S LITTLE, BUT SO'S DYNAMITE.
ACH! LET'S GET BACK TO BUSINESS. I VANT TO BUY DOT DAGGER QUICK, UND GO.
THEN PASS OVER THE MONEY, FELLA, 'CAUSE I'M ITCHING TO SPEND IT.
QUICK! I BUY DER DAGGER FOR $900. ISS DOT SETTLED?
SURE, BUT YER A SAP IF YA EXPECTS A BARGAIN.
WHY, FER $900 I COULD BUY YA DOZENS OF DAGGERS, JES AS GOOD, 'N' MAYBE BETTER.
JA, JA! I KNOW. BUT I VANT IT BECAUSE IT VAS IN MY FAMILY FOR CENTURIES. I AM VERY SENTIMENTAL.
OH, THA'S DIFFER'NT.
IT'S SOLD! YA GOT A BUM DAGGER 'N' I'M $900 TO THE GOOD.
HOORAY! AT LAST! AT LAST IT ISS MINE! DER DAGGER ISS MINE.
AFTER WOLFGANG AND HIS MEN RIDE MERRILY AWAY WITH THE DAGGER, WASH TURNS TO RIP IN SCORN.
YOU CHEAT! YOU TRAITOR! WOTTA CHEAP, DOUBLE-CROSSIN' CROOK YOU TURNED OUT TO BE! MY PAL! MY FRIEND! BAH!!
WELL! WHAT IF I DID SELL FRIEDA'S DAGGER TO WOLFGANG FOR $900? WHAT OF IT?
WHY, YOU CROOK, IT'S TH' KEY TO A TREASURE — A FORTUNE.
OH HO! NOT WITHOUT THIS PAPER, IT AIN'T.
WOTTA YOU MEAN?
I MEANS THAT THIS LI'L' PAPER IS THE REAL KEY TO THE TREASURE, 'CAUSE I TOOK OFF THE HANDLE, 'N' THA'S WHAT I FINDS INSIDE! ALL WOLFGANG GOT FOR $900 WAS THE EMPTY DAGGER.

HEY, FRIEDA! RIP'S SOLVED THE SECRET! HE FINALLY GOT TH' HANDLE OFF THE DAGGER, AN' FOUND TH' TREASURE MAP.
OH, YOU DARLINGS! HOW IN THE WORLD DID YOU DO IT?
AW, I DUNNO. I JES KEPT MONKEYING AROUN' 'N' OFF IT COMES.
BUT BEST OF ALL, RIP SOLD TH' EMPTY DAGGER TO WOLFGANG AN' TRICKED TH' OLD BUZZARD OUTA $900.
I DOESN'T TRICK NOBODY! A SQUARE-SHOOTER, THA'S ME. HE WANTS TO BUY THE DAGGER 'N' I SELLS IT. HE DOESN'T MENTION NO PAPERS IN IT, 'N' I DOESN'T INCLUDE NONE.
ANYWAY, MA'AM, I WOULDN'T OF SOLD YOUR DAGGER ONLY — WELL, YOU SAYS YOU CAN'T PAY TAXES ON THAT CASTLE O' YOURS, 'N' I THOUGHT MAYBE THIS $900 WOULD HELP.
!?
C'MON, LE'S SEE TH' TREASURE MAP.
DEAR ME, YES! I CAN HARDLY WAIT.
NOTSA FAST, THERE. IT AIN'T EVEN A MAP.
EAGERLY, WASH AND FRIEDA CROWD AROUND. BUT OH! HOW THEIR FACES FALL WHEN THEY SEE THE MESSAGE.
GOOD HEAVENS! IT'S IN CODE!
MY GOSH! WE MIGHT AS WELL HAVE NOTHIN' AT ALL. NOBODY COULD READ THAT CRAZY STUFF.
WELL — I ADMITS IT HAS ME STUCK SO FAR. BUT I HAS A HUNCH — 'N' IF I'M RIGHT, IT'S DEAD EASY; 'N' IF I'M WRONG, IT'S JES TOO BAD.
PUZZLE FANS: FOR YOUR OWN AMUSEMENT, SEE IF YOU CAN DECIPHER THE MESSAGE, AND LOCATE THE TREASURE.
RATS! YOU COULDN'T DECIPHER THIS GOOFY MESSAGE IN A MILLION YEARS.
WELL, MAYBE I KIN 'N' MAYBE I KINT. ALL I HOPES IS THAT FRIEDA'S GRAN'PA IS NAMED KLEY, TOO.
YES, ANTON KLEY.
ANTON KLEY, THA'S FINE. NOW SEE THIS LAS' LINE — "OƆ.EC.Ɔ.XO.U.C¢" — I FIGGERS MAYBE THA'S A SIGNATURE. ALSO, I FIGGERS THE "X" DOESN'T COUNT.
IN THAT CASE "OƆ.EC.Ɔ." SPELLS "A-N-T-O-N" AN' "O.U.C¢" SPELLS "K-L-E-Y." SAME NUMBER OF LETTERS. SEE?
OBOY! NOW WE'RE GETTIN' SOMEWHERE.
WHY, HOW SMART!
NOW LOOK WHAT HAPPENS TO THE MESSAGE WHEN WE KNOWS WHAT THE LAST LINE MEANS.
EEK EALT N E
LOO E TONE N L ON
EN
ANTON KLEY

RIP HAS MADE A FINE START AT DECIPHERING THE SECRET MESSAGE FOUND IN THE DAGGER.
EEK EALT N E
LOO E TONE N L ON
EN
ANTON KLEY
NOW, LE'S SEE. THE REST WE HAS TO GUESS AT. THAT FIRST WORD— IT WOULDN'T BE "MEEK" OR "PEEK"— MUS' BE "SEEK."
SWELL! AN' WOTTA YOU SEEK? IT'S EITHER "HEALTH" OR "WEALTH."
WEALTH, OF COURSE!
THA'S FINE. NOW WE KNOWS THE LETTER "S", AN' THAT FILLS OUT THE WORDS "LOOSE" AN' "STONE."
AN' "LIONS" TOO. AN' I BETCHA 'AT LAST WORD IS "DEN."
BLISTER ME! NOW WE HAS IT! "SEEK WEALTH UNDER LOOSE STONE IN LION'S DEN." WHOOPEE! IT'S SOLVED!!
WELL, BIG BOY, I GOTTA ADMIT YOU SURE PULLED SOME SMART TRICKS. NOW YOU REALLY GOT SOMETHING TO BRAG ABOUT, FOR A CHANGE.
WHO SAYS I BRAGS ?
YOU BIG WINDBAG, EVERYBODY SAYS SO. YOU'RE ALWAYS BRAGGIN'.
I NEVER BRAGS!
YOU MEAN YOU NEVER STOP. WELL, C'MON, LE'S HEAR HOW SMART YOU THINK YOU ARE, AFTER OUTWITTIN' WOLFGANG AN' SOLVIN' TH' DAGGER MYST'RY.
BAH! THA'S NOTHING! FOR A FELLA OF MY BRAINS, THA'S NOTHING!
I'M GOOD 'N' I KNOWS I'M GOOD. THEY'S NOBODY ALIVE KIN OUTSMART OR OUT-FIGHT ME, 'CAUSE I'M RIP O'DAY 'N' I'M HUSKY 'N' TOUGH 'N' THE BEST THERE IS AT EVERYTHING. BUT THA'S NOT BRAGGING — THA'S JES ADMITTING THE TRUTH.
WOLFGANG AND HIS MEN ARE JUBILANT. THE DAGGER IS THEIRS. EAGERLY, THEY BREAK OFF THE HANDLE, LITTLE DREAMING THAT THE PRECIOUS TREASURE NOTE HAS ALREADY BEEN REMOVED.
POW!
WOLFGANG'S EYES SNAP WITH FIENDISH GLEE, AS HE SNATCHES UP A SMALL SLIP OF PAPER.
AH! HERE IT ISS!
You bum! So you thinks you can outsmart old Rip O'Day! Ha! Ha!
TWICE HE READS THE STARTLING NOTE— THEN BLOWS UP IN A WILD, BOILING FIT OF ANGER.
I'LL KILL HIM! I'LL KILL HIM!!
Roy Crane

FRIEDA IS ANXIOUS TO START IN SEARCH OF THE HIDDEN TREASURE AS SOON AS POSSIBLE.
BUT I— I'M AFRAID.
WELL, BUST MY NECK! IF THA'S NOT A REAL LAUGH! YA HAS ME 'N' OLD TUBBSY TO PROTECT YA, 'N' YER AFRAID. HAW HAW HAW!
I KNOW, BUT—
AW, FORGIT IT, MA'AM. THEY'S ONLY ONE THING WRONG— THE NOTE SAYS THE TREASURE'S IN A LION'S DEN.
BUT WHERE'S THE LION'S DEN?
IN THE CASTLE. YOU SEE, MY GRANDFATHER WAS VERY ECCENTRIC —HE KEPT ALL SORTS OF HORRIBLE BEASTS, SUCH AS LIONS AND LEOPARDS, AS PETS.
HEAVENS! DO YOU WONDER THAT I'M AFRAID? LIONS— UGH!
LIONS, EH? SAY, THA'S GREAT! A LION IS ONE THING I AIN'T EVER HAD A CHANCE TO WHIP.
WHERE'S TH' CASTLE? C'MON— LE'S START DIGGIN' UP 'AT OLD TREASURE.
THA'S THE STUFF. LE'S UP 'N' GO. HOW ABOUT IT, MA'AM.
WE'LL HAVE TO HIRE A CAR. THE CASTLE'S 30 MILES.
OKAY! THA'S TUBBSY'S DOOTY WHILE I LOADS UP WITH AMMUNITION 'N' GITS IN MY WORKING CLOTHES.
WHOOPEE! AWAY WE GO!
IN YOU GO, BOYS.
WOLFGANG! IF THEY COULD BUT SEE THAT VILLAIN, AS HE SLIPS THRU A HOLE IN THE ROCKY CLIFF BELOW THE CASTLE WALL, THEIR MERRIMENT WOULD CEASE.
HELLO, HEINIE.
HOW'S DER BOY, HEINIE? DOT GIRL ISSN'T HERE YET, ISS SHE?
NOW, BOYS, HOW MANY TIMES I GOT TO TELL YOU DOT SHE ORDERED ME TO KEEP YOU OUDT?
LISTEN, YOU LUMP! DON'T TRY TO TELL ME VOT TO DO. DER BOSS ISS ME— NOT FRIEDA KLEY. NOW, DO YOU VISH TO SHARE DER TREASURE MIT US, OR GET A BUST ON DER SNOOZLE?
ACH! NO ROUGH STUFF. I DO VOTEFFER YOU SAY. YOU KNOW ME, I SHARE DER BLOOMING TREASURE.
HONK HONK!
TOOT HORN
JUST THEN A TRUMPET SOUNDS OUTSIDE, SIGNALING FOR THE DRAWBRIDGE TO BE LOWERED. FRIEDA AND HER FRIENDS HAVE ARRIVED.

UPON THE ARRIVAL OF FRIEDA AND HER FRIENDS, WOLFGANG GIVES A FEW HURRIED ORDERS AND DISAPPEARS WITH HIS MEN. IT IS A LONG TIME BEFORE HEINIE LOWERS THE CASTLE DRAWBRIDGE.
'S'ABOUT TIME HE LETS US IN.
HOW'S EVERYTHING, HEINIE? HAS WOLFGANG BEEN AROUND AGAIN?
NEIN, FRAULEIN. NO VUN HASS BEEN HERE.
Roy Crane
HI HO! WOT COULD BE MORE QUIET AN' PEACEFUL THAN THIS?
THIS IS A SPOOKY DUMP.
YES, THE NATIVES AROUND HERE THINK THE CASTLE IS HAUNTED.
AW, C'MON. LE'S DIG UP TH' TREASURE.
FRAULEIN, COULD I PLEASE SPEAK MIT YOU IN PRIVATE?
WHY-AH-CERTAINLY, HEINIE.
IS SOMETHING WRONG? WHAT IN THE WORLD HAS HAPPENED?
SH-H! COME DIS VAY.
THEY ENTER A DARK ROOM AND THE DOOR IS CLOSED. THE LOCK CLICKS. THERE IS AN UNCOMFORTABLE SILENCE—INKY BLACKNESS—THEN TERROR SEIZES FRIEDA.
LIGHTS! WHERE ARE THE LIGHTS? HEINIE! OPEN THAT DOOR!!
NO SOUND ANSWERS FRIEDA'S CRY. SHE BECOMES TERRIFIED AND SCREAMS.
HEINIE! LIGHTS! OPEN THAT DOOR! HELP!
THE LIGHTS COME ON WITH A BLINDING FLASH.
WOLFGANG!
SHUT UP!
DOT'S PRISONER NUMBER VUN. TIE HER UP.
WASH! RIP! HELP!!
Roy Crane
KICKING AND SCREAMING, FRIEDA IS CARRIED TO ANOTHER ROOM, DUMPED ON THE FLOOR, AND TIGHTLY BOUND.

WOW! 300 FEET TO TH' GROUND.
WONDER HOW I'D LOOK IN ONE O' THESE THINGS.
LITTLE REALIZING THE FATE THAT FRIEDA HAS MET, AT THE HANDS OF WOLFGANG, WASH AND RIP AMUSE THEMSELVES BY LOOKING AROUND THE CASTLE.
PRETTY SOON THE KEEPER COMES BACK.
VUN MOMENT, PLEASE, HERR TUBBS. FRAULEIN KLEY VISHES TO SPEAK MIT YOU.
HEY! DOESN'T SHE WANT ME, TOO?
G'WAN. THIS IS ROMANCE— NOT A FIGHT.
DIS VAY, HERR TUBBS, UND TURN TO DER RIGHT.
NOSSIR! YOU GO IN FIRST.
VOT'S DER MATTER? AFRAID UF DER DARK?
WASH STARTS TO ENTER THE DARKENED ROOM, THEN HESITATES, EVIDENTLY SUSPICIOUS
ALL RIGHT, I GO FIRST UND YOU FOLLOW. ACH! IMAGINE A GROWN MAN AFRAID UF DER DARK.
I'M NOT AFRAID, EITHER. I JUST DON'T WUNTA GO FIRST.
BUT ONCE INSIDE, WASH DOES FEEL AFRAID. HE CAN SEE NOTHING. THERE ARE ONLY THE FAINT SOUNDS OF RUSTLING GARMENTS, AND PEOPLE BREATHING.
HEY! STRIKE A MATCH. WHERE ARE YOU? I CAN'T SEE A THING.
BAM!
MY GOSH!
THE DOOR SLAMS. WASH'S HEART LEAPS TO HIS THROAT. HE JUMPS FOR THE DOOR, AND PULLS WITH ALL HIS MIGHT. IT'S LOCKED!
SUDDENLY THERE IS A BLINDING GLARE OF LIGHT, AND WASH FINDS HIMSELF ON THE UNCOMFORTABLE END OF SEVERAL REVOLVERS.
VELL, MY FRIEND, VE MEET AGAIN. NOW MAYBE YOU TELL VARE DOT TREASURE ISS HIDDEN, EH?
I-I DUNNO. I FORGOT.
OH HO! MAYBE DIS VILL HELP YOU TO REMEMBER
OW! OUCH! YOU'RE TWISTIN' MY ARM OFF.
DOT'S DER STUFF, MEN, MAKE HIM TELL.
I'LL DIE FIRST! I'LL NEVER TELL—OW! YOU'RE KILLIN' ME! HELP!
POW!
SOKKO!
BAM!

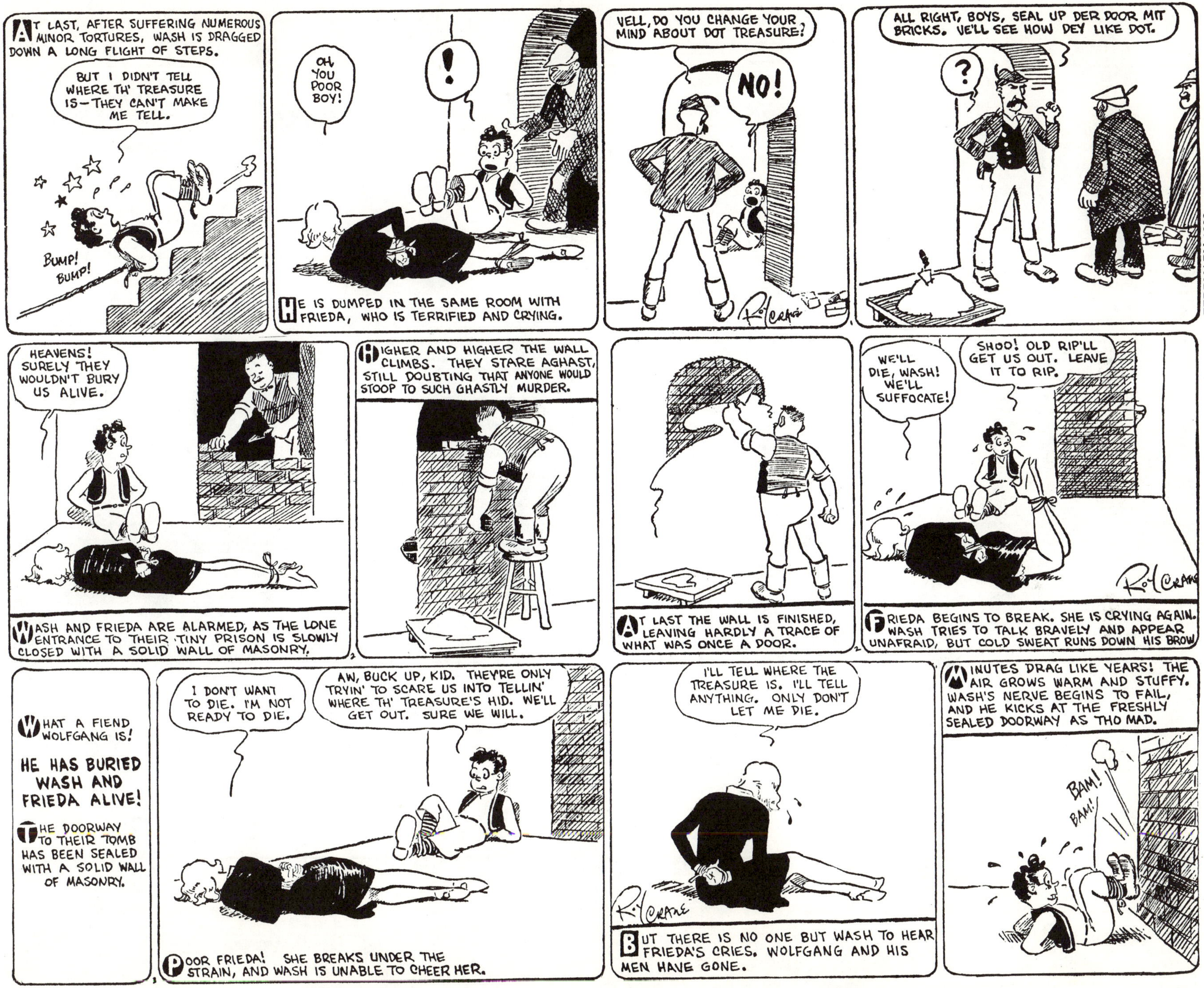

FEBRUARY 1932

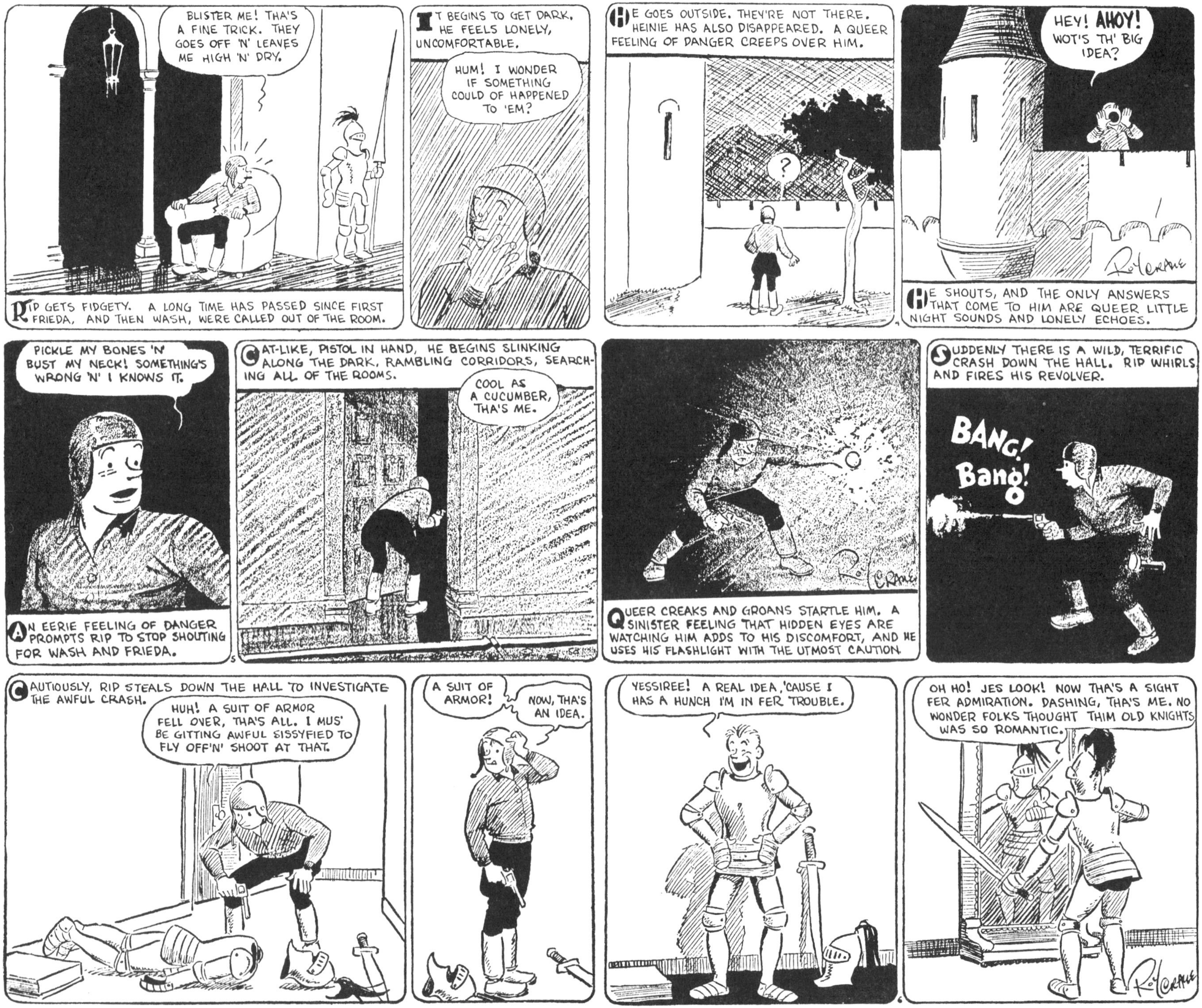
BLISTER ME! THA'S A FINE TRICK. THEY GOES OFF 'N' LEAVES ME HIGH 'N' DRY.
RIP GETS FIDGETY. A LONG TIME HAS PASSED SINCE FIRST FRIEDA, AND THEN WASH, WERE CALLED OUT OF THE ROOM.
IT BEGINS TO GET DARK. HE FEELS LONELY, UNCOMFORTABLE.
HUM! I WONDER IF SOMETHING COULD OF HAPPENED TO 'EM?
HE GOES OUTSIDE. THEY'RE NOT THERE. HEINIE HAS ALSO DISAPPEARED. A QUEER FEELING OF DANGER CREEPS OVER HIM.
?
HEY! AHOY! WOT'S TH' BIG IDEA?
Roy Crane
HE SHOUTS, AND THE ONLY ANSWERS THAT COME TO HIM ARE QUEER LITTLE NIGHT SOUNDS AND LONELY ECHOES.
PICKLE MY BONES 'N' BUST MY NECK! SOMETHING'S WRONG 'N' I KNOWS IT.
AN EERIE FEELING OF DANGER PROMPTS RIP TO STOP SHOUTING FOR WASH AND FRIEDA.
CAT-LIKE, PISTOL IN HAND, HE BEGINS SLINKING ALONG THE DARK, RAMBLING CORRIDORS, SEARCHING ALL OF THE ROOMS.
COOL AS A CUCUMBER, THA'S ME.
Roy Crane
QUEER CREAKS AND GROANS STARTLE HIM. A SINISTER FEELING THAT HIDDEN EYES ARE WATCHING HIM ADDS TO HIS DISCOMFORT, AND HE USES HIS FLASHLIGHT WITH THE UTMOST CAUTION.
SUDDENLY THERE IS A WILD, TERRIFIC CRASH DOWN THE HALL. RIP WHIRLS AND FIRES HIS REVOLVER.
BANG!
Bang!
CAUTIOUSLY, RIP STEALS DOWN THE HALL TO INVESTIGATE THE AWFUL CRASH.
HUH! A SUIT OF ARMOR FELL OVER, THA'S ALL. I MUS' BE GITTING AWFUL SISSYFIED TO FLY OFF 'N' SHOOT AT THAT.
A SUIT OF ARMOR!
NOW, THA'S AN IDEA.
YESSIREE! A REAL IDEA, 'CAUSE I HAS A HUNCH I'M IN FER TROUBLE.
OH HO! JES LOOK! NOW THA'S A SIGHT FER ADMIRATION. DASHING, THA'S ME. NO WONDER FOLKS THOUGHT THIM OLD KNIGHTS WAS SO ROMANTIC.
Roy Crane

NOW, BRING ON YER SPOOKS 'N' GOBLINS 'CAUSE I'M RIP O'DAY 'N' I AIMS TO TEAR THIS OLD CASTLE DOWN. AGAIN I STARTS PROWLING ABOUT IN MY OWN CAT-LIKE 'N' SILENT FASHION.
SCREECH!
BLISTER ME! WOT'S THAT?
CREAK!
SQUEAK!
HUH! I EVEN SCARES MYSELF. WELL—THEY'S CERTAIN'Y NO USE TRYING TO BE QUIET IN THIS FIRE WHISTLE.
SQUEAK!
SCREECH!
CLANK!
BLUMP!
K-REEK!
SO OFF I GOES, LOOKING FER TROUBLE. AHOY! MAKE WAY! HERE COMES THE HUMAN TANK.
CLANK!
BAM!
SQUEEEE!
WHAT I NEEDS IS A CAN OPENER.
JUST AS RIP ENTERS ANOTHER ROOM IN SEARCH OF WASH AND FRIEDA, HE REMEMBERS THAT HE HAS PUT ON THE SUIT OF ANCIENT ARMOR OVER HIS PISTOL.
THA'S SURE DUMB, BUT A SWORD'S BETTER IN THE DARK, ANYWAYS. HUM—I'LL JES TAKE A LOOK AROUND WHILE I'M HERE.
WOLFGANG! THE SINISTER, WAITING FIGURE OF WOLFGANG IS SUDDENLY CAUGHT IN THE BEAM OF LIGHT.
GET HIM, MEN! KILL DER BUMMER!
Whack! Bang Bang! Pow!
DARKNESS AGAIN—PISTOL SHOTS—SHOUTS—SCREAMS! AND THE AWFUL CLATTER AND SQUEAK OF RIP'S RUSTY ARMOR, AS HE LEAPS INTO ACTION.
HERE I AM! COME'N' GIT ME!
KILL HIM, BOYS! KILL HIM!
OW! HELP! MINE HEAD!
LIGHTS! LIGHTS!! SOMEBODY TURN ON DER LIGHTS.
WHAKO! Wham! CRASH! CRUNCH! BANG!
WHAT A BATTLE! PISTOLS, KNIVES, SWORDS, AND CHAIRS. MEN BATTLING FOR THEIR LIVES IN TOTAL DARKNESS.
I'M RIP O'DAY 'N' I NEVER KNOWS WHEN TO STOP. WHOOPEE! LE'S GO! GET A CANNON, YOU MUGS, 'N' LE'S MAKE THIS A REAL FIGHT.
SPLAT! SOKKO! Wham!
RIP'S SWORD IS KNOCKED OUT OF HIS HAND, BUT HIS IRON FIST IS ALMOST AS GOOD.
LIGHTS, DOT'S DER STUFF! NOW GET HIM!
OW! MINE FIST ISS BUSTED.
THA'S THE STUFF! HIT ME WITH YER FISTS 'N' I LAYS YOU ALL OUT.
KLINK!
Bam!
DARKNESS AGAIN! A FEW MORE CRASHES AND SHOTS AND SCREAMS—THEN UTTER SILENCE.

SQEEE!
CLUMP CLUMP!
THE SILENCE, FOLLOWING THE AWFUL BATTLE IN THE DARK, IS FINALLY BROKEN BY A NOISE LIKE THE SQUEAKING OF A RUSTY WINDMILL.
THE LIGHTS GO ON AND MR. RIP O'DAY, THE FIGHTING FOOL, SURVEYS THE HUMAN WRECKAGE WITH AN AIR OF COMPLETE SATISFACTION.
THA'S WHAT I THOUGHT. I KAYOES 'EM ALL.
HEY, WAIT! THIS AIN'T WOLFGANG! BLISTER ME — IF THAT MUG GOT AWAY I'LL—
!
SQUEAK!
HERE I AM, YOU LUMP. COME UND GET ME. HO HO HO! TRY UND GET ME!
BAM!
OH HO! LAYING FOR ME, WAS YOU? YOU BLANKETY-BLANKED RAT, I'LL — —
DOT'S DER STUFF! ATTACK ME UND LEARN A LESSON, YOU DUMMER.
KLINK!
POW!
POW!
SQUEE!
HEY! WOT THE—?
VELL! VELL! PRISONER NUMBER THREE.
CRASH!
AT LAST!
WONDERFUL, WASHIE! AND I ALMOST HAVE ONE OF MY HANDS FREE.
THE PRISONER'S DESPERATE EFFORT TO KICK A HOLE IN THE NEWLY CEMENTED WALL FINALLY SUCCEEDS.
OH, HOW GOOD THE FRESH AIR FEELS! BUT JUST THEN THERE IS AN AWFUL METALLIC CRASH OUTSIDE
Wham!
MY GOSH! WOT'S 'AT?
THEY EMERGE CAUTIOUSLY.
I THOUGHT I HEARD FOOTSTEPS.
SHH! LISSEN!
SILENCE — THEN IN THE DISTANCE CAN BE HEARD A WEIRD SCRAPING SOUND.
IT SOUNDS LIKE SOMEONE'S DRAGGING A SHOVEL. OH, DEAR! IT'S COMING NEARER.
WAIT. I'M GUNNA GET AN ARM LOAD OF BRICKS.

SHH! IT'S WOLFGANG! BUT WOT ON EARTH IS HE DRAGGIN' 'AT OLD SUIT OF ARMOR AROUND FOR?
FOR HEAVENS SAKE, WASH, DO SOMETHING! OH DEAR, IF HE CATCHES US.....!
GIMME ROOM! I'M GUNNA DO SUMPIN AWRIGHT.
WHACK!!
OBOY! I GUESS I'M NOTSA BAD AFTER ALL, EH, FRIEDA? I SURE KAYOED OLD WOLFGANG.
YOU DARLING!
BUT WHAT IN THE WORLD WAS HE GOING TO DO WITH THIS OLD SUIT OF ARMOR?
C'MON, FORGET IT. WE GOTTA FIND RIP.
UGH! WHAT HAPPENED? WHO HIT ME?
?
!
!
GEE WIZ! IT'S RIP.
OF COURSE IT IS, STUPID. GIT THIS TIN CAN OFFA ME.
I WAS FIGHTIN' 'N' SOMETHING HITS ME 'N' THA'S ALL I REMEMBERS UNTIL—WELL! WOTTER YOU LAUGHING AT?
OH, NOTHIN'. ONLY I CAN'T HELP THINKIN' WOTTA RIP-ROARIN' WILDCAT YOU CLAIM TO BE.
WELL! WOT OF IT?
HAW HAW HAW! EVEN WITH A SUIT OF ARMOR ON THEY KNOCK YOU OUT. THE TERROR OF THE UNIVERSE GETS BEAT UP. WHOOPEE!
NOW, WASH, I'M SURE RIP DID THE BEST HE COULD.
SURE—BUT TH' BIG WINDBAG COULDN'T DO MUCH. OMY, WOTTA MAN! RIP O'DAY, TH' FIGHTIN' FOOL! HAW HAW HAW!
SAY! YOU WANT A BUST ON THE NOSE?

WOTTA FIGHTER! HO HO HO! I THOUGHT YOU SAID YOU WERE GOOD.
PICKLE MY BONES 'N' BUST MY NECK! I AM GOOD! I'M THE BEST THEY IS.
GWAN! YER A SOFTIE. WHY, I HAD A PAL ONCE WHO—
OH, HE COULD, COULD HE? BLISTER ME—I'D LIKE TO MEET THAT FELLA "EASY" ONCE. JES ONCE, THA'S ALL.
I'D SHOW YOU WHO KIN FIGHT. I'D SHOW YOU IF I'M A WINDBAG. RIP O'DAY, THA'S ME, 'N' I'M A RIP-ROARING TOOTER 'N' I NEVER KNOWS WHEN I'M LICKED.
WELL, IN CASE YOU DON'T KNOW, BUDDIE, IT'S JUST HAPPENED.
IS ZAT SO? I'LL SHOW YOU. BRING ON YER PAL. BRING ON YER TOUGH GUYS 'N' LIONS 'N' TIGERS 'CAUSE I'M GITTING MAD 'N' I WANTS TO DO MY STUFF.
DEAR ME! DON'T GET SO EXCITED, RIP. HE'S ONLY TEASING.
PLEASE, BOYS, LET'S QUIT FUSSING AND FIND THE TREASURE.
SURE JUST AS SOON AS WE CAN STOP RIP FROM BRAGGIN'.
I NEVER BRAGS. FOR A FELLA OF MY STRENGTH THA'S NOT NECESSARY.
WE'LL PUT OLD WOLFGANG WITH THEM MUGS UP STAIRS THAT I LAYS OUT.
THEY'LL BE SAFE, 'CAUSE WHEN I HITS A GUY HE STAYS HIT-- WHY, BLISTER ME! THEY'RE GONE!
HUM! EVIDENTLY YOU DON'T HIT QUITE AS HARD AS YOU CLAIM.
I'LL SHOW YOU YET, YOU DUMPY DOODLE BUG! LOCK WOLFGANG IN THIS CLOSET 'N' WHEN I FINDS THEM OTHER MUGS—BOY, LOOK OUT!
THO WOLFGANG IS LOCKED IN A CLOSET, FRIEDA IS ALARMED BECAUSE HIS MEN GOT AWAY.
HEAVENS! I HOPE THEY'RE NOT STILL IN THE CASTLE.
AFTER THE BEATING I HANDED 'EM, MA'AM, THEY'LL BE IN A HOSPITAL.
AW, C'MON, YER SAFE WITH ME 'N' OLD TUBBSY.
SURE. SHOW US TO TH' LION'S DEN AN' WE'LL HAVE 'AT OLD TREASURE IN NO TIME.
AT LAST FRIEDA'S FEARS ARE QUIETED, AND SHE LEADS THEM TO THE DUNGEON DOOR.
BLISTER ME! IT'S LOCKED!
GEE! ISN'T THERE SOME OTHER WAY, FRIEDA?
LET ME SEE. I HAVEN'T BEEN HERE SINCE I WAS A LITTLE GIRL—OH, YES! I REMEMBER A SECRET PASSAGE.
AH! THA'S THE STUFF—A SECRET PASSAGE.
OBOY! 'AT'S A LOT MORE ROMANTIC.

THERE'S A SECRET DOOR HERE SOMEWHERE. I REMEMBER SEEING MY GRANDFATHER COME OUT OF IT ONCE. AH—HERE'S A BUTTON.
LOOK! IT OPENS!
BUT-BUT I THOUGHT YOU SAID THERE WAS NO DANGER.
GET YER GUN READY, SPORT. HERE WE GOES.
AW, HE'S ONLY KIDDIN'. IT'S AWRIGHT.
THEY CLIMB DOWN A RUSTY OLD LADDER.
AND PRETTY SOON RIP IS PEEPING CAUTIOUSLY INTO THE DUNGEON.
THA'S FINE. NOT A SOUL IN SIGHT.
© 1932 BY NEA SERVICE, INC. REG. U. S. PAT. OFF.
PSST! 'S'AWRIGHT. LOOKS LIKE NOBODY'S BIN IN THIS DUNGEON FER FIFTY YEARS.
HEAVENS! THIS IS AWFUL.
THE PLACE IS MUSTY AND HORRIBLY DEPRESSING, AND FRIEDA IS A BIT FRIGHTENED.
C'MON. LE'S DIG UP 'AT OLD TREASURE IN A HURRY AN' SCRAM.
THA'S THE STUFF. WHERE'S THE LION'S DEN?
SHH—NOT SO MUCH NOISE. I'M STILL AFRAID THAT WOLFGANG'S MEN MIGHT BE IN THE CASTLE.
© 1932 BY NEA SERVICE, INC. REG. U. S. PAT. OFF.
OH HO! THE MENAGERIE.
PSST! D'YOU NOTICE ALL TH' CAGES ARE EMPTY.
WHY, HOW STRANGE! MY ODD OLD GRAND-DADDY WAS WILD OVER HIS HORRID BEASTS.
TIGERS
LEOPARDS
HEY, LOOK! HERE IT IS AWRIGHT. TH' LION'S DEN!
AND EMPTY, TOO—SAY, THA'S LUCK. C'MON, LE'S BUS' RIGHT IN 'N' DIG UP THE TREASURE.
NO, NO, PLEASE!
HEY! WAIT, YOU IDIOT! HOW D'YOU KNOW IT'S EMPTY? LOOKIT THAT BIG HOLE.
NUBIAN LIONS
© 1932 BY NEA SERVICE, INC. REG. U. S. PAT. OFF.
AW, I KNOWS MY STUFF. RIP O'DAY, THA'S ME, 'N' IF CIRCUS FELLAS KIN HANDLE LIONS WITH A CHAIR 'N' A GUN, SO KIN I.

SHUX! THEY'S NO LIONS IN HERE. YA DOESN'T THINK I'M GUNNER WAIT ALL DAY TO DIG UP THAT TREASURE, I HOPES.
RIP—PLEASE!! COME BACK HERE—THAT CAVE MIGHT BE FULL OF LIONS.
TH' BIG SAP! WELL, IF HE'S FOOL ENOUGH TO GO IN THERE, SO'M I.
NUBIAN LIONS
THA'S THE STUFF, SPORT. YOU LOOK FOR THE LOOSE STONE WHILE I STAN'S GUARD.
OBOY! I FOUND IT! BUT FOR GOSH SAKES, KEEP YOUR EYE ON THAT HOLE. I DUN'T WUNTA BE ET ALIVE.
THA'S AWRIGHT, TUBBSY. A DEAD SHOT, THA'S ME 'N' I NEVER MISSES.
REG. U. S. PAT. OFF. © 1932 BY NEA SERVICE, INC.
HURRY—PLEASE! YOU FRIGHTEN ME TO DEATH
OBOY! LOOKY! AN IRON BOX! IT'S TH' TREASURE!
THA'S THE STUFF SPORT. ATTABOY!
NUBIAN LIONS
HERE IT IS, FRIEDA, AN' I WISH YOU THE VERY BEST OF LUCK.
YOU DARLING! OH, HOW CAN I EVER THANK YOU BOYS?
NOW LET'S GET OUT OF THIS DREADFUL PLACE.
WUZ IT GOLD, TUBBSY?
I DUNNO. TH' BOX WAS LOCKED. I THINK IT'S DIAMONDS, MAYBE.
NEVERMIND, WE CAN OPEN IT LATER.
WELL, I'LL BE BLISTERED! HEY—WHERE'S THE DOOR?
'AT'S FUNNY. I'DA SWORN WE CAME IN RIGHT BY THESE POSTS.
© 1932 BY NEA SERVICE, INC. REG. U. S. PAT. OFF.
'AT'S SURE FUNNY. I'D SWEAR I LEFT 'AT SECRET DOOR OPEN.
I SWEARS YA DID TOO, SPORT, 'N' IT WAS RIGHT ABOUT HERE.
OH, WE'RE ONLY LOST. I'LL LOOK AROUND THE OTHER WALLS.
FRIEDA RETURNS, LOOKING PALE AND WORRIED.
I—I COULDN'T FIND IT.
YEH, 'AT'S SOME DOOR.
WE BEEN EXAMINING THE WALL 'N' CAN'T EVEN FIND A CRACK.
GOOD HEAVENS! WHAT DOES IT MEAN, RIP? COULD WOLFGANG'S MEN—? OH, DEAR! YOU DON'T SUPPOSE THEY—?
AW, DON'T WORRY, MA'AM. WE'RE OKAY. IT JES MEANS WE HAS TO FIND A NEW WAY OUT, THA'S ALL.
REG. U. S. PAT. OFF. © 1932 BY NEA SERVICE, INC.

BOY, I DON'T LIKE THIS. 'AT SECRET DOOR DIDN'T CLOSE ACCIDENT'LY. SOMEBODY KNEW WE WERE DOWN HERE AN' SHUT IT ON PURPOSE.
I WISH WE'D NEVER FOUND THE TREASURE.
AW, YOU TWO MAKES ME SICK. WE'LL GIT OUT. FIGHTING 'N' JAIL-BREAKING, THEM'S MY SPECIALTIES.
LOOK! WOTTID I TELL YA? HERE'S A DOOR 'N' IT AIN'T EVEN LOCKED.
HO HO! IT WAS ONLY A CLOSET.
WELL, HERE'S ANOTHER ONE. LE'S TRY IT.
RIP THROWS IT OPEN AND---
ROY CRANE
REG. U. S. PAT. OFF. © 1932 BY NEA SERVICE, INC.
HORRORS! A LEOPARD IS INSIDE!! IT LEAPS FOR THE OPENING!!!
RIP SLAMS THE DOOR—BUT NOT IN TIME TO KEEP THE LEOPARD FROM WRIGGLING THRU.
BUS' MY NECK! HEY!
THE LEOPARD RUNS—FRIEDA IS IN THE WAY. THE BEAST SLASHES AT HER WITH HIS PAW AS HE LEAPS PAST.
POW!
BANG BANG!
REG. U. S. PAT. OFF. © 1932 BY NEA SERVICE, INC.
WASH AND RIP, FRIGHTENED STIFF, OPEN UP THE FIREWORKS, AND THE LEOPARD DISAPPEARS.
OMY GOSH! SHE'S DEAD! HE GOT 'ER!
MY FAULT, TOO! I OUGHT OF KEPT HER BACK.
ROY CRANE
LOOK—SHE'S COMIN' TO. SHE MUST OF ONLY FAINTED.
OH!! WHAT A FRIGHT—THAT AWFUL LEOPARD! OHHHH!
YOU POOR KID. GEE! WE SURE THOUGHT YOU WERE A GONER, FRIEDA. ARE YOU HURT?
NO. ONLY MY DRESS—I—I'M AFRAID I'M NOT VERY PRESENTABLE.
NO WONDER YA FAINTED.
GOSH! 'AT WAS TH' CLOSEST CALL I EVER SAW.
WHILE FRIEDA IS TRYING TO PIN HER DRESS TOGETHER, WASH AND RIP HOLD A COUNCIL OF WAR.
BUT GEE WIZ! WOT IF THERE'S WILD ANIMALS BEHIND ALL TH' DOORS?
GOTTER DO IT, SPORT. WE'LL NEVER GIT OUT WITH THAT TREASURE UNLESS WE TAKES A CHANCE 'N' YOU KNOW IT.
AWRIGHT, FOLKS, HERE'S ANOTHER DOOR, SO STAN' 'WAY BACK 'N' GIT READY FER TROUBLE.
© 1932 BY NEA SERVICE, INC REG. U. S. PAT. OFF.
ROY CRANE

MARCH 1932

CAUTIOUSLY, RIP TURNS THE HANDLE OF THE THIRD DOOR, AND PEEPS IN.
CAN'T SEE NOTHIN' YET.
CRASH!
?
*!
SOMETHING STRIKES THE DOOR A TERRIFIC WALLOP, AND RIP GOES HEAD OVER HEELS.
AND TWO SNARLING TIGERS SCRAMBLE OUT.
GRR-RRR!
!
BUST MY NECK! I THOUGHT YOU SAYS THESE BEASTS IS PETS.
DEAR ME! THIS IS GETTING WORSE. FIRST IT'S A LEOPARD, THEN TIGERS!
YEH. JUST FOR A CHANGE, I'M IN FAVOR OF SOME RABBITS JUMPIN' OUT AT US.
© 1932 BY NEA SERVICE, INC REG. U. S. PAT. OFF.
IN A TOUGH SPOT!
WASH, RIP, AND FRIEDA HAVE THE TREASURE.
BUT
THEY CAN'T FIND THEIR WAY OUT!
AND
A LEOPARD AND TWO TIGERS ARE RUNNING LOOSE IN THE SAME DUNGEON WITH THEM.
WE GOTTA DO SOMETHING. MAYBE I KIN HIT WUNNA THEM BABIES FROM HERE.
BETTER SAVE YOUR AMMUNITION, YOU SAP. THEY AREN'T BOTHERING US.
AN' B'SIDES, EAGLE EYE, YOU HAD PLENTY OF CHANCES AN' MISSED.
THA'S RIGHT— RUB IT IN! I S'POSE THAT GUY, EASY, COULD OF DONE BETTER, HUH?
REG. U. S. PAT. OFF. © 1932 BY NEA SERVICE, INC.
PLEASE, BOYS, LET'S NOT START THAT SILLY ARGUMENT AGAIN.
I- I'M THIRSTY.
I'M HALF STARVED.
WELL, I'M PLENTY SCARED AN' I'M NOT AFRAID TO ADMIT IT.
CRANE
JUST AS WASH, RIP, AND FRIEDA ARE BECOMING DOWNHEARTED, FRIEDA GIVES A CRY OF JOY.
MY GOODNESS! LOOK!
IT'S A HOLE IN THE CEILING.
BLISTER ME! IF ONLY WE HAD A LADDER.
NO! LIFT ME UP, RIP. LIFT ME UP.
ATTABOY, TUBBSY! KIN YA REACH IT?
HIGHER! GRAB MY ANKLES! NO, I'M STILL SHORT. 'S'NO USE, RIP.
Roy Crane
!
REG. U. S. PAT. OFF. © 1932 BY NEA SERVICE, INC
THEN TO RIP'S AMAZEMENT, WASH IS JERKED OUT OF HIS GRASP, AND DISAPPEARS IN THE HOLE.

WHAT IN THE WORLD HAPPENED?
I DUNNO. I'M HOLDING WASH, SO'S HE KIN REACH THAT HOLE IN THE CEILING 'N' HE SAYS HE CAN'T MAKE IT. THEN PRESTO! HE DISAPPEARS.
FROM ABOVE, STRANGE, MUFFLED FOOTSTEPS ARE HEARD, AND RIP GROWS ALARMED.
BUMP!
THUMP!
HEY, WASH! HEY! ARE YOU AWRIGHT?
THERE IS A LONG SILENCE.
YOU BLINKING DOODLE-BUG, ANSWER ME! HEY! WHAT'S HAPPENED?
THEN A FAR-AWAY GUTTURAL LAUGH.
HO HO HO!
BLISTER ME! THA'S NOT WASH!
HEAVENS! IT'S WOLFGANG! I'D KNOW HIS LAUGH ANYWHERE.
© 1932 BY NEA SERVICE, INC. REG. U. S. PAT. OFF.
RIP AND FRIEDA ARE STUNNED BY WASH'S SUDDEN DISAPPEARANCE THRU THE HOLE IN THE CEILING, FOLLOWED BY WOLFGANG'S CACKLE OF GLEE.
OH, RIP! WHAT SHALL WE DO?
STAY THERE! I HAS TO FIND A LADDER.
STOP! YOU ARE CUFFERED MIT FIREARMS, MITOUT ESCAPE.
!
WOLFGANG'S VOICE! IT SUDDENLY BOOMS THRU SOME HOLE IN THE WALL.
I GIF VUN MORE CHANCE. PUT DOWN DER TREASURE BOX UND PISTOLS, UND YOU UND DOT FOOL UF A GIRL GO FREE.
IS ZAT SO? WELL, HOW ABOUT MY BUDDIE?
REG. U. S. PAT. OFF. © 1932 BY NEA SERVICE, INC.
DO VOT I SAY! PUT DEM DOWN, VILE YOU HAF DER CHANCE. YOUR BUDDIE ISS ALREADY DEAD!!
!
!
WASH IS DEAD!
RIP AND FRIEDA CAN HARDLY BELIEVE IT!
ARE DUMBFOUNDED,
BUT PERHAPS WOLFGANG IS ONLY TRYING TO FRIGHTEN THEM WITH SUCH A YARN.
AGAIN COMES HIS VOICE FROM BEHIND THE WALL.
DO VOT I SAY! DROP DOT TREASURE BOX UND PISTOLS!
HEAVENS! LET HIM HAVE THE OLD MONEY.
NO. GIVE IT HERE.
MAKE UP YOUR MIND QUICK. I COUNT UP TO TEN, DEN I SHOOT. VUN, TWO, T'REE —
PSST! EDGE OVER BEHIND THIS POST. MAYBE WE KIN SCRAM.
REG. U. S. PAT. OFF. © 1932 BY NEA SERVICE, INC.
BANG!
?
A PISTOL SHOT! AND RIP TOPPLES OVER ON HIS SIDE.

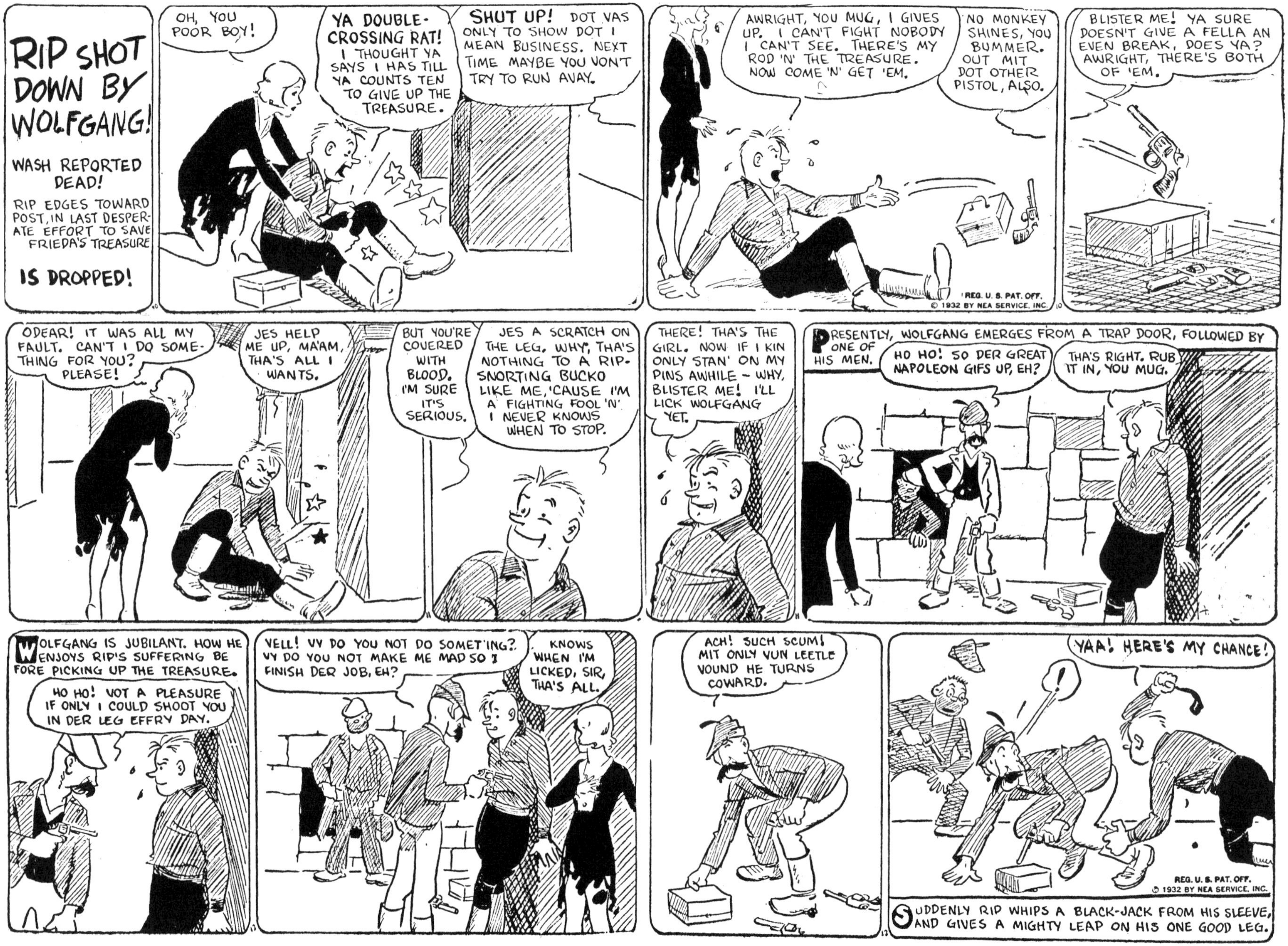
RIP SHOT DOWN BY WOLFGANG!
WASH REPORTED DEAD!
RIP EDGES TOWARD POST, IN LAST DESPERATE EFFORT TO SAVE FRIEDA'S TREASURE
IS DROPPED!
OH, YOU POOR BOY!
YA DOUBLE-CROSSING RAT! I THOUGHT YA SAYS I HAS TILL YA COUNTS TEN TO GIVE UP THE TREASURE.
SHUT UP! DOT VAS ONLY TO SHOW DOT I MEAN BUSINESS. NEXT TIME MAYBE YOU VON'T TRY TO RUN AVAY.
AWRIGHT, YOU MUG, I GIVES UP. I CAN'T FIGHT NOBODY I CAN'T SEE. THERE'S MY ROD 'N' THE TREASURE. NOW COME 'N' GET 'EM.
NO MONKEY SHINES, YOU BUMMER. OUT MIT DOT OTHER PISTOL, ALSO.
REG. U. S. PAT. OFF.
© 1932 BY NEA SERVICE, INC.
BLISTER ME! YA SURE DOESN'T GIVE A FELLA AN EVEN BREAK, DOES YA? AWRIGHT, THERE'S BOTH OF 'EM.
O DEAR! IT WAS ALL MY FAULT. CAN'T I DO SOMETHING FOR YOU? PLEASE!
JES HELP ME UP, MA'AM, THA'S ALL I WANTS.
BUT YOU'RE COVERED WITH BLOOD. I'M SURE IT'S SERIOUS.
JES A SCRATCH ON THE LEG. WHY, THA'S NOTHING TO A RIP-SNORTING BUCKO LIKE ME, 'CAUSE I'M A FIGHTING FOOL 'N' I NEVER KNOWS WHEN TO STOP.
THERE! THA'S THE GIRL. NOW IF I KIN ONLY STAN' ON MY PINS AWHILE ~ WHY, BLISTER ME! I'LL LICK WOLFGANG YET.
PRESENTLY, WOLFGANG EMERGES FROM A TRAP DOOR, FOLLOWED BY ONE OF HIS MEN.
HO HO! SO DER GREAT NAPOLEON GIFS UP, EH?
THA'S RIGHT. RUB IT IN, YOU MUG.
WOLFGANG IS JUBILANT. HOW HE ENJOYS RIP'S SUFFERING BEFORE PICKING UP THE TREASURE.
HO HO! VOT A PLEASURE IF ONLY I COULD SHOOT YOU IN DER LEG EFFRY DAY.
VELL! VY DO YOU NOT DO SOMET'ING? VY DO YOU NOT MAKE ME MAD SO I FINISH DER JOB, EH?
KNOWS WHEN I'M LICKED, SIR, THA'S ALL.
ACH! SUCH SCUM! MIT ONLY VUN LEETLE VOUND HE TURNS COWARD.
YAA! HERE'S MY CHANCE!
REG. U. S. PAT. OFF.
© 1932 BY NEA SERVICE, INC.
SUDDENLY RIP WHIPS A BLACK-JACK FROM HIS SLEEVE, AND GIVES A MIGHTY LEAP ON HIS ONE GOOD LEG.

WHAT A FOOL!
RIP IS PAINFULLY WOUNDED IN LEG.
HE IS COVERED BY ONE OR MORE PISTOLS!
YET HE IS IDIOT ENOUGH TO ATTACK WOLFGANG WITH ONLY A BLACK-JACK
BUT LOOK! HE DROPS WOLFGANG WITH A MIGHTY WHACK BEHIND THE EAR.
WHACK!
AND SO STARTLED IS FRITZ, THAT HIS FIRST SHOT GOES WILD.
DUNNER BLITZEN!
BANG!
IN THE MEANTIME, RIP THRUSTS WOLFGANG IN FRONT OF HIM AS A SHIELD. HE GRABS A PISTOL AND THE BATTLE IS ON.
ONE SHOT, THA'S ALL I NEEDS, 'CAUSE I'M RIP O'DAY 'N' I NEVER MISSES.
BANG! BANG!
POW!
BANG!
BANG! BANG! POW!
WOLFGANG'S HENCHMAN AND RIP ARE SHOOTING IT OUT, AS FRIEDA LOOKS ON IN TERROR.
ANOTHER SHOT! AND WOLFGANG'S MAN CRUMPLES UP LIKE A WET RAG.
OH HO! WHO SAYS RIP O'DAY CAN'T FIGHT?
POW!
'N' JES LOOKIT WOLFGANG—SHOT TWICE, THA'S WHAT. I GETS THAT FRITZ SO RATTLED HE SHOOTS HIS OWN BOSS
OH, RIP! THIS IS AWFUL! BOTH OF THEM ARE—THEY'RE DEAD.
AW, I GUESSES NOT, MA'AM, BUT A FAS' WORKER, THA'S ME, 'N' YOU KIN BETCHER LIFE YER TREASURE'S GUNNER BE SAFE FROM THEM OLD PIRATES NOW.
WELL, MA'AM, WE'RE SURE SITTING PRETTY. THAT OLD TREASURE'S SAFE AS YER AUNT SUSIE, WITH WOLFGANG 'N' HIS PAL LAID OUT.
BUT YOU FORGET THE OTHER TWO MEN STILL IN THE CASTLE.
AW, THEM BUM'S DOESN'T SCARE ME. IT'S ONLY WASH I WORRIES ABOUT. WE SURE GOTTER FIND THAT BOY.
COME, I'LL HELP YOU WALK, BUT I'M AFRAID YOU'RE AWFULLY HEAVY.
SORRY, MA'AM, BUT I GUESS IT'S THIS OLD LEG.
WAIT! I KNOW WHERE SOME STICKS ARE. THEY'D MAKE EXCELLENT CANES.
OH! RIP! RIP!!
ROY CRANE

HEAVENS! ANOTHER TIGER!
I HANDLES THAT BABY— WHY, BUS' MY NECK! I CAN'T EVEN WALK ANY MORE.
THA'S THE GIRL, HELP ME UP. I'D FORGOT THEM CATS WAS STILL HERE. HAVE TO BE MORE CAREFUL.
HE ONLY STARTLED ME. I'M— I'M NOT AFRAID.
WAIT—HERE'S WHERE I SAW THOSE STICKS. YOU'LL BE ABLE TO WALK WITH THEM.
IF IT'S ALL THE SAME TO YOU, MA'AM, I'D JUST AS LIEF HAVE AN AMBULANCE.
?
CRASH!
FRIEDA TRIPS OVER SOMETHING. AN IRON GRATING FALLS— AND THEIR RETREAT IS CUT OFF.
© 1932 BY NEA SERVICE, INC. REG. U. S. PAT. OFF.
WELL, PICKLE MY BONES 'N' BUS' MY NECK! WE AIN'T SITTING AS PRETTY AS I THOUGHT.
HEAVENS! AN IRON GATE.
PRISONERS AGAIN! WELL, I'VE GOT OUT OF WORSE DUMPS THAN THIS.
THERE'S NO OTHER EXIT, BUT MAYBE THERE'S A SECRET DOOR.
LOOK! HERE'S A BUTTON. MAYBE, IF I PUSH IT, WE'LL ——
CLANK!
PLUNK!
© 1932 BY NEA SERVICE, INC. REG. U. S. PAT. OFF.
BLISTER ME! A BLOOMING ROLLER-COASTER
ANOTHER TRAP DOOR! AND RIP AND FRIEDA, TERRIFIED, GO SHOOTING DOWN A STEEP INCLINE.
THEN, PLOP! OUT INTO THE CHILLING WATERS OF A SWIFT, MOUNTAIN RIVER
SPLOSH!
HO HO! THIS AIN'T SO BAD, IF ONLY YOU CAN SWIM.
CERTAINLY I CAN! AND I STILL HAVE THE TREASURE, TOO! BUT HOW'S YOUR LEG?
AW, IT'S AWRIGHT, IF I TAKES IT EASY. WE KIN CLIMB OUT ON THAT POINT AHEAD.
WE'LL HAVE TO SWIM HARDER, THEN. THIS STREAM'S FASTER THAN IT LOOKS.
© 1932 BY NEA SERVICE, INC. REG. U. S. PAT. OFF.

DEAR ME! THIS IS GETTING WORSE. WE'LL NEVER MAKE THAT POINT OF LAND, RIP.
AW, WELL. THEY'LL BE PLENTY MORE LANDINGS FARTHER ON.
BUT RIP SUDDENLY GROWS SILENT. HIS FACE FALLS.
YOU HEAR THAT NOISE, MA'AM?
BOTH LISTEN, AND THERE COMES TO THEM THE MIGHTY ROAR OF A WATER FALL, AHEAD.
ROY CRANE
© 1932 BY NEA SERVICE, INC. REG. U. S. PAT. OFF.

THE SOUND OF THE WATER FALL BECOMES A MIGHTY ROAR. THE RIVER GROWS WILDER AND SWIFTER.
TRY TO CATCH A ROCK.
OOF!
I'D AS LIEF TACKLE A RHINOCEROS.
FASTER AND FASTER THEY GO. THEY BECOME ALARMED. THEY ARE BEING SWEPT PAST THE LAST POINT OF LAND.
ROY CRANE
FROM SOMEWHERE THEY HEAR A SHOUT!
HEY! GRAB THIS STICK!
REG. U. S. PAT. OFF.
© 1932 BY NEA SERVICE, INC.

"GRAB THIS STICK", SOME ONE YELLS, AND HOW THEY GRAB! RIP AND FRIEDA HOLD ON FOR DEAR LIFE.
THANK HEAVENS! SAVED!
LOOK AT THE WATER FALL! OH, RIP! IT'S SIMPLY AWFUL.
WHO PULLED US OUT? THA'S WHAT I WUNTER KNOW.
JUST THEN A FAMILIAR FIGURE JUMPS OUT OF A TREE.
HA! I THOUGHT THEY'D BE THROWING YOU IN 'AT OLD RIVER, SOONER OR LATER.
WHY, WASHIE! YOU ANGEL! WE THOUGHT YOU WERE DEAD.
MY PAL, G. WASHINGTON TUBBS! WELL, BLISTER MY NECK!
ME DEAD?. NOT ME! WHO WOULDA BEEN AROUND TO SAVE TH' DAY?
ROY CRANE
REG. U. S. PAT. OFF.
© 1932 BY NEA SERVICE, INC.

RIP, FRIEDA, THE TREASURE!
ALL ARE SAVED BY NONE OTHER THAN THE WELL-TRAVELED AND DUMPY YOUNG MAN, G. WASHINGTON TUBBS HIMSELF.
WHEE! I GUESS I'M ALMOST AS GOOD AS RIP EVEN CLAIMS TO BE.
PLEASE, WASH, NO TEASING. RIP WAS WONDERFUL. HE WHIPPED WOLFGANG AND ANOTHER RUFFIAN, EVEN AFTER THEY'D SHOT HIM DOWN IN COLD BLOOD.
GEE! FELLA, I'M AWFUL SORRY. I DIDN'T MEAN ANYTHING, HONEST I DIDN'T. ARE YOU HURT BAD?
AW, IT'S JES A LITTLE SCRATCH ON THE LEG, SPORT. I'M AWRIGHT.
NEVER MIND. LE'S SEE AT LEG — MY GOSH! JUST AS I THOUGHT. IT'S A NICE, CLEAN BED AND PRETTY NURSES FOR THIS GUY.
WASH AND FRIEDA USE EVERY METHOD POSSIBLE, IT SEEMS, IN RUSHING RIP TO A HOSPITAL.
GOTTA HURRY. HE'S LOSING A LOTTA BLOOD.
AND FOR TWO DAYS, WASH SITS OUTSIDE THE HOSPITAL, WAITING TO SEE HIS FRIEND.
MEANWHILE, FRIEDA GOES TO HER VIENNA BANK WITH THE TREASURE BOX.
I WISH TO KNOW IF THIS IS—AH—VERY VALUABLE.
VELL, LADY, I VOULDN'T SNEEZE AT $17,000 CASH.
BUT THE OTHER THINGS— THE STOCKS AND BONDS
ACH HIMMEL! DER BONDS UND STOCKS! DUNNER VEDDER! LOOK—THOUSANDS OF SHARES—YOU ARE A VERY, VERY VEALTHY YOUNG LADY.
ROY CRANE
AT LAST WASH IS ALLOWED TO VISIT HIS FRIEND.
HOW'RE YOU FEELIN', RIP?
SWELL! SAY, I JES BEEN WISHING FOR YOU, SPORT, 'CAUSE I WANTS TO TALK OVER OUR SPLIT.
WOT SPLIT ?
WHY, THE SPLIT FRIEDA OUGHTA GIVE US FOR FINDING HER TREASURE 'N' EVERYTHING. NOW, MY IDEA'S TO SPLIT IT THREE WAYS.
WHY, YOU BIG ROBBER! YOU THINK I'M TH' KINDA BOZO 'AT HELPS PROTECT A GIRL'S PROPERTY AN' THEN STEALS IT BACK! NOSSIR! NEVER! I'MA SQUARE-SHOOTER.
AW, THA'S NOT STEALING. SHE'S A NICE KID 'N', IF WE KINDA HINTED, I BET SHE'D—
GET OUT! I LIKE TO DO GOOD FOR PEOPLE — I'M SATISFIED. AS FOR YOU, YOU WUNTED A SWELL FIGHT. WELL, WOTTA YOU KICKIN' ABOUT? YOU GOT IT!
ROY CRANE

NOSSIR! NO SELF-RESPECTIN' MAN WOULD DEMAND A BIG SPLIT ON FRIEDA'S TREASURE.
AW, DON'T GIT SORE! IF IT AIN'T RESPECTABLE, I'LL MARRY HER, THA'S WOT I'LL DO, 'N' NOBODY CAN SAY THA'S NOT RESPECTABLE.
WHAT? A BRAGGIN', BRAWLIN' MUG LIKE YOU?
SURE. WHY NOT? I NEEDS MONEY 'N' SHE NEEDS A BRAVE, HANDSOME MAN LIKE ME, TO KEEP AN EYE ON HER FORTUNE. THA'S A BREAK FOR BOTH OF US.
FLOWERS!
FROM FRAULEIN KLEY TO HERR O'DAY.
HO HO! I'M A HIT! LOOK! - SHE'S STUCK ON ME, AWREADY.
SHOO! SENDIN' FLOWERS DOESN'T MEAN ANYTHING! SHE PROB'LY THINKS YOU'VE DIED.

ONE DAY WASH IS RETURNING FROM THE HOSPITAL, WHEN A CLASSY, $12,000 AUTOMOBILE ROARS PAST HIM.
MY GOSH! FRIEDA— IN TH' BACK SEAT!!
I BET SHE'S GOIN' TO TH' HOSPITAL. BOY, WOTTA FORTUNE WE MUSTA FOUND, IF SHE KIN BUY CARS LIKE THAT! WOW!
HI, FRIEDA.
WHY, WASHIE!
YA DUMPY DOODLE BUG, SCRAM!! I'M TRYIN' TO GET MYSELF A WIFE.
© 1932 BY NEA SERVICE, INC. REG. U.S. PAT. OFF.

WHEN I MAKES LOVE TO YOU, MA'AM, THAT DUMPY DOODLE-BUG HAS TO SCATTER.
NOW, RIP, WASH IS A HERO. HE SAVED OUR LIVES AND THE TREASURE. AND I'M DYING TO KNOW HOW HE ESCAPED FROM WOLFGANG.
WHO'S A HERO?
SHOO! I COULD MAKE UP A SWELL STORY, IF I WUNTED TO, BUT WOT CHANCE HAVE I AGAINST A HORN-TOOTER LIKE RIP? NO, I BETTER ADMIT I WAS PLENTY SCARED WHEN THEY CAPTURED ME.
AN' WHEN I HEARD THOSE PISTOL SHOTS—BOY, I WENT COO-COO—I TRIED TO PUSH MY GUARD INTO A SORT OF WELL.
LEGGO!
IT WORKED, ONLY HE GRABBED ME, AN'—KER-PLUNK! BOTH OF US LANDED IN TH' RIVER
I MUSTA BIN A BETTER SWIMMER, 'CAUSE I GOT ASHORE. BUT I DIDN'T KNOW WOT TO DO THERE, SO I JUST STAYED. AN' WHEN YOU FOLKS CAME SPLASHIN' ALONG, I HELD OUT A STICK. GOSH! YOU CALL THAT HEROIC?
REG. U.S. PAT. OFF. © 1932 BY NEA SERVICE, INC.

APRIL 1932

PICKIN' A FIGHT WITH SEVEN SAILORS! WELL, OF ALL TH' FOOL STUNTS!
WELL, WHY NOT? I WHIPPED ALL SEVEN, DIDN'T I?
WE LOST OUR COATS, TOO.
AW, WELL! FRIEDA'S RICH. I'LL WRITE HER THAT A GOAT ATE 'EM 'N' SHE KIN SEND US SOME NEW SUITS.
WELL, I'M THRU! TH' NEXT TIME YOU GO STARTIN' A ROWDY ALLEY BRAWL, I STAY OUT. I DON'T EVEN KNOW YOU.
AW, SPORT! I THOUGHT ME 'N' YOU WOULD HAVE SOME SWELL TIMES TOGETHER— JES ONE GRAN' FIGHT AFTER ANOTHER.
NOT ME! I'M NO DINKY AMATEUR. I'MA BIG-LEAGUER, A SOLDIER OF FORTUNE. B'SIDES, I GET INTO ENOUGH TROUBLE WITHOUT LOOKING FOR MORE.
© 1932 BY NEA SERVICE, INC REG. U. S. PAT. OFF.
Roy Crane
SPIRITS ET BOISSONS
SOKKO!
WHAM!
OUCH!
PLOP!
HO HUM! WOTTA LIFE.
DAY AFTER DAY WASH WAITS PATIENTLY OUTSIDE CHEAP CAFES, WHILE HIS PAL IS INSIDE, STARTING ONE ROWDY BRAWL AFTER ANOTHER.
BLISTER ME! WOTTA MAN AM I!
AT THE END OF A WEEK RIP IS THE TERROR OF THE WATER FRONT, AND CAN WHIP ANY TWO MEN IN TOWN.
THEN ONE NIGHT THEY DISCOVER THAT THEY ARE BEING FOLLOWED.
PLOP!
HA! I'LL SHOW HIM.
© 1932 BY NEA SERVICE, INC. REG. U. S. PAT. OFF.
Roy Crane
YOU SAP! YOU'RE IN FOR IT, NOW. LOOK— HE'S A DETECTIVE!
BLISTER ME! THA'S NOT THE FIRST TIME I EVER HIT A COP, SO LE'S FORGET IT.
BUT THIS ONE'S A DETECTIVE, AN' HE MUSTA HAD A REASON FOR SHADOWING US.
MAYBE HE HAS AN IDEA I BEEN FIGHTING TOO MUCH.
SHOO! DETECTIVES DON'T FOLLOW PEOPLE TO KEEP 'EM OUTA FIGHTS, YOU SAP. IT'S MORE IMPORTANT THAN THAT.
GOSH! MAYBE THEY'RE GUNNA PUT US IN JAIL ABOUT THAT WOLFGANG AFFAIR.
NOW, SPORT, THA'S ALL BEEN SETTLED BY FRIEDA SO GO TO SLEEP. FORGET IT. WE'LL NEVER SEE THAT GUY AGAIN.
REG. U. S. PAT. OFF. © 1932 BY NEA SERVICE, INC.
BUT, WHEN THEY GET UP NEXT MORNING, THE SAME DETECTIVE IS OUTSIDE THEIR VILLA.

HUM! THA'S MORE SERIOUS, SPORT, THAN I THOUGHT. THAT DETECTIVE'S STILL OUT THERE.
LOOKS LIKE HE MEANS BUSINESS.
C'MON, LE'S SCOOT OUT THE BACK WAY 'N' GIVE HIM THE GO BY.
WELL, BLISTER ME PINK! ANOTHER ONE!
!
!
SAY! WHAT DO YOU GUYS WANT, ANYWAY? YOU BLINKING FLAT-FOOT, I'LL— —
HAF A CARE, MONSIEUR. I AM WELL PREPARE FOR TROUBLE.
OUT WITH IT, FLAT-FOOT. WOTTA YA SNOOPING AROUN' FOR, 'N' WOTTA YA WANT WITH ME?
WANT WEETH YOU, M'SIEUR? ABSOLUTELY NOTHING.
EET EES YOUR NOTORIOUS FRIEND, SPIKE DUFFLE, ZAT I AM CONCERN WEETH.
SPIKE DUFFLE?
HA HA! I GUESS TH' JOKE'S ON YOU, MISTER DETECTIVE. MY NAME'S TUBBS — NOT DUFFLE. G. WASHINGTON TUBBS.
SURELY YOU ARE NOT ZE GREAT SOLDIER OF FORTUNE? AH, THEN HAF MADE ZE BEEG BLUNDER. PARDON! PARDON!
HA! WOTTID I TELL YOU, RIP? I'M FAMOUS. HE'S HEARD ALL ABOUT ME.
SHUT UP, YA SAP! CAN'T YA SEE HE'S PUMPING YA?
WHO SPILLED TH' BEANS? ME?
YAS, YOU! YA TELLS THAT DICK YER NAME 'N' EVERYTHING.
WELL, WOT OF IT? HE SAID HE WAS LOOKIN' FOR ANOTHER GUY- NOT ME.
BUS' MY NECK! OF COURSE HE DID—HE'S SMART. BUT YA NOTICES THAT IT'S STILL YOU HE'S SHADOWING.
NOW, WOT I WANTS TO KNOW, SPORT, IS JES HOW SERIOUS A CRIME IT WAS THAT YOU COMMITTED.
BUT I DIDN'T COMMIT ANY CRIME. I NEVER COMMITTED A CRIME IN MY LIFE.
C'MON— THINK HARD. YOU'RE BOUND TO OF DONE SOMETHING.
NO SIR! NEVER! IT'S ALL A MISTAKE. I'M A MODEL YOUTH, AN' I DON'T EVEN KNOW TH' MEANING OF SIN.
ROY CRANE

BUT I NEVER COMMITTED A CRIME IN MY LIFE, RIP. I'M POSITIVE.
BAH! DETECTIVES DON'T SPEND THEIR TIME CHASING GOODIE-GOODIES.
THINK HARD, SPORT. DIDN'T YOU EVER MURDER ANYBODY OR ROB A BANK OR SET ANY HOUSES AFIRE?
OF COURSE NOT, STUPID. I TELL YOU I BIN A MODEL YOUTH.
'N' YOU NEVER ROBBED OR SWINDLED ANYBODY OR - - ?
OMY GOSH! I FORGOT!
AH HA! FORGOT WOT?
A FAKE INVENTOR NAMED JILOPPY! HE GOT ME AN' EASY IN A JAM OVER IN COSTA GRANDE — AN' THERE'S A REWARD OF $5000 FOR OUR CAPTURE.
REG. U. S. PAT. OFF. © 1932 BY NEA SERVICE, INC.
WASH AND RIP HURRY HOME, AND FIND THEIR SERVANT AS EXCITED AS THEY ARE.
WELL, WOT'S WRONG, TONY? HAVE THOSE DERN DETECTIVES BIN ON YOUR HEELS, TOO?
NO NO, M'SIEUR. A CABLEGRAM! EET EES FOR YOU.
WELL, I GOT NO TIME FOR CABLEGRAMS OR— HELLO! IT'S FROM HONG KONG, CHINA— OF ALL PLACES! NOW, WHO ON EARTH DO I KNOW IN CHINA?
READ IT, STUPID.
REG. U. S. PAT. OFF. © 1932 BY NEA SERVICE, INC.
"BEWARE, O FOOLISH GOAT, FOR THE ASIATIC DEMONS ARE SWEEPING TOWARD YOU."
WELL, BUS' MY NECK! 'N' IT AIN'T SIGNED.
THA'S SURE FUNNY, SPORT. I CAN'T FIGGER HOW ANYBODY IN CHINA WOULD KNOW YOUR ADDRESS.
I CAN'T FIGGER WHO'D EVEN WANTA KNOW IT.
MYSTERIOUS, THA'S WOT IT IS, 'N' I DOESN'T BLAME YA FOR BEING UPSET OVER THAT CABLEGRAM.
OH, I'M NOT AFRAID OF 'AT ASIATIC PERIL STUFF. IT'S THESE DETECTIVES WHO GET MY NANNY.
AN' I'M LEAVIN' TOWN. YESSIR, I'M GETTIN' WHILE TH GETTIN'S GOOD.
M'SIEUR TUBBS. ANOTHER CABLEGRAM
WELL, I'LL BE BLISTERED! THIS ONE'S FROM BANGKOK, SIAM.
MY GOSH! LISSEN: "THE RELENTLESS DEMONS OF THE ORIENT DRAW NEARER. BEWARE!"
REG. U. S. PAT. OFF © 1932 BY NEA SERVICE, INC.

MIDNIGHT. AND WASH AND RIP ARE STEALING QUIETLY AWAY FROM THEIR VILLA.
PRESENTLY THEY COME TO A WAITING CAR, ON A LONELY ROAD.
PSST! DRIVE US ANY PLACE THA'S FAR AWAY.
ARE YOU SURE NOBODY'S FOLLOWING US, RIP?
ABSOLUTELY, SPORT, ABSOLUTELY!
TAXI
REG. U. S. PAT. OFF. © 1932 BY NEA SERVICE, INC.
OBOY! THEN AT LAST I'M FREE.
SURE YA ARE! THA'S GIVING THEM DETECTIVES THE SLIP. IT'LL BE A WEEK BEFORE THEY WAKES UP 'N' FINDS US GONE.
CONFIDENT THAT DISTANCE HAS AT LAST HIDDEN THEIR IDENTITY, WASH AND RIP REGISTER UNDER ASSUMED NAMES AT A CHEAP HOTEL "SOMEWHERE IN FRANCE."
Mr. G. Washington – cowboy – New York City
Ripley Knight – giraffe breeder – Great Neck, Long Island
BUT OF COURSE THEY DO NOT DREAM THAT THE WILY SLEUTH HAS TAKEN AN ADJOINING ROOM, AND WATCHES THEIR EVERY MOVE.
NEITHER ARE THEY PREPARED FOR THE AMAZING DEVELOPMENT WHICH FOLLOWS.
A WHAT?
A CABLEGRAM! FOR YOU, M'SIEUR WASHEENGTON.
BLISTER ME! FROM CALCUTTA, INDIA.
"THERE IS NO ESCAPE, O STUPID GOAT, FROM THE THOUSAND SLEEPLESS EYES OF THE DREAD ORIENTAL MONSTER."
TUBBS
EUROPA
FRANCE
MR. G. WASHINGTON
EUROPA
FRANCE
THREE DAYS PASS, AND FROM INDIA, PERSIA, AND TURKEY COME THREE MORE MYSTERIOUS, THREATENING MESSAGES. WASH GROWS UNEASY. HIS SINISTER, UNSEEN FOE IS GETTING TOO CLOSE.
THEN, FROM NEAR-BY ITALY COMES THE MOST ALARMING MESSAGE OF ALL.
"BEWARE! THE ORIENTAL VIPER IS READY TO STRIKE."
NO WONDER WASH IS FRIGHTENED — THE UNKNOWN IS ALWAYS TERRIFYING. AND WASH KNOWS NEITHER WHAT MANNER OF PERIL TO EXPECT NOR FROM WHICH QUARTER TO EXPECT IT.
IF I CALL TH' COPS THEY'LL GET NOSEY AN' ARREST ME. MY GOSH, RIP— WOT'LL I DO?
BLISTER ME! HOW DOES I KNOW?
BY NEA SERVICE, INC. REG U. S. PAT. OFF.
THERE SEEMS NOTHING TO DO BUT TO WAIT AND HOPE FOR THE BEST.

WASH AND RIP SIT IN THE HOTEL CAFÉ ANXIOUSLY AWAITING THE ARRIVAL OF THE DREAD "ASIATIC MONSTER."
THEIR POCKETS ARE FILLED WITH LEAD PIPE, BLACK-JACKS, AND REVOLVERS. EACH STRANGER IS EYED WITH HOSTILE SUSPICION.
THIS SUSPENSE IS AWFUL. EVERY TIME TH' DOOR OPENS I NEARLY JUMP OUTA MY SEAT.
REG. U. S. PAT. OFF. © 1932 BY NEA SERVICE, INC.
MEANWHILE, A SLEEK CABIN-PLANE LANDS AT THE AIR PORT. IT ATTRACTS NO ATTENTION, FOR NO ONE SUSPECTS THAT IT HAS COME ALL THE WAY FROM CHINA. NO ONE DREAMS THAT THE RELENTLESS DEMON OF THE ORIENT IS INSIDE.
TWO MEN STEP FROM THE PLANE, AND ARE GREETED BY NONE OTHER THAN THE DETECTIVE WHO HAS BEEN SHADOWING WASH.
ROY CRANE
THE THREE GET IN A WAITING TAXI, AND DISAPPEAR
THIS SUSPENSE IS AWFUL.
WASH AND RIP HAVE BEEN WAITING HOURS, BUT THE SELF-STYLED "ASIATIC MONSTER" DOES NOT APPEAR. THE CAFÉ IS EMPTY, AND THE PROPRIETOR DOZES LAZILY BEHIND THE BAR.
I WEESH YOU TO TRY THEES SODA, GENTLEMAN. EET EES ON ZE HOUSE.
SURE, THANKS.
TASTES FUNNY
RIP! I FEEL QUEER. I-I'M GETTING WOOZY. I'M SLEEPY.
IT'S THAT SODA! GET UP, SPORT—I THINKS WE BIN DOPED!
ROY CRANE
© 1932 BY NEA SERVICE, INC. REG. U. S. PAT. OFF.
I'M WOOZY. I CAN'T STAND UP.
WE BIN GIVEN KNOCK-OUT DROPS! QUICK—GOTTA GET OUTA HERE
WHERE'S THAT BLANKETY BLANK PROPRIETOR? HE DID IT!
DOPED US, THA'S WOT HE DID. I'LL KILL 'IM, TOO. I'LL--
ROY CRANE
VOILA! ZEY SLEEP LIKE BABES, GENTLEMEN. EET EES NOW SAFE TO TAKE ZEM OUT.
© 1932 BY NEA SERVICE, INC. REG. U. S. PAT. OFF.

WHERE AM I?
WASH BLINKS HIS EYES. HE IS CONSCIOUS OF ONLY A THROBBING HEADACHE, A BLAZING SUN, AND THE MONOTONOUS SWISH OF WATER.
SLOWLY HE REALIZES THAT A FAMILIAR VOICE IS SPEAKING TO HIM.
?
THEY GOT US, SPORT. FED US KNOCK-OUT DROPS 'N' SHANGHIED US, THA'S WOT
STARTLED, WASH LOOKS AROUND. HE IS ON A TINY SAND BAR, APPARENTLY IN MID-OCEAN. TWO MEN, CALMLY PLAYING CARDS IN THE SHADE OF AN AIRPLANE, GLANCE AT HIM. THEN THE LARGER OF THE TWO FELLOWS BUCKLES HIS PISTOL ON, AND APPROACHES. HE IS MASKED.
!
OH, HO! SO YOU'RE THE ASIATIC MONSTER, EH?
NAY. THIS LOWLY PERSON IS BUT THE WITLESS ASSISTANT OF THAT LEARNED MASTER.
WELL! WOTTA YOU BIRDS GUNNA DO WITH US?
TO THE ETERNAL SORROW OF THE ENLIGHTENED PROFESSOR, YOU ARE TO BE USED IN ANOTHER OF HIS REGRETTABLE, THO HIGHLY IMPORTANT, SCIENTIFIC EXPERIMENTS.
YOU WILL BE MURDERED.
MURDERED !?!
IN THE NAME OF SCIENCE, YES. AS CHEMISTRY IS THE STUDY OF CERTAIN LEARNED MEN, HOMICIDE IS THE CALLING OF MY GIFTED MASTER. HIS TIRELESS AND SCHOLARLY RESEARCH IS A NOBLE EFFORT TO DETERMINE THE BEST MEANS OF ENDING HUMAN LIFE.
MY GOSH! THEY'RE CRAZY, RIP! THEY'RE MANIACS!
WHAT? THEY MURDERS PEOPLE 'N' CALLS IT SCIENCE? WHY, THEY'RE CRAZY!!
THEY'RE A COUPLA MANIACS!
ON THE CONTRARY, MY ENLIGHTENED MASTER IS A MOST GIFTED SCHOLAR. NO TWO MURDERS ARE ALIKE, AND THE SCIENTIFIC DATA COLLECTED IS AMAZING.
THEY'RE MAD-MEN! FIENDS!
NAY—CONSIDER THE CLEVERNESS OF YOUR OWN CASE, FOR AT HIGH TIDE THIS WORTHLESS SAND-BAR IS COVERED BY 12 FEET OF WATER.
YOU WILL BE TIED TO STAKES AND MAROONED. AND THE MERCILESS TIDE WILL RISE UNTIL EVEN THE HONORABLE NOSES DISAPPEAR—AND YOU WILL DROWN MOST MISERABLY. HA! IS IT MADNESS THAT CAN CONCEIVE SUCH INGENIOUS THINGS AS THAT?

MY GOSH, RIP! I DUN'T WUNTA DIE. I'M NOT READY.
PSST! LEAVE IT TO ME. WE'LL OUTSMART THESE BLOOMING MANIACS, THA'S WOT.
LISSEN, JUG-HEAD, HOW ABOUT GRANTING ME 'N' MY FRIEN' A LAS' REQUEST, HUH?
WELL SPOKEN, O' INSIPID NINNY. ASK WHAT YOU WISH.
WELL, I WUNTA WRITE A LETTER TO OLD EASY.
BAH! THA'S NOT MY STYLE. AFORE I DIES I WANTS TO ENJOY MYSELF.
ROY CRANE
YESSIR, ALL I WANTS IS FER YOU MUGS TO THROW AWAY YER GUNS 'N' MEET ME IN A GOOD OLD FIS' FIGHT. I DARES YA TO.
AND THIS PERSON REFUSES.
REG. U. S. PAT. OFF. © 1932 BY NEA SERVICE, INC.
THE SHREWD ORIENTALS CAME HERE, NOT TO ENJOY A BOXING MATCH, O BRAYING ONE, BUT IN THE INTEREST OF SCIENCE.
YOU OVERGROWN MANIAC! YOU'LL NEVER DROWN RIP O'DAY!
WHAM! I LAYS 'EM DOWN 'N' THEY STAYS DOWN, 'CAUSE I'M BIG 'N' STRONG 'N' I'M GITTING MAD.
POW!
NOW FER THAT GUN! I'M A FIGHTING FOOL 'N' I AIMS TO DIE WITH MY BOOTS ON.
ROY CRANE
OH HO! NOW'S WHEN YOU GITS YOURS, YOU BLINKING IDOL, 'CAUSE I AIMS TO PULL THIS OLD TRIGGER.
PULL AWAY, O FOOL. YOU WILL FIND THAT THE PISTOL IS NOT EVEN LOADED.
© 1932 BY NEA SERVICE, INC. REG. U. S. PAT. OFF.
BLISTER ME! HE'S RIGHT—THE BLOOMING GUN AIN'T LOADED.
NEITHER IS MINE. SO I RECKON WE'RE EVEN.
CLICK
EVEN? THERE AIN'T A MAN ALIVE THA'S EVEN WITH ME, 'CAUSE I'M BIG 'N' BAD 'N' THE FIGHTINGEST FOOL AFOOT.
SURE. I'VE HEARD WHAT A BULLY YOU ARE. BUT, FELLA, YOU CAN'T HIT.
THA'S A LIE! I KIN KNOCK OVER A HORSE.
ROY CRANE
© 1932 BY NEA SERVICE, INC. REG. U. S. PAT. OFF.
YOU'RE TOO FAT. TOO SLOW. I HAD NO IDEA YOU WERE SUCH A SOFTIE.
I'LL SHOW YOU! I'LL — — OOF! OW!
PLOP!
BAM!

HOW THE FISTS FLY!
WHAM! BAM! SOKKO!
AND THAT FIGHTING FOOL, MR. RIP O'DAY, IS GETTING A CLASSY, SCIENTIFIC BEATING AT THE HANDS OF THE TERRIBLE ASIATIC MONSTER.
WHY DON'T YOU FOLD UP, FAT BOY, AND ADMIT YOU'RE TOO CLUMSY?
WHO SAYS I'M CLUMSY? WHY, YOU KNOCK-KNEED WHOZIS, I'M JES BEGINNING TO FIGHT.
WATCH THIS! JIU JITSU, THA'S WOT IT IS, 'N' THA'S MY SPECIALTY. I'M THE BEST THEY IS.
GOOD! YOU OUGHT TO DO BETTER.
NO, YOU'RE STILL TOO FAT. TOO CLUMSY. I'M DISAPPOINTED.
BUS' MY NECK- I'LL KILL YOU! THEY AIN'T NOBODY KIN MAKE A FOOL OF RIP O'DAY.
ROY CRANE
WELL, FAT BOY, ARE YOU READY TO BE TIED TO THE STAKE AND DROWNED?
HELP ME UP, SOMEBODY! I'LL FIGHT THAT BLINK-ING CHINAMAN TILL I CROAKS.
NO YOU WON'T EITHER. THIS IS ALL NONSENSE. 'AT GUY'S NO MORE A CHINAMAN THAN I AM.
THERE NEVER WAS BUT ONE FELLA COULD FIGHT LIKE HIM — AN' 'AT'S OLD EASY.
C'MON, I KNOW YOU! OFF WITH 'AT MASK, Y'BIG SAP, AN' KINDLY EXPLAIN WOT TH' HECK'S TH' BIG IDEA.
?
ROY CRANE
SUDDENLY, THE "ASIATIC MONSTER" REMOVES HIS MASK AND A TRICK MUSTACHE. WASH GIVES A SHOUT OF JOY.
WHOOPEE! I KNEW IT! I KNEW IT! IT'S OLD EASY!
BLAZES! BUT I'M GLAD TO SEE YOU, LADDIE. BEEN LOOKING ALL OVER THE WORLD FOR YOU.
HERE. MEET MY FRIEND, LIEUTENANT SING LO. GREAT GUY. BEEN FIGHTING AROUND SHANGHAI IN THE SAME SQUADRON.
AND SO YOU'RE RIP O'DAY? BLAZES, FELLA, I SURE HOPE THERE'S NO HARD FEELINGS OVER OUR LITTLE SCRAP.
AW, THA'S FUN. I LIKES FIGHTING. 'N' MAYBE, AFTER I RESTS A BIT, WE KIN HAVE ANOTHER ONE, HEY?
ROY CRANE
© 1932 BY NEA SERVICE, INC. REG. U. S. PAT. OFF.

I DON'T GET TH' BIG IDEA, EASY, OF SCARIN' A PAL WITH ALL 'AT ASIATIC MONSTER STUFF.
WAS A LOW-DOWN, DIRTY TRICK, PODNER, AND I ADMIT IT.
YOU SEE, I SPENT WEEKS LOOKING FOR YOU. THEN THAT WAR SCARE CAME IN CHINA — I DIDN'T WANT TO MISS IT, SO I PUT A DETECTIVE AGENCY ON YOUR TRAIL.
WELL, SUH, THOSE FELLAS MESSED THINGS UP PLENTY. TREATED YOU LIKE A CRIMINAL, AND SCARED YOU.
YOU BET THEY DID.
STRUCK ME FUNNY, SO I DECIDED TO CARRY THE JOKE ON, AND GIVE YOU A REAL SCARE.
YEH. 'AT WAS SOME JOKE. YOU GOT A GREAT SENSE OF HUMOR, YOU HAVE!
ROY CRANE
LISSEN, EASY, I DON'T GET ALL THIS — YOU BIN GALLOPIN' 'ROUND TH' MAP, FIGHTIN' WARS AN' LOOKIN' FOR ME — WELL, GEE WIZ! WHERE'S YA WIFE?
MY WIFE?
CERTAINLY! TH' GIRL YOU MARRIED WHILE IN WEST POINT. YOUR MOTHER TOLD ME ALL ABOUT IT.
AND DIDN'T SHE MENTION ALL THE TROUBLE IT CAUSED? AND HOW THE MARRIAGE WAS ANNULLED?
YEH, BUT MY GOSH! I THOUGHT TH' TROUBLE WAS OVER. I THOUGHT SURE YOU'D MARRY AGAIN.
WELL, WE DIDN'T. SO THAT'S THAT.
WHY NOT, EASY? DID SHE LOVE SOMEBODY ELSE? OR DID SHE —?
NOW, LADDIE, LET'S JUST FORGET IT. SOME THINGS ARE BETTER WHEN LEFT UNSAID.
LADDIE, I PREFER NOT TO DISCUSS IT, AND THAT'S FINAL.
BUT, GEE WIZ, EASY! CAN'T A FELLA TELL A PAL WHY HE DIDN'T GET MARRIED, WHEN HE WAS S'POSED TO?
IT'S A PERSONAL MATTER, SUH, THAT CONCERNS NOBODY BUT ME.
BUT I'M YOUR PAL. YOUR FRIEND. WE BIN THRU THICK AN' THIN TOGETHER.
LISSEN — DID SHE JILT YOU?
BLAST YOU! GET IN THAT PLANE AND SHUT UP!
!
ROY CRANE
FURTHERMORE — IF YOU REFER TO THAT HOME TOWN GIRL AGAIN, S'HELP ME, PODNER, I'LL CLIP YOU ONE. SAVVY?
YESSIR.
AND NEVER AGAIN DOES WASH DARE MENTION HIS FRIEND'S STRANGE AND SHATTERED ROMANCE.

MAY 1932

AFTER SEVERAL DAYS IN FRANCE:
LADDIE, HOW'D YOU LIKE TO GO ON A CRUISE THRU THE SOUTH SEA ISLANDS, AND PICK UP THAT TREASURE O' YOURS, OFF BORNEO.
OBOY! HOW'D WE DO IT?
OH, I SAVED A COUPLE THOUSAND OUT O' THAT CHINESE SCRAP. I'LL BUY A BOAT, AND WE'LL TURN SAILORS.
SAY! 'AT'S GREAT! AN' RIP'LL BE CRAZY ABOUT IT.
SUH, I HADN'T COUNTED ON TAKING THAT WINDBAG ALONG.
BUT RIP'S A PAL OF MINE, TOO. I COULDN'T DITCH A PAL.
IN THAT CASE, PODNER, I RECKON THE TRIP'S OFF. I'M SORT OF A LONE WOLF AND DON'T RUN IN PACKS.
© 1932 BY NEA SERVICE, INC. REG. U. S. PAT. OFF.
THINK I'D PUT UP WITH THAT CHESTY BUMPKIN ON A 5000 MILE SAILING TRIP? BLAZES, NO! HE STAYS BEHIND.
BUT I CAN'T JUST UP'N' DITCH HIM. POOR RIP! I'M TH' ONLY PAL HE'S GOT. HE'D BE HEARTBROKEN.
'SCUSE ME FER BUTTING IN, SPORT, BUT, SEEING AS I'M LEAVING RIGHT AWAY, I --
LEAVING?
YEAH. YA SEE, ME 'N' SING LO BEEN GITTING ACQUAINTED, 'N' HE AST ME TO FLY BACK TO CHINA WITH HIM.
© 1932 BY NEA SERVICE, INC. REG. U. S. PAT. OFF.
I SURE HOPES YA AIN'T SORE BECAUSE I ACCEPTS. I NEVER BEEN TO CHINA, SEE, 'N' I --
OH, AT'S AWRIGHT, RIP. NO HARD FEELINGS. YOU GO AHEAD. I UNDERSTAND PERFECTLY.
WORKS OUT PERFECTLY, PODNER. YO WANT TO GET RID OF RIP, AND HE WANTS TO GET RID O' YOU.
THE TWO FRIENDS TRY TO BID A CASUAL, GRUFF FAREWELL, BUT THEIR VOICES BREAK.
I-I HOPE WE MEET AGAIN SOME DAY, RIP.
YEAH. WE SURE HAD SOME SWELL FIGHTS TOGETHER, SPORT.
I'D THROW A FAREWELL PARTY FOR YOU IF-IF I WASN'T S'BROKE.
AW, THA'S AWRIGHT. JES TELL FRIEDA, IF YA EVER SEES HER AGAIN, TO SAVE MY REWARD FER ME, THA'S ALL.
THEN RIP STEPS INTO THE PLANE. THERE IS A ROAR, A CLOUD OF DUST—AND HE IS GONE.
REG. U. S. PAT. OFF.
© 1932 BY NEA SERVICE, INC.

Y'KNOW, EASY, YOU'RE TH' ONLY REAL BUDDIE I EVER HAD. GEE, BUT IT'S GOOD TO BE TOGETHER AGAIN.
SURE IS, LADDIE.
I DON'T MISS RIP AT ALL. HONEST, YOU'RE A REAL GUY, A PRINCE, A MAN'S MAN. NO GRANDSTAND STUFF ABOUT YOU. WHY, YOU'RE—
AW, DRY UP. YOU'RE GETTING MUSHY.
THERE—SEE THAT BOAT, PODNER? SHE'S THE ONE I'M BUYING FOR OUR CRUISE TO THE SOUTH SEAS.
WOT? WE'RE GUNNA SAIL TH' OCEAN IN A TOY LIKE THAT?
MISHAP
WE'LL DROWN! WE CAN'T GO TO TH' SOUTH SEAS IN THAT DINKY TOY.
RATS! MEN HAVE SAILED AROUND THE WORLD IN BOATS NO BIGGER THAN THAT.
YEH. AN' MEN HAVE GONE TO TH' BOTTOM IN LOTS BIGGER ONES, TOO.
SAY! YOU GETTING YELLA? YOU GETTING THE IDEA YOUR DUMPY CARCASS IS PRECIOUS?
OF COURSE NOT, STUPID. ONLY I--
THEN PIPE DOWN! I CAN'T AFFORD TO BUY THE LEVIATHIAN.
WE'LL TAKE IT, SKIPPER.
Roy Crane
REG. U. S. PAT. OFF.
© 1932 BY NEA SERVICE, INC.

BOY! WE MIGHT SINK, BUT WE SURE WON'T STARVE.
EASY SPENDS MONEY LIKE WATER AND HE AND WASH WORK ALL DAY, STOWING AWAY THE SUPPLIES THAT HE BUYS.
BLAZES, PODNER! WE'RE ALMOST READY TO SAIL.
THERE'S A LOTTA THINGS NEED FIXIN FIRST. F'RINSTANCE 'AT OIL LAMP IN TH' CABIN—IT'S ABOUT TO FALL DOWN.
REG. U. S. PAT. OFF.
© 1932 BY NEA SERVICE, INC.
THAT REMINDS ME—I FORGOT TO BUY SOME CARPENTER TOOLS.
AN' SOAP AN' FISHIN' STUFF, TOO—AN' TRINKETS TO TRADE TO TH' NATIVES. SHOO! WE'RE NOT HALF READY.
Roy Crane

WASH AND EASY ARE CAREFREE AND HAPPY. THEY TALK EXCITEDLY OF THEIR TRIP TO THE SOUTH SEAS, NEVER DREAMING THAT THEY ARE TO MEET WITH MISFORTUNE BEFORE EVEN THE ANCHOR IS RAISED.
MISHAP
?
THE MISFORTUNE OCCURS WHEN A PASSING MOTOR-BOAT CAUSES THEIR VESSEL TO PITCH VIOLENTLY.
THERE IS A CRASH OF GLASS IN THE CABIN—THEN A BURST OF SMOKE AND FLAME.
GOSH AMIGHTY! TH' LAMP BUSTED!
REG. U. S. PAT. OFF.
© 1932 BY NEA SERVICE, INC
ROY CRANE
SMOKE AND FLAME BURST FROM THE CABIN, AS THE LIGHTED LAMP TUMBLES FROM ITS PERCH.
QUICK! GRAB A BUCKET.
MORE WATER! FASTER! FASTER!
WITHIN A MOMENT, THE CABIN IS A RAGING INFERNO. THE FLAMES SPREAD. THE HEAT BECOMES TERRIFIC.
SOON THE ENTIRE BOAT IS ABLAZE. WASH AND EASY CAN STAND IT NO LONGER. THEY DIVE OVERBOARD AND SWIM, DEJECTEDLY, FOR SHORE.
MISHAP
ROY CRANE
© 1932 BY NEA SERVICE, INC. REG. U. S. PAT. OFF.
WELL, I-I GUESS 'AT FINISHES OUR GOOD OL' TRIP TO TH' SOUTH SEAS.
RECKON SO, LADDIE.
ROY CRANE
HONEST, I COULD BUST OUT 'N' CRY.
YEAH. HARD LUCK— BOAT'S GONE, SUPPLIES GONE, AND MONEY'S GONE.
YOU MEAN WE'RE ON TH' BEACH? WE'RE BROKE?
EXACTLY! WE'RE WIPED OUT.
© 1932, BY NEA SERVICE, INC. REG. U. S. PAT. OFF.

WOT'LL WE DO, EASY? NO BOAT- NO MONEY. GEE WIZ! WE'RE UP AGAINST IT.
SHUX! THIS ISN'T THE FIRST TIME WE'VE BEEN ON THE BEACH. WHY WORRY?
BECAUSE I GOT TH HABIT OF EATING THREE MEALS A DAY, 'AT'S WHY.
BAH! GETTING SOFT. WHAT YOU NEED IS A GOOD WAR.
I CAN'T THINK OF ANY, CLOSE BY. WE COULD JOIN TH FRENCH FOREIGN LEGION, THO.
NIX! LONG ENLISTMENTS, BUM PAY, AND NO GLORY.
OR HOW 'BOUT GOING HOME?
YOU MEAN TO STOW AWAY ON SOME SHIP? NOW, THAT'S AN IDEA, PODNER- A NOBLE IDEA.
© 1932 BY NEA SERVICE, INC. REG. U. S. PAT. OFF.
OUI, M'SIEUR. ZE BEEG GREY ONE.
HAW HAW! EET SAILS TONIGHT.
?
?
WASH AND EASY INQUIRE IF ANY SHIPS ARE SAILING FOR AMERICA. TO THEIR BEWILDERMENT, THEY ARE GREETED WITH HOOTS OF LAUGHTER.
BUMS! THEY THINK THEY'RE KIDDING US.
NEVERMIND. WE'LL ASK SOMEBODY ELSE.
WE WANT TO GO TO AMERICA, BUDDIE. NOW, IS THAT GREY SHIP GOING THERE, OR NOT?
YOU WEESH TO GO ON ZE GREY SHIP? HAW HAW HAW!
AGAIN THAT BURST OF LAUGHTER! THEY CAN'T UNDERSTAND IT.
REG. U. S. PAT. OFF. © 1932 BY NEA SERVICE, INC.
HOW ABOUT IT, PODNER— STILL GAME TO STOW AWAY ON THAT SHIP?
SURE. WHY NOT?
FROM THE WAY THOSE FRENCHMEN GAVE US THE LAUGH, SHE'S PROB'LY THE TOUGHEST OLD TUB AFLOAT.
OH, WELL! I GUESS ALL SHIPS ARE TOUGH ON STOWAWAYS.
I DON'T MIND, AS LONG AS SHE TAKES US HOME.
GOOD BOY! JUST FOR THAT I'LL OPEN THE BANK.
MY GOSH! I THOUGHT WE WERE BROKE.
EMERGENCY FUNDS, LADDIE. GOING TO NEED LOTS O' FOOD AND WATER. HERE, YOU GET 'EM WHILE I GATHER DRIFTWOOD FOR A RAFT.
REG. U. S. PAT. OFF. © 1932 BY NEA SERVICE, INC.

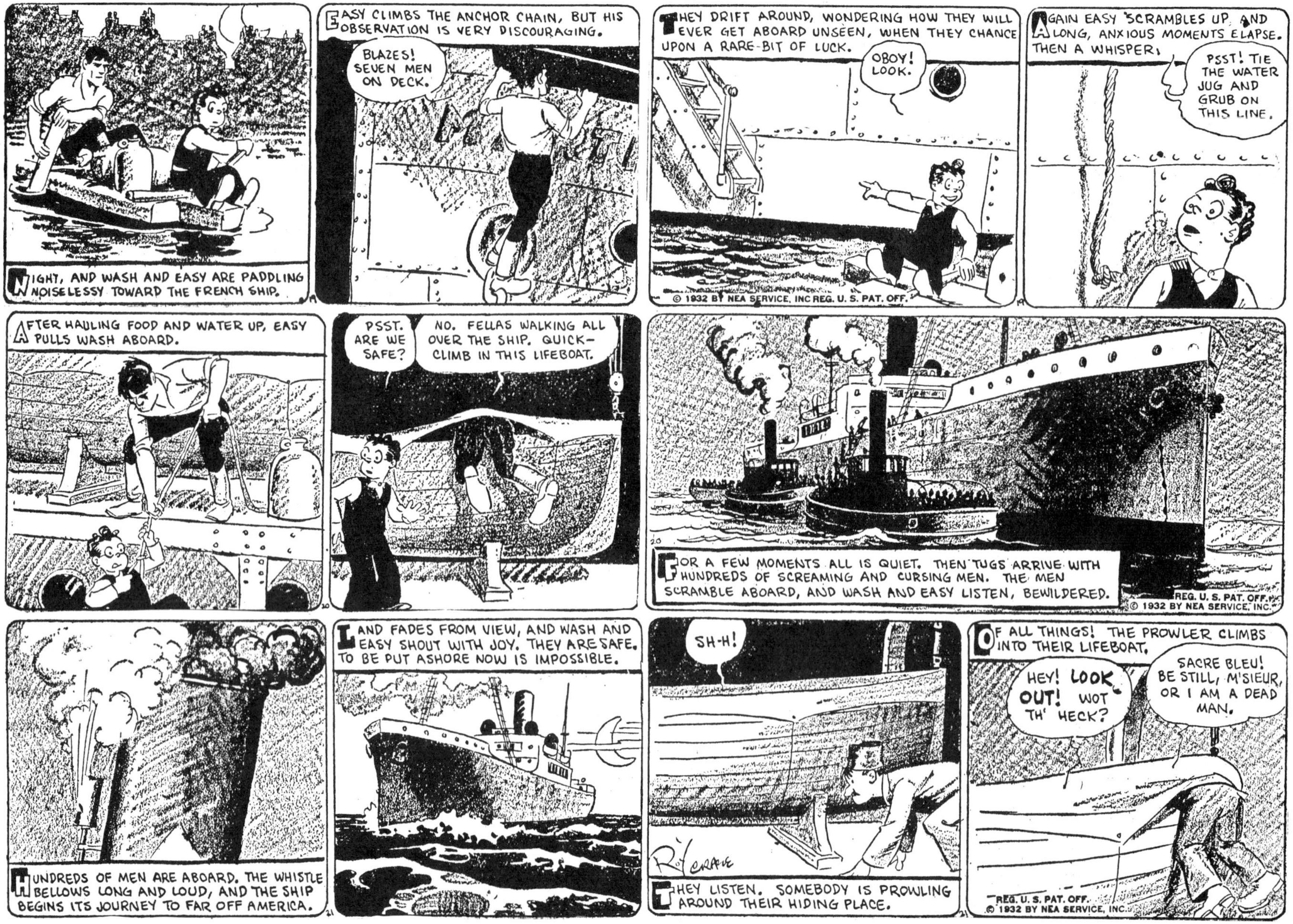
NIGHT, AND WASH AND EASY ARE PADDLING NOISELESSY TOWARD THE FRENCH SHIP.
EASY CLIMBS THE ANCHOR CHAIN, BUT HIS OBSERVATION IS VERY DISCOURAGING.
BLAZES! SEVEN MEN ON DECK.
THEY DRIFT AROUND, WONDERING HOW THEY WILL EVER GET ABOARD UNSEEN, WHEN THEY CHANCE UPON A RARE-BIT OF LUCK.
OBOY! LOOK.
© 1932 BY NEA SERVICE, INC REG. U. S. PAT. OFF.
AGAIN EASY SCRAMBLES UP AND ALONG, ANXIOUS MOMENTS ELAPSE. THEN A WHISPER.
PSST! TIE THE WATER JUG AND GRUB ON THIS LINE.
AFTER HAULING FOOD AND WATER UP, EASY PULLS WASH ABOARD.
PSST. ARE WE SAFE?
NO. FELLAS WALKING ALL OVER THE SHIP. QUICK-CLIMB IN THIS LIFEBOAT.
FOR A FEW MOMENTS ALL IS QUIET. THEN TUGS ARRIVE WITH HUNDREDS OF SCREAMING AND CURSING MEN. THE MEN SCRAMBLE ABOARD, AND WASH AND EASY LISTEN, BEWILDERED.
REG. U. S. PAT. OFF.
© 1932 BY NEA SERVICE, INC.
HUNDREDS OF MEN ARE ABOARD. THE WHISTLE BELLOWS LONG AND LOUD, AND THE SHIP BEGINS ITS JOURNEY TO FAR OFF AMERICA.
LAND FADES FROM VIEW, AND WASH AND EASY SHOUT WITH JOY. THEY ARE SAFE. TO BE PUT ASHORE NOW IS IMPOSSIBLE.
SH-H!
THEY LISTEN. SOMEBODY IS PROWLING AROUND THEIR HIDING PLACE.
OF ALL THINGS! THE PROWLER CLIMBS INTO THEIR LIFEBOAT.
HEY! LOOK OUT! WOT TH' HECK?
SACRE BLEU! BE STILL, M'SIEUR, OR I AM A DEAD MAN.
REG. U. S. PAT. OFF.
© 1932 BY NEA SERVICE, INC.

GET OUT! WHO ARE YOU?
A CONVICT, M'SIEUR. FOR HEAVENS SAKE HELP ME TO ESCAPE— SAVE ME!
BUT HOW?
I DON' KNOW—ONLY HELP ME. THEY DO NOT RETURN FROM GUIANA, M'SIEUR. EE EES ZE LIVING DEATH— ZE DRY GUILLOTINE! I WEEL DIE!
BUT WE'RE ONLY A COUPLA STOWAWAYS.
STOWAWAYS ON THEES SHIP? NON, NON, M'SIEUR. I DO NOT BELIEVE ZAT.
REG. U. S. PAT. OFF. © 1932 BY NEA SERVICE, INC.
YOU ARE JESTING. WHY, NO WAN EES ZAT CRAZY. THEES EES A CONVICT SHIP.
!
WHAT! THIS IS A CONVICT SHIP??
FOR HEAVEN'S SAKE, M'SIEUR— NOT SO LOUD!
BLAZES! A BLINKING CONVICT SHIP— AND THEY SAID SHE WAS GOING TO AMERICA.
OUI, M'SIEUR. TO SOUTH AMERICA. FRENCH GUIANA AND ZE TERRIBLE DEVIL'S ISLAND PENAL COLONY.
MY GOSH, EASY! WOT'LL WE DO?
GIVE OURSELVES UP, OF COURSE.
NON, NON! ZEY WILL PUT YOU IN IRONS.
BUT WE CAN'T STAY HERE, MAN. THEY'RE BOUND TO SEARCH FOR YOU— THEY'LL FIND US, TOO.
WOW! WOTTA MESS! EITHER WAY WE GET PUT IN IRONS.
BAH! TH' ONLY CONVICT SHIP AFLOAT— AN' WE HAD TO STOW AWAY ON IT. WOTTA BREAK!
HUM! NOT QUITE DAYLIGHT YET. MAYBE WE CAN ESCAPE.
LA MARTINIERE
ESCAPE?
SURE. WE'LL SIMPLY BORROW THEIR LIFE-BOAT— IT'S WORTH TRYING.
WONDERFUL! M'SIEUR, YOU HAF ZE MASTER MIND.
SQUEEEEE
BLAZES! WHAT A RACKET!
LA MARTINIERE
BUT THEN COMES THE TRYING ORDEAL OF LOWERING THE BOAT.
THE PULLEYS SQUEAK HORRIBLY. THEY FEEL CERTAIN THAT, AT ANY MOMENT, THEY WILL BE DISCOVERED.
REG. U. S. PAT. OFF. © 1932 BY NEA SERVICE, INC.

THANK GOODNESS! NOBODY SAW US — WE GOT AWAY.
COME ON! ROW LIKE BLAZES.
SHE'S OUT OF SIGHT! NOW UP WITH THE SAIL. WE'RE OFF FOR AFRICA. WE'RE FREE!
M'SIEUR, YOU HAF SAFE MY LIFE. PIERRE LUPI WILL NEVAIR FORGET.
WHOOPEE, WE'RE FREE!
WASH, EASY, AND THE CONVICT SHOUT WITH JOY. THEY WRING EACH OTHERS HANDS AND LAUGH AND CRY. THEY HAVE ESCAPED FROM THE FRENCH PRISON SHIP.
GAY AND CONFIDENT, THEY TURN TOWARD AFRICA. BUT TOWARD NOON THEY SIGHT A SHIP, AND THE CONVICT BECOMES DEATHLY PALE AND SILENT.
WOW! MAYBE THEY MISSED TH' LIFEBOAT AN' TURNED BACK.
BETTER CLIMB THE MAST, LADDIE, AND GIVE HER A LOOK. SHE'S COMING CLOSER.
WHAT DOES SHE LOOK LIKE, PODNER?
MY GOSH! FASTER!! SHE'S A DEAD RINGER FOR TH' CONVICT SHIP.
EASY QUICKLY CHANGES THE COURSE, BUT THE SHIP'S COURSE IS CHANGED ALSO.
AND SOON THEY HEAR THE CRACK OF RIFLES — AND BULLETS WHIZZING PAST THEM.
IT'S HOPELESS. WE BETTER GIVE UP.
BUT, WITH A CRY OF DESPERATION, THE CONVICT JUMPS OVERBOARD.
NON NON! I WILL NEVAIR RETURN TO GUIANA.

SOON THE PRISON SHIP IS ALONGSIDE, AND WASH AND EASY ARE GAZING DEJECTEDLY INTO THE MUZZLES OF A DOZEN RIFLES. CONVICTS STARE AT THEM FROM EVERY PORTHOLE.
NON NON! LET ME DROWN.
AH! THEES MUS' BE A SECOND OFFENSE. HE DON' LIKE DEVIL'S ISLAND.
30 LASHES WITH ZE WHIP—THEN PUT ZEM IN IRONS!
EH BIEN! IT IS STRANGE. THERE ARE THREE CONVICTS, YET THE REPORT SHOWS THAT ONLY ONE WAS MISSING.
MY FRIEND AND I ARE NOT CONVICTS, SUH. WE ARE AMERICAN STOWAWAYS.
IMPOSSIBLE! THEY LIE!! HERE—LET ME SEE ZAT REPORT.
Roy Crane
REGARDE! EET EES TRUE. THEY MUS' BE STOWAWAYS, FOR WE HAF NO RECORD OF THEM.
HUM! IF ZEY ARE AMERICANS THEY WILL HAF PASSPORTS.
!
?
WELL! WHERE ARE THEY?
LOST, SUH. MY BOAT CAUGHT FIRE. I LOST EVERYTHING.
AND I SUPPOSE YOURS BURNED TOO, EH?
NOSSIR. Y'SEE, SIR, I PUT A $10 BILL AN' MY PASSPORT IN MY SHOE FOR SAFE-KEEPIN'—AN' GUESS WOT HAPPENED? WELL, SIR, TH' DERN THINGS WORE OUT.
BAH! THROW ZE IMPOSTERS IN A CELL!
Roy Crane
LOOK AT OUR CLOTHES. BLAZES, MAN! CAN'T YOU SEE WE'RE NOT CONVICTS?
CLOTHES DO NOT MAKE ZE MAN. LA LA! YOU T'INK I FREE EVERY CRIMINAL WHO SMUGGLES STREET CLOTHES ABOARD?
BUT YOU GOT NO RECORD OF US.
DO NOT WORRY. I SHALL SEND TO FRANCE FOR IT.
BLAST YOU! THIS IS AN OUTRAGE! AN INJUSTICE! WE DEMAND OUR RIGHTS!
RIGHTS? A CONVICT HAS NO RIGHTS.
YOU MONKEY-FACED DODO, YOU'LL SWING FOR THIS! WE DEMAND A TRIAL! WE---
TURN ZE HOSE ON THEM.
Roy Crane

JUNE 1932

ENOUGH. TURN OFF ZE WATER.
EASY SOON QUITS SHOUTING FOR JUSTICE, AND HE AND WASH ARE GLAD TO BE PUT IN A CELL.
THEY STARE IN ASTONISHMENT. 639 MEN ARE JAMMED TOGETHER LIKE SARDINES. THE PLACE IS FOUL, STIFLING. THE SIX PORTHOLES ARE CLOSED. THE HEAT IS TERRIFIC. SEASICK MEN ARE SPRAWLED ON THE STEEL FLOOR.
ROY CRANE
WHAT AN ASSORTMENT OF HUMANITY.
MILD-EYED EMBEZZLERS. SHY, FRIGHTENED COUNTRY LADS. MALAYS, ARABS, NEGROES. CITY BOYS, HARD AND WIRY. MURDERERS, THIEVES, ANARCHISTS. HAIRY, TATTOOED BRUTES FROM THE FOREIGN LEGION AND OTHER TOUGH REGIMENTS OF AFRICA.
REG. U. S. PAT. OFF.
© 1932 BY NEA SERVICE, INC.
NOBODY TRIES TO KID WASH AND EASY. NOBODY OFFERS SYMPATHY. EXCEPT FOR THE HOSTILE GLARE OF THE TOUGHER CONVICTS, THEY ARE TOTALLY IGNORED.
THERE ARE NO SEATS, SO THEY MAKE THEMSELVES AS COMFORTABLE AS POSSIBLE IN TWO EMPTY HAMMOCKS.
THEN ONE OF THE TOUGHER CONVICTS GIVES HIS COMPANIONS THE WINK.
PSST! WATCH ME HAF SOME FUN.
!
THAT'S MY HAMMOCK!
ROY CRANE
BLAZES! NOBODY CAN PICK ON A BUDDIE O' MINE.
YOU GET BACK, EASY. I'M FIGHTIN' MY OWN BATTLES.
HOHO! HE WANTS TO FIGHT THE CHAMP OF THE FOREIGN LEGION.
NOT THAT WAY, YOU BUM. I'LL GET YOU TH' WAY YOU GOT ME.
I THOUGHT SO— HE'S YELLER!
THEY HOOT AND JEER AT WASH UNTIL HIS EARS BURN, BUT HE DOESN'T FIGHT.
THAT NIGHT, HOWEVER, HE POCKETS A PIECE OF BROKEN GLASS AND DROPS NOISELESSLY FROM HIS HAMMOCK.
ROY CRANE
?
TWEET TWEET
AND THE NEXT MORNING HIS ENEMY IS FOUND LYING ON THE STEEL DECK. BESIDE HIM DANGLES THE SEVERED END OF HIS HAMMOCK. FROM THEN ON WASH IS TREATED WITH THE UTMOST RESPECT.

WASH HAS MADE A NEW ENEMY. BUT WHY WORRY ABOUT IT? HIS ENEMY HAS BEEN TAKEN TO THE INFIRMARY.
BESIDES, FIGHTS ARE COMMON. THEY OCCUR EVERY DAY, WHILE CONVICTS SING TO DROWN OUT THE NOISE.
IN OTHER CAGES THERE ARE TWO MORTAL COMBATS WITHIN THREE DAYS. BUT LIFE IS CHEAP WHERE THEY ARE GOING, AND NO ONE IS EVEN PUNISHED.
DEVIL'S ISLAND
REG. U. S. PAT. OFF. © 1932 BY NEA SERVICE, INC.
ROY CRANE
THE CHANCES ARE 10 TO 1 THAT A CONVICT WILL NEVER LIVE OUT HIS SENTENCE, ANYWAY. IT'S A TOSS UP WHETHER HE LIVES THRU EVEN THE FIRST YEAR.
LIFE ABOARD THE CONVICT SHIP SETTLES DOWN TO A DREARY ROUTINE OF SLEEPING AND EATING.
BAH! A PIG WOULDN'T EAT THIS STUFF.
AW, DRY UP. IT'S FREE, ISN'T IT?
IN EACH CAGE THERE IS A SINGLE WASH-BUCKET, WHICH SERVES MORE THAN A HUNDRED MEN.
OH, WELL! I CAN'T KICK. ONLY ABOUT TEN REALLY USE IT.
THE BRIGHT SPOT OF EACH DAY (IN FAIR WEATHER) IS A 15 MINUTE WALK ON DECK, WHILE THE SAILORS TURN THE HOSE ON THE CAGES. THEN EVERYONE IS CHEERFUL.
BUT WHEN THE SEA IS ROUGH, THE PORTS AND HATCHES ARE CLOSED, AND THE AIR BECOMES MORE FOUL THAN EVER. HALF THE MEN BECOME SEASICK, AND THEIR CLOTHES ARE STOLEN AND TRADED TO THE SAILORS FOR TOBACCO.
SIXTEEN DAYS PASS. AND THE SUN BEATS DOWN ON THE STEEL DECK ABOVE, MAKING THE HOLD A VERITABLE OVEN.
MA FOI! SURELY EET EES NOT THEES HOT IN GUIANA.
HOTTER, I EXPECT. THEY SAY TH' HENS THERE LAY FRIED EGGS.
THE REPORT GOES AROUND THAT THEY ARE NEARING GUIANA, AND ANXIOUS FACES APPEAR AT EVERY PORT.
THE CONVICTS FAIRLY SIZZLE IN THE HEAT, BUT THEY STOP BOASTING OF THEIR CRIMES AND THEIR WOMEN, AND TALK OF NOTHING BUT ESCAPE.
HOW OPTIMISTIC THEY ARE!
THEY SAY THE GUARDS ARE SO FAT THEY CANNOT RUN.
LA LA! THEN ESCAPE WEEL BE EASY. WE WEEL ALL RUN AWAY TOGETHER.
YES, WE WEEL ALL GO THRU ZE JUNGLE TO BRAZIL.
PSST. I AM GOING TO STEAL A BOAT AND SAIL TO VENEZUELA. WEEL YOU JOIN ME, COMRADES?
NOT US. WE'LL BE FREE BY THEN.
SURE. THEY CAN'T HOLD US. THEY GOT NO RECORD.
REG. U. S. PAT. OFF. © 1932 BY NEA SERVICE, INC.

LAND!
IT IS NOT UNTIL THE NINETEENTH DAY THAT THE COAST OF FRENCH GUIANA IS SIGHTED.
IT IS ONLY A FAINT, GREEN LINE ON THE HORIZON. BUT, OH, THE EXCITEMENT! HOW THE CONVICTS CLAMOR FOR THE FIRST SIGHT OF THEIR NEW LAND!
BUT THE SIX PORTHOLES ARE FOR THE TWELVE STRONGEST MEN, AND THE LESS FORTUNATE MUST BE CONTENT WITH RELAYED INFORMATION.
WHAT IS IT LIKE?
DO YOU SEE THE PRISON? DO YOU SEE DEVIL'S ISLAND?
NO—ONLY A MUDDY RIVER. WE ARE GOING UP IT.
AND TREES. MA FOI! I HAF NEVAIR SEEN TREES SO GREEN, SO THICK!
SLOWLY THE CONVICT SHIP STEAMS UP THE MARONI RIVER, AND, FOR THE FIRST TIME, WASH AND EASY LEARN THAT THEY ARE NOT BEING SENT TO DEVIL'S ISLAND.
DEVIL'S ISLAND, THEY LEARN, IS FOR POLITICAL ENEMIES ONLY. THO IT GIVES ITS NAME TO THE ENTIRE PENAL COLONY, NOT MORE THAN 20 OF THE 7,000 CONVICTS ARE ACTUALLY IMPRISONED THERE
ILE ROYALE—FOR THOSE WHO ATTEMPT TO ESCAPE TOO OFTEN
DEVIL'S ISLAND. FOR TRAITORS
ILE ST. JOSEPH. WHERE SOLITARY CONFINEMENT DRIVES MEN MAD.
ONLY A FEW DOZEN ARE KEPT ON ISLANDS AT ALL.
BR. GUIANA
ST. LAURENT
DEVIL'S ISLAND
DUTCH GUIANA
FRENCH GUIANA
BRAZIL
THE VAST MAJORITY ARE ON THE MAINLAND.
THAT IS WHERE WASH AND EASY WILL GO—UP THE RIVER TO ST. LAURENT, THE HEART OF A NETWORK OF JUNGLE PRISONS.
REG. U. S. PAT. OFF. © 1932 BY NEA SERVICE, INC.
THERE ARE TWO MELANCHOLY BLASTS OF THE WHISTLE. AND THE CONVICT SHIP SWINGS SLOWLY TOWARD THE WHARF OF ST. LAURENT.
SOON THE CONVICTS SWARM ASHORE, GAY AND NOISY, EAGER TO SEE WHAT THEIR NEW LAND IS LIKE.
AH! WOMEN! YELLOW, BLACK, BROWN, AND WHITE. AND HOW DAINTY AND PRETTY SOME OF THEM ARE.
HOW GREEN ARE THE TREES! HOW DELIGHTFUL! OH, THEES WEEL BE WANDERFUL!
OO LA LA! AND ESCAPE WEEL BE EASY. LOOK—DUTCH GUIANA EES ONLY ACROSS ZE RIVER.
REG. U. S. PAT. OFF. © 1932 BY NEA SERVICE, INC.

BEFORE BEING TURNED OVER TO THE PRISON AUTHORITIES, EACH CONVICT IS CAREFULLY CHECKED.
THEES ARE ZE MEN, M'SIEUR LE COMMANDANT, OF WHOM I SPOKE.
OUI, OUI. ZE MEN WHOSE RECORDS WERE LOST, EH?
BEG PARDON, SUH. BUT WE'RE STOWAWAYS. WE NEVER HAD ANY RECORDS. IT'S A BLASTED OUTRAGE, SUH.
AH, YES. I SUPPOSE, I SUPPOSE. I MUS' REMEMBER TO CONDUCT AN INVESTIGATION. MEANWHILE, MY GOOD MAN, YOU SHALL BE ALLOWED SPECIAL PRIVILEGES. AH, YES, EVEN TO CREAM EEN ZE COFFEE.
BAH! WHAT WE WANT IS JUSTICE!
REG. U. S. PAT. OFF. © 1932 BY NEA SERVICE, INC.
SILENCE, FOOL! BACK TO YOUR PLACE! SPECIAL PRIVILEGES WITHDRAWN.
CAMP DE LA TRANS
ONLY RAGS OF MEN, GAUNT AND ILL, ARE THERE TO WATCH THE CONVICTS MARCH THRU THE GRIM GATE OF THE PRISON.
NUMBER 52, 367.
NOT UNTIL WASH AND EASY ARE INSIDE THE HIGH STONE WALLS, AND ARE HANDED PRISON GARB, DOES THE LAST RAY OF HOPE DISAPPEAR.
THEN, FOR THE FIRST TIME, COMES THE AWFUL REALIZATION THAT THEY ARE REALLY CONVICTS, REAL CONVICTS.
OH! HOW AWFUL!
REG. U. S. PAT. OFF. © 1932 BY NEA SERVICE, INC.
WASH AND EASY ARE NOT PLACED IN CELLS. THEY ARE LOCKED IN A LONG, HOT BUILDING WITH OVER A HUNDRED OTHERS.
A NICE, CHILLY RECEPTION, EH?
MY GOSH! IS THIS ALL THEY SLEEP ON?
THERE ARE NO BEDS, NO BUNKS—NOT EVEN BLANKETS. JUST A LONG LINE OF BARE PLANKS ALONG EACH WALL.
HEY, BUDDIE, THESE TWO BOARDS OCCUPIED?
NON. ONE FELLA, HE DIE YESTERDAY. ONE FELLA TODAY. HELP YOURSELF.
REG. U. S. PAT. OFF. © 1932 BY NEA SERVICE, INC.
WASH CATCHES HIS BREATH. SHIVERS. THESE ARE NOT MEN. JUST SHELLS OF MEN. GAUNT, BEATEN, AND HUNGRY. - FEVER-RIDDEN WRECKS.

NOT ENOUGH SALT ON TH' MEAT.
EES ALWAYS ZAT WAY, COMRADE. NEVAIR ENOUGH OF ANYTHING.
A SLAB OF BREAD, A HUNK OF BOILED MEAT FOR ZE DINNER. FOR SUPPER, ONLY A CUP OF RICE. FOR BREAKFAST, COFFEE. NOSSING MORE.
AH, YOU SINK YOU CAN LIVE ON ZAT – AND WORK? NON NON, EES IMPOSSIBLE. NEVAIR ENOUGH. ALWAYS ZE SAME.
HOW AWFUL! NEVER ANY DESSERT, OR FRUIT, OR EGGS, OR VEGETABLES ?
© 1932 BY NEA SERVICE, INC. REG. U. S. PAT. OFF.
NON NON! ZE SAME EVERY DAY. EET NEVAIR VARY. NEVAIR! AND ALWAYS ZE TERRIBLE HEAT, ZE BURNING FEVER. AH, EET NO TAKE LONG IN GUIANA, COMRADE, TO SICKEN AND DIE.
THE NOON HOUR OVER, EASY IS PUT TO WORK IN THE COFFIN FACTORY, AND WASH IS SENT OUT WITH A ROAD GANG.
THE FIERCE TROPIC SUN BEATS DOWN WITH ALL ITS FURY. THE HEAT IS TERRIFIC. WASH'S BARE FEET BLISTER. HE'S WRINGING WET.
MY GOSH! IS IT ALWAYS THIS HOT?
ALWAYS! NIGHT AND DAY.
OBOY! RAIN – NOW WE CAN REST AN' COOL OFF A BIT.
NON NON. WE KEEP ON WORKING. AND AFTER ZE RAIN EET WEEL BE EVEN HOTTER.
GEE WIZ! I DON'T SEE HOW PEOPLE STAND IT.
AH, WAIT UNTIL ZE FEVER HIT YOU. EES MUCH WORSE. ONLY ZE STRONG SURVIVE. HALF ZE CONVICTS DIE ZE FIRST YEAR.
REG. U. S. PAT. OFF. © 1932 BY NEA SERVICE, INC.
AFTER A WEEK OF PRISON LIFE, WASH AND EASY BEGIN TO WILT. THE DEADLY TROPICAL CLIMATE IS ALREADY SAPPING THEIR STRENGTH.
WOW! A MONTH OF THIS AN' WE'LL BE LIKE THESE OLD TIMERS.
LISSEN, EASY, THERE'S NO TWO WAYS ABOUT IT. WE GOTTA ESCAPE.
NOT SO FAST, PODNER. WAIT TILL WE GET ONTO THE ROPES.
NOSSIR, RIGHT AWAY. AN' I KNOW TH' VERY GUY TO ESCAPE WITH. NAME'S DEAD-PAN. TOMORROW HE AN' TWO OTHERS ARE STARTIN' THRU TH' JUNGLE TO BRAZIL.
BAH! DOES HE KNOW WHAT A JUNGLE IS, LIKE?
BOY, HE OUGHTA! HE'S BEEN HERE 'LEVEN YEARS. TRIED TO ESCAPE SIX TIMES, AN' ALMOST MADE IT EVERY TIME.
GOOD! LOOK HIM UP, LADDIE. SEE IF HE'LL TAKE US.

LISSEN, DEAD-PAN, ME AN' MY BUDDIE WUNTA ESCAPE. WE WONDERED IF WE COULD JOIN YOUR PARTY.
HUM! YOU GOT MONEY FOR PAY YOUR SHARE?
YEH. I THINK EASY'S GOT $5 HID SOME PLACE.
POOF! EES ONLY HALF ENOUGH.
BUT LISSEN! WE C'D GET BY ON THAT. I'M SURE WE COULD. WHY, WE'D LIVE MOSTLY OFFA WILD FRUIT AN' BERRIES AN' THINGS.
FOOD EES NOT ALL. YOU NEED MONEY FOR MANY SINGS — A CANOE, AXES, BLANKETS.
NON NON, MY FRAN. BETTER LUCK NEX' TAM.
!
© 1932 BY NEA SERVICE, INC. REG. U. S. PAT. OFF.
WHAT DID HE SAY, PODNER?
HE WON'T TAKE US. SAID WE DIDN'T HAVE ENOUGH DOUGH.
I WAS AFRAID O' THAT.
HE SAID NOBODY COULD ESCAPE ON WOT WE GOT. BUT IT'S BEEN DONE, EASY. I KNOW IT HAS. THEY LIVE ON TH' JUNGLE.
TELL YOU WHAT, PODNER. $5 IS ENOUGH FOR ONE. WHY DON'T YOU TAKE IT? AND I'LL JOIN YOU LATER.
HA! SO 'AT'S TH' KIND OF A PAL YOU THINK I AM? NOSIR, IT'S YOUR DOUGH. YOU TAKE IT, AN' I'LL STAY BEHIND.
BUT I WON'T MIND, LADDIE. HONEST, I WON'T. I'LL GET OUT SOMEHOW.
NOT ON YOUR LIFE! WE GOT IN THIS MESS TOGETHER — AN' I GUESS WE KIN GET OUT TOGETHER.
REG. U. S. PAT. OFF. © 1932 BY NEA SERVICE, INC.
DEAD-PAN ESCAPES!
HARDENED FUGITIVE MAKES 7TH BREAK FOR FREEDOM.
IS MISSING AT NOON ROLL-CALL. PLUNGES INTO DENSE JUNGLE WITH TWO COMPANIONS. HEADS FOR BRAZIL, 200 MILES AWAY.
OTHERS ALSO VANISH!
TWO LIFERS HEAD FOR OPEN SEA IN DUG-OUT CANOE.
PRISONERS IN UPROAR AT DOUBLE ESCAPE. GUARDS CALM; WILL NOT BEGIN SEARCH UNTIL AFTER MID-DAY NAP.
REG. U. S. PAT. OFF. © 1932 BY NEA SERVICE, INC.
TUBBS DESPONDENT
BEMOANS BUM LUCK AS CONVICTS CHEER.
LACK OF EXTRA FIVE SPOT KEEPS HIM FROM BEING WITH THOSE AT LIBERTY.

JUST THINK—ONLY $5 AN' I'D BE FREE, TOO.
UNTIL WASH LEARNS THE FATE OF THE TWO LIFERS, WHO HEADED FOR VENEZUELA IN A DUG-OUT CANOE, HE CONSIDERS HIMSELF THE UNLUCKIEST PERSON ALIVE.
APPARENTLY, ALL WENT WELL WITH THE LIFERS UNTIL THEY REACHED THE MOUTH OF THE RIVER, A PLACE NOTORIOUS FOR ITS TREACHEROUS CURRENTS.
REG. U. S. PAT. OFF. © 1932 BY NEA SERVICE, INC.
AND THEIRS IS THE SAME HORRIBLE FATE OF COUNTLESS OTHER DARING CONVICTS. NOTHING BUT THE OVERTURNED CANOE IS FOUND.
GEE WIZ! IS IT ALWAYS DANGEROUS TRYIN' TO ESCAPE?
DANGEROUS? MA FOI! ONLY HALF WHO TRY EET COME BACK ALIVE.
TWO WEEKS PASS WITHOUT ANY NEWS OF DEAD-PAN. THEN ONE DAY, GUARDS FIND HIM AND A COMPANION FLOATING DOWN THE RIVER, HALF DEAD FROM STARVATION.
NO ONE KNOWS WHAT HAPPENED. THEIR CLOTHES ARE IN SHREADS, AND APPARENTLY THEY HAVE BEEN LOST IN THE JUNGLE FOR DAYS.
THE FATE OF THE OTHER COMPANION IS A MYSTERY. SUPPOSEDLY, HE EITHER STARVED TO DEATH, OR DIED IN AGONY FROM EATING SOME POISONOUS FRUIT.
WHAT AN INGLORIOUS END!
OUT OF FIVE MEN WHO ESCAPED, NOT ONE REMAINS AT LARGE. ONLY TWO ARE STILL ALIVE. THEY ARE WRECKS, AND WILL BE PLACED IN SOLITARY CONFINEMENT FOR MONTHS
REG. U. S. PAT. OFF. © 1932 BY NEA SERVICE, INC.
OH, WELL! I GUESS THERE'S WORSE THINGS THAN THIS.
AFTER SEEING THE TERRIBLE TOLL EXACTED BY THE SEA AND JUNGLE ON THOSE WHO TRY TO ESCAPE WASH AND EASY FEEL PRETTY LUCKY THAT THEY WERE LEFT BEHIND.
BUT, OH, HOW BLUE THEY ARE! IT SEEMS THEY WILL NEVER GET OUT OF PRISON. THEIR BESEECHING LETTERS TO THE AUTHORITIES ARE IN VAIN.
ONE DAY WASH SEES A STRANGELY FAMILIAR FACE.
WHY, IT LOOKS LIKE THE FELLA WHO CLIMBED INTO TH' LIFE-BOAT WITH US.
© 1932 BY NEA SERVICE, INC. REG. U. S. PAT. OFF.
PIERRE! I HARDLY KNEW YOU. YOU'VE AGED TEN YEARS.
TWENTY, MY FRAN. I HAVE JUST RETURN FROM SEEX WEEKS IN SOLITARY CONFINEMENT. AH, HOW GLAD I AM TO SEE YOU.

MAN, YOU LOOK HALF DEAD A'READY. HOW MUCH LONGER YOU GOT TO SERVE?
FORTY YEARS. TWEN'Y EEN PRISON — TWEN'Y EEN EXILE.
POOR OLD PIERRE!
AH, YOU SINK I NEVAIR SEE MY BELOVED FRANCE AGAIN, EH? HA! PIERRE EES SMART. PIERRE GOING ESCAPE.
YEH? 'AT'S WOT DEAD-PAN SAID.
POOF! ZAT DEAD-PAN, HE EES DUMB. SEVEN YEARS AGO I ESCAPE — ZEY CATCH ME ONLY LAS' JANUARY.
WELL, BUDDIE, I SURE WISH YOU BETTER LUCK THAN TH' TIME WE RAN AWAY WITH TH' LIFE BOAT.
AH, MY FRAN, I DON' FORGET ZAT. NEVAIR! YOU TOOK ME WIZ YOU — AND I GOING TAKE YOU WIZ ME.
REG. U. S. PAT. OFF. © 1932 BY NEA SERVICE, INC.
WHAT'S GOING ON?
IT'S PIERRE. HE WUNTS US TO ESCAPE WITH HIM.
WE HAVEN'T ENOUGH MONEY STUPID.
PIERRE HAS. HE'S GOT GOBS OF IT.
WHAT BELONG TO PIERRE, MY FRAN, BELONG TO YOU. IN ALL ZIS WORL' YOU ARE ZE ONLY WANS WHO EVER HELP POOR OLD PIERRE — AND PIERRE DON' FORGET.
BLAZES — THERE'S A GREAT GUY! BUT HOW ABOUT THE RISK?
POOF! WIZ PIERRE, MY FRANS, ZARE EES NO RISK. EVERTHING EES ARRANGE.
GOOD OLD PIERRE!
FELLA, YOU'RE A LIFE SAVER — YOU BET WE'LL ESCAPE WITH YOU.
TRES BIEN! MEET ME AT ZE CHINAMAN'S SHOP TOMORROW NOON. EVERYTHING IS ARRANGE.
OBOY! I CAN HARDLY BELIEVE IT.
BLAZES! THINK OF IT. TOMORROW WE'LL BE FREE. FREE! NO MORE FEVER! NO MORE STALE GRUB.
REG. U. S. PAT. OFF. © 1932 BY NEA SERVICE, INC.
WAIT'LL I GET OUT! BOY, I'M GUNNA EAT HAM'N' EGGS AN' PIE SIX TIMES A DAY.
I'M GOING TO SPEND THE REST OF MY LIFE IN BED — A REAL BED, WITH SPRINGS AND CLEAN SHEETS.

DAWN. COFFEE IS OVER. THE CONVICTS MARCH THRU THE PRISON GATES TO THEIR DAILY LABOR.
EVERY MOVE IN WASH'S BODY TINGLES WITH EXCITEMENT. HE COUNTS EACH MINUTE, EACH SECOND. THE HOURS DRAG LIKE YEARS.
AT LAST!
BONG! BONG!
THE ZERO HOUR!
THE TIME HAS COME FOR HIM TO JOIN HIS COMPANIONS—TO ESCAPE.
HE WIPES THE COLD PERSPIRATION FROM HIS FACE. PUTS DOWN HIS PICK. CLIMBS SLOWLY OUT OF THE DITCH.
G-GETTING A DRINK OF WATER, SIR.
GET IT.
R. Crane
© 1932 BY NEA SERVICE, INC. REG. U. S. PAT. OFF.
SLYLY, WASH WATCHES FOR A CHANCE TO ESCAPE.
PRESENTLY THE GUARD TURNS HIS BACK, AND IN A FLASH WASH IS GONE.
IF SOMEBODY STOPS ME I'LL—I'LL DIE.
REG. U. S. PAT. OFF. © 1932 BY NEA SERVICE, INC.
BUT NO ONE STOPS HIM. NO ONE EVEN NOTICES HIM.
THE CHINAMAN'S STORE IS REACHED IN PERFECT SAFETY. HE NEVER DREAMED THAT ESCAPE WOULD BE SO EASY.
BREATHLESS, WASH DASHES THRU THE CHINAMAN'S BACK DOOR. PIERRE IS THERE. EVERYTHING IS IN READINESS FOR THE ESCAPE.
OBOY! WHERE'S EASY?
GEEV HIM TAM. EES EARLY YET.
BONG!
BUT THE MINUTES PASS. THE CHURCH CLOCK CHIMES AGAIN, AND EASY IS STILL MISSING.
NOON. THE STREETS ARE DESERTED. CONVICTS HAVE BEEN MARCHED BACK TO PRISON. IT IS TIME TO LEAVE.
GEE WIZ! MAYBE HE GOT CAUGHT.
OUI. WE HAF BETTER GO. WE CAN WAIT NO LONGER.
R. Crane
BUT I CAN'T RUN OFF AN' LEAVE EASY BEHIND.
MA FOI! WHAT YOU GOING TO DO? RETURN TO PRISON, AND BE PUT IN SOLITARY? NON NON. BETTER YOU FORGET HIM AND COME WIZ ME.
REG. U. S. PAT. OFF. © 1932 BY NEA SERVICE, INC.

JULY 1932

EASY ARRIVES AT THE LAST MINUTE.
GEE WIZ, FELLA! WE THOUGHT YOU'D BIN CAUGHT.
HAD TROUBLE. A BLASTED GUARD HAD HIS EYE ON ME ALL MORNING.
NEVAIR MIND—ZIS WAY. HURRY.
THEY DODGE THRU BACK ALLEYS TO THE JUNGLE.
THEN TURN TO THE RIVER, WHERE A MAN IS WAITING FOR THEM IN A BOAT.
YOU'RE LATE.
AND ROW TOWARD A SMALL SLOOP.
LA LA! OLD PIERRE EES SMART. NO DUG-OUT CANOE FOR PIERRE. HE HIRE A REAL BOAT.
REG. U. S. PAT. OFF. © 1932 BY NEA SERVICE, INC.
R. CRANE
WASH LOOKS OVER THE SKIPPER WHOM PIERRE HIRED—AND SOMETHING ABOUT THE MAN GIVES HIM THE CREEPS.
PSST! DO YOU TRUST THIS GUY, PIERRE?
NO. BUT EES NOT EVERY WAN, MY FRAN, WHO WILL RISK CARRYING CONVICTS.
THEY CLAMBER ABOARD.
GO BELOW. CHANGE YOUR CLOTHES, AND THROW THEES PRISON OUTFIT OVERBOARD.
THEY ARE SURPRISED TO FIND TWO OTHER ESCAPED CONVICTS BELOW. ONE IS A TOOTHLESS WRECK.
REG. U. S. PAT. OFF. © 1932 BY NEA SERVICE, INC.
!
!
THE OTHER—YE GODS! THE OTHER IS WASH'S ENEMY, THE BULLY WHOSE SKULL HE CRACKED WHILE ABOARD THE CONVICT SHIP. WASH HAS NOT SEEN HIM SINCE.
WASH GULPS AND TURNS PALE AT THE SIGHT OF HIS ENEMY, ABOARD THE SAME VESSEL. BUT THE ENEMY BARELY NOTICES HIM.
I THINK HE MUST OF FORGOTTEN ME, EASY.
MAYBE, BUT KEEP AN EYE ON HIM, PODNER. HE'S A BAD ACTOR.
MEANWHILE, THE ESCAPE FARES BADLY.
THERE IS NO WIND, AND THE CONVICTS BECOME DESPERATE. THE SLUGGISH CURRENT HAS CARRIED THEM A SCANT QUARTER MILE.
GEE WIZ! AT THIS RATE WE'LL NEVER GET AWAY.

The convicts are frantic. The wind has failed them. They are becalmed, helpless.
DO SOMETHING, FOOL! ANY MINUTE THE GUARDS'LL FINISH THEIR NAP, AN' START AFTER US.
YES, AN' WE'LL BE CAUGHT BEFORE WE'RE OUTA SIGHT OF ST. LAURENT.
MA FOI! BUT WHAT CAN WE DO?
BLAZES! GET SOME PADDLES.
NON NON! ZAT MAKE PEOPLE SUSPICIOUS. ZEY SEE WE ARE IN A HURRY.
MY GOSH! TH' JUNGLE'S BETTER'N THIS. LE'S TAKE TO TH' JUNGLE.
OUI, OUI! ZE JUNGLE!
WAIT! YOU FEEL ZAT? A BREEZE! SACRE BLEU! A BREEZE! WE ARE MOVING!!
REG. U. S. PAT. OFF. © 1932 BY NEA SERVICE, INC.

As the breeze freshens, and hurries them toward the open sea and freedom, the escaping convicts take heart.
Meanwhile, however, the guards begin the chase. Every possible avenue of escape is to be closed. One launch speeds down-stream, another up-stream.
Wireless messages are sent out, requesting the Dutch officials to cut them off if they cross the river.
And every jungle trail for miles around is carefully guarded.
ROY CRANE
REG. U. S. PAT. OFF. © 1932 BY NEA SERVICE, INC.

The fugitives are but a few miles from St. Laurent, when the prison launch is sighted.
WE ARE DOOMED!
Instantly, wild excitement breaks loose.
QUICK! EVERY WAN BELOW! KEEP OUT OF SIGHT.
ROY CRANE
Breathlessly, the fugitives wait for the worst to happen — but, to their amazement, the launch races by without stopping.
© 1932 BY NEA SERVICE, INC. REG. U. S. PAT. OFF.

OH, THE SIGH OF RELIEF WHEN THE PRISON LAUNCH PASSES WITHOUT STOPPING. HOW THE CONVICTS YELP WITH GLEE!
BUT THE BURLY SKIPPER QUICKLY PUTS A STOP TO THE REJOICING.
FOOLS! PRESENTLY ZEY WEEL TURN AROUND AND COME BACK. AND ZAT TIME—HA!—YOU WEEL NOT BE SO LUCKY.
TRUE! TRUE! NEX' TAM ZEY WEEL SURELY STOP.
WE ARE DOOMED! THEY WEEL COME ABOARD—THEY WEEL FIND US.
LA LA! WHAT SHALL WE DO?
VERY SIMPLE! WE'LL GO ASHORE AND THEY CAN SEARCH THE BOAT ALL THEY LIKE.
© 1932 BY NEA SERVICE, INC. REG. U. S. PAT. OFF.
WHEN THEY'VE FOUND NOTHING, AND HAVE LEFT, THE SKIPPER CAN PICK US UP AGAIN.
AH, AN EXCELLENT PLAN! I PUT ZE CONVICTS ASHORE, EH? AND AFTER ZE GUARDS SEARCH ZE BOAT, I COME BACK. AH, MOS' EXCELLENT!
RIGHT! AND JUST TO MAKE SURE YOU COME BACK, I'LL TAKE YOUR GUN.
NON, NON, NON! YOU CAN TRUST ME—GEEV EET BACK.
LIKE BLAZES I WILL! TAKE THE COMPASS, BOYS, AND EVERYTHING OF VALUE.
SAY, PARD, YER OKAY. MAKE I'M LIKE IT.
THE CONVICTS SCRAMBLE ASHORE, LEAVING THE SKIPPER TO GRUMBLE AND CONTINUE DOWN RIVER ALONE.
Roy Crane
REG. U. S. PAT. OFF. © 1932 BY NEA SERVICE, INC.
AND THEY ARE JUST IN TIME, TOO, FOR THE PRISON LAUNCH IS SIGHTED COMING BACK ALMOST IMMEDIATELY.
SURE ENOUGH, THE PRISON LAUNCH STOPS.
AHOY! HAVE YOU SEEN ANY ESCAPED CONVICTS?
NO, M'SIEUR. ONLY SOME NEGROES IN A CANOE.
BETTER SEARCH. HIS BOAT, MEN. IT'S OLD LE FEVRE, THE BIGGEST SCALAWAG IN GUIANA.
THE GUARDS GO ABOARD.
REG. U. S. PAT. OFF. © 1932 BY NEA SERVICE, INC.
MEANWHILE, THE HUNTED CONVICTS CHUCKLE WITH GLEE, FOR THEY ARE SAFE IN THE JUNGLE.

AFTER MAKING SURE THAT NO CONVICTS ARE ABOARD THE SLOOP, THE PRISON LAUNCH SPEEDS BACK TOWARD ST. LAURENT.
THEN THE CONVICTS WHOOP AND YELL, AND SWARM TRIUMPHANTLY OUT OF THE JUNGLE.
WHOOPEE! AWAY WE GO.
AN HOUR LATER THEY REACH THE RIVER MOUTH.
THEN A SPANKING BREEZE AND A ROLLING SEA, AND GUIANA FADES FAST FROM VIEW. FREE! FREE! AT LAST THEY'RE FREE!
REG. U. S. PAT. OFF. © 1932 BY NEA SERVICE, INC.
AT LAST, FREEDOM SEEMS ASSURED, AND TEARS OF JOY RUN DOWN PIERRE'S LEATHERY CHEEKS.
I AM SO HAPPEE, MY FRAN. SOME TAM I SINK I NEVAIR GOING ESCAPE ZAT AWFUL PRISON—NEVAIR WEEL I SEE MY BELOVED HOMELAND AGAIN.
AND NOW I AM FREE. EES TOO GOOD TO BE TRUE. I GOING HEAR MUSIC AGAIN. I GOING WEAR SHOES, AND SEE MY LEETLE FARM AND MY PEEGS AND SHEEP.
AND MY LEETLE GRAND-DAUGHTER, M'SIEUR, MY LEETLE BABETTE, WHO SAY A PRAYER EVER' NIGHT FOR POOR OLD PIERRE—I GOING SEE HER, TOO. I GOING KEES HER LEETLE HANDS—WANCE MORE—AND HOLD HER ON MY KNEE.
REG. U. S. PAT. OFF. © 1932 BY NEA SERVICE, INC.
OH, M'SIEUR, NO WAN KNOW HOW HAPPEE I AM. MY HEART, SHE EES ABOUT TO BURST. MY PRAYER EES ANSWERED. I AM GOING HOME.
I AM FREE. MY HEART EES FULL WEETH SONG. AH, TO SINK, MY FRAN, ZAT I WEEL AGAIN SEE MY BELOVE' HOMELAND, MY LEETLE GRAND-DAUGHTER.
BUT HOW YOU GOING TO GET BACK TO FRANCE, PIERRE, WITHOUT A PASSPORT?
OH, EES NOT SO HARD WHEN WAN HAF MONEY.
THE SKIPPER SUDDENLY SNORTS AND LOOKS UP.
MONEY? YOU HAF MUCH MONEY, M'SIEUR?
NON, NON. ONLY A LEETLE. WHY DO YOU ASK?
WHO KNOWS? PERHAP IF YOU HAF ENOUGH I TAKE YOU TO FRANCE MYSELF.
REG. U. S. PAT. OFF. © 1932 BY NEA SERVICE, INC.
EASY SQUIRMS UNCOMFORTABLY, AND RECALLS HOW A GUARD REFERRED TO LE FEVRE AS THE BIGGEST SCALAWAG IN GUIANA.

GR-R-R
FOR A LONG TIME THE SKIPPER SCOWLS IN GLOOMY SILENCE. SO EVIL IS HIS TEMPER, THAT EASY IS ALMOST AFRAID.
I WISH I HADN'T GIVEN THAT GUY'S GUN BACK TO HIM.
AW, LET 'IM GROWL. HE ENJOYS IT.
BUT WHEN THE CONVICTS BEGIN TALKING OF GOOD THINGS TO EAT, HIS FACE BRIGHTENS.
HUNGRY, EH? LA LA! THEN LET US CELEBRATE OUR GOOD FORTUNE. MAIS OUI! GO BELOW, MY BOYS, AND OPEN CANS OF PEACHES AND PINEAPPLE.
ROY CRANE
IMMEDIATELY, THERE IS A RUSH FOR THE CABIN.
WHOOPEE! A FEAST!
PEACHES AND PINEAPPLE! OO, LA LA! WAT COULD CONVICTS ENJOY MORE THAN ZAT?
© 1932 BY NEA SERVICE, INC. REG. U. S. PAT. OFF.
HE SAY TO LOOK UNDER ZE STARB'RD BUNK.
MAIS OUI! BUT EES NOTHING THERE.
THE SKIPPER IS LEFT ALONE ON DECK. THE CONVICTS ARE BELOW, EAGERLY SEARCHING FOR CANNED PEACHES.
HEY! WHERE YOU SAY EES ZE PEACHES?
!
PIERRE STARTS UP THE COMPANION-WAY — BUT STOPS IN AMAZEMENT.
BEFORE HIM STANDS THE SKIPPER, PISTOL IN HAND, PIG-EYES BLAZING.
PEACHES? PEACHES? HA! YOU SINK I FEED YOU PEACHES?
ROY CRANE
THE MAN MUST BE MAD! HE STARTS SHOOTING!!
REG. U. S. PAT. OFF. © 1932 BY NEA SERVICE, INC.
BANG!
BANG!
Bang!
ALL OF THE CONVICTS ARE IN THE CABIN WHEN THE SKIPPER, APPARENTLY GONE MAD, STARTS SHOOTING AT THEM.
ROY CRANE
THERE IS NO WARNING — NO TIME TO DUCK. PIERRE IS THE FIRST TO FALL. HE CLUTCHES HIS STOMACH, AND CRUMPLES TO THE FLOOR WITHOUT EVEN A MOAN.
MORE SHOTS! SCREAMS! PANDEMONIUM!!
REG. U. S. PAT. OFF.
© 1932 BY NEA SERVICE, INC.

FORTUNATELY, SOMEONE HAS THE PRESENCE OF MIND TO SLAM AND BOLT THE CABIN DOORS.
!
SLAM!
CLICK!
BUT THE MANIAC IS STILL AT LARGE, AND PIERRE AND THE TOOTHLESS WRECK LIE ON THE FLOOR, BLEEDING.
LOOK OUT! HE'S BREAKING THE GLASS IN TH' PORTHOLES.
EASY IS DESPERATE. HE GRABS THE PISTOL WHEN IT IS THRUST THRU THE OPENING.
BANG!
REG. U. S. PAT. OFF. © 1932 BY NEA SERVICE, INC.
AND GETS IT, TOO!
BUT IT'S EMPTY. THAT WAS THE LAST SHELL.
THE CONVICTS ARE TERRIFIED AND HELPLESS— UNTIL THE CRAZED SKIPPER MAKES THE MISTAKE OF THRUSTING HIS REVOLVER THRU A PORTHOLE.
MON DIEU! ZEY GRAB MY PEESTOL! I AM LOST! I AM DESTROY!
WHOOPEE! WE GOTTIM! HE'S UNARMED.
COME ON— LET'S MOB HIM!
THROW 'IM TO THE SHARKS!
WAIT— ZE SHOT GUN! SACRE BLEU! I ALMOS FORGET ZE SHOT GUN.
AN EYE FOR AN EYE, MEN.
ALL TOGETHER— LET'S GO!
© 1932 BY NEA SERVICE, INC REG. U. S. PAT. OFF.
THEY THROW OPEN THE DOORS, LITTLE DREAMING THAT CERTAIN DEATH IS JUST AROUND THE CORNER.
ALL TOGETHER, MEN! LET'S GO!
MOB HIM! KILL HIM!
WHEN THE SKIPPER IS NOT IN SIGHT, EASY DRAWS BACK.
WAIT. HE MIGHT BE LAYING FOR US WITH A HATCHET, OR SOMETHING.
BANG!
© 1932 BY NEA SERVICE, INC REG. U. S. PAT. OFF.
SLAM!
CLICK!
WHAT A PREDICAMENT!
FIVE MEN, TWO OF THEM WOUNDED, HELPLESSLY CAGED IN A TINY CABIN WHILE A MANIAC ROAMS THE DECK.

THE RAGING SKIPPER BEGINS FIRING HIS SHOT GUN THRU THE CABIN PORT HOLES.
POW!
AND THE CONVICTS RETREAT THRU A SMALL OPENING INTO THE HOLD. THERE, THEY HUDDLE IN THE DARKNESS, DEJECTED, MISERABLE.
POOR OLD PIERRE! I'M AFRAID HE'S DONE FOR.
YEAH—HE JES LAYS THERE 'N' BLEEDS.
GEE WIZ! WOT'LL WE DO, EASY?
WAIT UNTIL THE BLASTED MANIAC BREAKS IN, I RECKON. THEN FIGHT LIKE BLAZES AND HOPE FOR THE BEST.
HE AIN'T GOING TO BUST IN. HE KNOWS WE'D BUTCHER HIM WIT' HATCHETS.
WAIT AND SEE, STUPID. THERE'S NO FOOD OR WATER ON DECK. HE'S GOT TO BREAK IN, OR STARVE.
?
© 1932 BY NEA SERVICE, INC. REG. U. S. PAT. OFF.
DEAD MEN TELL NO TALES! THAT'S THE SKIPPER'S PHILOSOPHY. HE'S NOT ACTUALLY CRAZY. HE'S AN UNSCRUPULOUS OLD RASCAL, GREEDY FOR MONEY.
BAH! WHAT EES A FEW CONVICTS MORE OR LESS?
BUT THE ATTEMPT TO MASSACRE HIS PASSENGERS HAS FAILED. THEY ARE BARRICADED IN THE HOLD, WELL ARMED WITH HATCHETS — WAITING.
WHAT'S MORE, THEY HAVE ALL THE FOOD AND WATER. THE SKIPPER IS ALARMED.
AHOY, DOWN THERE!
WOTTA YOU WANT?
I GEEV WAN MINUTE TO TURN OVER ZE MONEY AND HATCHETS, OR I COME DOWN WIZ MY SHOT GUN.
WE DARE YOU TO!
COME AHEAD! YOU'LL GET TH' HATCHETS, ALL RIGHT.
© 1932 BY NEA SERVICE, INC. REG. U. S. PAT. OFF.
THE SKIPPER CHANGES HIS TACTICS, AND TRIES DIPLOMACY IN PLACE OF THREATS.
LEESTEN TO REASON, BOYS. WHAT ARE YOUR TERMS FOR A TRUCE?
FEED YOURSELF TO THE SHARKS, SUH, AND WE'LL CALL EVERYTHING SQUARE.
YAH, YAH! HE'S YELLA! HE'S AFRAID TO COME AFTER US.
HOO-EE! WE GOT THE OLD BILLY-GOAT LICKED.
WOT'S MORE, WE GIVE YOU ONE MINUTE TO THROW AWAY YOUR GUN, AND LET US OUT.
LET YOU·OUT?? SACRE BLEU! I SINK ZE BOAT FIRST.
I DROWN YOU LIKE RATS! I SHOW YOU!
REG. U. S. PAT. OFF. © 1932 BY NEA SERVICE, INC.

BY GAR, I SHOW ZEM! I SINK ZE BOAT! I DROWN ZEM LAK RATS!
THE TRAPPED CONVICTS GROW A BIT ALARMED, AS MORE AND MORE WATER POURS INTO THE HOLD.
THEY HOLD A CONFERENCE OF WAR, AND PRESENTLY SLUG SNYDER EMERGES FROM BELOW WITH A HATCHET BETWEEN HIS TEETH.
HE CRAWS AFT, TRUSTING THAT THE SKIPPER IS TOO BUSY TO SEE HIM.
BUT THE SKIPPER DOES SEE HIM — GRABS HIS SHOT GUN! SLUG HEAVES THE HATCHET WITH ALL HIS MIGHT!
!?
© 1932 BY NEA SERVICE, INC. REG. U. S. PAT. OFF.
WHACKO!! THE HATCHET STRIKES THE SKIPPER SQUARE IN THE FOREHEAD.
SLUG LEAPS, EAGER TO CONTINUE THE BATTLE.
BUT THE SKIPPER IS OUT, COMPLETELY OUT!
REG. U. S. PAT. OFF. © 1932 BY NEA SERVICE, INC.
SLUG HESITATES ONLY LONG ENOUGH TO SEARCH HIS POCKETS FOR MONEY, THEN DUMPS THE LIMP BODY TO THE SHARKS.
AND, AS FAR AS HE IS CONCERNED, THE GORY DEED IS FORGOTTEN.
AWRIGHT, YOU GUYS, GIT SOME GRUB TO COOKIN' — I'M HUNGRY.
YES, SIR! YOU CAN PUT SLUG SNYDER DOWN AS BEING A HARD HOMBRE.
CONVICTS VICTORIOUS!
SKIPPER IS DUMPED OVERBOARD.
FUGITIVES YELP WITH GLEE. COMPLETE FREEDOM A CERTAINTY.
WHOOPEE! GOOD TIMES ARE HERE AGAIN. HOORAY FOR EVERYTHING!
CAN THE CELEBRATION, PODNER. WE GOT WOUNDED TO CARE FOR. YOU AND SLUG LOOK AFTER PIERRE AND TOOTHLESS. I'LL RUSTLE A MEAL.
AND LISTEN, LADDIE. TELL PIERRE HIS PRAYERS ARE ANSWERED. HE'S FREE! HE'S GOING TO SEE HIS LITTLE GRAND DAUGHTER AGAIN — AND HOLD HER ON HIS KNEE.
WASH REAPPEARS, HIS EYES FILLED WITH TEARS.
IT'S TOO LATE, EASY. PIERRE IS DEAD!
!
© 1932 BY NEA SERVICE, INC. REG. U. S. PAT. OFF.

POOR, KINDLY, OLD PIERRE! WE OWE EVERYTHING TO HIM, EASY.
TO THINK THAT HE HELPED OTHERS TO FREEDOM, YET COULDN'T GAIN IT HIMSELF. BLAZES - WHAT IRONY!
THEY BURY PIERRE IN AN UNMARKED, WATERY GRAVE, AND TURN SORROWFULLY TOWARD THE SOUTH, IN SEARCH OF LAND.
EARLY THE NEXT MORNING THEY SIGHT A FORBIDDING JUNGLE, AND FOLLOW THE COAST WESTWARD.
PROB'LY BRITISH GUIANA.
REG. U. S. PAT. OFF. © 1932 BY NEA SERVICE, INC.
BUT NOT UNTIL THE THIRD DAY DO THEY CONSIDER IT SAFE TO LAND.
MUST BE VENEZUELA.
IF IT IS, WE'RE SAFE. THEY CAN'T TAKE US BACK TO PRISON FROM THERE.
Roy Crane

AUGUST 1932

THE ESCAPED CONVICTS TURN INTO A SMALL HARBOR, HOPING THAT THEY HAVE REACHED VENEZUELA AND SAFETY.
THE HARBOR IS DESERTED EXCEPT FOR A FEW FLOATING ORANGES AND A JUNKY STEAMER.
HOTEL DEL
Roy Crane
REG. U. S. PAT. OFF. © 1932 BY NEA SERVICE, INC.
BUT THERE IS A TOWN, BLINDING WHITE, AND FANNED BY GENTLY SWAYING PALMS. IT IS TYPICALLY LATIN AMERICAN, SIZZLING HOT, ILL-PAVED, AND DIRTY. AS USUAL, THE MOST PRETENTIOUS BUILDINGS ARE THE BARRACKS, THE JAIL, AND THE CHURCHES.

WE'LL NOSE AROUND AND SEE WHAT COUNTRY THIS IS.
THE ESCAPED CONVICTS ANCHOR ABOVE THE TOWN, NOT DARING TO TIE UP AT THE WHARF.
IMMEDIATELY, SOLDIERS SPRING FROM THE BUSHES AND RUN TOWARD THEM. THE CONVICTS ARE SCARED STIFF.
AH, HA! AMERICANOS, EH?
YES, SUH. THREE FUN-LOVING COLLEGE BOYS OUT FOR A LARK.
WE WERE LOOKING FOR THE PANAMA CANAL.
REG. U. S. PAT. OFF. © 1932 BY NEA SERVICE, INC.
LET ME SEE YOUR PASS-PORTS.
WELL, SUH, NOW THAT'S A COINCIDENCE. WE WERE JUST LOOKING FOR 'EM OURSELVES, AND COULDN'T FIND 'EM. WE SUSPECT FOUL PLAY, SUH, AND APPEAL TO YOU FOR ASSISTANCE.

THREE AMERICANOS WEETHOUT PASSPORTS, EH? BETTER YOU SEARCH THE BOAT, PEDRO.
TUT TUT, COLONEL! LET'S GO DOWN TO THE BAR AND TALK THIS OVER LIKE GENTLEMEN.
OYE! OYE! EES BEEN A FIGHT, MI TENIENTE! MANY BULLET HOLES—AND A MAN EES EEN BED, WOUNDED!
OH HO! JUST AS I THOUGHT! REVOLUTIONISTS!!
SAY, LISTEN, GENERAL! YOU GOT US ON THE WRONG PEG. WE'RE--
SILENCE, YOU REBEL! YOU ARE UNDER ARREST!
REG. U. S. PAT. OFF. © 1932 BY NEA SERVICE, INC.

IT'S GETTING TO BE A DAWGONE HABIT. NO SOONER DO WE GET OUTA ONE BUM JAIL UNTIL WE'RE DUMPED IN ANOTHER.
OH, THIS ISN'T SO BAD. IN FACT, FOR A LATIN AMERICAN JAIL, IT'S DOWNRIGHT ELEGANT. WHY, BOY, THIS TIME WE GOT A PRIVATE ROOM WITH BATH.
DON'T JOKE AT A TIME LIKE THIS, YOU IDIOT. THEY THINK WE'RE REVOLUTIONISTS. WE'RE LIABLE TO BE SHOT.
NAH! BUT EVEN SO, IT'D BEAT ONE O' THOSE SLOW, HUNGRY GUIANA FADE-OUTS.
BUT WOTTLE WE DO?
TAKE IT EASY AND LET THE GOVER'MENT FEED US, MAKE THE USUAL SQUAWKS TO THE AMERICAN CONSUL, AND SWAT MOSQUITOS. THAT'S ALL WE CAN DO.
REG. U. S. PAT. OFF. © 1932 BY NEA SERVICE, INC.

AHOY, YOU IN TH' NEXT CELL! WOT COUNTRY'S THIS?
THE REPUBLIC OF PANAZUELA, SEÑOR.
TH' HECK YOU SAY! AN' WHERE'S TH' FIGHTIN'?
FIGHTING? WAT FIGHTING?
WHY, TH' REVOLUTION, OF COURSE.
POOF! EES BEEN NO REVOLUTION EEN PANAZUELA EEN SEEXTEEN YEARS.
WELL, CAN Y'BEAT THAT, EASY? THEY PINCH US FOR BEIN' REVOLUTIONISTS, AN' THERE'S NOT EVEN A REVOLUTION.
OH, THERE EES TALK, SEÑOR. PLENTY OF TALK. AND MOS' EVER' DAY THEY EXECUTE SOME RADICAL, BUT THAT EES ALL.
© 1932 BY NEA SERVICE, INC. REG. U. S. PAT. OFF.

CRASH! POW! BOOM! Brroom! Ding Dong!
MIDNIGHT. THE LITTLE PORT OF LA GRIPPE, PANAZUELA, IS SUDDENLY SHAKEN BY A SERIES OF TERRIFIC EXPLOSIONS, PISTOL SHOTS, AND CLANGING OF BELLS.
WASH HAS NEVER HEARD SUCH A FRIGHTFUL DIN. HE AND EASY RUN TO THE WINDOW, CONFIDENT THAT THE RUMORED REVOLUTION HAS BECOME A REALITY.
WHOOPEE! WOTTA BATTLE!
VIVA LA REVOLUCION! COME ON, YOU REBELS!
IF TH' REBELS WIN, WE'RE FREE. THREE BLOOMIN' CHEERS FOR TH' REBELS!
SOMEBODY'S CALLING US.
LOUDER! WE CAN'T HEAR FOR ALL TH' SHOOTIN'.
I SAY, GO BACK TO BED, YOU FOOLS! EES NOT A REVOLUTION— EES ONLEE NATIONAL EENDEPENDENCE DAY.
REG. U. S. PAT. OFF. © 1932 BY NEA SERVICE, INC.
WELL, IT SOUNDED LIKE A BATTLE, ANYWAY.
WASH AND EASY ARE DISGUSTED TO THINK THAT THEY MISTOOK AN INDEPENDENCE DAY CELEBRATION FOR A REVOLUTION.
BUT, WHEN MORNING COMES, PEOPLE BEGIN TO REALIZE THAT SOMETHING HAS REALLY HAPPENED. A RED FLAG FLUTTERS ABOVE THE BARRACKS.
AND STRANGE, RAGGED SOLDIERS PATROL THE STREETS.
REG. U. S. PAT. OFF. © 1932 BY NEA SERVICE, INC.
AND THEY EXECUTE A LOT OF POLITICIANS, INCLUDING THE MAYOR. THEN THE PEOPLE BECOME ALARMED, AND HIDE ALL THEIR VALUABLES. THEY KNOW THE REVOLUTION HAS COME.
CARRAMBA! I AM THE NAPOLEON OF THE WEST.
THE REBEL GENERAL IS A FIERY OLD BOY. HE SURPRISES AND CAPTURES THE FEDERAL GARRISON BY ATTACKING UNDER COVER OF A FIREWORKS CELEBRATION.
NEXT, HE MAKES HIS NAME FEARED, BY A WHOLESALE MASSACRE OF HIS ENEMIES. NOW, HE SWOOPS DOWN ON THE LOCAL CALABOOSE.
CALL OUT THE PREESONERS.
ATTENTION, YOU MANGY BURROS! I AM A MAN OF FEW WORDS. I NEED RECRUITS.
REG. U. S. PAT. OFF. © 1932 BY NEA SERVICE, INC.
ANY OF YOU WHO WEESH TO JOIN MY ARMY, ARE FREE! THE REST WILL BE SHOT! TAKE YOUR CHOICE.
VIVA EL GENERAL!
VIVA LA REVOLUCION
WE WEESH TO FIGHT!
AND SO, AMONG THE OTHERS, HE ADDS WASH AND EASY AND SLUG TO HIS RAGGED MOB

WELL. WE'RE IN TH' ARMY, BUT LOOK AT US — NO SHOES, NO UNIFORMS, NOT EVEN HATS.
WE GOT RIFLES. THAT'S AS MUCH AS THESE OTHER BUCK PRIVATES GOT.
BUT I WUNTA LOOK LIKE A SOLDIER IF I'M GUNNA BE ONE.
REBELS IN THESE COUNTRIES, LADDIE, AREN'T SOLDIERS. THEY'RE GLORIFIED BANDITS. THEY'LL STEAL ANYTHING FROM A HEN'S EGG UP.
BUT DON'T THEY EVEN HAVE UNIFORMS?
NAH! THEY SEW RED STRIPES DOWN THE LEGS O' THEIR OVERALLS, AND THINK IT'S CLASS.
REG. U. S. PAT. OFF. © 1932 BY NEA SERVICE, INC.
SHOO! THIS IS A HECK OF A WAR.
NOT FOR A MARRIED MAN. HE HAS ALL THE COMFORTS OF HOME. HE TAKES HIS WIFE ALONG, AND SHE COOKS, AND CARRIES HIS PACK, AND EVERYTHING.
ROY CRANE
WASH AND EASY RUN ACROSS THE REBEL GENERAL AND A GROUP OF OFFICERS, TEARING THEIR HAIR OVER SOME NEW RUSSIAN MACHINE GUNS.
BLAZES, PODNER! HERE'S A BREAK FOR US.
VACUUM CLEANE
WELL, STUPID, WHO ARE YOU?
PRIVATE EASY, SUH, FIFTH INFANTRY.
PROFESSIONAL SOLDIER, SUH, AND FORMER CAPTAIN IN MEXICAN AND GUATEMALAN REVOLUTIONARY FORCES, SPANISH FOREIGN LEGION, KANDELABRAN ROYAL ARTILLERY, AND CHINESE AIR CORPS — COLONEL OF INFANTRY, HONDURAS, AND COMMANDER CUCUMBRIAN LIGHT ELEPHANT BRIGADE. AT YOUR SERVICE, SUH.
ROY CRANE
REG. U. S. PAT. OFF. © 1932 BY NEA SERVICE, INC.
CARRAMBA! AND DO YOU ONDERSTAN' A MACHINE GUN? WE HAF TRY ALL MORNING TO GET ONE ASSEMBLE.
GIVE ME FORTY MINUTES, SUH, AND I'LL HAVE THE WHOLE BUNCH ASSEMBLED.
WANDERFUL!
AS EASY ASSEMBLES THE MACHINE GUNS IN NEAR-RECORD TIME, THE REBEL OFFICERS CANNOT CONCEAL THEIR DELIGHT.
EXCELLENT, MI SOLDADO! EXCELLENT! I NEED MEN LIKE YOU. I GEEV YOU COMMAND OF THE MACHINE GUN COMPANY.
I ACCEPT, SUH, ON TWO CONDITIONS. FIRST, THAT MY PODNER IS MADE LIEUTENANT. SECOND, THAT WE GET PAID IN ADVANCE EVERY MONTH, AND IN GOLD.
'STA BUENO, MI CAPITAN. BUENO!
REG. U. S. PAT. OFF. © 1932 BY NEA SERVICE, INC.
TENIENTE GARCIA! CONDUCT THEES GENTLEMEN TO THEIR QUARTERS AND SEE THAT THEY RECEEF UNIFORMS AND A MONTH'S PAY AT ONCE.

HAPPY DAYS ARE HERE AGAIN!
EX-CONVICTS LEAP FROM HOOSEGOW TO ARMY COMMANDS! BECOME BIG SHOTS OVER NIGHT! POCKETS ARE LINED WITH GOLD, AND FAME AND FORTUNE BECKON.
WHEE! AT THIS RATE WE'LL BE GENERALS BY MIDNIGHT.
NO MORE OVERALLS—NO MORE GOING BARE-FOOTED FOR US, LADDIE.
COME ON, BOZO, LE'S CELEBRATE. LE'S BURN UP TH' TOWN.
WE OUGHT TO BEGIN WHIPPING OUR COMPANY INTO SHAPE. CHANCES ARE THOSE INDIANS NEVER SAW A MACHINE GUN.
RATS! I GOTTA BUST LOOSE. I HAVEN'T SEEN A SHOW OR A PRETTY GIRL IN MONTHS.
OKAY. JUST ONE NIGHT OUT, THEN WE SETTLE DOWN.
REG. U. S. PAT. OFF. © 1932 BY NEA SERVICE, INC.
WASH AND EASY, EAGER FOR EXCITEMENT AFTER MONTHS OF IMPRISONMENT, WANDER INTO A GAY CABARET. THE PLACE IS FULL OF OFFICERS AND PRETTY GIRLS, AND A MARIMBA BAND CAN HARDLY BE HEARD FOR THE MERRY-MAKING.
HEY! THIS STUFF AIN'T GOT NO KICK!
?
NEXT TO THEIR TABLE SITS ANOTHER AMERICAN, BELLOWING LOUDLY AND ANNOYING EVERYONE. HE SEEMS STRANGELY FAMILIAR.
SUDDENLY HE TURNS AROUND, AND THEY RECOGNIZE THEIR MOST BITTER ENEMY.
BULL DAWSON!
YOU BUM! I THOUGHT YOU WERE DOING A STRETCH IN ATLANTA.
!
DAWSON NEARLY JUMPS OUT OF HIS SEAT WHEN EASY SPEAKS TO HIM.
INSTANTLY, HE IS ON HIS FEET, EYES GLITTERING WITH HATRED.
YOU BLASTED STOOL PIGEONS!
HERE'S WHERE I SETTLES OLD SCORES! AND THIS TIME, BY THUNDER, I SETTLES 'EM FER KEEPS!

HE DONE ME DIRT! I'LL RUIN 'IM! I'LL KILL 'IM!
BEFORE EASY CAN REGAIN HIS FEET, DAWSON IS ON TOP OF HIM, STOMPING, AND POUNDING HIM WITH A CHAIR.
THE CABARET IS IN AN UPROAR. WASH DASHES IN TO AID HIS FALLEN COMRADE AND GETS SMEARED.
STOP THAT FIGHT! STOP EET!!
TURN ME LOOSE! I'M NOT LICKED! I'LL KILL THAT GUY! I'LL KILL 'IM!
I HASN'T FINISHED HIM. LEAVE GO, I SAY! LEAVE GO!! I'LL BUST HIS BLASTED NECK!!
CARRAMBA! YOU SINK I ALLOW MY MOS' VALUABLE MEN BE KEEL THEES WAY? AWAY! TAKE THEM AWAY.
© 1932 BY NEA SERVICE, INC. REG. U. S. PAT. OFF.

THERE'S GOING TO BE TROUBLE. EASY IS BURNING UP. HE PACKS A GUN, AND IS SO MAD THAT HE CAN HARDLY DRILL HIS MEN.
I'LL KILL THAT GUY!
THE WORLD AIN'T BIG ENOUGH, BY THUNDER, TO HOLD ME AN' THAT BLASTED SWAB.
DAWSON IS PLENTY HOT, TOO, AND IS EAGER TO CONTINUE THE FIGHT.
THEN ALONG COMES THE GENERAL, AND MAKES MATTERS WORSE.
I HAF A DANGEROUS MEESION FOR YOU, MI CAPITAN.
YES, SUH.
REG. U. S. PAT. OFF. © 1932 BY NEA SERVICE, INC.
YOU ARE TO GO WEETH SEÑOR DAWSON AFTER A CARGO OF ARMS AND AMMUNITION.
WHAT!! ME GO WITH THAT SNAKE?

BLAZES! YOU ASK ME TO GO ON A CRUISE WITH MY WORST ENEMY?
I ASK NOTHEENG. I COMMAND EET.
LET ME ESPLAIN, SEÑOR. I NEED ARMS AND AMMUNITION. I HAF HIRE THEES DAWSON TO SMUGGLE THEM TO ME.
HE'S A NO-GOOD CROOK, THAT GUY.
CARRAMBA! HE EES WORSE! HE EES A TRAITOR! HE EES WAT YOU CALL THE POLO CAT. HE PLAN TO BETRAY ME, AND SELL TO THE ENEMY MY MUNITIONS.
REG. U. S. PAT. OFF. © 1932 BY NEA SERVICE, INC.
AH! NOW I GET IT. I'M BEING SENT ALONG TO KEEP 'IM FROM DOUBLE-CROSSING YOU.
EXACTLY! EXACTLY! TAKE A MACHINE GUN. KEEP OPEN THE EYES. AND EEF HE TRY TO GET FONNY—SHOOT TO KEEL.

OUGHT TO BE ABLE TO HANDLE DAWSON WITH ALL THIS HARD-WARE, EH, LADDIE?
EASY TAKES WASH AND A DOZEN PICKED MEN. THEY HAUL A MACHINE GUN AND A SMALL BRASS CANNON ABOARD THE JUNKY STEAMER.
AND FORTIFY THEMSELVES ON THE FOREPEAK.
WHEN DAWSON COMES ABOARD AND SEES THEM, HE NEARLY EXPLODES.
WHAT! THIM BLASTED SWABS ABOARD MY SHIP?
THE MEELITARY ESCORT, SEÑOR. THEY WEEL ACCOMPANY YOU.
LOUD MOUTHED DAWSON SQUAWKS EVEN LOUDER THAN USUAL.
I DOESN'T NEED NO MILITARY ESCORT!! GIT THIM SWABS OFF'N MY SHIP AFORE I THROWS 'EM OFF!
THEY REMAIN! FURTHERMORE, YOU WEEL TAKE ORDERS FROM CAPITAN EASY.
I QUITS! I REFUSES TO GO, BY THUNDER! YER BLASTED MUNITIONS KIN BLINKIN' WELL ROT FER ALL I CARES.
YOU HEAR THAT? I QUITS!! I MUTINIES!! I HAS THE ONLY SHIP IN PORT, YOU LOP-EARED BANANA, AN' I TAKES ORDERS FROM NOBUDDY!
CAPITAN EASY! ARRES' THEES BUM FOR TREASON.
NOT ME! YOU WON'T ARREST ME FER TREASON. I AIN'T PART O' YER BLINKIN' ARMY.
OUCH! HEY! NOT SO BLOOMIN' RECKLESS!
TRAITOR! MUS' I EXECUTE YOU LIKE A DOG—OR WEEL YOU OBEY ORDERS?
OUCH! I GIVES UP! I STARTS FER TH' AMMUNITION THIS VERY MINUTE.
THE BLASTED LOP-EARED GALOOTS! THEY'LL PAY FER THIS. NOBUDDY KIN GIT TH' BEST O' BULL DAWSON, BY THUNDER!

BLAZES! WHAT ARE YOU DOING HERE?
THAT'S MY BUSINESS.
AFTER LEAVING LA GRIPPE, EASY IS SURPRISED TO LEARN THAT DAWSON'S MATE IS NONE OTHER THAN SLUG SNYDER.
LISTEN, PARD. TURN THEM GUYS OVER TO THE FRENCH POLICE, AND YOU'LL MAKE YOURSELF SOME MONEY.
NEVERMIND! I HAS OTHER PLANS FER TH' SWABS.
AFTER LESS THAN 24 HOURS AT SEA, DAWSON ANCHORS NEAR A LOW, LONELY ISLAND.
LIVELY THERE! LE'S GIT THEM BLOOMIN' MUNITIONS ABOARD.
REG. U. S. PAT. OFF. © 1932 BY NEA SERVICE, INC.

STAY ABOARD, LADDIE, AND KEEP YOUR EYES OPEN. I'M GOING ASHORE WITH DAWSON.
O.K.
TWO BOATS PULL AWAY, LOADED WITH MEN AND PICKS AND SHOVELS.
LIVELY THERE, ME BULLY BOYS. UP AND AT 'EM.
TO EASY'S AMAZEMENT, BULL ORDERS HIS MEN TO DIG UP THE GRAVES AND TOMBS OF A SMALL CEMETARY.
AND THEY DIG. BUT UNEARTH, NOT HUMAN BONES AND COFFINS, BUT BOX AFTER BOX OF RIFLES AND AMMUNITION.
REG. U. S. PAT. OFF. © 1932 BY NEA SERVICE, INC.
Ro-Crane

LIVELY THERE! UP AND AWAY! GIT THEM RIFLES ABOARD.
EASY YAWNS. HE EXPECTS NO TROUBLE UNTIL THE LOADING IS FINISHED. PERHAPS HE GROWS CARELESS, OR DROWSY—
ANYWAY, HE FAILS TO SEE DAWSON DISAPPEAR INTO THE JUNGLE.
AHOY! OPEN THE DOOR, QUICK! IT'S ME—BULL!
BAM!
AND BEFORE HE MISSES HIM, HIS ARCH ENEMY IS A MILE DOWN THE ISLAND.
REG. U. S. PAT. OFF. © 1932 BY NEA SERVICE, INC.
Ro-Crane

AT BULL'S KNOCK, A STUNNING, BLACK-EYED SEÑORITA RUNS OUT.
OH, CHICO! I AM SO GLAD YOU HAF RETURN.
QUICK, DOLL, GIT INTO A BATHING SUIT. THEY'S A COUPLE O' GUYS I WANTS YOU TO HELP ME RUIN.
AH! YOU WEESH I SHOULD MAKE THE GOO-GOO EYES WIS THEM, YES?
ALL YOU DOES, BABY, IS TO LOOK PRETTY, 'N' WEEP. YER GUNNA BE LOLA FEDORA, THE PRESIDENT'S DAUGHTER, 'N' YOU GITS CAPTURED BY OL' BULL DAWSON.
HOW SILLEE! NO WAN EES THE FOOL ENOUGH, CHICO, TO BELIEF THAT.
© 1932 BY NEA SERVICE, INC. REG. U. S. PAT. OFF.
CRANE
THESE SAPS ARE! THEY AIN'T SEEN A PRETTY DOLL FER MONTHS. YOU GOT TH' LOOKS, BABE—YOU KIN MAKE 'EM B'LIEVE ANYTHING.
REMEMBER, DOLL, YER GUNNA BE LOLA FEDORA, DAUGHTER OF THE PRESIDENT.
AND I AM TO BE CAPTURE BY THE TERRIBLE DAWSON MAN. OH, CHICO—EES GOING TO BE SO FONNY.
'N' YOU WEEPS, BABY. DON'T FORGIT TO WEEP. YER HEART IS BROKE—YOU APPEALS TO THE BRAVE AMERICANOS TO PERTECK YOU.
AH! I WEEL VAMP THEM.
THA'S TH' STUFF. MAKE SAPS O' THEM. NOW, ON WITH YER SWIMMIN' SUIT, 'N' I SEND A GUY BACK TO CAPTURE YOU.
REG. U. S. PAT. OFF. © 1932 BY NEA SERVICE, INC.
?
Roy CRANE
BULL RETURNS TO CAMP AS THO NOTHING HAD HAPPENED. EASY EYES HIM SUSPICIOUSLY, BUT SAYS NOTHING.
EASY IS MORE WATCHFUL. SHORTLY AFTER BULL'S RETURN, HE NOTICES THAT SLUG WANDERS INTO THE JUNGLE.
THEN THERE IS THE BLOOD-CURDLING SCREAM OF A WOMAN.
HELP!
?
LOOK SMART! GET READY FOR TROUBLE.
!
Roy CRANE
REG. U. S. PAT. OFF. © 1932 BY NEA SERVICE, INC.
EASY REMAINS WHERE HE IS. HE SUSPECTS THAT THIS IS A RUSE OF DAWSON TO DRAW HIM INTO A TRAP— AND HE'S DETERMINED TO FALL INTO NONE OF DAWSON'S TRAPS.
HELP!!
HELP!!
?
?
HE WATCHES BULL INTENTLY, BUT CRAFTY OLD DAWSON PRETENDS TO BE AMAZED.

SEPTEMBER 1932

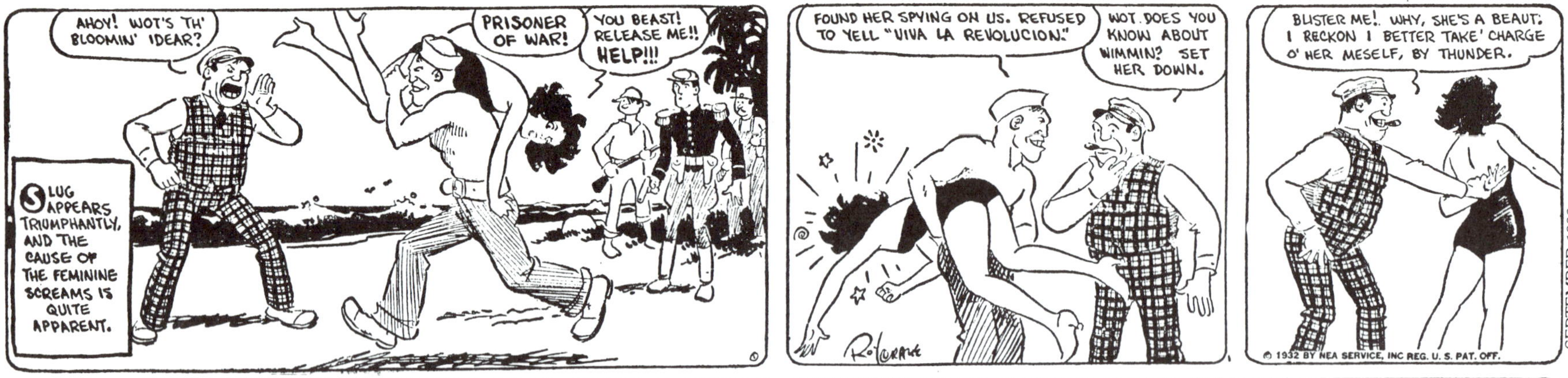

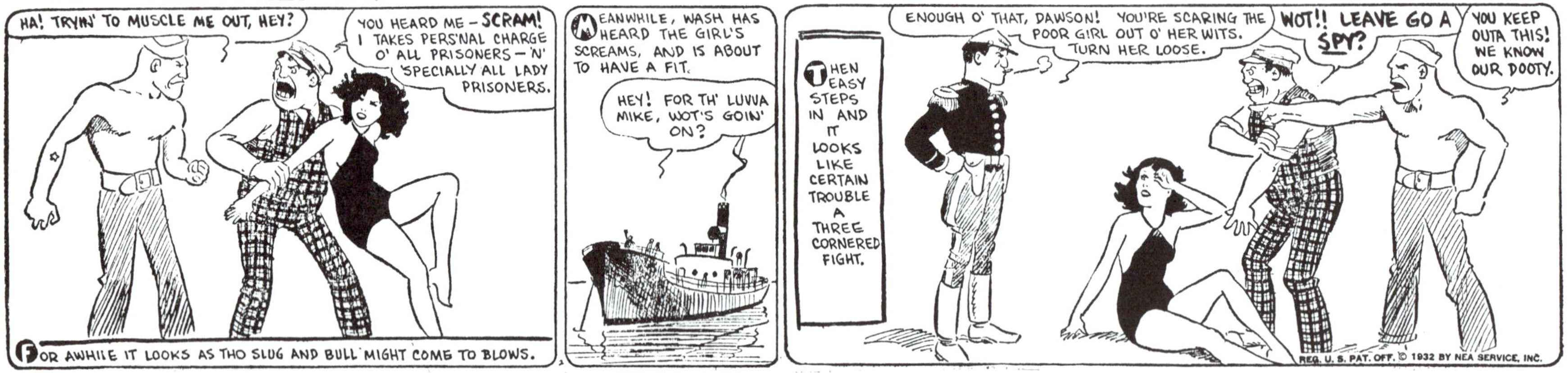

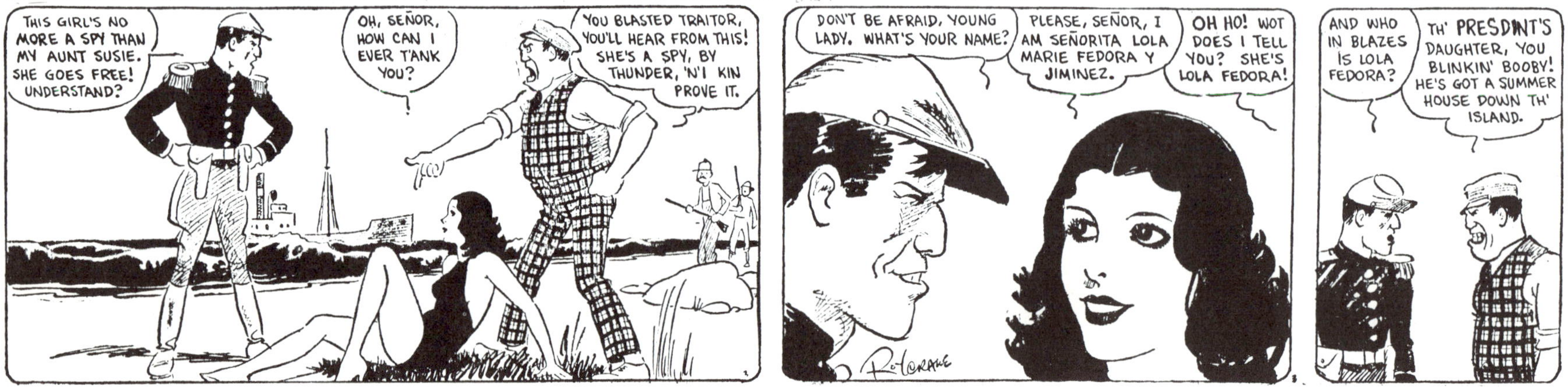

BLAZES! THAT TRUE? YOU THE PRESIDENT'S DAUGHTER?
COURSE SHE IS, YOU LOP-EARED GALOOT. AIN'T SHE ADMIT HER NAME IS LOLA FEDORA?
SUDDENLY, THE GIRL BURSTS INTO TEARS, AND SINKS TO THE GROUND.
I DEVOTE TO YOU MY LIFE, SEÑOR. I BECOME FOR YOU THE SLAVE.
ONLY DO NOT TAKE ME AWAY. THEY ARE CRAZED WEETH THE WAR, THEES REBELS. THEY WEEL TORTURE AND KEEL ME. OH, SEÑOR, I BEG OF YOU — SAFE ME — PROTEC' ME — DON' LET ME DIE.
DESPERATELY, SHE CLINGS TO EASY, SOBBING AS THO HER HEART WOULD BREAK.
ROY CRANE
REG. U. S. PAT. OFF.
© 1932 BY NEA SERVICE, INC.
IT GETS OVER BIG, TOO. EASY FORGETS THE WAR AND DUTY AND EVERYTHING BUT THIS GORGEOUS, HELPLESS FEMALE.
HE HAS ENOUGH ROPE, BLAST HIM. NOW LEAVE HIM HANG HIS SELF.
SLY BULL DAWSON CHUCKLES. HE HAS TRICKED HIS ENEMY INTO A DANGEROUS TRAP.
FOR EASY, GALLANT OLD EASY, IS SMITTEN WITH THE GLAMOROUS BEAUTY OF LOLA FEDORA.
SURELY HE WILL REFUSE TO ARREST SO CHARMING A GIRL. HE WILL SET HER FREE. THEN BULL WILL DENOUNCE HIM AS A TRAITOR — AND EASY WILL BE SHOT.
ROY CRANE
BUT HARK! WHAT IS THIS? EASY SPRINGS A SURPRISE.
SORRY, MA'M. I LIKE YOU, BUT MY DUTY IS TO TAKE YOU PRISONER.
!
© 1932 BY NEA SERVICE, INC. REG. U. S. PAT. OFF.
MR. DAWSON IS MORE OR LESS DUMBFOUNDED. WHY, HE NEVER DREAMED EASY COULD BE SO HARD-HEARTED.
THA'S TH' STUFF. TREAT 'ER ROUGH. DUMP 'ER DOWN TH' HATCH.
RELEASE ME! HELP!! THEY ARE TAKING ME AWAY!
HONEST, LADY, I GOT TO DO THIS. IF I TURNED YOU LOOSE HERE THAT BLASTED DAWSON WOULD HAVE ME SHOT.
DO NOT SPEAK WEETH ME. YOU HAF BETRAY ME. I HATE YOU!
YOU WILDCAT! LISTEN — I'LL THINK O' SOME WAY TO GET YOU FREE SOON AS WE HIT LA GRIPPE. TRUST ME.
ROY CRANE
© 1932 BY NEA SERVICE, INC.
OBOY! WOTTA PRIS'NER! WOTTA QUEEN! WOTTA GIRL!
YOU'VE FALLEN FOR HER TOO, EH? I RECKON THAT MAKES IT UNANIMOUS.
REG. U. S. PAT. OFF.

I AIN'T LICKED YET, BY THUNDER!
NO SOONER DOES EASY TAKE LOLA ABOARD THAN DAWSON DUCKS INTO THE JUNGLE AGAIN.
ON YER TOES, YOU BLINKIN' MUMMY! GIT SOME WOOD TOGETHER. -I WANTS THAT FIRE LIT IN HALF AN HOUR, AN' I WANTS A HEAP O' SMOKE. SAVVY?
SI, SEÑOR.
FIVE MINUTES LATER HE COMES ABOARD WITH THE LAST OF THE MUNITIONS.
UP WITH TH' ANCHOR, ME BULLY BOYS. WE'RE OFF.
REG. U. S. PAT. OFF.
© 1932 BY NEA SERVICE, INC.
AND THEN BEGINS THE MOST DANGEROUS PART OF THE VENTURE. THE FATE OF AN ARMY, OF AN ENTIRE NATION, DEPENDS UPON THE SUCCESS OR FAILURE OF THIS SHORT VOYAGE HOMEWARD.
I'M EXPECTING TROUBLE, PODNER. TAKE A COUPLE O' MEN AND GUARD THE ENGINE ROOM.
SURE.
GO AFT, CORPORAL. IF ANYBODY THROWS A CABLE OR ANYTHING OVERBOARD THAT MIGHT DISABLE THE PROPELLER, USE YOUR GUN.
SI, SEÑOR.
STATION THREE SENTRIES, SERGEANT, ONE TO WATCH FOR SHIPS, THE OTHERS TO GUARD AGAINST A SURPRISE ATTACK FROM THE CREW.
'STA BUENO.
AS FOR MYSELF, I'LL WATCH MY COMPASS AND MAKE SURE DAWSON GOES BACK THE SAME WAY HE CAME OUT.
THEY AIN'T NO MAN ALIVE, BY THUNDER, KIN OUTSMART OLD BULL DAWSON.
BULL CHUCKLES AS HE WATCHES EASY'S EFFORTS TO GUARD AGAINST A SURPRISE ATTACK.
BULL IS SUPREMELY CONFIDENT. A THICK COLUMN OF SMOKE RISES FROM THE ISLAND FAR ASTERN, AND EASY, BEING FORWARD, DOES NOT SEE IT.
SMOKE! SIGNAL SMOKE.
REG. U. S. PAT. OFF. © 1932 BY NEA SERVICE, INC.
BUT A LOOK-OUT ON A SCHOONER TWENTY MILES AWAY SEES IT, AND SHOUTS THE NEWS TO HIS COMMANDER.
PSST! WE ROUNDS AN ISLAND ABOUT DAWN, BABY. GIT SEASICK — ANYTHING WOT'LL DIVERT EASY'S ATTENTION.
DEPEND ON ME, CHICO.

DAWN. EASY IS UP EARLY, WATCHFUL AS A HAWK.
WAT EES THE TROUBLE, DARLEENG? EES SOMETHEENG WRONG?
ROUNDING AN ISLAND, THAT'S ALL. GOOD PLACE TO FIND TROUBLE.
OOO! CATCH ME!
YOU HURT?
MY ANKLE—I TURN HER ON THE ROPE. OH, CHICO, HOLD ME TIGHT—I THINK I GOIN' TO FAINT.
REG. U. S. PAT. OFF. © 1932 BY NEA SERVICE, INC.
NOT ONLY IS EASY'S ATTENTION DIVERTED, BUT THE SENTRY'S AS WELL-OTHERWISE, THEY WOULD SURELY NOTICE THE TWO SCHOONERS JUST AROUND THE ISLAND.

MY ANKLE—I THEENK EES BROKEN, CHICO. I TURN EET ON THE ROPE. OO—HOW EET HURT!
BLAST YOU! BACK TO YOUR LOOKOUT. I'LL ATTEND TO THE LADY.
SI, SEÑOR.
CARRAMBA! SAILEENG SHEEPS, MI CAPITAN. COME QUEEK!
OH, CHICO, YOU HAF DESERTED ME.
BLAZES! GIVE THE ALARM! EVERYBODY READY FOR ACTION.
REG. U. S. PAT. OFF. © 1932 BY NEA SERVICE, INC.
YOU, DAWSON! STEER AROUND THOSE BOATS!
WOT! GIT OUTA TH' BLOOMIN' CHANNEL 'N'SINK MY SHIP? NO, BY THUNDER!
Ro-Crane

THERE IS NOTHING SUSPICIOUS-LOOKING ABOUT THE TWO FISHING BOATS—
EXCEPT THAT THEY ARE SO ANCHORED ON EACH SIDE OF A NARROW CHANNEL AS TO FORCE DAWSON TO STEER BETWEEN THEM.
REG. U. S. PAT. OFF. © 1932 BY NEA SERVICE, INC.
AH, HA! A TRAP! THE STEAMER PLOWS INTO A SUBMERGED ROPE, CONNECTING THE BOATS—AND THEY ARE DRAWN ALONGSIDE.
A HORDE OF YELLING, TRIUMPHANT, FEDERAL SOLDIERS BURSTS FROM BELOW. THE BATTLE IS ON.
CRANE

Panel	Text
1	Federal soldiers are swarming aboard by the dozens.
2	"Fight, blast you, fight! Back to your places." So sudden and unexpected is the attack that Easy's men are on the point of surrendering.
3	RAT-TE-TAT-TAT-TA-TAT! He wastes a precious moment rallying them — then jumps to his machine gun.
4	And still the Federals swarm aboard. From both sides they come. It seems nothing can stop them.
5	"Wow! Easy must be in trouble." At the sound of firing, Wash dashes up the engine room steps.
6	And runs into three Federal soldiers.
7	"Help!" "Bang! Bang!" "Pow!" "Bang!" He is nearly scared out of his wits. He shoots. There are also shots from below.
8	"Lights! Turn out th' lights." And the Federals tumble down the steps.
9	"Attaboy! Lights out — everybody in a safe place. We'll show 'em." Flushed with a sudden victory, Wash eagerly prepares for a more determined attack.
10	"Bang! Bang! Pow! Bang!" ENGINE ROOM. He hasn't long to wait either. Here they come — a full dozen of them.
11	"Yah, yah! Try it again. I dare you to." ENGINE ROOM. But it is suicide, rank suicide, to charge from the blinding glare of the sun into utter darkness. The poor Federals are mowed down like so many weeds.
12	"Boy, oboy! Wotta swell gen'ral I'd make." Temporarily, at least, Wash is triumphant.

WHILE WASH IS HOLDING THE ENGINE ROOM, EASY WREAKS HAVOC WITH HIS MACHINE GUN. FULLY HALF OF THE FEDERALS ARE WIPED OUT IN LESS THAN A MINUTE.
RAT-TA-TATTA-TA-TAT
THE REMAINDER TAKE REFUGE IN THE CABINS AFT.
ON YER BLOOMIN' FEET, BLAST YOU! GIT TO THE PORT-HOLES 'N' FIGHT.
BANG
POW
REG. U. S. PAT. OFF. © 1932 BY NEA SERVICE, INC.
THE TABLES TURN. EASY'S MACHINE GUN JAMS. SNIPERS BEGIN PICKING OFF HIS MEN WITH ALARMING SUCCESS.
THEN THE FEDERALS BRING A MACHINE GUN OF THEIR OWN INTO ACTION, AND EASY'S REMAINING MEN ARE PANIC STRICKEN.
RATTA-TA-TATTA-TAT-TA
BLAZES! I'M GETTING THE TAR BEAT OUT O' ME.
HIS MACHINE GUN JAMMED, HIS FEW REMAINING MEN ON THE VERGE OF MUTINY, EASY TURNS IN DESPERATION TO THE LITTLE BRASS CANNON.
BULLETS ARE SPATTERING ALL AROUND HIM AS HE GETS IT INTO POSITION AND FIRES POINT BLANK AT THE ENEMY.
BRROOM!
POW!
MACHINE GUNNERS AND SNIPERS ARE SMEARED ALL OVER THE PLACE.
REG. U. S. PAT. OFF. © 1932 BY NEA SERVICE, INC.
SUDDEN PANIC SEIZES THE FEDERALS. THEY BREAK AND RUN FOR THE BOATS. THEY'VE HAD ENOUGH.
BALOOM!
AGAIN EASY FIRES THE LITTLE BRASS CANNON.
REG. U. S. PAT. OFF. © 1932 BY NEA SERVICE, INC.
Ka-rash!
AND THE BATTLE BECOMES A SLAUGHTER. THE FEDERALS ARE CRUSHED, ALL BUT ANNIHILATED.

LOOK, MI CAPITAN! THE FEDERALS HAF SURRENDER. THEIR BOAT EES SEENK.
TAKE CHARGE, CORPORAL. TEND TO WOUNDED AND PRISONERS. I-I GOT TO SEE WHAT'S BECOME O' MY BUDDIE.
HEY, PODNER!
GEE WIZ, FELLA! IT'S A GOOD THING YOU YELLED-YOU ALMOST GOT SHOT.
ARE YOU O.K., LADDIE?
O.K? I'LL SAY I'M O.K. I WIPED OUT A WHOLE ARMY ALMOST SINGLE HANDED.
BOY, HOW I SLAY 'EM! TH' FEDS ARE PILED SO HIGH DOWN THERE THEY ALMOST FALL IN TH' SMOKESTACK.
GOOD WORK, NAPOLEON. NOW, LET'S SETTLE A FEW SCORES WITH DAWSON.
ENGINE ROOM
ROY CRANE
REG. U. S. PAT. OFF. © 1932 BY NEA SERVICE, INC.

WITH THE SUDDEN SURRENDER OF THE FEDERAL TROOPS, BULL DOES SOME QUICK THINKING.
QUICK-HIT ME IN TH' EYE.
HUH?
WHAT?
BLAST YOU! HIT ME IN TH' EYE AFORE I---OW!!
YOU MUST OF WENT CRAZY.
WHOP!
CRAZY, HEY? THEY DOESN'T COME NO SMARTER THAN BULL DAWSON, YOU BLASTED BOOBY. NOW, GIT A ROPE AN' TIE ME UP.
THA'S TH' STUFF. AN' IF YOU EXPECTS TO GIT OUTER THIS MESS ALIVE, SHIPMATE, BUTT YER NOODLE AGAINST TH' WALL AN' ACK LIKE YOU WAS KNOCKED UNCONCIOUS.
ROY CRANE
REG. U. S. PAT. OFF. © 1932 BY NEA SERVICE, INC.

GEE WIZ! YOU AREN'T GUNNA SHOOT BULL, ARE YOU?
MY ORDERS, PODNER, ARE TO KILL HIM LIKE A DOG WHEN HE PULLS ANY DIRTY WORK. AND I AIM TO OBEY ORDERS.
AHOY! OPEN TH' DOOR, SOMEBODY! GIT ME LOOSE!!
?
?
FIRST MATE
WHAM!
REG. U. S. PAT. OFF.
?!!
DON'T STAND THERE GAWKIN', YOU BLINKIN' PELICAN! GIT ME LOOSE! THIM BLASTED FED'RALS NEARLY RUINT US.
© 1932 BY NEA SERVICE, INC.
ROY CRANE

WASH AND EASY ARE DUMBFOUNDED TO FIND BULL LOCKED IN A CABIN AND THOROUGHLY TIED.
GEE WIZ! LOOKIT HIS BLACK EYE.
STOW THE GAB, MATEY, AN' GIVE A SHIPMATE A HAND.
THIM BLASTED SOJERS DERN NIGH RUINT OLD SLUG 'N' ME. SAPS, THA'S WOT WE WAS. WE TRIES TO LICK TH' WHOLE KABOODLE O' THIM WITH OUR FISTS.
WOW!
WHEN WASH AND EASY HAVE LEFT:
BY GOLLY, SKIPPER, THAT WAS THE SMARTEST TRICK I EVER SEEN. THEY DIDN'T SUSPECT A THING.
BLAST 'EM! THEY SURE RUINT MY PLANS O' TURNIN' OVER TH' MUNITIONS TO TH' FED'RALS, THO.
ROY CRANE
BUT JUST WAIT! I'LL SETTLE THEIR BLOOMIN' HASH. THERE AIN'T NO MAN ALIVE, BY THUNDER, WOT KIN OUTSMART BULL DAWSON AN' GIT AWAY WITH IT.
IMAGINE SLUG AN' BULL ATTACKIN' THAT ARMY OF FEDS WITH THEIR FISTS. WHY, IT'S A WONDER THEY WASN'T KILLED.
BAH! YOU B'LIEVE THAT YARN, LADDIE?
DON'T YOU?
BLAZES, NO! I'D BET MY LIFE BULL WAS IN CAHOOTS WITH THOSE BIRDS.
BUT, EASY, IF HE WAS IN CAHOOTS WITH 'EM, HOW'D HE GET A BLACK EYE? AN' WHO TIED HIM UP?
I DUNNO.
ROY CRANE
THAT'S WHY I LET HIM GO. I COULDN'T PROVE ANYTHING ON HIM. I COULDN'T SHOOT HIM JUST ON SUSPICION. SHUX! I RECKON THE OLD FOX OUTSMARTED ME.
UPON THE RETURN OF THE MUNITIONS SHIP, LA GRIPPE GOES WILD WITH EXCITEMENT. THE WATERFRONT IS CROWDED WITH MOTOR TRUCKS, TOOTING FREIGHT TRAINS AND SOLDIERS.
PSST—NOW'S YOUR CHANCE TO ESCAPE. SLIP OVER THE SIDE, MA'AM, AND SWIM ASHORE CASUAL LIKE.
OH, SEÑOR! 'OW CAN I EVER TANK YOU.
THEN THE GENERAL BUSTLES ABOARD, VERY EXCITED.
CARRAMBA! W'Y YOU TAKE SO LONG?
ATTACKED BY FEDERALS, SUH. OUTNUMBERED 12 TO 1. THEY BOARDED OUR SHIP, SUH, AND—
NEFERMINE THE BUM ESCUSES. WARE EES THE MUNITIONS? DID YOU SAFE THE MUNITIONS?
YES, SUH. EVERYTHING IS SAFE AND SOUND.
ROY CRANE

OCTOBER 1932

LOLA! WHAT IN BLAZES YOU DOING HERE ???
OH, CHICO, I WANT TO GO 'OME. THEY SAY MY FATHER IS EEN COMMAND OF THE FEDERAL ARMY NOT FAR AWAY. I AM TRYING TO FINE HEEM.
BUT YOU CAN'T GO THRU THE LINES, YOU LITTLE IDIOT.
BUT I AM SO AFRAID—SO ALONE. I MUS' FINE MY FATHER. OH, DARLEENG, SAY YOU WEEL HELP ME.
YOU POOR KID—I'LL—I—NAH! I WON'T LISTEN! YOU CAN'T GO! IT'D BE SUICIDE.
THEN I WEEL REMAIN WEETH YOU. WE WEEL 'OLD 'ANDS, AND YOU WEEL NOT ALLOW THE BATTLE TO FRIGHTEN ME. YES?
RATS! ON YOUR WAY! SCRAM! GET OUT! THIS AIN'T ANY LADIES' WAR.
© 1932 BY NEA SERVICE, INC. REG. U. S. PAT. OFF.

IMPOSSIBLE! THERE'S GOING TO BE A BATTLE—YOU CAN'T STAY HERE.
VEREE WELL, THEN. I WEEL WALK ACROSS TO THE FEDERAL LINES AND FINE MY FATHER.
YOU'LL DO NOTHING OF THE KIND. YOU'RE GOING TO A PLACE O' SAFETY.
I WEEL GO ANYWHERE I PLEASE.
BLAZES! DO I HAVE TO TURN YOU OVER MY KNEE AND GIVE YOU A SPANKING? NOW BEAT IT!!
STOP, OR I WEEL SCREAM.
SCREAM ALL YOU WANT TO, LADY, BUT YOU'RE GOING BACK O' THE LINES—AND YOU'RE GOING TO LIKE IT.
OH, HO! IT WORKED, BY THUNDER! HE'S LEFT HIS BLOOMIN' POST.
© 1932 BY NEA SERVICE, INC. REG. U. S. PAT. OFF.

HEY! WAKE UP, STUPID. TELL TH' GEN'RAL I HAS NEWS FER HIM WOT'LL KNOCK HIM COLD.
G.H.Q.
Z-Z-Z
DAWSON'S CUNNING PLAN OF REVENGE BEGINS TO UNFOLD.
I KNOWED IT, BY THUNDER! I KNOWED HE HAD A YELLER STREAK.
WHO, YOU IDIOT?
YER BLOOMIN' PET, THE BRAVE 'N' DASHIN' CAPTING EASY. HE'S DESERTED!
WAT?
I SAYS HE'S DESERTED. HE UP 'N' QUITS TH' BLINKIN' ARMY JUST BEFORE TH' BATTLE. I SEEN 'IM WITH ME OWN EYES.

A DESERTER, THA'S WOT HE IS — A YELLER-LIVERED QUITTER.
BAH! I DO NOT BELIEF IT. CORPORAL, COMMAND CAPITAN EASY TO REPORT TO ME EENSTANTLY.
LATER:
CAPITAN EASY, SEÑOR GENERAL, EES NO WARE TO BE FOUN'.
CARRAMBA! EET EES TRUE!
FIND HEEM! FIND CAPITAN EASY! BREENG TO ME THAT TRAITOR, DEAD OR ALIFE.
REG. U. S. PAT. OFF. © 1932 BY NEA SERVICE, INC.
AND TWENTY HORSEMEN DASH OFF IN SEARCH OF THE UNSUSPECTING VICTIM.
YOU ARE UNDER THE ARREST.
WHAT THE BLAZES? I'M CAPTAIN EASY, SUH, OF THE MACHINE GUN COMPANY.
I AM AWARE OF THAT FACT, SEÑOR. FORWARD — MARCH!
REG. U. S. PAT. OFF. © 1932 BY NEA SERVICE, INC.
EASY IS DUMBFOUNDED. HE THINKS THAT THERE HAS BEEN SOME MISTAKE.
UNTIL HE SEES BULL DAWSON STANDING BESIDE THE GENERAL. INSTANTLY, HE REALIZES THAT, 'SOMEHOW, DAWSON HAS FRAMED HIM.
I DEMAND A REASON, SUH, FOR MY ARREST.
BECOS, SEÑOR, YOU HAF DEESOBEY ORDERS AND LEF' YOUR POST EEN TIME OF DANGER. BECOS YOU ARE A COWARD, A DESERTER, AND A TRAITOR.
BUT, SEÑOR GENERAL, I —
ENOUGH! YOU WEEL BE COURTMARTIAL AND SHOT AT WANCE.
THEN EASY RUNS AMUCK. BEFORE BEING SHOT, HE IS DETERMINED TO SETTLE SCORES WITH THE LOUT WHO FRAMED HIM.
POP!
WAK!
KA-RASH
© 1932 BY NEA SERVICE, INC. REG. U. S. PAT. OFF.
BUT HE IS DENIED THAT SATISFACTION. SOLDIERS BEAT HIM TO THE GROUND.

THE SUNDAY STRIPS

Wash Tubbs
REG. U. S. PAT. OFF.
HEY! TELL THAT GUY TUBBS THIS IS THE LAST TIME I'M GONNA COME TO COLLECT THIS BILL, SEE.
HUM! I WONDER WOT'D HAPPEN IF UNCLE WASH DIDN'T COME ACROST.
HE SAYS YER A BIG WINDBAG, AN' HE WUN'T PAY IT. WOT'S MORE, HE SAYS IF YOU DUN'T QUIT PESTERIN' HIM, HE'LL KNOCK YER BLOCK OFF.
OH, HE DID. DID HE? ONE SIDE, YOUNGSTER, ONE SIDE!
POW!
I DUNNO WOT IT'S ALL ABOUT, BUT I'D BET MY LIFE THAT WALLACE IS AT TH' BOTTOM OF THIS.

MAY 1931

Wash Tubbs
REG. U. S. PAT. OFF.
CUTTIT OUT, YA BIG SAP! OW! OUCH!
THIS, YOUNG MAN, IS JUST ON GEN'RAL PRINCIPLES. IF I CATCH YOU GETTIN' INTO ANY MISCHIEF, I'M GONNA SETTLE YOU GOOD AN' PROPER.
YEH, AN' HE'LL BUST HIS FIST DOIN' IT, TOO.
CRASH!
I'LL FIX 'IM, TH' BIG STIFF!
© 1931 BY NEA SERVICE. INC.
HEY! ENT YA GUNNA LICK ME, UNCLE WASH? ENT YA GUNNA GIMME A WALLOPIN'?
NOT ON Y'LIFE! YOU'RE GOIN' TO BED WITHOUT YOUR SUPPER!
5-17

Wash Tubbs
HOLD TH' END OF THIS ROPE A MINUTE, WILL YA, UNCLE WASH?
REG. U. S. PAT. OFF.
WHOOPEE! IT WORKED!
© 1931 BY NEA SERVICE, INC.
R. CRANE

Wash Tubbs
REG. U. S. PAT. OFF.
LOST YOUR UNCLE, EH? BUT WHAT MAKES YOU THINK A GANG OF BANDITS KIDNAPPED HIM?
NOTHIN' SHORT OF THAT, MISTER, COULD EVER DRAG MY UNCLE AWAY FROM ALL THESE CLASSY DAMES. NOTHIN'!
© 1931 BY NEA SERVICE, INC.
R. CRANE
5-31

Wash Tubbs
OBOY!
HEY! WAKE UP, UNCLE WASH – YA GOTTA BITE.
6-7

JUNE 1931

Wash Tubbs
KLANK'S JUNK YARD
SAFE
WELL! WOTTA YOU DOIN' HERE?
HONEST, UNCLE WASH, I DIDN'T BUST 'EM.
©1931 BY NEA SERVICE, INC.
6-14

Wash Tubbs
REG. U. S. PAT. OFF.
WELL, WELL! A CIRCUS IN TOWN, EH? HOW IT BRINGS BACK MEMORIES, WALLACE, OF TH' TIME I WAS WITH A CIRCUS.
I WAS GOOD, TOO. I COULD DO ALL SORTS OF TRICKS.
HELP! WOT TH'-?
WHEE! YOU KIN STILL DO 'EM.
AW, LISSEN TO REASON, OFFICER.
BAH! I OUGHTA WAITED TILL HE BOUGHT ME A TICKET BEFORE I PLAYED ANY PRANKS.
© 1931 BY NEA SERVICE, INC.
6-21

Wash Tubbs
MY DEAR YOUNG MAN, DON'T YOU KNOW THIS POND IS ENTIRELY TOO SHALLOW FOR SWIMMING?
SURE.
C'MON IN, UNCLE WASH. TH' WATER'S SWELL
HUM! 'AT'S NOTTA BAD IDEA.
ATTABOY! LE'S SEE IF YA CAN GET BOTTOM.
© 1931 BY NEA SERVICE, INC.
AW, HECK! CAN'T YA TAKE A JOKE, YA BIG SPINACH?
SMAK! SMAK!

Wash Tubbs
HERE, YOUNG FELLA, TAKE THIS DOLLAR AN' SHOW YOURSELF A BIG TIME WHILE I'M GONE. MIKE HOGAN'S SICK, AN' I'M DRIVIN' HIS WATER WAGON TODAY.
REG. U. S. PAT. OFF.
HAVE YA GOT ANYTHING FER A DOLLAR, MISTER, WOT'LL COLOR A LOTTA WATER?
MY STARS! FOR A DOLLAR YOU COULD COLOR THE OCEAN.
NOW, WHILE UNCLE WASH IS EATIN' LUNCH—
OBOY! I'M SHOWIN' MYSELF A BIG TIME, AWRIGHT.
© 1931 BY NEA SERVICE, INC.

JULY 1931

HEY, Y'WANTA PLAY BALL WITH ME?
SIR! ARE YOU ATTEMPTING TO FLIRT WITH ME?
OBOY! HERE'S WHERE I HAVE SOME FUN.
REG. U. S. PAT. OFF.
Wash Tubbs !!!
AW, RATS!
OUCH!
BUT OFFICER, I WUZ ONLY STANDIN' THERE, HONEST I WUZ, WHEN ALL OF A SUDDEN—
TELL IT TO THE JUDGE.
© 1931 BY NEA SERVICE, INC.

Wash Tubbs
THANK GOODNESS! AT LAST YOUR MOTHER'S BACK FROM EUROPE, AN' HAS SENT FOR YOU TO COME HOME.
I DUN'T WUNTA GO, YA BIG SAP.
WATCH THAT KID, CONDUCTOR — HE'S TH' WORLD'S WORST.
DON'T WORRY. TOUGH KIDS ARE DUCK SOUP TO ME.
AH! AT LAST! HE'S GONE! NOW, I CAN LIVE IN PEACE.
© 1931 BY NEA SERVICE, INC.
9-19

Wash Tubbs
SAY, BABY, ANOTHER 40 LESSONS AND YOU'LL BE A WONDER.
GEE! YOU'RE SUCH A PEACHY INSTRUCTOR, WASHIE. I WONDER IF YOU'D MIND TEACHING MY COUSIN, SUSAN ANN, TO SWIM WHEN SHE VISITS ME?
OBOY — I LIKE TO TEACH GIRLS.
AND THEN HE MEETS SUSAN ANN —
WHAT DO I DO FIRST?
GWAN, AN' KICK. YOU'LL LEARN.
© 1931 BY NEA SERVICE, INC.
9-26

From here until 10/18/31 Roy Crane took a break and was replaced by a ghost artist (possibly Wood Cowan?).

Wash Tubbs
OH, WASHIE! ISN'T IT LUCKY I FOUND YOU, NOW BE A GOOD BOY AND TAKE MYRTLE CANOEING
I'LL RIDE UP IN FRONT
COME ON—CLIMB IN
I'M SORRY, MYRTLE, BUT YOU'LL HAVE TA PADDLE — I CAN'T REACH THE WATER!
8-16

WASH TUBBS
GEE, WE'VE HAD A GREAT TIME AT THIS PICNIC GROUNDS, WASH. FIRST ON THE TEETER-TOTTER- THEN THE SLIDE---- THEN THE TENNIS COURT--- AND NOW THIS DANDY SWING. I'LL BET YOU'VE BEEN HERE BEFORE!
OH, SURE! AND, BELIEVE ME, I KNOW ALL THE ROPES AROUND HERE
OH YEAH!
8-23
REG. U. S. PAT. OFF.
© 1931 BY NEA SERVICE, INC.

WASH TUBBS
BOY! THIS IS SOME DOWNPOUR----BUT, WHADDA I CARE? I AINT GOIN' ANY PLACE
REG. U. S. PAT. OFF.
HERE, LADY, YOU KIN BORROW MY UMBRELLA
THANKS, YOU'RE A GENTLEMAN!
GLUB--- HELP!
I'LL TEACH YOU TO PLAY TRICKS ON ME!
© 1931 BY NEA SERVICE, INC.
8-30

WASH TUBBS
AW, COME ON AN' SWIM AROUND, WASH!
NUTHIN' DOIN'! I AINT MOVING AN INCH. I'M GONNA STICK RIGHT HERE AND GET A GOOD SUN BATH
REG. U. S. PAT. OFF.
GOSH! WASHIE SURE DOES CHANGE HIS MIND IN A HURRY!
© 1931 BY NEA SERVICE, INC.
9-6

Wash Tubbs
SURE! I JUST RENTED THIS BIKE TO HAVE SOME FUN---WATCH ME! I KEN RIDE WITHOUT TOUCHIN' THE PEDALS!
GOSH! THAT WAS GREAT! NOW SEE IF YA CAN RIDE WITHOUT TOUCHIN' THE HANDLEBARS.
© 1931 BY NEA SERVICE, INC. 9-19

WASH TUBBS
NOW FOR A NICE PEACEFUL REST!!
SAY, MISTER, WILL GIMME A PENNY FOR SOME CANDY?
HAVEN'T ANY CHANGE, LI'L FELLA. RUN ALONG AND DON'T BOTHER ME!
WELL, MEBBE YOU'LL TAKE ME TO A MOVIE!
I HAVEN'T TIME FOR A MOVIE!
HOW 'BOUT BUYIN' ME A SODY?
AW, LET ME ALONE! GO FLY A KITE
SURE, BUT WILL YA GIMME A DIME TA BUY IT WITH!
BY GOLLY YOUR PERSISTANCY WINS. COME ON!
© 1931 BY NEA SERVICE, INC.

WASH TUBBS
YOU GET THE OLD CAMP FIRE GOING, WASHIE AND I'LL FIX THE COFFEE.
NO SOONER SAID THAN DONE, MABLE!
WELL, AINT I THE DUMMY! I NEVER GO ON A PICNIC WITHOUT FORGETTING SOMETHING.
I'M THE CONSTABLE OF THESE HERE PARTS, SON--- AN' I JUST THOUGHT I'D TELL YA THATCHA CAN'T START A FIRE HERE.
I KNOW DERN WELL I CAN'T, MISTER----UNLESS YOU'LL BE KIND ENOUGH TO LOAN ME A MATCH.
© 1931 BY NEA SERVICE, INC.
9-27

WASH TUBBS
GOSH, IT'S GREAT TO CALL ON A GIRL WHO MAKES SWELL FUDGE FOR YA. AINT I THE LUCKY GUY?
REG. U. S. PAT. OFF.
HEY! COME OUT HERE, MOLLY! QUICK!
HUH! AFTER MIDNIGHT AND YOU'RE STILL HERE. BEAT IT---AND BE QUICK ABOUT IT.
WHY, WHAT'S THE MATTER, WASHIE ??
YER FUDGE AND YER OLD MAN ARE BOTH BOILIN' OVER!
Z-I-P
© 1931 BY NEA SERVICE, INC.

WASH TUBBS
WASHIE! YOU SAID YOU'D READ ME THAT POEM YOU WROTE ABOUT US
WELL, HERE GOES--- "WE'VE ALWAYS BEEN THE BEST OF FRIENDS---OF THAT THERE IS NO DOUBT-----
SNIP!
"---I ONLY HOPE WE NEVER HAVE A SERIOUS FALLING OUT" !!
REG. U. S. PAT. OFF.
© 1931 BY NEA SERVICE, INC.

WASH TUBBS
ALWAYS GET A KICK OUTA SCARIN' FOLKS, GUESS I'LL GO OVER AND SPRISE BETTY T'NITE!
BO-O-O-H
OH, MAN, WHATTA KICK! THAT'S SCARIN' 'ER
REG. U. S. PAT. OFF.
© 1931 BY NEA SERVICE, INC. 10-18

Roy takes over again...

REG. U. S. PAT. OFF.
Wash Tubbs
WE WANT TUBBS! WE WANT TUBBS!
AH, MY PUBLIC!
PUT ME IN, COACH. PUT ME IN — TH' FANS ARE YELLIN' FOR ME.
WE WANT TUBBS —
— TO SIT DOWN!
© 1931 BY NEA SERVICE, INC.
Roy Crane

Wash Tubbs
BEHOLD THE POOR DUB, DESTINED TO SIT ON THE SIDELINES THRUOUT THE SEASON WHILE THE BIG, STRONG LADDIES GRAB ALL THE GLORY AND ALL THE FAIR GIRLIES.
BEHOLD, ALSO, AN END RUN THAT IS LIKE UNTO THE WILD AND THUNDERING STAMPEDE OF CATTLE OVER THE WESTERN PLAINS.
THEN SEE OUR HALF PINT HERO GETTING SMEARED PLENTY WHEN THE RUN GOES OUT OF BOUNDS
SPLAT!
POW!
Roy Crane
AH, WELL! BUT THIS IS A TALE WITH A HAPPY ENDING, FOR THE WOUNDS OF YE HOPELESS DUB ARE PROOF THAT HE WAS IN THE BIG GAME.
YOU POOR BOY!
MY HERO!

Wash Tubbs
BOY, CIVILIZATION'S TOO TAME FOR ME. I'M GUNNA GET MY THANKSGIVING DINNER LIKE TH' OLD PIONEERS USETA DO.
TURKEYS GEESE AND OLD ROOSTERS
MEATS, POULT
GOBBLE GOBBLE
$5
YESSIR, I'M GUNNA SHOOT IT.
$5
GOBBLE GOBBLE GOBBLE
BANG! BANG! BANG! POW! BAM! POW
WELL, I'MA TWO-TAILED HIPPOPOTAMUS!
© 1931 BY NEA SERVICE, INC.

Wash Tubbs
OBOY! OF ALL TH' LUCK — A BEAR, RIGHT IN MY OWN BACK YARD!
BANG! Bang! POW!
!
HEY! WHO TH' HECK'S BIN AIRIN' MY BEAR SKIN RUG?
© 1931 BY NEA SERVICE, INC.
11-29

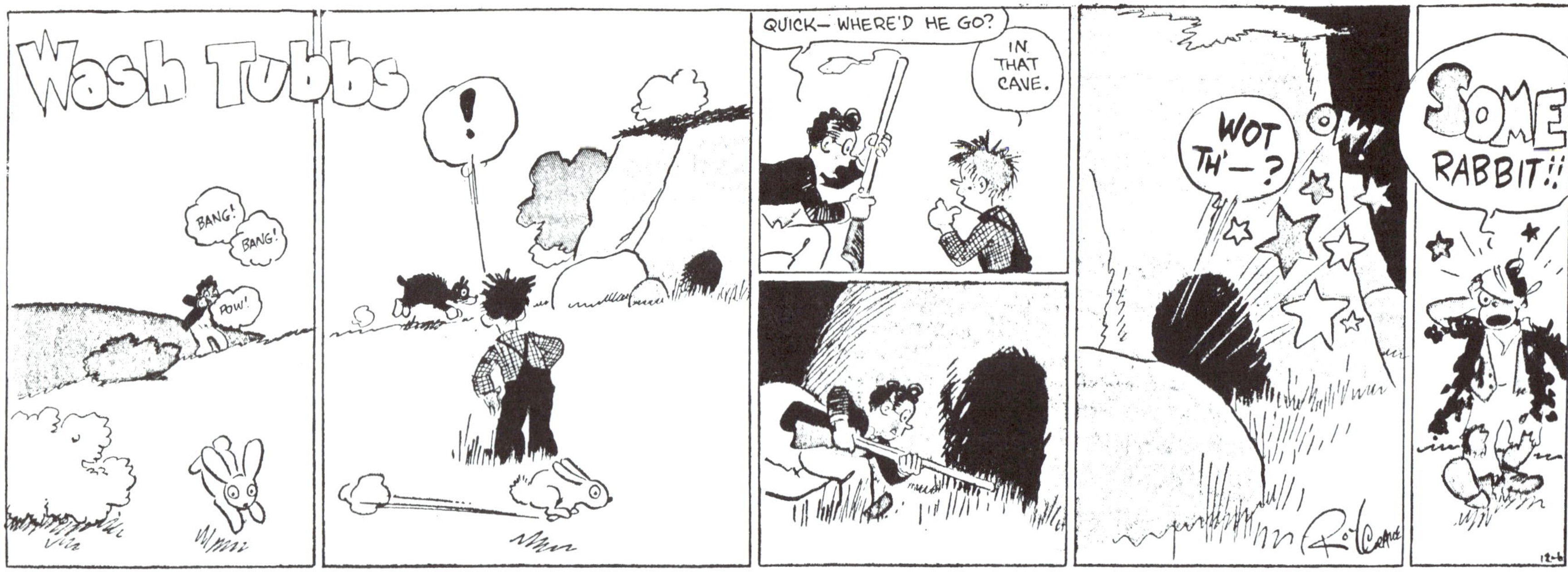

DECEMBER 1931

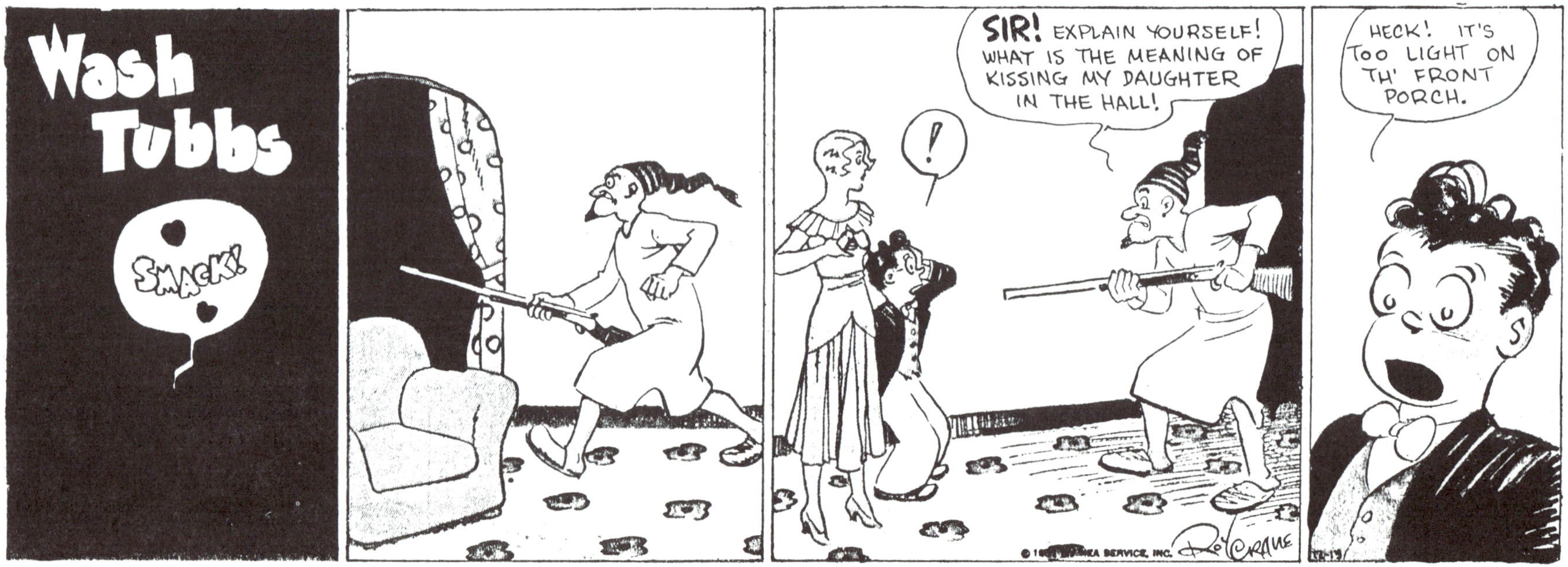

Wash Tubbs
'AT'S TH' STUFF, BOYS. BUILD A SNOW MAN AROUND ME, AN' WE'LL HAVE SOME FUN.
YOU OLD SKINFLINT! WHERE'S MY CHRISTMAS PRESENT?
MY STARS ALIVE!!
HOHOHA! THAT SURE WUZ A SWELL JOKE ON HIM.
HE HEEE! HE DIDN'T KNOW IT WAS ONLY OLD WASH IN THERE.
?
A JOKE ON ME, HEY?
Roy Crane
© 1931 BY NEA SERVICE, INC.
HA!
THERE'S YOUR CHRISTMAS PRESENT, YOU YOUNG WHIPPER-SNAPPER!
!
POW!
12-20

REG. U. S. PAT. OFF.
Wash Tubbs
HEY, MISTER, HELP US MAKE SOME SNOWBALLS, WILL YA? WE WANTA CHUNK A GUY.
SURE, BOYS - ANYTHING TO OBLIGE.
THERE! 'AT OUGHTA BE ENOUGH TO ROUTE AN ARMY.
THANKS, MISTER. NOW FOR TH' FUN!
!
SPLAT!
WHAM!
POW!
SOKKO!
© 1931 BY NEA SERVICE, INC.
Roy Crane
12-27

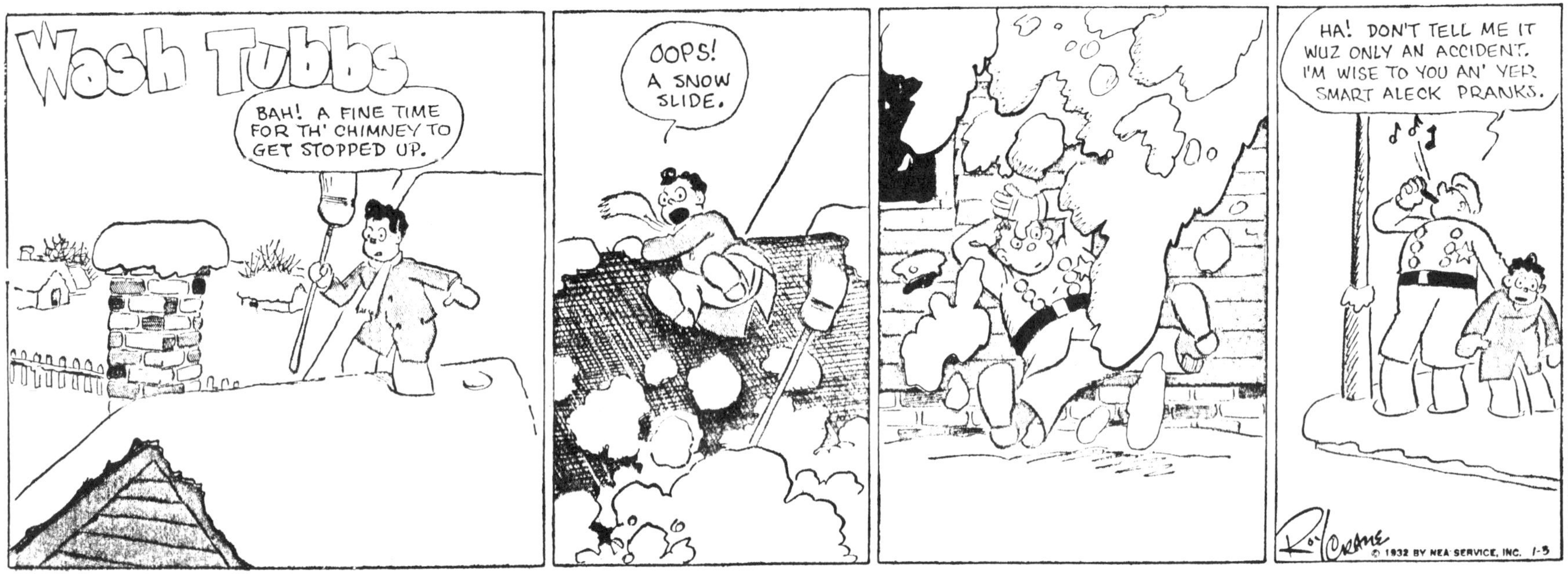

JANUARY 1932

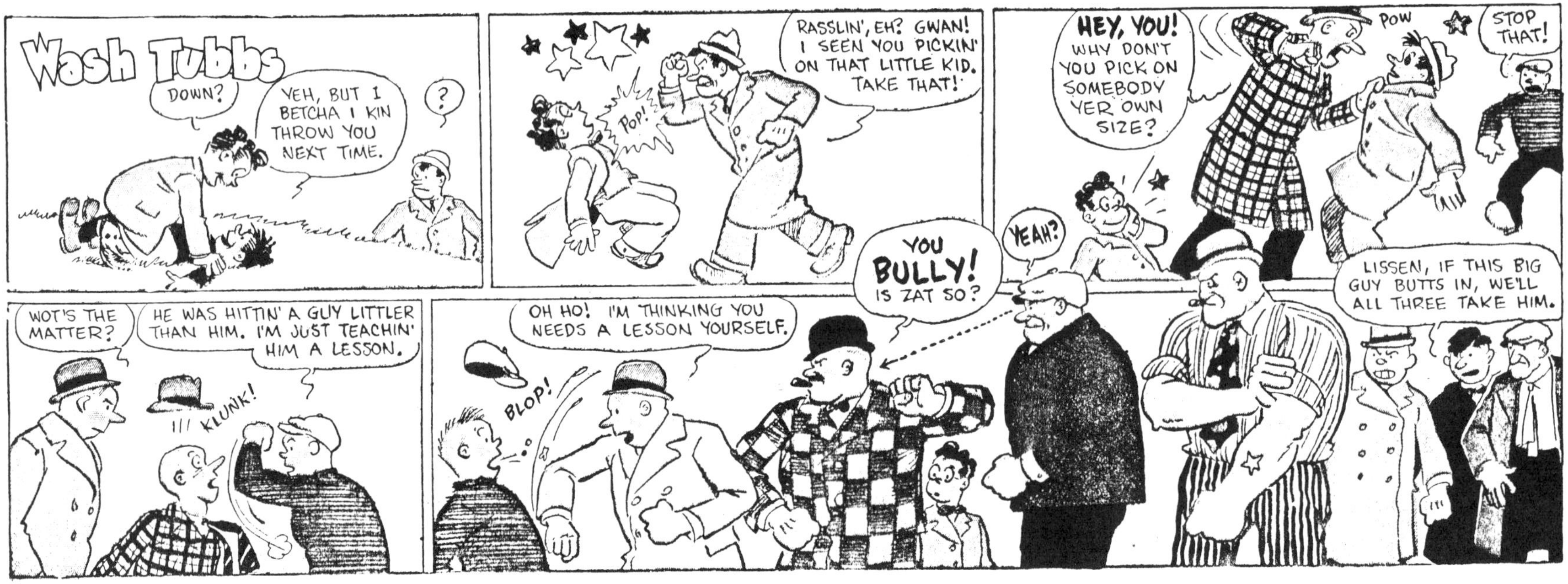

Wash Tubbs
KIN WE THOW THNO BALLS AT YOU, MITHTER?
SURE, BOYS. HAVE YOUR FUN. YOU COULDN'T HURT ANYBODY, ANYWAY.
?
POW!
!
?
?
LITTLE BOY, LET ME SHAKE THE HAND OF THE FUTURE GREATEST BASEBALL PITCHER OF THE WORLD.
?
Roy Crane
© 1932 BY NEA SERVICE, INC. 1-17

REG. U. S. PAT. OFF.
OBOY! IF THERE'S ANYTHING I LIKES, IT'S A GOOD OLD MASQUERADE PARTY.
Wash Tubbs
HUM! THAT GUY WILL BEAR WATCHING.
I KNOW WOT I'LL DO. INSTEAD OF RINGIN' TH' BELL, I'LL JUST HOP IN A WINDA AN' SURPRISE 'EM.
HA! I GOTCHA! AND DON'T GIMME THE OLD GAG ABOUT YOU WAS ONLY WAITING FOR A STREET CAR, EITHER.
BUT HONEST, OFFICER, I WAS GOIN' TO A PARTY.
© 1932 BY NEA SERVICE, INC. 1-24
Roy Crane
A PARTY? THA'S RIGHT, BO, THA'S RIGHT. YOU'RE GOING AS MY GUEST TO A BIG RECEPTION AT THE JAIL HOUSE!

Wash Tubbs
REG. U. S. PAT. OFF.
HEY! BUSTER FELL IN THE AIR HOLE.
BAW!
DANGER
?
WHERE? WHERE?
HE'S CAUGHT UNDER THE ICE. HE NEVER CAME UP.
BAW!
DANGER
MY GOSH! THERE'S NOT A MINUTE TO LOOSE.
DANGER
ALAS! I DID MY BEST, BOYS, BUT ALL I COULD FIND WAS THIS OLD TOY DOG.
OH, GOODY! THAT'S BUSTER!
GEE! THANKS A LOT, MISTER.
ANGER
Roy Crane
© 1932 BY NEA SERVICE, INC. 1-31

Wash Tubbs
REG. U. S. PAT. OFF.
HO HUM! GUESS I'LL GO FOR A SPIN.
WHEE! HOW'S THIS FOR SPEED?
MY GOSH! I FORGOT MY DOG.
IT MUST BE 20 MILES BACK TO TOWN.
BUT I WOULDN'T LOSE THAT PUP FOR TH' WORLD.
GEE! I HOPE HE ISN'T GONE.
AH! NICE DOGGIE. STILL WAITIN' FOR ME.
Roy Crane
© 1932 BY NEA SERVICE, INC. 2-7

Wash Tubbs
WOW! SOME SNOW.
KEEP YOUR EYE PEELED FOR A DIME, BUDDIE. I JUST DROPPED ONE.
SURE THING, MISTER.
AN', BY TH' WAY— IF YOU HAPPEN TO RUN ACROST TH' RAILROAD STATION, LET ME KNOW. I PARKED MY CAR THERE.
© 1932 BY NEA SERVICE, INC.
2-14

Wash Tubbs
BAH! A FLAT TIRE! AN' NO WONDER! I RAN OVER A HORSE SHOE.
OBOY! A HORSE SHOE BRINGS GOOD LUCK.
LISSEN, STUPID! HAVE YOU GOT TH' CRUST TO TELL ME IT'S BROUGHT ME GOOD LUCK? A PUNCTURE—NO SPARE TIRE—AN' 20 MILES TO TH' NEAREST GARAGE.
?
AH! I KNOW WOT'S THE MATTER. YA GOTTA THROW IT OVER YA SHOULDER TO GET GOOD LUCK. GO AHEAD. TRY IT.
WELL, WE SURE NEED SOME LUCK.
© 1932 BY NEA SERVICE, INC.
CRASH!

Wash Tubbs
OW! OUCH! HELP! MUR-DER!! POLICE!
OUCH! LET ME GO! YOU'RE KILLING ME!
HURRY, OFFICER! THERE MAY NOT BE A MINUTE TO LOSE.
JIMINY! THAT SOUNDS LIKE THE REAL STUFF.
HEY! WOT'S COMIN' OFF HERE? WHERE'S THE FIGHT?
WHY, NO ONE'S FIGHTING, SIR. THAT WAS ONLY MY PET PARROT YOU HEARD.
© 1932 BY NEA SERVICE, INC.
YER PARROT, HEY?
YES! YOU SEE, I AM A DENTIST, AND I USED TO KEEP THE LITTLE FELLOW IN MY OFFICE.
OW! OUCH! ARK-K!
2-28

LISSEN, WASH! YOU WANTA MAKE $5? THEN GO OUTSIDE AND RUN THAT BLANKETY-BLANK RED ROADSTER OF MINE OFF THE DOCK. I'M SICK OF IT! I NEVER WANTA SEE IT AGAIN.
Wash Tubbs
HUM! THIS DOESN'T LOOK SO JUNKY TO ME. 'AT GUY'S CRAZY.
OH, WELL! I SHOULD WORRY WOT HE DOES, AS LONG AS I GET MY MONEY.
KER-PLUNK!
© 1932 BY NEA SERVICE, INC.
WELL, EDDIE OLD BOY, I CAME BACK TO COLLECT MY FIVE BUCKS.
OH, NO!
YOU DON'T GET PAID TILL YOU'VE PUSHED THIS BLASTED CAR OF MINE OFF THE DOCK.
3-6

MARCH 1932

Wash Tubbs
REG. U. S. PAT. OFF.
WOTTA FIX! MY DOGS HURT AN' I DUN'T WUNTA WALK HOME AN' I HAVEN'T GOT CAR FARE.
AH! LUCKY, LUCKY! HERE'S A FELLA GOIN' MY WAY.
BUT GEE WIZ! HE'S PASSIN' MY CORNER LIKE SIXTY.
OW! HE'S OUT IN TH' COUNTRY! HE'S DOIN' EIGHTY! HE'LL NEVER STOP.
BAH! HOW COULD I TELL HE WAS WUNNA THOSE BIRDS TRYIN' TO BUST TH' TRANSCONTINENTAL SPEED RECORD?
TUBBSVILLE 42 MILES
3-19 © 1932 BY NEA SERVICE, INC.

AW, LISSEN, HAVE A HEART, CONDUCTOR. I TELL YA I LEFT MY MONEY IN MY OTHER PANTS.
MAKES NO DIFFERENCE. SCRAM! GET OFF!
Wash Tubbs
BUT LISSEN, CANCHA TRUST ME? I'LL PAY YA BACK. HONEST I WILL.
CASH OR WALK!
BUT MY DEAR CONDUCTOR—
GET OFF BEFORE I KICK YOU OFF! WE DON'T OPEN CHARGE ACCOUNTS. AND IT DOESN'T DO ANY GOOD TO ARGUE.
OH, IT DOESN'T? WELL, THIS IS MY CORNER, ANYWAY. YAAA! YAAA!
© 1932 BY NEA SERVICE, INC.
3-20

COMIC SCRAP BOOK

LOOK here, kids! What a lot of fun you can have with this idea! Pictures for a comic scrapbook. Just cut them out and paste them in. New pictures will be furnished at later dates and soon you'll have a fine scrapbook of your comic character friends.

HERE'S Wash Tubbs, the greatest adventurer of them all. He's been a lot of places and seen a heap of things. Why, once he was the sheriff in the world's toughest town. And, to prove it, here he is, all dressed up in his sheriff's outfit! He'll look fine in your scrapbook.

APRIL 1932

COMIC SCRAP BOOK

DON'T overlook the fun you can have with a Comic Scrapbook! Just cut the sketches out and paste them in. Here are Willis and Lillian, the two kids who help "The Willets" entertain you every Sunday. Other sketches will appear from time to time.

WHEN Willis and Lillian said they would pose,
They must have been overly willing, gosh knows.
In fact, a small battle was caused by the stunt,
They both were so anxious to stand up in front!

MAY 1932

COMIC SCRAP BOOK

HERE'S another picture for your comic scrapbook! It's Willis again, and this time he has his hound with him. Willis, you know, helps to entertain you every week on this page. Watch for other comic character sketches which are coming at later dates.

To his dog Willis said, "Come on, fella, sit up,
Just to show all the kids you're a smart little pup!"
And the dog answered, "Yip, yip!" which means, in dog land,
"Sure I will—for that wiener you have in your hand."

Wash Tubbs
BZ-Z-Z-Z
BEES
OUCH!
?
HEY! WOT TH' HECK?
!
!
REG. U. S. PAT. OFF.
© 1932 BY NEA SERVICE, INC. 5-22
COMIC SCRAP BOOK
ONCE more Wash Tubbs steps out in some classy clothes. And he thinks he's dressed up plenty good enough to step into your comic scrapbook. Also, he promises to keep right on entertaining you on this page each week. Watch for more sketches of comic characters
THREE cheers for Wash! He's all togged out
In funny clothes galore.
He got this suit when he was in
A crazy foreign war.

Wash Tubbs
BAH! THIS LAKE HASN'T ANY FISH. I HAVEN'T HAD A BITE ALL DAY.
DISGUSTED, 'AT'S WOT I AM. PLUMB DISGUSTED.
I MIGHT AS WELL THROW MY BAIT AWAY 'N' GO HOME.
WORMS
!
WORMS
REG. U. S. PAT. OFF.
© 1932 BY NEA SERVICE, INC.
5-29

REG. U. S. PAT. OFF.
Wash Tubbs
MEOW!
DANG THEM CATS!
WELL, I'M PREPARED. I'M TIRED OF NEVER FINDIN' ALL TH' BRUSHES 'N' CLOCKS 'N' SHOES I THROWS AT 'EM. THIS TIME I GOT BRICKS.
CRASH!
CHEAP-SKATE!
© 1932 BY NEA SERVICE, INC.
Roy Crane 6-6
COMIC SCRAP BOOK
GEE! Wasn't it nice of the two Willet kids to forget their little brother-and-sister scraps long enough to put on this friendly stunt for you? You bet it was! So, forward, march—right into your comic scrapbook. Just cut their pictures out and paste them. And watch for more sketches of comic characters, which will come to you from time to time.
BOTH Willis and Lil thought they'd give you a thrill
If they put on a funny parade.
They dressed up a bit, till they felt they looked fit
And 'twas then that this picture was made.

Wash Tubbs
AND I PRONOUNCE YOU MAN AND WIFE!
JUSTICE OF THE PEACE
REG. U. S. PAT. OFF.
I HAVE A SURPRISE FOR YOU, DARLING. MAMA AND PAPA AND AUNTIE AND THE WHOLE FAMILY ARE COMING TO LIVE WITH US. ISN'T THAT HEAVENLY?
OH! OH! OH!!
WOTTA N'AWFUL NIGHTMARE!
Roy Crane © 1932 BY NEA SERVICE, INC.
LISSEN, BABY, I JUST HAD A DREAM ABOUT YOU. THIS IS TH' END. OUR DATE IS ALL OFF! I NEVER WUNTA SEE YOU AGAIN!
6-12

JUNE 1932

REG. U. S. PAT. OFF.
Wash Tubbs
LAWSY! AIN'T NOBODY EATIN' THEIR FOOD TODAY.
AIR
LINES
?
GOOD GOSH! IT'S RAINING FISH! AN' FRIED ONES AT THAT!
OW! LOOK! PORK CHOPS AN' A SARDINE CAN!!
© 1932 BY NEA SERVICE, INC.
QUICK, DOCTOR, LOOK ME OVER. I THINK I'M GOIN' CRAZY. I'M SEEIN' THINGS.
?
Roy Crane
6-19
COMIC SCRAP BOOK
HAIL the conqueror! Your friend Wash Tubbs seems to have conquered a nice striped tiger. But how long is the beast going to remain quiet? Better paste the sketch in your Comic Scrapbook before something happens. Then watch for more sketches of comic characters.
WASH TUBBS is sitting pretty now,
To him this stunt is fun!
But, if the tiger starts to growl,
We'll betcha Wash will run!

Wash Tubbs
WELL, WELL! A BATHING BEAUTY STYLE SHOW, EH?
MISS 1890
REG. U. S. PAT. OFF.
MISS 1910
A TRIFLE MORE DARING.
AH! NOT BAD.
MISS 1920
MISS 1932
!
6-26
Roy Crane
MISS 1950
© 1932 BY NEA SERVICE, INC.

COMIC SCRAP BOOK

THE two youngest members of the Willets family are in again. This time they're doing a song and dance for you—and your Comic Scrapbook. Of course you'll have to imagine the song part of it. But anyway, paste them in your Comic Scrapbook while we have them in a cheerful mood.

COMIC SCRAP BOOK

ON one of his thrilling adventures, Wash Tubbs landed in the quaint land of Sneezia and promptly got the job of engineer on funny ol' Ajax, the only engine in the vicinity. Wash thinks this picture of himself at the throttle will fit nicely in your Comic Scrapbook. Better paste it in before the strange train falls apart.

IN Sneezia Wash Tubbs took charge of quite a funny train.
He'd make it puff and puff, but all the puffing seemed in vain.
Then, once, he got it up a hill, upon its narrow track.
Poor Wash forgot the brakes and so the blamed train rolled right back.

COMIC SCRAP BOOK

USUALLY Ma is doing the dishes, Lil having a date, Willis is pestering her, and Pop is snoozing. But this time we caught all of the Willets together and, despite the fact that Pa doesn't look so pleased over the reading-over-the-shoulder stunt, this makes a nice picture for your Comic Scrapbook.

HERE is the Willets family. All four of them at once. And three of them are pulling off one of their daily stunts. Pa's trying to read the paper, but for him it's just too bad. The rest are butting in again. No wonder he is mad!

COMIC SCRAP BOOK

WASH TUBBS sure has had a lot of experiences in his time. Some years ago he worked on a street car. Imagine that! And here's a picture of him, on the job. Cut it out and paste it in your Comic Scrapbook. More pictures of comic characters will be printed from time to time.

WASH once was a conductor and
It gave him quite a thrill.
He'd catch his breath; be scared to death
On starting down a hill.

Wash Tubbs
REG. U. S. PAT. OFF.
?
GWAN! SCRAM! WOTTA YOU KEEP FOLLOWING ME AROUND FOR?
AW, HAVE A HEART, MISTER. YOU'RE TH' ONLY BIT OF SHADE IN TH' PARK.
RoY CRANE
© 1932 BY NEA SERVICE, INC.
COMIC SCRAP BOOK
WHEN Wash Tubbs sees thrilling adventure in the offing he's so excited he can't express himself. Maybe that's why he often hies on his way via a freight train. Trains go everywhere. So does Wash! But this time, let them both go right into your Comic Scrapbook. Then watch for more sketches of other comic characters.
WASH TUBBS is never happier,
Or filled with more hurray,
Than when adventure beckons him
And he is on his way.
8-28

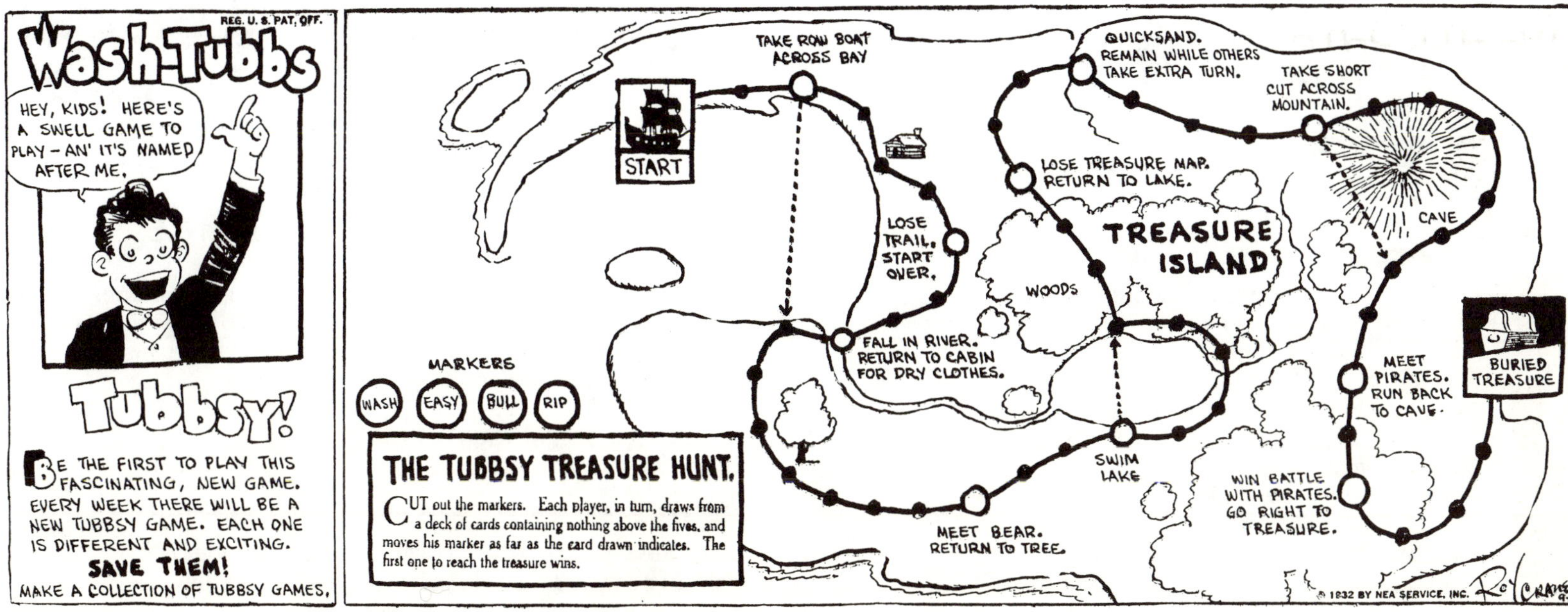
Wash Tubbs
REG. U. S. PAT. OFF.
HEY, KIDS! HERE'S A SWELL GAME TO PLAY - AN' IT'S NAMED AFTER ME.
Tubbsy!
BE THE FIRST TO PLAY THIS FASCINATING, NEW GAME. EVERY WEEK THERE WILL BE A NEW TUBBSY GAME. EACH ONE IS DIFFERENT AND EXCITING.
SAVE THEM!
MAKE A COLLECTION OF TUBBSY GAMES.
START
TAKE ROW BOAT ACROSS BAY
QUICKSAND. REMAIN WHILE OTHERS TAKE EXTRA TURN.
TAKE SHORT CUT ACROSS MOUNTAIN.
LOSE TREASURE MAP. RETURN TO LAKE.
TREASURE ISLAND
CAVE
LOSE TRAIL. START OVER.
WOODS
FALL IN RIVER. RETURN TO CABIN FOR DRY CLOTHES.
MEET PIRATES. RUN BACK TO CAVE.
BURIED TREASURE
MARKERS
WASH
EASY
BULL
RIP
SWIM LAKE
WIN BATTLE WITH PIRATES. GO RIGHT TO TREASURE.
MEET BEAR. RETURN TO TREE.
THE TUBBSY TREASURE HUNT.
CUT out the markers. Each player, in turn, draws from a deck of cards containing nothing above the fives, and moves his marker as far as the card drawn indicates. The first one to reach the treasure wins.
© 1932 BY NEA SERVICE, INC.
RoY CRANE 9-4

TERRY and the Pirates by MILTON CANIFF

COLLECTOR'S EDITION
The complete reprint. Each volume 11 x 7½, jacketed, gold stamped, numbered, 320 pages:
Vol. 1 (1934-1935): sold out
Vol. 2 (1935-1936): $32.50, few left!
Vols. 3-6 (1936-1940): sold out
Vols. 7-12 OF THE GREAT HARDCOVER EDITION AT ALMOST HALF PRICE!
$19.95!

PAPERBACK EDITION
Going over all of Terry & The Pirates by Caniff once again in an affordable format! Each volume is 64 pp., 8½ x 11, color cover. The first 8 volumes covering up to 1939 are out and a new one is issued every 3 months.
Vols. 1-5: $5.95 each; vol. past #5: $6.95 each
Special Offer:
Vols. 1-4 slipcased: $25
Vols. 5-8 slipcased: $25
SUBSCRIBE!
Get any 4 volumes past or future: $25, free P&H

WE HAVE HUNDREDS OF VERY SATISFIED SUBSCRIBERS!

MISSING ANY VOLUMES?

FLYING BUTTRESS CLASSICS LIBRARY

Bill Blackbeard
Series Editor

The Complete 1924-1943
WASH TUBBS®
AND CAPTAIN EASY
by Roy Crane

Each volume of this quarterly 18 volume reprint contains 192 pages of action of this classic which inspired so many adventure strips to come. Available in either a handsome jacketed gold stamped hardcover, or paperback. In a handy 11 x 8½ format with 3 strips per page.
Hardcovers: $32.50 each
Paperbacks: $16.95 each
ALL VOLUMES IN STOCK

SUBSCRIBE!
Only $80 for any 4 hardcovers ($130 separately)
Only $50 for any 4 paperbacks ($67.80 separately)

NBM
35-53 70th St.
Jackson Heights, NY 11372